W9-BRC-940

MARGARET TRUMAN'S

MURDER AT THE CDC

BY MARGARET TRUMAN

Souvenir

White House Pets

Harry S. Truman

Women of Courage

Letters from Father: The Truman Family's Personal Correspondence

Bess W. Truman

Where the Buck Stops: The Personal and Private Writings of Harry S. Truman

First Ladies

The President's House: A First Daughter Shares the History and Secrets of the World's Most Famous Home

THE CAPITAL CRIMES SERIES

Murder in the White House

Murder on Capitol Hill

Murder in the Supreme Court

Murder in the Smithsonian

Murder on Embassy Row

Murder at the FBI

Murder in Georgetown

Murder in the CIA

Murder at the Kennedy Center

Murder at the National Cathedral

Murder at the Pentagon

Murder on the Potomac

Murder at the National Gallery

Murder in the House

Murder at the Watergate

Murder at the Library of Congress

Murder in Foggy Bottom

Murder in Havana

Murder at Ford's Theatre

Murder at Union Station

Murder at The Washington Tribune

Murder at the Opera

Murder on K Street

Murder Inside the Beltway

Monument to Murder

Experiment in Murder

Undiplomatic Murder

Internship in Murder

Deadly Medicine

Allied in Danger

Murder on the Metro

MARGARET TRUMAN'S

MURDER AT THE CDC

A CAPITAL CRIMES NOVEL

JON LAND

A TOM DOHERTY ASSOCIATES BOOK • NEW YORK

This is a work of fiction. All of the characters, organizations, and events portrayed in this novel are either products of the author's imagination or are used fictitiously.

MARGARET TRUMAN'S MURDER AT THE CDC

A Forge Book
Published by Tom Doherty Associates
120 Broadway
New York, NY 10271

www.tor-forge.com

Forge® is a registered trademark of Macmillan Publishing Group, LLC.

Library of Congress Cataloging-in-Publication Data

Names: Land, Jon, author. | Truman, Margaret, 1924–2008.
Title: Margaret Truman's Murder at the CDC : a capital crimes novel / Jon Land.
Other titles: Murder at the CDC
Description: First edition. | New York : Forge, 2022. | Series: Capital crimes ; 31 | "A Tom Doherty Associates book" |
Identifiers: LCCN 2021039439 (print) | LCCN 2021039440 (ebook) | ISBN 9781250238894 (hardcover) | ISBN 9781250238887 (ebook)
Subjects: LCSH: Private investigators—Fiction. | LCGFT: Thrillers (Fiction). | Detective and mystery fiction. | Novels.
Classification: LCC PS3562.A469 M36 2022 (print) | LCC PS3562.A469 (ebook) | DDC 813/.54—dc23
LC record available at https://lccn.loc.gov/2021039439
LC ebook record available at https://lccn.loc.gov/2021039440

Our books may be purchased in bulk for promotional, educational, or business use. Please contact your local bookseller or the Macmillan Corporate and Premium Sales Department at 1-800-221-7945, extension 5442, or by email at MacmillanSpecialMarkets@macmillan.com.

First Edition: 2022

Printed in the United States of America

0 9 8 7 6 5 4 3 2 1

For Tom Doherty

The heroes writers create may get remembered,

but the legends who bring them to the page never die.

Nearly all men can stand adversity, but if you want to test a man's character, give him power.

—ABRAHAM LINCOLN

MARGARET TRUMAN'S

MURDER AT THE CDC

PROLOGUE

APRIL, 2017

The tanker lumbered through the night, headlights cutting a thin swath out of the storm raging around it.

"I can't raise them, sir," said Corporal Larry Kleinhurst, walkie-talkie still pressed tight against his ear.

"Try again," Captain Frank Hall said, from behind the wheel.

"Red Dog Two, this is Red Dog One, do you read me? Repeat, do you read me?"

No voice greeted him in response.

Kleinhurst pressed the walkie-talkie tighter. "Red Dog Three, this is Red Dog One, do you read me? Repeat, do you read me?"

Nothing again.

Kleinhurst lowered the walkie-talkie, as if to inspect it. "What's the range on these things?"

"Couple miles, maybe a little less in this slop."

"How'd we lose both our lead and follow teams?"

Hall remained silent in the driver's seat, squeezing the steering wheel tighter. Procedure dictated that they rotate the driving duties in two-hour shifts, this one being the last before they reached their destination.

"We must be off the route, must have followed the wrong turnoff," Kleinhurst said, squinting into the black void around them.

Hall snapped a look the corporal's way. "Or the security teams did," he said defensively.

"*Both* of them?" And when Hall failed to respond, he continued, "Unless somebody took them out."

"Give it a rest, Corporal."

"We could be headed straight for an ambush."

"Or I fucked up and took the wrong turnoff. That's what you're saying."

"I'm saying we could be lost, sir," Kleinhurst told him, leaving it there.

He strained to see through the big truck's windshield. They had left the Tooele Army Depot in Tooele County, Utah, right on schedule, at four o'clock p.m., for the twelve-hour journey to Umatilla, Oregon, which housed the Umatilla Chemical Depot, destination of whatever they were hauling in the tanker. The actual final resting place of those contents, Kleinhurst knew, was the Umatilla Chemical Agent Disposal

Facility, located on the depot's grounds, about which rumors ran rampant. He'd never spoken to anyone who'd actually seen its inner workings, but the tales of what had already been disposed of there, including weapons that could wipe out the world's population several times over, was enough to make his skin crawl.

Which told Kleinhurst all he needed to know about whatever it was they were hauling, now without any security escort.

"We're following the map, Corporal," Hall said from behind the wheel, as if needing to explain himself further, a nervous edge creeping into his voice.

He kept playing with the lights, in search of a beam level that could better reveal what lay ahead. But the storm gave little back, continuing to intensify the farther they drove into the night. Mapping out a route the old-fashioned way might have been primitive by today's standards, but procedure dictated that they avoid the likes of Waze and Google Maps, out of fear that anything Web-based could be hacked to the point where they might be rerouted to where potential hijackers were lying in wait.

A *thump* from the ragged, unpaved road shook Hall and Kleinhurst in their seats. They had barely settled back down when a heftier jolt jarred the rig mightily to the left. Hall managed to right it with a hard twist of the wheel that squeezed the blood from his hands.

"Captain . . ."

"This is the route they gave us, Corporal."

Kleinhurst laid the map between them. "Not if I'm reading this right. With all due respect, sir, I believe we should turn back."

Hall cast him a condescending stare. "This your first Red Dog run, son?"

"Yes, sir, it is."

"When you're hauling a shipment like what we got, you don't turn back, no matter what. When they call us, it's because they never want to see whatever we're carrying again."

With good reason, Kleinhurst thought. Among the initial chemicals stored at Umatilla, and the first to be destroyed at the chemical agent disposal facility housed there, were containers of GB and VX nerve agents, along with HD blister agent. The Tooele Army Depot, where their drive had originated, meanwhile, served as a storage site for war reserve and training munitions, supposedly devoted to conventional ordnance. In fact, the military also developed and stored nonconventional munitions there in secret, within a secure area of the base known by few and accessible to even fewer.

The normal route from Tooele to Umatilla would have taken just under ten hours via I-84 west. But a Red Dog run required a different route, entirely off the main roads, in order to avoid population centers. The point was to steer clear of anywhere people resided and avoid the kind of attention an accident or spill would cause, necessitating a much more winding route, which Hall and Kleinhurst hadn't been given until moments prior to their departure. A helicopter had accompanied them through the first stages of the drive, chased away when a mountain storm the forecasts had made no mention of whipped up out of nowhere and caught the convoy in its grasp. Now two-thirds of that convoy had dropped off the map, leaving the tanker alone, unsecured, and exposed, deadly contents and all.

Kleinhurst's mouth was so dry he could barely swallow. "What exactly are we carrying, sir?"

Hall smirked. "If I knew the answer to that, I wouldn't be driving this rig."

Kleinhurst's eyes darted to the radio. "What about calling in?"

"We're past the point of no return. That means radio silence, soldier. They don't hear a peep from us until we get where we're going."

Kleinhurst watched the rig's wipers slap at the pelting rain collecting on the windshield, only to have a fresh layer form the instant they had completed their sweep. "Even in an emergency? Even if we lost our escorts miles back in this slop?"

"Let me give it to you straight," Hall snapped, a sharper edge entering his voice. "The stuff we're hauling in this tanker doesn't exist. That means *we* don't exist. That means we talk to nobody. Got it?"

"Yes, sir," Kleinhurst sighed.

"Good," said Hall. "We get where we're supposed to go and figure things out from there. But right now . . ." His voice drifted as he stole a glance at the map.

Suddenly, Kleinhurst lurched forward, straining the bonds of his shoulder harness to peer through the windshield. "Jesus Christ! Up there, straight ahead!"

"What?"

"Look!"

"At *what*?"

"Can't you see it?"

"I can't see shit through this muck, Corporal."

"Slow down."

Hall stubbornly held to his speed.

"Slow down, for God's sake. Can't you see it?"

"I can't see a thing!"

"That's it! Like the world before us is gone. You need to stop!"

Hall hit the brakes and the rig's tires locked up, sending the tanker into a vicious skid across the road. He tried to work the steering wheel but it fought him every inch of the way, turning the skid into a spin through an empty wave of darkness.

"There!" Kleinhurst screamed.

"What in God's name . . ." Hall rasped, still fighting to steer, when a hole opened out of the storm like a vast maw.

He desperately worked the brake and the clutch, trying to regain control. He'd been out in hurricanes, tornados, even earthquakes. None of those, though, compared to the sense of airlessness both he and Kleinhurst felt around them now, almost as if they were floating over a massive vacuum that was sucking them downward. He'd done his share of parachute jumps for his Airborne training, and the sensation was eerily akin to those first few moments in free fall before the chute deployed. He remembered the sensation. It was not so much like being unable to breathe; it was more like being trapped between breaths for an absurdly long moment.

The rig's nose pitched downward, everything in the cab sent rattling. The dashboard lights flickered and died, and the world beyond was lost to darkness as the tanker dropped into oblivion.

And then there was nothing.

PART ONE

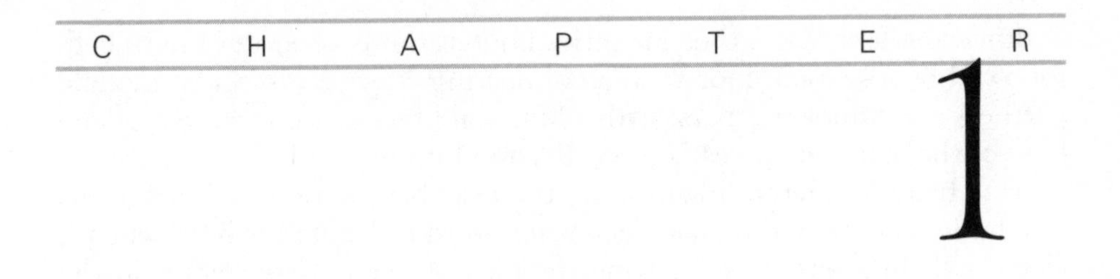

CHAPTER 1

WASHINGTON, DC; THE PRESENT

Are you sure about this, Mac?"

"No, Robert," Brixton's best friend, Mackensie Smith, said. "I'm not. That's why we're having this conversation."

Brixton adjusted the notepad in his lap and readied his pen. "Tell me about her."

He knew the bulk of the associates in Mac's law firm used iPads these days, but Brixton still favored pen and paper. Mac made it a practice to almost never close his office door, but Brixton watched him do just that now and then retake the leather armchair in the office's sitting area.

"She's twenty-five, beautiful, and whip smart."

"In other words, nothing like the man she claims is her father. And you're forgetting something."

"What?"

"Her name, Mac. I will need that, you know."

Mac returned the smile that Brixton had hoped might put him more at ease. "Alexandra. Alexandra Parks. Parks being her mother's name."

"Next question: Have you considered using an investigator with more objectivity?"

Mac looked thrown by that for a moment. "Not even for a second. It has to be you, Robert. You're the only one who understands what this means to me. Like another chance at something I never thought I'd experience again."

Mac had been one of Washington's top criminal lawyers for years, a go-to guy when a case seemed hopeless. But after losing a son and his first wife to a drunk driver on the Beltway—and seeing the drunk get off with what Smith considered a slap on the wrist—he closed his office and accepted a professorship at The George Washington University Law School, where he'd taught fledgling attorneys about the real world of being a lawyer.

While his stint in academia had been satisfying, the call of the courtroom became too loud to ignore. After many long, heated discussions with his second wife, Annabel Reed-Smith, herself a former attorney and now owner of a pre-Columbian art gallery in Georgetown, he resigned his post at the university and hung out his shingle again.

Not surprisingly, his modest return to the law ballooned into a booming practice once more. A single office and reception area gave way to a suite of offices for associates, then an entire floor as those associates multiplied, followed by a second floor with a connecting stairwell to accommodate partners and junior partners, with additional office space reserved for the likes of the firm's top investigator—Brixton himself.

Mac had considered downsizing, the year before, only to change his mind. He had started to scale back when word leaked of his involvement, along with Brixton's, in destroying the most dangerous conspiracy in the nation's history. Though the actual facts of that conspiracy were known to extraordinarily few, rumors of Mackensie Smith's involvement in its destruction were known to many. The result was an unprecedented number of calls and inquiries looking to hire his firm. Although Mac had earned the right to be discriminating about which cases he took on, the client load necessitated an expansion, and the firm had relocated to the vacant and newly renovated top two floors of the city's Warner Building, located on Pennsylvania Avenue Northwest.

Brixton knew Mac loved the work, loved the action, loved the fact that the firm had license to avoid the kind of lobbying efforts and representation of politicos that had so soured Mac on the law in general—and on backroom politics specifically. The latest infusion of cash from hourly billings and retainers was substantial enough for the firm to take on more than its share of pro bono work. And when COVID-19 had forced the closure of Annabel's art gallery, she had returned to the law to head up that department with the firm in its new space.

"You understand what it's like to lose a child, what it does to you, as well as I do," Mac continued, referring to Brixton losing his own daughter, Janet, to a terrorist bombing.

"I was lucky in one respect," Brixton told him. "I had another kid."

"And now, maybe, I do too. I worry that's clouding my judgment, not seeing all this clearly. I want it to be true too much."

"What's she like?"

Mac cast his gaze out the window, a tell Brixton knew indicated he was uncomfortable addressing the subject. The Warner Building's location, detached from the cluster of government offices, iconic and otherwise, left it without much of a view to offer, but the building was a mere five-minute walk from the Federal Triangle Metro stop, which featured access to the Orange Line, the Silver Line, and the Blue Line, assuring easy access for the firm's lawyers and its clients. Much of the world might have moved online for meetings, but initial client meetings went much better in person and, being old-fashioned, Mac always suggested coming in as opposed to logging on.

"Charming, charismatic, full of personality, and beautiful. In other words, you're right, Robert. Nothing like me."

Brixton made some more notes. "Beauty really is in the eye of the beholder, Mac."

"The way everyone was looking at her in The Capital Grille, there must be a lot of beholders."

"That's where you met the first time?"

Mac nodded. "Her choice. Turns out it's her favorite place to eat in the city, too."

"Like father, like daughter."

"I didn't know restaurant choice was genetic."

"Tell me more," Brixton urged.

"Did I mention how bright she is?"

"'Whip smart' was the term you used," Brixton said, without consulting his notes.

"Neuroscience and organic chemistry major at MIT, if you can believe it. That's the Massachusetts Institute of Technology."

"I think I heard that someplace."

Mac smiled and shook his head. "I sound like a doting father, don't I?"

Brixton nodded. "You do."

"For a daughter I've known for all of a week."

Brixton weighed his next words carefully. "Tell me about Alexandra's mother."

"Beverly Parks. New York socialite and head of the family's magazine empire."

"The name sounds familiar."

"Beverly or Parks, Robert?"

"Parks, for sure." Brixton hesitated. "And this was twenty-five years ago?"

Mac met his gaze. "The answer's yes, Robert."

"I didn't ask a question."

"You wanted to. Something like 'It was an affair, wasn't it?'"

"I would've been more tactful in my phrasing."

"I was married at the time. My first wife and son were still alive. It was the worst mistake of my life—at least that's the way I've always looked at it."

"Until a week ago."

"Do you blame me?"

"Not at all, Mac. We all have a right to be happy and fulfilled. I know that better than anyone."

Mac nodded, smiling. "Speaking of which . . . Have I told you recently how wonderful it is to see you and Flo back together? Annabel and I feel like we have a social life again."

Brixton smiled back. "Not that I'm much fun anymore."

"You mean since you quit drinking."

"It snuck up on me, Mac. Sometimes you don't know how far you've fallen until you can't look up and see the light anymore."

Brixton had blamed his breakup with longtime girlfriend Flo Combes on the malaise that had overtaken him. He'd gotten too accustomed to doing business over dinner and drinks, until the two became virtually indistinguishable. But when the business dried up, the dinner, and especially the drinks, had remained. That had all changed a year ago, when Brixton had climbed back on the horse—almost literally, given that he had proposed to Flo outside her New York clothing boutique after clip-clopping up the street in a horse-drawn carriage. She had dropped down to the pavement, where Brixton knelt on bended knee, and hugged him tight.

"Can I take that as a yes?" he'd asked her.

She'd moved back to Washington. COVID had led Flo to close her New York boutique, leaving her clinging to the DC venue for dear life. Fortunately, Brixton had remained steadily employed through the pandemic, living in Arlington instead of the city proper, a location far friendlier to their finances. The truth was, Brixton had found himself happy to be able to provide for Flo while retail continued to struggle. It felt like redemption to him, a means to make amends after a breakup that had been entirely his fault.

"I know that feeling," Mac said, shocking Brixton back to the present and the matter at hand. "I fell into a pit for a time after the accident."

"That wasn't your fault."

"But I've never stopped replaying that night in my mind. What I could have done differently, what might have happened if I hadn't been out of town. Maybe they'd still be alive."

"Have you ever heard the word *maybe* used in a positive light?"

"Not off the top of my head."

"What about in terms of whether Alexandra Parks is really your daughter? Have you confirmed all this with a DNA test?"

"I don't have to. I know she's my daughter."

Brixton weighed not just his best friend's words but also the veil of certainty through which he'd said them. "But you don't know her, do you?"

"That's why you're here, Robert. There's something I haven't told you yet."

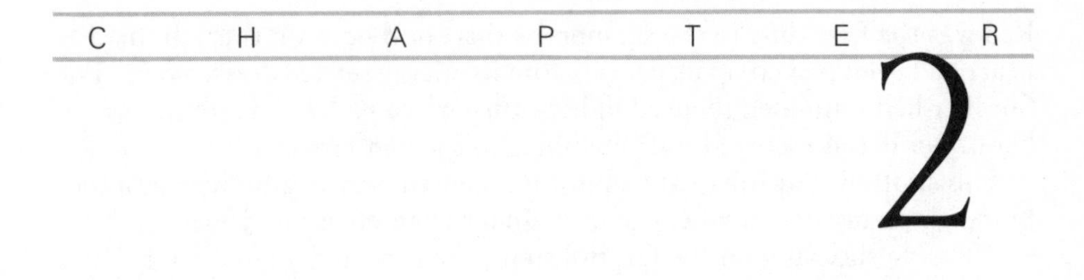

WASHINGTON, DC

"*All units, we have a Code Red. Repeat, shots fired! We have a Code Red. Secure all positions and personnel, and remain in place until you receive the all clear.*"

Kelly Loftus was just coming off her shift as part of the Speaker of the House's Capitol Police protective detail when a piercing squeal, followed by that message, was transmitted over the earpiece that was a permanent fixture for USCP's Department of Protective Services. Fortunately, the Speaker was in her office at the time, enabling her four-person detail to immediately lock down the suite of rooms. Nobody in, nobody out, and all those present ordered to the conference room in the back, where it would be easier to secure them. That process had taken on a new meaning and urgency since the Capitol Building had been overrun by insurrectionists looking to thwart tallying up the presidential electors.

It was the first time in the months since Kelly had been on the job with the Capitol Police that her adrenaline kicked in. That had been a far more regular occurrence in her job as a homicide detective for the Baltimore Police Department, or BPD, as it was known in the city, until her tenure and future there were summarily ended for no other reason that her telling the truth. She left one maelstrom for another—her assignment to Protective Services right off the bat rankled those who'd been passed over for promotion. There were claims of reverse racism and sexism, given that Kelly was female and African American. All told, she had no friends remaining on the force she'd left, and none in the offing on the force that she'd joined.

In fact, her new position was the product of an agreement whereby she had agreed to relinquish her detective shield with the BPD in exchange for being placed in another law enforcement job at a comparable rank and salary. Kelly would do even better with the Capitol Police, moneywise, given all the overtime, but she knew she'd miss the action that came with being a homicide detective. She took great pride in putting bad guys away so they couldn't kill anyone else, and great satisfaction in every case she cleared, just as she'd lose sleep over an investigation in which she couldn't make a case to nail a suspect she knew was guilty.

That was hardly a concern, working a protective detail for the Capitol Police. There was nothing in her new job to lose sleep over. This Code

Red was the first time in the six months that she'd been on this job that her heart had even picked up its pace, before it quickly settled down again. The Speaker had remained secured in her office while Kelly and another member of her detail escorted staff members to the conference room.

She spotted a uniformed Capitol policeman wearing body armor and brandishing an assault rifle, standing guard at an emergency exit.

"It was a shooting on the Capitol steps," he reported, before Kelly had a chance to pose a question. "Word is, it's bad."

MINUTES EARLIER

The hand of God is upon you! He is my shepherd and I shall not want!"

Those were the last words high school sophomore Ben McDonald heard before the shooting started. He and the cluster of other students from the Gilman School, their Baltimore prep school, were on a field trip to the Capitol Building, the first such trip they had taken since academic life had returned to a degree of normalcy, following the endless coronavirus nightmare. Everyone had shown up in their school uniforms, the buses had left on schedule, and the students felt like pioneers, explorers blazing a trail back into the world beyond shutdowns and social distancing.

The reduction in Capitol tour group size was still in force and had necessitated the two busloads of students to be divided into five groups of fifteen, give or take, with three chaperones allotted to each. The group with Ben and his twin brother, Robbie, had gone first, and they had found themselves lingering on the Capitol steps, taking pictures and chatting away with their local congressman and senator, who'd come out to greet and mingle with the students on the steps at the building's east front.

"Why are you still wearing a mask?" one of them had asked the congressman, but Ben had already forgotten the answer.

He remembered checking the time on his phone just before he heard the first shots. Ben thought they were firecrackers at first, realizing the truth a breath later, when the screams began and bodies started flying.

"I am doing the Lord's work! I am a sacrifice to his Word!"

Somehow Ben gleaned those words through the screams and incessant hail of fire. The shots were coming so fast he wasn't sure if the shooter was firing on semi- or full auto. The boy never actually saw the gunman as more than a shape amid the blur before him, which enveloped his vision like a dull haze, though the thin, sheer curtain drawn over his eyes didn't keep him from recording bodies crumpling, keeling over, tumbling down the steps. The force of a bullet's momentum slammed a classmate into him, sparing Ben the ensuing fusillade that turned the other boy's back into a pincushion.

Robbie!

The panic and shock of those initial seconds had stolen thoughts of his brother from him. He wheeled about, covered in the blood of a boy who had dropped off the scene.

"Robbie!"

Did he cry out the name or only think it? The steps around him looked blanketed in khaki and blue, the pants and blazers that made up the Gilman uniform. The sound of gunfire continued to resound in his ears, but he wasn't sure the shooter was still firing, because no more bodies seemed to be falling. People were running in all directions, crying and screaming. Ben remained frozen out of fear for his brother.

"Robbie!"

He saw his brother's sandy blond hair draped down from one of the marble steps onto another. Nothing else at first, just the hair. Maybe he had dived atop a friend who'd been wounded, to spare that kid more fire—that was Robbie. But there was no one beneath him, and . . . and . . .

He wasn't moving. His arms were stretched to the sides at angles that looked all wrong. Ben dropped to his knees next to Robbie, his pants sinking into pooling patches of blood that merged and thickened beneath him. He felt something pinching him along the right side of his rib cage and saw his blue shirt darkening with a spreading wave of red in the last moment before he collapsed next to his brother.

By the time Kelly hustled the last stragglers into the conference room and got them settled, someone had tuned a flat-screen TV to CNN, which was already broadcasting the immediate aftermath of the shooting on the Capitol Building's east steps, which led up from the beautiful Capitol lawn that adorned the Capitol plaza. She found herself transfixed by the scene for a few moments before she took her post at the door. There was no report on the number of casualties yet, but CNN's camera caught more than a dozen fallen bodies, a few already being tended to by a combination of bystanders and Capitol Police personnel, including EMTs who'd rushed outside from their station inside the building when the shooting subsided. A report indicated that one of the dead was a sitting U.S. congressman.

She saw a cluster of khaki pants and blue blazers, school uniforms, strewn over a section of the steps, evidence that students from some school were among the victims—maybe even accounted for the bulk of the victims. All boys, at first glance. Kelly figured they were collateral damage for whatever the shooter's real target on those steps had been. Or maybe he was just a lunatic looking to make a point, a broken and desperate man who had delivered his frustrations onto these innocent kids in a deadly manner. How he had managed to get what must have been a semiautomatic assault rifle, at the very least, past all the security measures in place baffled her. She supposed the shooter could have been a practiced pro who knew his way around such things. Kelly had to take up her door post before CNN weighed in with any further information on the specifics. By the time the lockdown ended, though, she fully expected that to change.

She had handled more than her share of random street violence and shootings back in Baltimore. One of these had led to the chain of events that had brought her here, and she was lucky for that, in some respects, given that her actions could have just as easily ended her career in law enforcement of any kind. Now, instead, here she was, in a kind of a career purgatory, without much room for advancement and lacking in options, given that no police department, big or small, would want anything to do with her, once they did a deep enough dive into her background.

Kelly thought once more of the innocent victims who'd had the misfortune of being on the Capitol steps when the shooting erupted and felt instantly guilty about bemoaning her own fate. Such tragedy had a way of putting things in their proper perspective, and she realized she was lucky to be where she was, even if it wasn't exactly where she wanted to be.

She'd be far more comfortable rushing to the scene of the shooting, of course, but for now, anyway, this was as close as she was going to get, left to replay the looped CNN footage over and over in her head. It was playing there again when she remembered something she'd spotted that looked out of place: a stationary figure swinging *toward* the shooter instead of away.

And what she was certain he did next would give her an excuse to check out the scene as soon as the Speaker's office received the all clear.

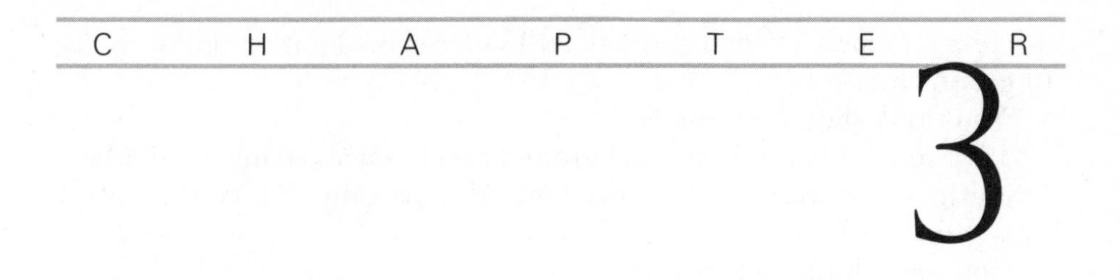

CHAPTER 3

WASHINGTON, DC

What is it you haven't told me, Mac?" Brixton prodded, when his friend lapsed into silence.

"Did I tell you Alexandra's mother died recently?"

"Answer my question, Mac."

Smith forced a smile. "And I thought I was the lawyer here."

"You are, and still a damn good one, to boot. Now answer my question."

"I wanted Alexandra to take a DNA test," Mac said, remaining evasive, "but I kept losing my courage every time I started to bring the subject up."

"Because you're afraid of the results?"

"More like I didn't want to hurt her feelings. Her mother passed only recently, and it was something in her private papers that alerted Alexandra to the truth. It couldn't be about money, because she's the sole familial heir to Beverly's estate. I look at her and I know she's my daughter. I don't need a DNA test to tell me what I already know."

"And yet here we are."

"What I know and what can be proven are two different things, Robert."

"Now who sounds like the lawyer?"

Mac didn't have to force a smile this time. "I told her she'd be hearing from you."

"Even though I hadn't taken the case yet?"

"I would've gotten down on bended knee and begged, if I had to. Hey, it worked for you, didn't it?"

"That was different."

"So is this."

Brixton looked down at the notepad and saw he hadn't made many notes at all. "How'd Alexandra take the news that you were going to bring in an investigator?"

"I didn't put it in those words."

"How did you put it?"

"That you were a friend, an associate. She's ready to cooperate."

"Normally, the people I deal with aren't cooperative. Do you have a picture of the young woman?"

"On my phone."

“Text it to me. I’ll run it through AFIS’s facial recognition program, see if I get any hits.”

“You think she’s a criminal?”

“It’s a standard part of the background check you asked me to do, Mac.”

Smith tapped the side of his head melodramatically. “Of course. What I was thinking?”

“You were thinking like a father.”

“Not many parents need private investigators to run background checks on their kids,” Mac said, frowning.

“That’s because not many parents meet their kids for the first time at age twenty-five. Why didn’t Beverly ever tell you about her?”

“You want the truth, Robert?”

“I’ll find it anyway.”

“She’d just turned forty, married three times, without kids. I think she decided to have a kid on a whim. I think I just happened to be in the right place at the right time—or wrong place and wrong time, depending on how you look at it. It was during my high-powered lawyering days, and we moved in the same social circles.”

“She used you, in other words.”

Mac shrugged. “It could also be that she didn’t want to destroy my marriage. You know, do the right thing.”

“But you don’t think so.”

“Beverly was a figurative chess player, Robert. Always thinking two steps ahead in every phase of her life. And she made a point of telling me she was using birth control.”

Brixton made some fresh notes and flipped to the second page of the pad. “What’s Alexandra do?”

“She was just hired by the Centers for Disease Control.”

“In Atlanta?”

“No, their offices here in Washington, over on E Street.”

Brixton knew the building, had looked at potential space there before Mac had offered him an office at his firm.

“Up here, they’re involved in pretty humdrum stuff involving mostly responding to congressional requests for information,” Mac continued, “and providing technical assistance on public health policy and legislative initiatives.”

“So how does an MIT graduate with degrees in organic chemistry and neuroscience fit that job description?”

“Alexandra’s job is to make sense of complicated stuff for Capitol Hill simpletons like us.”

“Hey, speak for yourself, Mac.”

“She’s even briefed the president twice already. On one occasion, his entire cabinet was present.”

“Impressive,” Brixton commented, making another note.

"I thought so."

"Her taking this job—did it have anything to do with the fact that you were in Washington?"

Mac shook his head. "No, she was already working at the CDC when her mother died and an inspection of her papers revealed the birth certificate."

"Her mother never told her anything about you prior to that?"

Mac shrugged. "She claimed Alexandra's father was her late third husband. The timeline worked, pretty much. I first met Beverly about a month after his death."

"How long did the affair last?"

"We were talking about Alexandra, Robert," Mac said, bristling at Brixton's question.

"And that's what we're doing," he followed, leaving it there.

"A few months, maybe a bit longer."

"If a witness gave that answer in court, what would you do?"

"Ask him to be specific."

Brixton laid the notepad on the cocktail table set before them. "So tell me how long the affair lasted."

"Three months almost to the day." Mac managed a smile. "You're quite good at this, you know."

"That's why I'm here, why you've put up with me for so long."

Mac's expression grew reflective, distant in an almost whimsical way. "I've come to measure time differently as of late, like my life started at the same time Alexandra was born twenty-five years ago. I start asking myself what she might have been doing on a certain day, on this Christmas or that Thanksgiving, a birthday or two."

"A lot of holes to fill in."

"I need you to use your shovel on several of them, Robert."

"One in particular," Brixton said, coaxing his friend back to the subject at hand.

Mac took a deep breath and let it out slowly, finally getting to what he'd been reluctant to raise. "I think Alexandra's in trouble."

Brixton fought the urge to reach for his pad again, remaining still in his chair, his gaze locked with Mac's.

"That dinner at The Capital Grille," he continued. "Twice she had to leave the table because of phone calls. I know that's hardly unusual in this town, but even I turned mine off for this, our first meeting. And even when she came back, I don't think she kept her eyes off the screen for more than ten seconds, as if expecting a text or another call."

"Maybe she was just confirming a meeting for the next day or dealing with the residue from an earlier one."

Mac shook his head slowly. "She was nervous, Robert, and scared, too. That's the moment I knew she must be my daughter, because I knew that look—from the mirror, just before a big case is going to start."

"Did you ask what was bothering her?" Brixton wondered.

"It was our first meeting," Mac said, leaving it there.

"Anything else on that end?"

"Remember what you told me about your time with SITQUAL?" Mac asked, referring to the civilian security arm of the State Department, where Brixton had spent five years.

"I told you a lot."

"The part about trust."

Brixton nodded. "You never knew if the guy who just walked through the door had come there to kill you."

"Hypervigilance, you called it. That describes Alexandra all through dinner." Something changed in Mac's expression. "I think she's in some kind of danger, Robert."

"Personal or professional?"

"Either, both, neither—I don't know. I guess I should have expressed my concerns and asked her straight out, but things were going so well and I didn't want to . . ."

"I understand, Mac," Brixton said, when Smith's voice trailed off. Then, to change the subject and put his friend more at ease, he asked, "What's Annabel think of all this?"

"She can't wait to meet her, can't wait to make her stepdaughter a part of her life, too."

"Long lunches and shopping excursions?"

"To Flo's shop, of course. Speaking of which, we all must get together, Alexandra included."

"That would be wonderful."

"Thanksgiving maybe. A true family gathering."

"Even better." Brixton readied his pen again. "This isn't about me checking to make sure Alexandra is really your daughter, is it?"

"I'd like to be certain, but no, it's not. I need to know if I'm right about her being in some kind of trouble."

"You used the word 'danger' before."

"Same thing, Robert."

"Not always. If she made a mistake she's trying to work her way out of, that's one thing. If something she's working on is getting attention from the wrong kind of people, that's something else again."

"The last time she was near a chemical was senior year at MIT. She's in the information business up here."

"A piece of it that she came by, then. How direct do you want me to be with her about this, Mac?"

"As direct as you need to be, so long as you don't leave her thinking I'm nothing but an overprotective father."

"Which you are."

Mac managed to crack a smile at that. "Of course I am. But that doesn't mean she has to know it."

"Tell me more about her job."

"All boilerplate stuff normally."

"Normally," Brixton echoed.

Mac's stare hardened. "My gut tells me that 'normal' doesn't even begin to describe whatever it is Alexandra's gotten herself into."

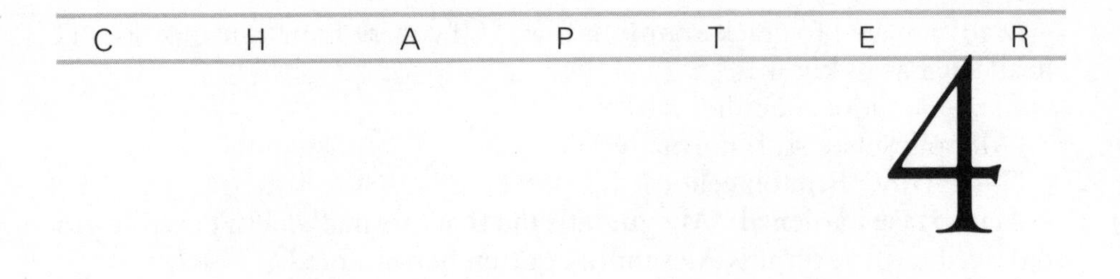

CHAPTER 4

WASHINGTON, DC

All clear," Kelly heard in her earpiece. "Repeat, we are all clear of the Code Red. Single suspect is confirmed down."

Moments later, the Speaker's office resumed its more typical hustle and bustle and Kelly's replacement arrived for the next shift. She could feel the tension in the building, as she made her way toward the main doors, everyone she passed in the halls glued to their phones in pursuit of more information about the shooting. For her part, Kelly couldn't get her mind off those schoolkids, the very definition of wrong place at the wrong time. She was going to head straight to her car, but then she changed her mind and headed to the east front of the Capitol instead.

Kelly could spot the kaleidoscope of flashing lights as she rounded the corner of the building, enough heartache and pain revolving within them to make her wonder why she'd come here instead of going straight to her car. She supposed it involved the classic cliché of the old fire dog who still springs to life every time he hears the bells go off. Her new role in Protective Services said nothing about her instincts as a trained investigator who somehow believed there might be something she could contribute, maybe something she could spot that no one else had yet.

Her Capitol Police badge got her through the initial perimeter, but the FBI had already established a second perimeter around the east steps themselves. Forensics teams wearing the familiar dark windbreakers with "FBI" stenciled on the back were already at work, sharing the space with paramedics and ambulance EMTs, who had to carve a path through a forest of those windbreakers to lug the body bags down the steps. A tarpaulin containing the outline of a body rested not far from the foot of the steps, surrounded by law enforcement officials. The fact that a trio of uniformed Capitol policemen were being interviewed off to the side by a pair of what Kelly took for FBI agents was enough to tell her that her three Capitol Police colleagues had likely been the ones who felled the shooter, saving potentially dozens of lives.

She didn't dare draw any closer to the steps themselves but trained her eye on the area that had commanded her attention on CNN, back in the Speaker of the House's office. She spotted a Capitol Police detective who'd recently transferred from Protective Services, interviewing witnesses inside the cordoned-off area. She waited until he was finished to grab his attention.

"Everything good inside the Speaker's office?" John Bremmers asked her.

"Besides the tension you'd expect after this," Kelly said, gesturing toward the scene beyond them, ready to tell Bremmers what she'd just realized in the Speaker's office. "Speaking of which, I think I spotted something on CNN's looped footage. It was just a glimpse, could be nothing, but have any of the witness statements mentioned a man drawing a gun in the vicinity of where those kids were?"

Bremmers checked to make sure no one was in earshot and then spoke softly even though there wasn't. "He was one of ours. Undercover."

"On the Capitol steps?" Kelly posed, still processing that.

"Stationed there to prevent exactly what happened." Bremmers lowered his voice to a whisper. "He's the one who took out the shooter."

"CNN's reporting it was a couple of uniforms."

"Because that's what we told them. You need to keep this under your hat, Kelly."

"No problem," she told him, leaving it there.

Bremmers started to back away. "Investigative work's in your blood. You should consider requesting a transfer."

"I kind of like being in the prevention business instead," Kelly told him, not bothering to elaborate.

There was nothing more she could do here, no support she could provide, and there was no more to see anyway. Before taking her leave, she found herself studying the area of the east steps where the high school kids had been, where they had fallen.

Kids . . .

She was no stranger to seeing dead bodies that hadn't been old enough to vote yet, not with the level of juvenile violence in Baltimore. While this scene felt much different from those, Kelly had seen enough. She turned and walked off, feeling her heart settle as she charted the route across the Capitol lawn to where she'd parked her car. Then she spotted a woman seated alone on a park bench facing First Street. The woman sat motionless, unblinking, making Kelly think she might have suffered some kind of seizure or stroke, perhaps even was deceased.

"Ma'am?" she said, positioning herself in front of the woman and making sure her Capitol Police badge was in plain sight. "Ma'am?"

The woman stirred at that and regarded her dimly, before resuming her empty stare. Her tangled hair hung flat and smelled unwashed. Her simple clothes, a plain blouse and slacks, draped over her thin frame, as if she'd lost considerable weight since originally purchasing them. She wore flat, well-worn shoes showing cracks down the sides.

Kelly sat down next to her, with the woman's tattered and torn handbag set between them. "Are you all right, ma'am? Do you need help of any kind?"

For a long moment, the woman did nothing at all. Then she turned toward Kelly.

"I know why he did it," the woman said blankly.

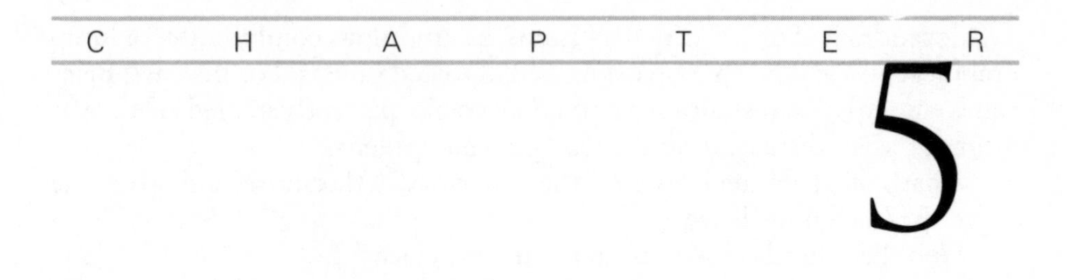

CHAPTER 5

WASHINGTON, DC

Isn't it awful?" Alexandra Parks asked Brixton from across the table where they'd met for a late lunch, her eyes straying from a television mounted on the wall behind the bar, which was covering the shooting on the Capitol steps nonstop.

"That's why I took the seat facing away from the screen," he told her. "If I start watching, I won't be able to stop."

"My dad told me all about you," she said.

"Care to give me the highlights?"

"He called you his best friend."

"He called you his daughter."

"He did?"

Brixton nodded. "He didn't have much doubt on the subject."

"Then why are we here?"

"He wants to be sure. Make sure his heart and brain are on the same page."

Alexandra chuckled. "Lawyers have no hearts. Jury's still out on private investigators."

"I wasn't always a private investigator."

"Right. My dad told me you used to be a cop, and a secret agent or something."

"Security specialist attached to the State Department," Brixton said, not elaborating further.

"What's a security specialist?"

"Kind of like a secret agent."

Brixton had come straight to Chopsmith from his meeting at Mac's office, listening to coverage of the Capitol steps shooting the whole time on his phone. He'd chosen the place mostly because the restaurant was easy walking distance from the CDC's Washington office on E Street Southwest, which was a far cry from the agency's sprawling headquarters in Atlanta. But Chopsmith was also an establishment he favored enough to make it a destination stop, especially for lunch, since it was just off the beaten path and less likely to be frequented by the politicos who sucked the air out of any establishment they frequented. It was bright, open, and airy, now back at full capacity at long last, with the diminished risk of COVID-19.

Alexandra had ordered Wharf Louis, a sumptuous combination of lump crabmeat and grilled shrimp over a bed of mixed greens. For his part, Brixton went with the restaurant's namesake staple, perfectly grilled steak over a similar salad display, described as "gourmet greens."

"That's what my dad ordered the other day," Alexandra said, after the server had taken his leave.

"He's the one who introduced me to this place."

Alexandra Parks was exactly as advertised. Actress beautiful with an athlete's build. She had an easy, unforced smile and looked like the kind of young woman destined to succeed in whatever she chose as her calling. Her blond hair tumbled past her shoulders, a few strands occasionally straying over her face. She brushed these back with a wave of her hand or a shake of her head, and both motions looked effortless, because everything she did looked effortless. But Alexandra's emerald green eyes flashed like a cat's, missing nothing and occasionally twisting back toward that flat-screen television mounted behind the crowded bar. Brixton willed himself not to follow her gaze. Otherwise, he knew he'd fixate on the incident, start seeing it through an investigator's lens. Once activated, that was a part of his brain he couldn't turn off.

"So what happens now?" Alexandra asked him.

"We enjoy our lunch and get to know each other better."

"Spoken like a long-lost uncle."

"To go with your long-lost father. And thank you."

"For what?" Alexandra asked him.

"Saying 'uncle' and not 'grandfather.'"

"But you are a grandfather, Robert. My dad told me."

Brixton hadn't expected Alexandra to refer to Mac as "Dad" so easily. He took that as a sign of maturity and acceptance. He wondered how it had felt, learning the truth from papers after the death of her mother.

"My grandson's fourteen."

"Your daughter must have married young."

"She was just out of college."

Alexandra wrinkled her nose at that. "Not for me."

"My daughter Margot's, what, a millennial?"

Alexandra nodded. "And I'm Generation Z. Just made the cut."

"There you go." She took in a few breaths and leaned backward, crossing her arms, the events unfolding on the flat-screen forgotten for now. "So what's next? You administer a DNA test or something?"

Brixton shook his head.

"Forget your swab, Robert?"

"It's not necessary. You're Mac's daughter. I don't need a DNA test to tell me that."

"You an expert on people?"

"I'm an expert on eyes."

"Windows to the soul, right?"

"You have your father's eyes—only the second person I've ever met with that shade."

Alexandra looked down almost shyly, then back up again. "But I can take one, right?"

"If you want. Say the word and I'll make the arrangements."

She leaned forward. "You didn't ask why."

"Because it's none of my business."

"The answer to your question is, eyes aside, I want to be a hundred percent sure. For Mac's sake."

"You didn't call him 'Dad' this time."

"Slip of the tongue."

Brixton knew the time had come to get to the real reason behind this lunch. "He's worried about you."

"I'm a big girl, Robert."

"Does he have a reason to be worried, Alexandra?"

"He has the right." She pointed at her eyes. "Remember?"

"That's not what I asked you."

Brixton watched her stiffen a bit. "So he sent you here to pry."

"Like you just said, he has the right."

"So why didn't he ask me himself?"

"What would you have said?"

"That there was nothing to worry about."

Brixton managed a tight smile. "That's why he didn't bother to ask."

For a long moment, it looked as if Alexandra wasn't going to respond. Then she spoke suddenly.

"It's work-related, involving the Centers for Disease Control. I'm not allowed to talk about it."

Brixton let her words, and Alexandra herself, settle a bit. He'd detected a nervous edge to her voice, something just beneath the surface, tinged with anxiety. It was the first time her naturally smooth veneer cracked a bit, followed by an artificial smile that was in stark contrast to the one she wore like a second skin.

Mac was right. Alexandra was scared.

"You mind if I call you *Uncle* Robert?"

"I've always wanted to be an uncle."

"Good. Because you can always trust your favorite uncle, and I need someone I can trust."

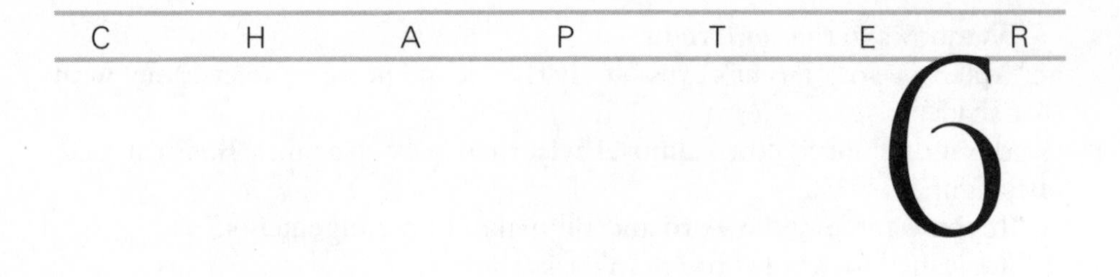

CHAPTER 6

WASHINGTON, DC

I know why he did this.

Not *who* did this, something Kelly Loftus would have expected someone to say, but *why*. She slid a bit closer to the woman on the bench, the smell of mousy, unwashed hair growing stronger.

"Are you talking about the shooter, ma'am?"

"No one would listen to him," the woman said, without regarding her.

"Do you mean why he just killed all those people on the Capitol steps?"

The woman turned her way, as if noticing she was there for the first time. "I'm sorry."

"Were you acquainted with the shooter, ma'am? Did you recognize him? Was he familiar to you?"

But the woman had lapsed into silence again, and Kelly realized she could be a potential accomplice or accessory to the shooting, not just a witness. Around her, people continued to stream across the Capitol lawn, many holding their phones to follow the shooting's aftermath on social media, maybe the local or national news. A few, protesters advocating this conspiracy or that, came with their signs and placards in evidence. They wore T-shirts of different colors, all emblazoned with a large Q consistent with the QAnon movement Kelly had never been able to make any sense of.

"I didn't look, I couldn't bring myself to look," the woman said suddenly. "I heard the shots and . . ."

Kelly elected not to press her, waited for to her continue. Her gaze looped down to the handbag that rested between them, noticing for the first time the brown tape that was meant to blend in with the battered leather. The edges had peeled upward to reveal a nasty tear. Kelly spotted a similar patch on the bag's underside, also peeling, adding to the sadness that hung over the woman like a cloud.

"I could have stopped it," the woman resumed abruptly.

Kelly felt something flutter inside her stomach.

"I could have stopped him."

A chill coursed up Kelly's spine.

"I got here too late. I heard the shots and I knew."

"What was it that you knew, ma'am?" Kelly asked, feeling and sounding very much like a detective again.

The woman regarded Kelly as if seeing her for the first time. "I should go. I need to go."

Kelly laid a hand on the woman's shoulder to keep her in place as gently as possible. "I'm with the Capitol Police, ma'am. My name is Kelly Loftus. What's yours?"

"It doesn't matter. Nothing matters anymore."

"How did you know the man that did this, ma'am?"

The woman shrugged herself from Kelly's hold. "I need to leave. I need to go."

Just then, a heated argument broke out a few yards away, between the QAnon protesters and a group of students chanting "Bullshit!" An exchange of blows between the parties seemed inevitable, more violence on a day that had already seen its share of it.

"Stay here, ma'am," Kelly said, rising from the bench. "I'll be right back. You need to stay here so I can help you. Okay?"

The woman managed a nod, not acknowledging the escalating situation just a few yards from them.

"Capitol Police!" Kelly shouted, flashing her badge as she moved between the battling groups. "Move along, all of you! Let's go! I said *now*!"

The warring factions froze. Kelly yanked back her jacket, exposing her holstered pistol and the walkie-talkie that she unclipped from her belt.

"Central, this is Loftus," she started, without depressing the button. "We have a situation, east front on the Capitol lawn, First Street entrance."

The students and QAnon members hurled some final insults at each other then began dispersing in opposite directions, while others streaming onto the lawn to join the crowd of spectators flowed right past them. Kelly waited until she was reasonably sure the potentially violent situation had been defused before turning and heading back to the woman seated on the bench.

But she was gone.

A forlorn, empty feeling struck Kelly smack in the gut. She'd had a witness with potentially vital information about the mass shooting that had just taken place on the Capitol steps right in her grasp, only to let her slip away.

Then she saw the trail of contents from the woman's handbag scattered over the grass, leading away from the bench.

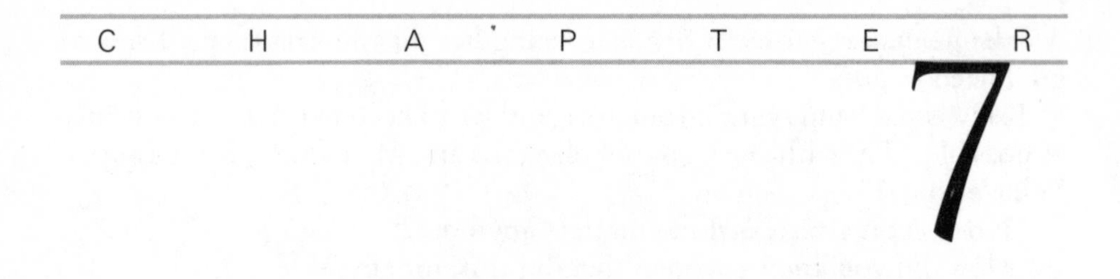

CHAPTER 7

WASHINGTON, DC

"I could use your help," Alexandra continued. "Your advice, anyway."

Brixton nodded once to urge her on.

"I'm involved in something that's a little out of my element."

He waited for her to resume.

"Maybe more than a little."

"You mention this to your father?"

She shrugged. "I told him over dinner, and one too many glasses of wine, that I could use a good lawyer. You know, a joke."

"I'm guessing he didn't laugh."

A single nod this time. Mac had seen right through his newfound daughter when she made that joke, just as Alexandra had seen right through Brixton in terms of the real purpose of this meeting. The DNA test that was no more than a pretext for Mac to facilitate this meeting in order for Brixton to glean something the doting father himself had been unable to.

"How much did my father tell you about what I do for the CDC?"

"Not a lot, beyond the fact that you brief congressional personnel—I'm guessing by dumbing down all the scientific jargon."

"And some of them don't get it no matter how much we dumb the information down," Alexandra acknowledged. "I could tell you some stories . . ."

"I'm sure you could. But whatever this thing you're involved in is, I'm guessing it has nothing to do with briefing anybody."

Their meals arrived and they lapsed into silence while the server set the sumptuous-looking food down before each of them, smiling before he took his leave. Neither Brixton nor Alexandra made a move for their forks.

"We're also tasked with providing technical assistance on public health policy and legislative initiatives, and sometimes we engage with scientific experts on topics of interest. That's taken on greater meaning now, with safety protocols post-COVID."

"It seems like there was never a *pre*-COVID sometimes, doesn't it?" Brixton commented.

"More like all the time, especially in terms of those safety protocols, and education in general."

Brixton had a feeling she was getting to the point. And, in that moment,

Alexandra leaned forward over her crab-and-shrimp salad, checking the tables around them to see if anyone might be listening.

"Do you have any idea how many calls our office fields every day, Uncle Robert?"

Brixton couldn't help but smile at being called that. "No."

"Neither do I, exactly, but it's a ton, and a great portion of them come from the general public to report something. Plenty of these calls come complete with theories about anything from mosquito sprayers to municipal water departments being involved in massive conspiracies. They wake up sick one morning, or have someone close to them get diagnosed with cancer, and they want to blame hostile action. Someone in the deep state poisoning this or that. We actually field more calls like that than headquarters in Atlanta."

"That's because this is Washington. That two-oh-two area code carries its own baggage."

"The vast majority of these calls get logged and ignored—I probably shouldn't be telling you that," Alexandra said, so abruptly it almost seemed like an extension of the same sentence.

"I wasn't born yesterday, kid."

She grinned. "I like that."

"What?"

"You calling me 'kid.' Means we're bonding, Uncle Bob."

"Ugh . . . Nobody ever calls me Bob. Or Bobby."

"Just Robert?"

"Yup."

She cupped her chin in her hands, elbows canted on either side of her untouched salad. "Tell me a story, Uncle Robert."

Brixton remembered he hadn't touched his plate either, and he didn't want the steak to get cold. "I'd rather listen to you finish yours."

"You understand I can't tell you everything, not even most of it," Alexandra said, her tone more serious. "By telling you even this much, I've probably violated a dozen rules."

"This is Washington," he told her. "Rules get broken every day. And I'm your Uncle Robert, remember? We're practically family."

She smiled, relaxing again. "The receptionist put one of those crackpot calls through to me. You know, low person on the totem pole and all that sort of shit."

"But she must have had reason to believe this call was different."

"The receptionist is a *he*."

"Oops. Sorry."

"But you're right. This call was different."

"What can you tell me about it, Alex?" Brixton asked, growing more familiar with the daughter of his best friend.

"Not much."

"Pretend I'm a priest."

She started to pick at her salad, while Brixton began working on his steak, ignoring the bed of greens under it.

"Let me put it another way," he offered. "How can I help?"

"I've been thinking about that since my dad suggested we meet."

Again, Brixton willed himself to be patient and waited for her to continue.

"Like I said, *Uncle Robert*, the receptionist put the call through, and I listened to the caller issue some wildly outlandish claims that were so crazy they actually made a degree of sense."

"And that scared you?"

"Terrified me, would be a more accurate way to put it, if they were true."

"So you followed the claims up."

Alexandra nodded. "And I think there might be something to them."

"You pass this up the office's chain of command?"

"I wanted to speak with you first."

"Make an appointment to see whoever you report to. Today, if at all possible; tomorrow at the latest. You don't want your name tarnished in any way in this town, because it never goes away. Like a scar, and also like a scar, it's what everybody notices first."

"You want me to do what's best for my career."

Now it was Brixton who leaned forward across the table, leaving his sliced steak to cool and his greens to warm. "In this case, I want you to follow procedure, which is the same thing."

Alexandra leaned back and poked a fork at the crabmeat nestled in her salad. "I can see why my dad has so much faith in you. Can I think about it?"

"Take all the time you need."

"If this turns out to be true, Uncle Robert," Alexandra said, an edge creeping into her voice she couldn't chase away, "time is our biggest problem."

They went back to their meals and made small talk. It turned out that Alexandra loved baseball, though as a Yankees fan, she wasn't quite ready to accept the hometown Nationals yet, nor the Washington Football Team. The "business" between them concluded, Brixton enjoyed just getting to know her better and telling her stories about her father, especially his greatest courtroom moments, which he knew Mac, being a portrait in modesty, would never share with her on his own.

They parted with a long embrace that was hardly befitting a first meeting, because it hadn't felt like that at all.

"Can I call you tomorrow to tell you what I decided to do?" Alexandra asked, after they'd exited the restaurant.

"You can call me anytime, for any reason."

Alexandra hugged him again, tighter this time, before they headed in different directions.

Brixton stopped in the shade to turn his phone back on. He felt a quiver in the pit of his stomach when he saw voicemails and missed calls from Margot, his daughter, who'd recently moved to Virginia. He didn't listen to any of the messages, just quickly pressed the Call icon to ring her back.

"Dad?"

"What's wrong? What's the matter?"

"It's all over the news. Haven't you seen it?"

"I was—"

"The shooting at the Capitol!" Margot screeched, her voice dull and scratchy, as if she'd been crying.

Brixton's stomach dropped for his feet. The sidewalk felt like it was tilting, and he stretched a hand to a nearby building to keep his balance. He was trembling, the surface of his arms pricked by gooseflesh.

"Max was there," his daughter continued, referring to his grandson, "with other kids from Gilman, on a school field trip. I . . . I . . . I haven't been able reach him, Dad."

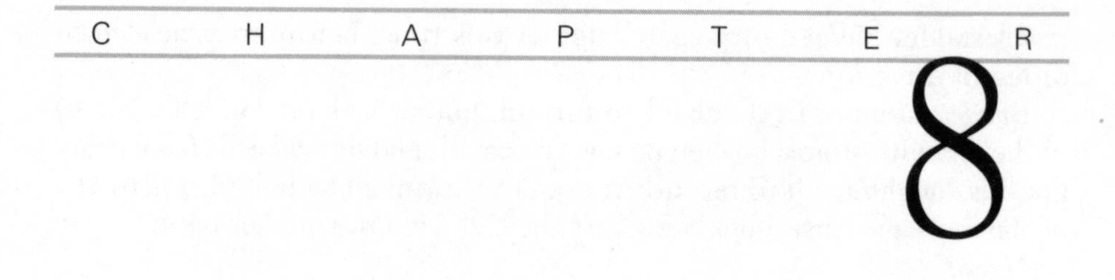

CHAPTER 8

WASHINGTON, DC

Kelly Loftus sat in her car, windows open and air-conditioning blasting, to help bring her body temperature down after a wild trek that had her dodging pedestrians and vehicles alike to collect the contents of the now missing woman's handbag. Those contents had been scattered across First Street Southeast, continuing west on Independence Avenue for a brief stretch. The trail ended just before a bus stop, just after Kelly had swung right at the intersection, leaving her to think the woman had fled the area via a Maryland Transit Administration bus.

The process of retrieving the items spilled from her handbag had been like chasing the wind—more of a soft breeze, fortunately, since it didn't entirely forestall Kelly's efforts to recover as much of what had slipped through the tear in the woman's handbag as she could. She would snatch one item off the grass or pavement, only to see another kicked by a pedestrian or blown into traffic.

Kelly had moved at a panicked pace, desperate to find this woman who clearly had vital information about the mass shooting that was now just over an hour old.

I could have stopped it.

The woman could only have meant the shooting, Kelly had thought, stooping to retrieve one piece of paper and then stamping her foot down on another to keep it from drifting into traffic.

I could have stopped him.

Kelly took that to mean the shooter, which meant the woman must have been acquainted with him—closely, in all probability. Next came a host of business cards that had tumbled from the woman's torn handbag and were left to the whims of the wind.

She performed what must have looked like a crazed pirouette to snatch them up, with the items she'd already retrieved either pocketed or still held in a clump in her free hand. Kelly wasn't giving a lot of thought to forensics, fingerprints, preserving the chain of evidence; keeping that chain of evidence from being swept away was her first and only priority.

I got here too late. I heard the shots and I knew.

Where had she come from? Where had the shooter come from? The woman's voice had been tinged by guilt and remorse, as if she bore as much responsibility as the gunman. Her expression was more than dazed, though, more than sad. It was also forlorn and hopeless—residue, Kelly assumed, of a tortured psyche.

Kelly continued to scoop up items along the scattershot trail leading to the bus stop, hoping for a driver's license, stray envelope or bill, maybe a blank check. Something that might reveal the woman's name and address.

No one would listen to him.

Not only had the cadence of the woman's tone changed with those words, so had the intent and the tense, suggesting that the shooter had tried to report something that had gone unheeded. Reported to *whom*, though?

And now Kelly found herself seated in her car in a lot reserved for Capitol employees, on Delaware Avenue, across from the Russell Senate Office Building. What she hadn't been able to fit into the pockets of her jacket she had carried loose in both hands, pressed up tight against her body to avoid losing it to the next whim of the wind.

At first glance, there wasn't much to glean from any of what she had managed to retrieve in spite of pissed-off pedestrians she had shouldered aside and equally pissed-off drivers who were forced to break or swerve as she'd rushed out into the street. The business cards were of the type you could pull from a bulletin board or lift from a stack left on a counter somewhere. The host of receipts going back at least a year were from a variety of stores, from gas to food to medications to coffee. As near as Kelly could tell, the woman always paid cash, rendering the receipts worthless unless she could track down their locations and perhaps triangulate a general area where she must live. In all she had recovered, there was nothing that, initially anyway, included a name, address, or phone number for the woman, although a single tattered page, which bore evidence of tire tracks, contained four phone numbers, all handwritten in the same scratchy scrawl.

She settled back behind the wheel, the pile of recovered items divided between her lap and the passenger seat. Her cell phone was wedged into its caddy, though Kelly had no memory of how it had gotten there. She thought about calling her direct superior, a captain in the Protective Services division of the Capitol Police, and telling him everything. That would be the wisest and most prudent thing to do. But then she'd have to explain why she'd left a potentially vital witness with firsthand knowledge of the mass shooting unattended, then let her walk off and disappear. And if there was nothing she could glean from the gathered materials—business cards, receipts, a lipstick container missing its top, that compact, and wrapped, loose pieces of caramel candies that must have been the woman's favorite—it could very well mean that the investigating authorities would gain nothing from them, either.

Kelly was still too amped up, her thoughts too jumbled, to make much sense of anything here in a Capitol parking lot. She had kept her place in Baltimore, preferring the forty-mile commute over the extreme rents fetched within Washington, DC, itself or the nearby Virginia suburbs, despite the awful traffic that on some days stretched to three hours, round trip. Normally, she took the MARC train, but line maintenance had curtailed service to the point that, even with traffic, driving had become her best means of getting to work. That was especially true when she worked the Speaker's overnight detail or split shift, as had been the case today, to conform to the Speaker of the House's travel schedule.

She needed to drive home, collect her bearings, and take a fresh look at the recovered contents of the woman's handbag tonight, in lieu of the sleep Kelly knew wouldn't be in the offing until she settled her thinking down. Or she could just turn everything over, offer a lame explanation of what had transpired, with just enough left out to avoid the kind of recriminations that could cost Kelly her job. She was behaving like this was her case, when it was as far from that as it got.

What was she thinking?

She should call the head of her department, turn everything over, and let him push it further up the chain. With the chaos at the Capitol, her indiscretion might even fly under the radar. She pulled her phone from the caddy, already preparing the story she would tell her boss.

Then she spotted the folded-over strip of paper that had slipped from her lap to the floor mat of her SUV.

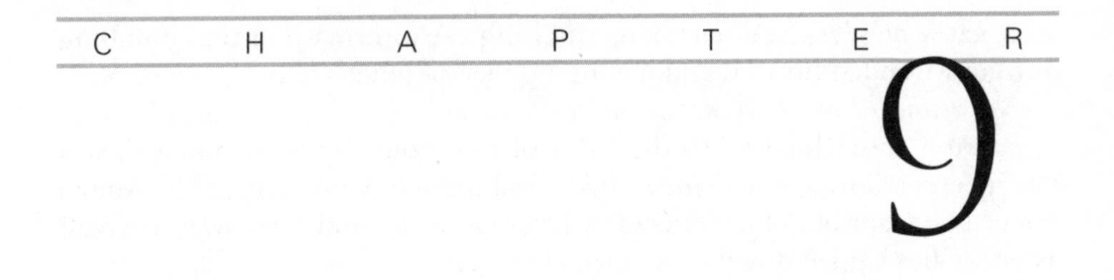

CHAPTER 9

WASHINGTON, DC

Brixton couldn't find his breath, almost like he had forgotten how to breathe. He trotted across the Capitol lawn, gasping by the time he reached the outskirts of the cordoned-off east front steps, where controlled chaos still ruled the day. All the bodies had been removed, and he caught glimpses of yellow flags denoting where each had fallen. When he got closer, he knew, there would be blood, lots of it.

He bent over and laid his hands on his knees, willing his breathing to settle and his heart to stop slamming up against his rib cage. He wondered if he might be having a heart attack, then banished the thought as quickly as it had come.

Because he had to find out what had happened to Max. He was clinging to the hope—and prayer—that the boy had avoided the spray of assault rifle fire that had felled so many of his classmates, seven so far at last count, with another listed in critical condition and several more hospitalized. Brixton had turned his phone to on-scene reporting on the Metro ride over. The number of confirmed dead had risen to eighteen, with at least that many wounded, some critically as well. Reports from the scene mentioned kids from Max's school being among both groups, and a website he checked while listening claimed that eight high school freshmen visiting the Capitol from a Baltimore prep school had been among those who did not survive the shooting—eight, not the seven that other outlets were reporting, meaning the one who was critical hadn't made it.

Based on what Brixton had been able to string together, it had now been more than three hours since the shooting had occurred, explaining how all the dead and wounded had already been removed from the scene. Margot said she'd called Max a dozen times, only to have the phone go straight to voicemail. Brixton took that as a far better sign than if the phone had rung unanswered. Perhaps the kids were told to shut off their phones or leave them on the bus.

Brixton finally recovered enough of his breath and senses to stand up straight again, warding off a wave of dizziness that threatened to overcome him. The scene felt surreal, like a dream he couldn't wake from. The whole way over he'd had flashbacks to the terrorist bombing that had claimed the life of his daughter Janet at a Washington restaurant, right before his eyes. How helpless he'd felt then, watching the aftermath of that bombing unfold, wounded himself and having no idea of Janet's fate.

Not again. Please, God, not again . . .

Brixton eased his way to the front of the crowd squeezed up against a hastily erected rope line manned by a combination of uniformed DC Metro police and Capitol Police officers. All were wearing body armor. A few held assault rifles tipped downward across their chests.

Initial, unconfirmed reports said the shooter had been dressed in a National Guard uniform, falling in behind an arriving twelve-man security detachment permanently assigned to supplement security at the Capitol Building. Brixton could picture the man waiting patiently nearby, having schooled himself on the Guard's deployment schedule. That was enough to confirm that this was no random act undertaken by a depraved mind acting on impulse.

No, the shooter had done his homework to ensure he could reach the steps without attracting any undue attention while carrying an assault rifle. Brixton imagined such National Guard shifts were staggered and rotated daily to avoid just this kind of infiltration. There would have been a window, somewhere between one and two hours, and if the shooter was patient and committed, that would have posed little problem for him.

"Excuse me," Brixton kept saying, as he shouldered his way forward. "Excuse me."

As he reached the front, he realized his breath was coming in short, shallow heaves. The panic that must have claimed his features was enough to get a Metro cop he didn't recognize to take notice.

"You okay, pal?"

Brixton eased an ID wallet from his pocket with a trembling hand—not his private investigator identification but a backup he always carried, from his days with SITQUAL, because the State Department seal opened far more doors and the ID came with no expiration date.

"My grandson goes to the school," he said to the cop, who was still regarding his ID.

"Name?"

"Robert Brixton."

The cop remembered it from his check of Brixton's ID. "I mean your grandson's name."

"Max Gregory. He's fourteen, a freshman."

The cop's expression didn't change but he leaned in toward his shoulder-mounted mic. "Base, this is three two. I've got a relative of one of the students involved in the shooting."

A pause followed.

"Roger that," the cop finally said into the mic, and looked back toward Brixton. "All relatives are being taken to a secure room inside the Capitol. If you slide under the rope, I'll escort you there."

Brixton ducked beneath it and felt dizzy again when he stood all the way back up.

"You okay?" the cop asked him.

"What do you think?"

"Yeah," was all the cop said, and Brixton fell into step alongside him, wishing there was a railing he could hold on to.

They bypassed the Capitol's east steps in favor of a side emergency exit door manned by Capitol policemen on either side. But that didn't stop Brixton from turning his gaze toward the site of the carnage, seeing it all unfold through his trained eye. Placement of the forensics team and small flags indicating the points where spent shells had been recovered told him where the shooter had been standing. Based on the largest cluster of flag outlines for fallen bodies, the positioning would have given him a straight sight line to where Max and the other kids had been clustered.

"Hey, buddy, you wanna stop for a sec."

Brixton hadn't realized how much he was laboring. "I want to find my grandson."

"You're no good to him in a cardiac unit."

Brixton nodded. "I'm okay. Let's go."

The cop grudgingly led him on, straight up to the emergency exit, where one of the Capitol policemen used an old-fashioned key attached to a chain on his belt to open the door. The cop led Brixton through and along a hallway he didn't recall ever being down before. He thought this might be a nesting of rooms once reserved for tour groups, long closed, thanks to security measures enacted post-9/11. It made sense. Rooms large enough for tour groups would also have ample space to accommodate families stricken with terror over the fates of their sons and daughters.

"This room is where families are being reunited with their kids," the cop said, as they drew closer to a door guarded by another pair of Capitol policemen. "So if your grandson made it . . ."

"Thanks for your help," Brixton told him.

The cop brought him all the way to the door. "Good luck, Mr. Brixton. And, by the way, the State Department changed their logo." He managed a smile, both compassionate and reassuring. "You should update your ID."

One of the other Capitol cops opened the door for Brixton to enter. Brixton brushed past him into the long-shuttered tour group gathering point, with his breath bottlenecked in his throat. He'd never felt air so thick, so clogged with emotion. He heard sobbing. He heard voices amid a sea of indistinguishable faces and a smattering of the familiar khaki pants and blue blazer Gilman School uniform he recalled Max wearing every time he picked his grandson up. He was afraid to look deeper than that, afraid that he wouldn't spot Max. He was frozen in place, needing to remind himself to breathe again.

"Poppi!" he heard a shrill voice cry out.

And then Max jumped into his arms.

CHAPTER 10

WASHINGTON, DC

Kelly saw that it was a piece of loose-leaf paper, the kind with serrated edges torn awkwardly from a standard spiral notebook of the sort that kids used to cram in their backpacks, one for each subject. A handwritten note that bore a tire mark from being run over. It was stained with grime, still sodden along its right side, and marred by a jagged, diagonal tear. The fact that the page had been folded over was a blessing in that it had shielded the handwritten content from being lost for good. Instead, it was merely damaged and compromised.

Some of the words on the most sodden portions had run together, and others had been wiped out beyond recognition. Kelly saw that still more of the writing was indecipherable, as she carefully peeled the top edge back to unfold the page and reveal a chicken scratch scrawl of words that had likely filled a page, only about half of which was still intact. The topmost portion had been lost to the whims of the air and street, but the rest seemed to be a note written to the slovenly woman on the Capitol plaza, likely by the shooter, and beginning in the middle of a sentence:

> . . . wish there had been another way, wish this hadn't been forced upon me by—

The rest of that sentence was lost to a tear, and the remainder of the note picked up in the middle of the next one.

> . . . do not seek this but nor do I shun my duties before the eyes of—

The sentence ended there, thanks to the same tear. Kelly mentally filled in *God* after "of" to see if that made sense. She recalled something she had heard in the reports she'd seen on her CNN app, which she brought up to learn the latest they had on the shooting. And sure enough, one of the few things witnesses were certain of was that the shooter had made not one, but two biblical references.

The hand of God is upon you! He is my shepherd and I shall not want!

That had been followed, moments later but before the shooting started, by another.

I am doing the Lord's work! I am a sacrifice to his Word!

Plenty of crazies behind mass shootings deluded themselves into believing they were doing the work of God. So, screaming out that intention, along with memorializing it in a final note, was hardly unusual.

She read on, picturing the woman from the Capitol lawn finding this note on her kitchen table, thinking back to those words she'd spoken on the bench, which continued to haunt Kelly.

I could have stopped it.

Which could only mean she was well acquainted with the shooter. The shock the woman had displayed indicated he was someone close to her. All indications pointed to her husband. That made the most sense. Meanwhile, the circumstances suggested the shooter wasn't a crazy, not a zealot, but a man with a specific reason for coming to the Capitol today. Kelly went back to the note, hoping it might contain some hint as to what that reason might be, trying to decipher what she could from fragments, filling in the blanks while finding an occasional complete thought.

> I know you'll never forgive me.

Kelly had a sense from the broken and interrupted sentences that surrounded that line that the writer was referring to something he had done already as opposed to what he was planning. Starting to feel stiff and cramped in the confines of her car seat, she began to see this as a puzzle with some missing pieces, which might nonetheless yield a coherent picture. Kelly read on, wanting to at least get to the end of the note before doing a more thorough job of assembling the puzzle, back home in Baltimore. The bottom portion of the hand-scrawled note with its bleeding letters had the least remaining, but there was a nearly whole line that stuck out.

> . . . failed to heed my warnings no matter how much I tried to . . .

Back to the point that the shooter had tried desperately to have his warnings about something or other heeded by one or more people, who'd turned a deaf ear to his claims. But why had that led him to open fire on the crowded Capitol steps?

That thought triggered another in Kelly's mind: Why today? Sure, it could have been chosen at random, nothing more than fate and a chance to blame, but she didn't think so. Enough of the note was intact for her to see that all the handwritten words clung to the respective lines on the page of loose-leaf paper. The penmanship was neat, measured, and precise, though a bit jumpy in spots, as if the author's hand had begun to shake for a moment. And the tear down the side of the page had been pristine, no "kadoobies"—the tiny shreds of paper left over when one tears a sheet of paper from a spiral notebook.

. . . not survive this, nor do I deserve . . .

Everything in this note pointed to the shooting being anything but random. He had come here with a purpose, knowing he was going to die, willing to sacrifice himself.

For what, though?

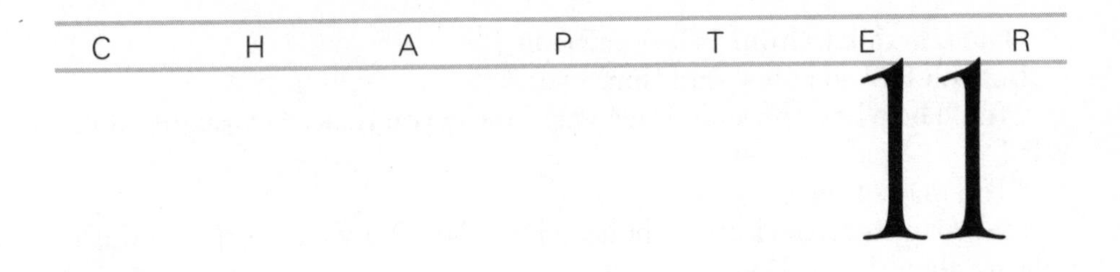

CHAPTER 11

WASHINGTON, DC

Brixton didn't want to let go of his grandson, as if Max might slip away from him forever.

"My friends, Poppi, my friends!" Max sobbed into Brixton's ear, his ears dampening the shoulder of his jacket. That made Brixton wonder what had become of his grandson's blazer and why he was wearing the kind of Capitol-branded T-shirt that was sold pretty much everywhere around DC. "I watched them—"

Brixton eased him away. "Don't say it. You can think it, but don't say it. When you say it, when you make the words, it's like going through it all over again."

The boy nodded, his lips trembling.

"Why didn't they let you call your parents?" Brixton asked him gently.

"I lost my phone. I had it out, was taking pictures, when—" Max stopped, as if remembering his grandfather's counsel.

Brixton had been forty-two when Max was born, fourteen years ago. He and Marylee had had Margot straight out of college, working on starting a family from the time they were married. Both were old school that way. It turned out to be one of the few things they really had in common, though they managed to stay together. Old school, too. A young father first, and then a young grandfather.

Like father, like daughter, Brixton thought, since Margot had Max at the same age Brixton and Marylee had had her.

"I told them that and they said they'd call my parents to tell them I was okay," Max continued.

Brixton realized that task now fell on him, and he started to reach for his phone.

"Don't bother," his grandson advised. "I was just on the phone with Mom and Dad before you walked in. The cops said they realized they'd been dialing the wrong number. They're on the way here now."

As if on cue, Brixton's phone rang, with "MARGOT" lighting up the caller ID.

"I'm with him now," Brixton greeted.

"Oh, thank God! Thank God, Dad!"

"He's fine," Brixton said, casting Max a wink.

"Did you talk to him? Is he okay *really*?"

Brixton looked at his grandson. "Yes."

"You'll help him through this, right? I mean you've been through it yourself."

"Too many times."

Margot paused, having caught herself too late. "I didn't mean . . . I wasn't talking about Janet, Dad."

"I know."

"You were a cop; you were a special operator. What was it they called your type?"

"A door kicker," Brixton told her, referring to the kind of operative who liked to be first through the door on a raid. "And I left SITQUAL and State to get away from that."

"You can't get away from it, Dad. It's everywhere now."

He looked at his grandson again, closer. "I know. We're waiting for you. Drive carefully."

"Count on it."

Brixton watched Max swallow hard as he pocketed his phone.

"Nobody will tell us how many kids died, Poppi." He paused to scan the room. "There's a bunch of them missing."

"There were some wounded, too," Brixton said, not wanting to fill in too many blanks for his grandson.

"Bad?"

"It's never good."

Max swallowed hard again. He had dark hair and features, his hair hanging in twisted ringlets that framed his face the same way his mother's curls framed hers. But Max had Brixton's eyes, steely and sharp, what some might call a gunfighter's eyes. Brixton looked in those eyes and saw the boy's strength and resilience, had never been more impressed with him.

Max grabbed hold of his sleeve with a surprisingly strong grip and pulled him aside, into a corner of the room. "I need to tell you something. Can I tell you something?"

"Of course," Brixton nodded.

"I saw the shooter. I mean I saw him, noticed him before he started . . ."

Brixton put his hand on the boy's shoulder. "I don't want you talking about this."

"I want—I *need* to talk about it, Poppi. I should have spoken up. I knew something was wrong, something was off about him."

"You can't beat yourself up over this, Max!"

"I'm not! Okay, maybe I am, but that's not what I need to tell you. See, when I looked at him, he was looking back—not at me alone but at all of us, all the kids from my school. Then he started shooting." Max sighed, then took a deep breath. "Because it was us he came here to kill, Poppi. I think we were his targets."

CHAPTER 12

BALTIMORE, MARYLAND

Kelly promised herself she'd eat something when she got home but ended up only guzzling a twenty-four-ounce water—well, twenty-three ounces, these days—instead. Going back to her days as a homicide cop, investigations tended to become all-consuming for her. She wouldn't eat, wouldn't sleep, wouldn't drink. Ended up dehydrated and exhausted, with a constantly rumbling stomach. She'd lie in bed, creating a flowchart in her mind, assembling the pieces of the case in big, broad fashion. A mental wall-length murder board.

Which she intended to fashion physically, in this case, assembling a puzzle as best she could with the disjointed pieces of the incomplete note that had been torn, sodden, run over, and soiled with grime.

She lived in the Ashburton Townhomes complex on North Rosedale Street in Baltimore, just northwest of downtown. She had a parking space directly outside her front door and there was plenty of room inside for a single person, including a spacious kitchen that Kelly didn't get very much use out of and an equally spacious living room that she did. That living room featured a big driftwood coffee table she'd purchased at a store in Harbor East, positioned directly before the couch, upon which she placed the pile of items she'd managed to recover from the handbag belonging to the woman who'd disappeared from Capitol plaza. There was no rhyme or reason to those items, and she hoped to make some sense of their content through the rest of the evening.

What am I thinking?

Kelly had information, potentially vital to an all-hands-on-deck investigation, which she had failed to turn over. Part of it was stubbornness, part of it was the itch to feel like a detective again, and the rest was territoriality. She'd found the note, so it was hers to follow up. Simple as that.

Of course, if she hadn't broken protocol and left a potential material witness alone to vanish, there would have been no clues to recover. She would have listened to the rest of the woman's story and then brought her to her superiors or the head of the FBI detail that was already on the scene. Losing the woman changed all that, left Kelly with no more than the scattered possessions she had desperately rushed about the streets and sidewalks to recover.

Kelly put off eating until later. She set the tattered and badly damaged piece of loose-leaf paper inside a plastic sleeve that detectives used to safeguard evidentiary documents, to protect it from any further degradation. Chain of evidence had gone out the window a long time ago, since the note had been lost to the whims of the wind. But it still might contain vital evidence that her own scrutiny, or any naked eye, might miss, so it needed to be preserved, first and foremost.

Then she set the plastic sleeve alongside her laptop and opened a Word document. She typed in a huge, bold font, adjusting the document so it was wider than it was high, to maximize how much could be squeezed onto each line. This, even though the vast bulk of the sentence fragments left far more space than the scant remaining letters occupied.

She typed everything in order, double-spacing to the next line every time she came to what she judged to be the end of a sentence or thought.

> . . . wish there had been another way, wish this hadn't been forced upon me by—
>
> . . . do not seek this but nor do I shun my duties before the eyes of—
>
> I know you'll never forgive me.
>
> . . . failed to heed my warnings no matter how much I tried to . . .
>
> . . . not survive this, nor do I deserve . . .
>
> . . . and now millions will . . . result
>
> . . . can no longer live with my . . .
>
> . . . Sena . . .

After she finished typing those fragments in a large, bold typeface, she printed the two pages out and used scissors to turn each entry into an individual strand. Kelly supposed she could have managed the same effort on her computer, but the laptop screen was too small for the scrutiny she wanted to give the finished product. Beyond that, this was how she preferred to work, her mind far more adept at responding to printed matter than that which was digitally displayed.

She arranged the fragments to replicate the contents of the note atop her driftwood coffee table, forgoing the couch in favor of sitting on her knees to complete the effort, and then standing up to review the product of her work. The handwritten note, as far as she could tell, consisted of a single paragraph, so she arranged the fragments with that in mind.

__________ wish there had been another way, wish this
hadn't been forced upon me by __________ beyond
__________ only I had known that __________ do
not seek this but nor do I shun my duties before the eyes
of __________ I know you'll never forgive me.
__________ the pain __________ was another way
__________ my fault . . . failed to heed my warnings
no matter how much I tried to . . . __________
__________ the fate that r __________ suf __________
not survive this, nor do I deserve __________ because no
one else deserves to d__________ . . . and now millions
will __________ result . . . can no longer live with my . . . hate
me __________ time you read this __________
Sena __________ __________ I can only
__________ loving hus __________

That was it. For those portions of the note that had been damaged by exposure to the elements and roadbed, there were techs who specialized in restoring the original content to some degree. As for the jagged portion of the page that was missing along the right-hand side, those words, and their message, were lost forever.

Kelly had hoped that, once assembled this way, the note would make more discernible sense, that she'd be able to glean something from it she hadn't been able to before. Only there was too much missing. It was like playing a game of Scrabble, but with missing words and sentences instead of letters.

She had no choice but to improvise, promising herself she'd spend only another hour at this before forcing herself to eat. If nothing else, it would take her mind off losing a potential vital witness. Assembling the note in search of meaning and context was an act of redemption more than anything else.

Her next task was to try to use index cards to fill the blank sections on the coffee table with content. For example, she added "I only" before *wish* in the first line. The process became maddening as Kelly struggled to add sense to a tattered message that defied her effort at every turn.

She tried a different tack by reading backward. She believed "loving hus" to be confirmation of what she had suspected already: that the shooter was the husband of the woman she'd found languishing on the Capitol lawn bench. The couple likely owned only a single car; since it seemed the woman had left the area by bus, it figured that she also had come to Washington through some means of public transportation. That meant the shooter's car must still be in the general area of the Capitol, and she was certain that a combination of Capitol Police, DC Metro, and the FBI were scouring the area for it. Assuming that the shooter had carried no ID on him, they would print and photograph his bullet-riddled corpse in order to run him through various systems in search of a match.

Kelly found herself wondering how the woman had known where her husband was heading, but the note gave no indication of that. It might have been in the portion that was missing. But she didn't think so, believing that the final words were a kind of good-bye, filling in the blanks to form "Your loving husband." A name would likely have followed *husband*, but that, too, was gone now.

Instead of continuing to focus on what she didn't know, Kelly decided to concentrate on what she could reasonably deduce. For instance, the shooter apparently believed he was acting to spare suffering for others. He felt that his hand had been forced, that he had no choice, consistent with reciting religious phrases in the moments before he opened fire. The phrase "my fault" suggested the shooter was acting under some degree of guilt, something that led Kelly off on another tangent.

She kept an ancient fluorescent desk lamp on the workstation she'd bought from Wayfair. The desk lamp had been her father's and had followed her from high school to college to all the places she'd lived since. She tilted the lamp itself straight toward her, squinting against the blinding brightness.

When that effort failed to produce the desired result, she pulled a magnifying glass from the desk drawer and held it in front of the plastic.

Nothing.

She looked away, took a deep breath, rubbed the life back into her eyes. When she looked down at the note again, a portion jumped out at her:

> . . . and now millions will . . . result . . .

She looked at the space between *will* and *result*, estimating the number of letters that would fill that space and then extrapolating what words might fill the gap. On a whim, she returned to her laptop and typed three words, eight spaces in total. Same size font, only bold print in all caps to indicate it was her addition. Then she printed it and cut the fresh words from the page.

Back at the coffee table she set the new section into the gap. It fit perfectly, giving her a chill when she read the result in total.

> . . . and now millions will **DIE AS A** result . . .

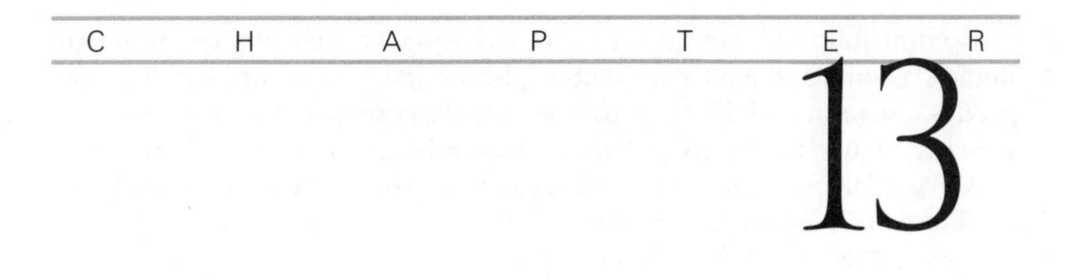

CHAPTER 13

BETHESDA, MARYLAND

Brixton waited until they reached his daughter's home in Bethesda, close to Walter Reed Hospital, where she worked as a hospital administrator, to press the issue further.

Because it was us he came here to kill, Poppi. I think we were his targets.

Those words had stuck with him from the moment his grandson uttered them, but he backed off pushing the boy for more until he had settled down sufficiently for his mind and memory to sharpen, the haze of shock clearing. The FBI and Capitol Police had wisely avoided questioning the surviving Gilman School students at the scene, going so far as to request only voluntary statements from anyone who thought they remembered something that might prove helpful in getting to the bottom of why this had happened. A few kids elected to give statements, once their parents had arrived on the scene, while everything was still fresh in their minds. Margo and her husband, Zeke, though, wanted no part of that. They wanted Max out of there the moment they arrived, remaining only long enough to speak briefly with the FBI special agents manning the room.

The family's move back to the area had allowed Brixton not only to get to see his grandson more but also to get to know his son-in-law better. Zeke was short for Ezekiel, and the opportunity to become a partner at a leading Washington lobbying law firm had been the reason for the move. Mackensie Smith had given the firm a big thumbs-up in terms of reputation and legacy, while still professing a loathing for that kind of lawyering in principle.

Zeke was African American, and if there was nothing else to like about how the world had changed, at least there was the fact that mixed-race kids fared far better today than ever before. It seemed to him it was hardly even an issue anymore. And for his part, Brixton couldn't be happier to have his surviving daughter and her family so close. Being able to spend more time with Max and Margot had become an unrivaled blessing. He tried to schedule everything around Max's football, basketball, and lacrosse games, but there were times he couldn't, and he regretted every game he missed.

"Can I talk to you, Dad?" Margot said, after Max had gone upstairs to shower and change his clothes. "Wash the death off of them" was the way the boy had put it, but his attempt at humor didn't take.

Brixton followed Margo into the sprawling kitchen of their beautiful Bethesda home in the Fort Sumner neighborhood, known for its trees, block parties, an annual Halloween parade, and Christmas lights that would be switched on like clockwork just after Thanksgiving, three weeks from now.

Margot hugged him as soon as they reached the kitchen. "Thanks, Dad."

"For what?" Brixton asked her.

"Being there when I needed you."

"What are fathers, and grandfathers, for?" He grasped her shoulders and rubbed them reassuringly. "And I'm always there for you, you know that."

Margot seemed to have something else on her mind. "I don't want you getting involved in this."

"In what?"

She scoffed at his response. "You know."

Brixton did. "It's a federal case, Maro," he said, using the nickname that owed its origins to the fact that as a young girl, Margot couldn't pronounce her own name without leaving out the *G*. "I don't think anyone's going to want my help."

Brixton thought about what Max had said about the shooter having targeted the kids from his school, directing his fire straight at them. It was something he hadn't yet shared with Margot, and now had no intention to. But it was something Max would have to share when he gave his statement to the FBI. Brixton wondered if any of the other kids had made the same observation, but he doubted it. If nothing else, as a grandfather, Brixton had embedded in the boy's mind the need to always stay vigilant, to keep a constant focus on your surroundings, and to never take anything, or anyone, for granted.

"I know how you get when it's personal, Dad."

"I was a lot younger back then, Maro," he told his oldest daughter, knowing she was referring to his actions in the wake of Janet's death.

Margot managed a smile. "But not too old to get married again. Have you set a date for the wedding?" she asked him, as eager to change the subject as he was.

"Not yet. I'm leaving all that to Flo."

Just then, Max appeared in the kitchen doorway, his hair twisted into ringlets that dripped with water.

"I need to talk to Poppi," he said to his mother.

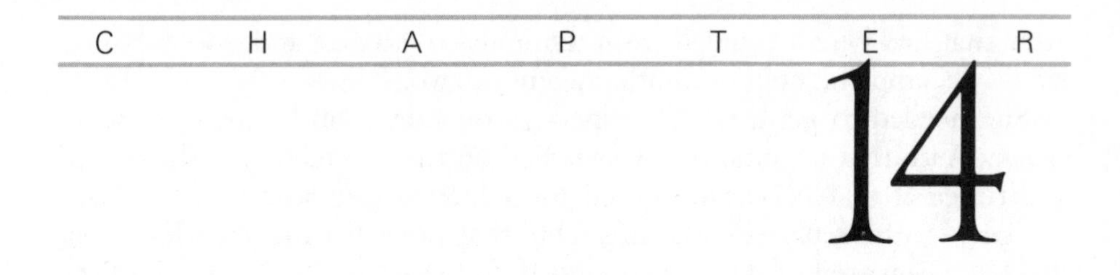

CHAPTER 14

BALTIMORE, MARYLAND

> . . . and now millions will **DIE AS A** result . . .

Kelly's attention had frozen on that fragment, her addition making for a perfect fit in terms of both size and content.

As a result of *what*? And who were these millions—*where* were these millions? Could this have been the shooter's warning that had gone unheeded?

> . . . failed to heed my warnings no matter how much I tried to . . .

And who exactly had he tried to warn?

Kelly's cell phone rang; the Capitol Police office calling. She let it go to voicemail, stricken by fear someone might have witnessed her actions after she'd left work and now she'd face obvious recriminations. More likely, the call was simply to advise her of a shift change, especially in view of the shooting. But she'd grown increasingly paranoid since the seeds of her departure from the Baltimore Police Department were sowed. She hadn't learned to trust again, at least professionally, and had begun to question whether she ever would. Then she went back to the note jumbled across her coffee table.

Its message was becoming clearer, but it was still too elusive to make sense of. Kelly decided to put off eating longer, to try something different in the hope of adding more pieces to the puzzle. Eating had become a problem for her since her dismissal from Baltimore Homicide—not eating too much, but too little. She'd lost her appetite on what had become a permanent basis, couldn't remember a time where she didn't have to force herself to eat meals she normally would have devoured. She knew it was the kind of condition she'd likely not be able to remedy on her own, but professional help was not on her life menu at this point; the last thing she wanted to do was dredge up a recapitulation of her final months with the BPD.

Kelly grabbed her phone and held her breath while checking the message that had come in from headquarters. Fortunately, it was only to advise her that extended shifts were commencing immediately and would continue into the foreseeable future. She still had tomorrow off, but her shift the day after that had been extended from ten hours to sixteen and, she was sure, would be supplemented by another agent or two.

She needed to get a fresh perspective on this, a bird's-eye view, so to speak. With that in mind, Kelly switched on the one television she owned and tuned it to CNN. She waited for a loop of the scene on the Capitol steps to be replayed—the moments that preceded the shooting, what had been captured of the shooting itself, followed by the aftermath of the carnage. The network had used a combination of professional news feeds, security camera footage, and jumpy cell phone footage to assemble a montage that approximated a moment-by-moment rendering of the events. It lasted just over three minutes in all, and Kelly DVR'd it so she could replay the footage at a slower speed.

First, she watched it three more times at normal speed, confirming that the shooter's fire had started on the high school students on the far right of the Capitol's east front steps, looking up from the base, almost out of the frame. The fire had then moved sideways across the stairs in deliberate fashion, the bodies tumbling like dominoes from right to left, while those who'd avoided the bullets rushed in panic out of the frame or ducked down and pressed themselves low.

Kelly then watched the rendering at slower speed, freezing the frame occasionally to check for something she might have missed. Something was plaguing her—specifically, whether the shooter had come here with specific targets in mind. The context of his note, even with so much missing, indicated rational, motivated, premeditated thinking. That left Kelly certain that the shooter hadn't come to the Capitol just to fire on the steps and claim as many random victims as he could. No, he had come there with clear intent.

Since he had fired on the prep school students, all boys, first, logic dictated that she consider them his primary targets. Which of course made no sense. Maybe he had a son who'd attended the Gilman School and had suffered some terrible wrong that his father had sought to avenge. Could it really be that simple?

Otherwise, opening fire on the kids first made no sense. The precision of the man's fire indicated a man well-practiced and seasoned with a firearm, if not from actual combat experience, then certainly from hours at the range. Kelly just couldn't accept the fact he had shot those kids without malice aforethought.

She could make no sense of the anomaly, wishing she had a clear angle from the shooter's point of view at the bottom of the steps. Lacking that, she went back to the beginning of the tape once more, focusing on the Gilman kids in their khaki pants and blue blazers, in slow motion. They occupied only a small quadrant of her flat-screen. Just before the shooting began, the kids were being addressed by a senator she recognized but couldn't name. The picture shifted a bit, returning in the very seconds before the first shots rang out as the kids were taking selfies with that senator and a few other dignitaries. She recognized one of them as David Leopold, a congressman from Maryland, because he had been named as one of the shooter's victims, pronounced dead on the scene. Again, could it simply be that he had been the target all along and the kids were just collateral damage? No, because if that were the case, why would the shooter have kept firing from right to left after Leopold had already been downed?

There wasn't much to see, once the shooting began and chaos broke out. Even when she slowed the recording as much as she could, Kelly could no longer follow anything but a mad rush of bodies interspersed with the victims going down. Twice, at that slow speed, she was certain she could see a mist of blood spray outward on impact with two of those who were shot.

Kelly decided to take a break from the footage and the fragmented note to do a fresh inventory of the items from the handbag belonging to the woman she'd let slip away. She'd scooped up everything in her path, so she'd likely retrieved at least a few items that had not dropped from the woman's handbag at all, including what looked like an orange plastic bracelet, which she'd taken for some kind of token given in return for a small donation to this cause or that.

Closer inspection, though, revealed it to be something else entirely, and Kelly realized with a chill what that was.

CHAPTER 15

BETHESDA, MARYLAND

"Alone," Max added, also in his mother's direction.

Margot looked toward Brixton. "Just remember what I said," she said softly, but firmly.

Brixton raised his arms in concession. Max watched his mother walk past him, leaving them alone in the kitchen.

"Want something to drink?" Brixton wondered, moving toward the refrigerator.

"Sure. How 'bout a beer?"

Brixton turned from the now open door. "They lower the drinking age to fourteen?"

"I'll be fifteen next month."

"They lower the drinking age to fifteen, then?" he said back to his grandson, and snatched a Diet Coke.

"You can have one, if you want," Max said to him.

"I'm off the sauce."

"Sauce?"

Brixton realized Max must never have heard that term before. "Also known as alcohol."

"Why? You have a problem or something?"

That's what Brixton loved about kids. They said what was on their minds. Sneaky as hell other times, but they didn't hold anything back.

"Not with alcoholism, Max. The biggest problem was my waistline."

"You got fat?"

"More like I didn't feel like working out too many mornings because I'd been out the night before. It was after my fiancée moved to New York, after we broke up."

Max nodded knowingly. "You were lonely."

"Comes down to cause and effect. Drinking wasn't an effect of her leaving me; it was the cause. Too many late dinners."

Max nodded as if he understood that, but Brixton didn't think he did. He forced himself to let the boy talk about whatever he wanted to on his own time, to not push him at all. He'd looked older at the Capitol, more like a young adult. Wearing a warm-up suit for one of the sports he played, though, gave him the look of a boy again. The kitchen's bright lighting also seemed to highlight the youthful terror that clung to his eyes. Normally big and bright, they had now gone shifting and uncertain.

"You've shot people, right?" Max asked, those doe-like eyes aimed downward.

"Yes," Brixton said, not elaborating.

"When you were a cop?"

"Two when I was a cop."

"What about after, when you were working security for the State Department?"

Brixton didn't bother to correct his grandson on the actual job description of SITQUAL. He opted for the truth in his answer.

"I don't know."

"You don't—"

"A few."

"You mean a lot."

Max had never raised such issues before with him, other than looking at his grandfather with worshipful eyes as a young boy because he thought Brixton was a spy. Like James Bond. He'd never discussed the issue before with his grandson, had never discussed those particulars of his SITQUAL experience with anyone, not even Mac. Those closest to him knew better than to ask, but kids lack such filters, and this was something Max needed to talk about tonight, after the horror he'd experienced.

"Somewhere between a few and a lot," Brixton heard himself saying.

"I looked up SITQUAL once," his grandson confessed.

"What'd you find?"

"A lot about their work as a private security company." Max finally looked up all the way and met Brixton's gaze. "But that wasn't your department, was it?"

"No."

"You worked for a part of the company that isn't on their website."

"That part of SITQUAL closed not long after I left."

"I know—at least, I read stuff on the internet about it. There was that incident in the Middle East."

"I was gone by then."

"They identified a couple assassins as working for SITQUAL. Real black-ops shit."

The boy tensed over how Brixton might react to his use of that word, but Brixton ignored it.

"It's true," he admitted.

Max swallowed hard. "And is that what you did for them? An assassin?"

"No."

"But you killed people."

"Only when they were trying to kill me or whoever I was assigned to protect at the time," Brixton said, leaving it there.

Of course, he left out mention of the nighttime raids launched against enemy encampments, undertaken to preempt attacks uncovered by intelligence. The raids had normally involved multiple organizations, while avoiding use of active duty military. No SEALs or Delta Force, to keep the circle small and not involve the Joint Special Operations Command. Some in that world called the teams Brixton had been a part of the last true gunslingers in that they were truly accountable to no one. Get in, kill a bunch of guys, get out. No action reports, no pushing anything up the chain of command, no commendations, no medals.

"Oh," Max said, in a tone that gave away none of whatever he was feeling. "What does it feel like?"

"What does *what* feel like?" Brixton asked, even though he knew where his grandson was going with this.

"Killing someone."

"You don't have time to think about it. And when you finally do, you know what you did just saved a lot of lives."

"Like the death penalty in advance."

The kid had a point. "More or less." In fact, it was the best description of those raids he'd ever heard.

"So you were doing good."

"I like to think so. If I didn't, I would have stopped. It wasn't like the military, Max. I was free to quit at any time."

"So you liked it."

A tough one, Brixton thought. "I liked the work. The shooting was a part of it."

"You mean the killing."

"If you aim straight," Brixton conceded.

"Did you aim straight?"

"Most of the time."

The boy swallowed hard, looking his grandfather straight in the eye when he posed his next question. "Will you teach me how to shoot?"

"Only if your parents say it's okay."

"They won't."

"Then you'll have to convince them."

Max took a deep breath before resuming. "You think the shooter today liked what he did, killing my friends and the others?"

"I think he was dead before he had a chance to."

Max's expression, his features, changed, and he was suddenly no more than a tall, gangly, and handsome boy. "Why did he do it?"

"We may never know, Max. Sometimes we never find out for sure."

That was the first quasi lie Brixton had told his grandson. Dressing like a National Guardsman, timing his approach after clearly studying the Guard shift rotation for supplementing the guards around the Capitol—that and more suggested a clear purpose and motivation, as opposed to a random, impulsive act. The attack had been clearly mapped out in detail. He had known exactly what he was doing the whole time.

Which made Brixton see this another way. Max had insisted, back at the Capitol, that the shooter had specifically targeted the boys from his school. Tour groups had returned to the building in big numbers, to the point that there was often a waiting list to accommodate all those looking for a cherished slot sometime between the hours of 8:45 and 3:30. The shooter could have learned that much on the internet. And if these kids had for some inexplicable reason been his targets, their particular school's tour wouldn't have been difficult to ferret out, either. The timing of the man's approach had been perfect, in that respect.

"Earth to Poppi," Max was saying, snapping his fingers in front of Brixton's face. "Earth to Poppi."

"What?" Brixton asked, roused from his contemplative trance.

"You were somewhere else. You didn't even hear what I was saying."

"What were you saying?"

"I was asking you what you would've done if you were there."

"If I were you?"

"If you were me."

"So I'd be fourteen—"

"Almost fifteen."

"In which case you did everything right. I couldn't have done anything more, even as a trained fourteen-year-old special operative."

Brixton's attempt to inject a bit of humor drew a smile from Max before his eyes went glassy.

"I have this friend named Ben. We play the same sports. His twin brother got shot and then he got shot. The shooting stopped and I could tell Ben's twin was dead, but he was bleeding, so I took off my blazer and pressed it hard against the spot where the bullet must've been—you know, to stop the bleeding."

Brixton just nodded.

"They took my blazer for evidence . . . my shirt, too." Max looked down at his chest beneath the warm-up suit's top. "Are they going to give me my blazer back? I want my blazer back."

Brixton noted that Max had said nothing about his shirt.

"They wouldn't tell me anything about Ben," Max continued, before Brixton could respond. "I asked about a hundred times while they had us in that room, but they wouldn't tell me. Kept saying they'd request an update and get back to me. But they never did. I kept asking, but they never did. You can find out for me, right? You know people you can call."

Before Brixton could respond, the boy broke down, fat tears streaming down his cheeks. Brixton moved to him, and Max threw his arms around his grandfather like he'd never let go. Brixton said nothing, just stroked the boy's hair, losing his hand in a drying tangle of ringlets.

Max sniffled as he pushed himself away, his eyes coming back to life. "There's something else I need to tell you, Poppi, something really important I think I saw when—"

"Ahem," Margot said from the door.

Both Max and Brixton turned her way.

"You need to eat something, Max. Even if you're not hungry, you need to eat."

Max looked back at his grandfather.

"She's right," Brixton told him, forcing himself to agree with his daughter, even though he really wanted to know what else his grandson had to tell him. "We can finish talking later."

"But—"

"Later," Brixton reiterated, wondering what it was Max had seen.

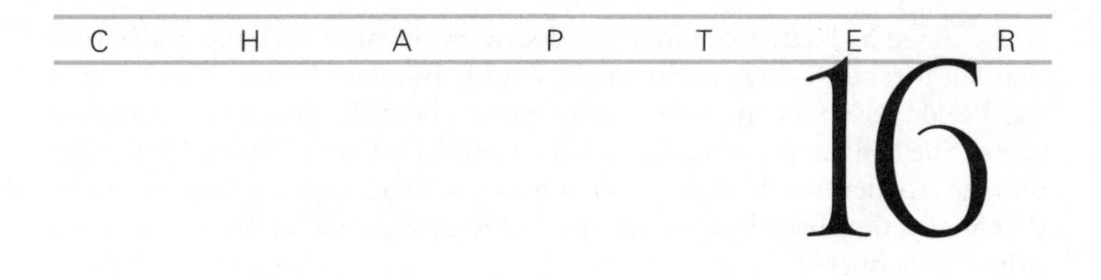

BALTIMORE, MARYLAND

A hospital wristband! The orange bracelet was a hospital wristband!

Kelly was too exhilarated by the discovery to wonder why she hadn't made the connection earlier. It had seemed so innocuous, easily confused with something people hand out in return for a small cash donation outside a store or shopping mall.

She took it in hand to inspect it, readying the magnifying glass it turned out she didn't need. A bar code ran across the top. Kelly knew this allowed hospital personnel to access the patient's medical records. Beneath the bar code was a birth date, account number for that visit to the hospital, and the name of the primary physician of, presumably, the woman who'd vanished from the Capitol plaza earlier in the day.

There was no hospital or patient name displayed, but the latter would be a cinch to find, once the hospital was identified. Kelly knew there would be an identifier somewhere within the symbols, numbers, and letters displayed on the soft plastic. The bracelet was in pristine condition, save for being trampled by pedestrians and maybe even a tire or two. It hadn't been torn off but carefully cut to keep it reasonably intact.

The woman Kelly had come upon sitting on the Capitol lawn bench must have been a hoarder of some kind; the cluttered contents of her handbag were more than enough to tell Kelly that. There were receipts for virtually everything, some of the dated ones going back several years, to a time when the handbag was likely in far better condition, if not new. Some had been in the handbag for so long that they were clumped together when Kelly retrieved them from the grass, sidewalk, or pavement. She hadn't bothered separating them yet.

Kelly focused again on the hospital wristband, using the magnifying glass this time to make sure she hadn't missed anything. And, sure enough, she spotted some scratchy writing on the inside of the band, two letters: P R.

She took those to be the woman's initials, pictured a nurse or technician using them to make sure she was affixing the band around the proper wrist. From that point on, everyone who examined the patient would have asked for the person's date of birth, to confirm they had the right individual. Even with such repetition and redundancy, hospitals still made treatment errors, but the number had been greatly curtailed since practices like this were instituted.

As elated as Kelly felt about the discovery, it came with the realization that she'd taken things as far as she could, and dared, on her own. This was no longer a treasure hunt sort of game where she got to play detective again. She had happened upon a piece of evidence that might enable the authorities to identify the shooter, or at least a woman who was likely his wife. Potentially, they had already done that but were withholding the information from the public.

The simple fact was that she had no idea how far the investigation had progressed, none at all. She had a friend at the FBI with whom she had been close at one point, and occasionally a bit more than that, and she trusted him well enough. Xander Peel was a real up-and-comer with the Baltimore field office, on the fast track to much bigger things. The kind of guy, in other words, who would know what to do with what she had to give up.

Kelly jogged her phone to "CONTACTS," scrolled to the *P*s, and pressed his number.

"As I live and breathe," he answered, in his typically smooth, newscaster voice.

"I guess you still have my number stored."

"Under 'Favorites,' actually. Old habits die hard, Kel."

"Busy day?"

"Have you been watching the news?"

"Living it, actually."

Kelly heard Xander Peel chuckle on the other end of the line. "That's right. I seem to remember you moving your talents down to DC. Capitol Police."

"Protective Services," Kelly confirmed for him.

"Explains why we've been out of touch."

"You still had my number, X. And my talents were moved for me."

"I remember that, too." He hesitated, his tone tighter and less airy when his voice returned. "Can I assume you didn't call to ask me to dinner?"

"You can. But dinner's not a bad idea. Are you working the mass shooting at the Capitol?"

"DC field office is in charge, with HQ following every step. We've been on hold up here, but so far they haven't needed our support."

"I've got some information that can change that," Kelly told him. "Have they ID'd the shooter yet?"

"Not that I know of."

"Yes or no, X?"

"No, which is strange, because initial thinking was he had a military background for sure. But I guess not, since his fingerprints aren't on record anywhere, and facial recognition software also drew a blank."

"What if I could fill it in?"

A brief silence followed, before Peel's voice returned. "Keep talking, Kel."

Kelly eyed the orange hospital bracelet before her. "Got a pen handy?"

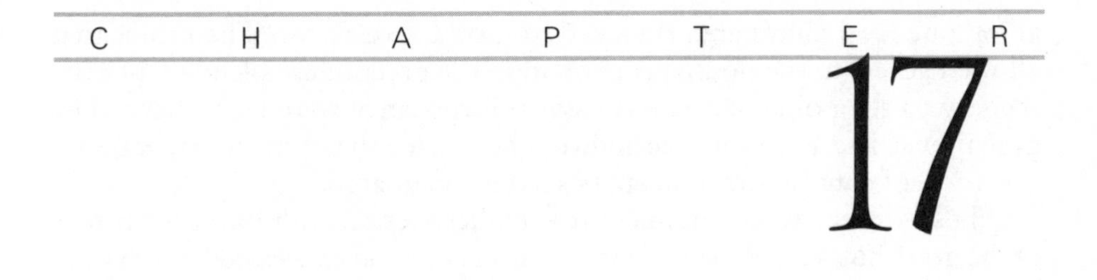

AURORA, COLORADO

The orchids were in bloom, and Dr. Efram Lutayne couldn't tear himself away from them. He could sit out here and just stare at their regal majesty, taking pride in all the care and love that had brought them to this point. They were his pride and joy, close to a stand-in for the human companionship that he neither had nor wanted. Their beauty made him forget about the wheelchair that a stroke had bound him to fifteen years ago, as well as the cause to which he'd dedicated the bulk of his professional life, all the ugliness in stark contrast to the contents of the greenhouse that lent his life all the beauty it needed.

There were times when Lutayne whiled away not just hours but entire mornings or afternoons out here. He'd come to embrace a world in which he had erased his digital footprint entirely. No cell phone, no internet, no record that this sprawling property nestled at the base of the Rocky Mountains, in the literal middle of nowhere, was in his name. He was off the grid, nothing but satellite television to connect him to the outside world, the bill paid on a yearly basis by a third party with no apparent link to him.

He enjoyed his white orchids most of all, because they left the most to the imagination and seemed the most alive. Their flowers were always richer than his purple, pink, or blue varieties, even though he found the blue to be the boldest and most striking to the eye. He found the white orchids, though, to be the most calming, as if their lack of color rendered them a blank space, which seemed appropriate for a man whose past was an utter blank to everyone but himself. The strikingly beautiful blue orchids represented spirituality and contemplation, neither of which endeared them to Lutayne, since he had long ago lost any semblance of spirituality and preferred not to contemplate the long, lost period of his life. White orchids, on the other hand, represented purity, something he longed for in the face of spending too much of his life sowing the seeds for the deaths of tens of millions. Gazing at their unfinished beauty was almost enough to make him forget all that.

Almost.

Upon coming to Aurora, he had the home he'd purchased renovated around his need for a wheelchair. The drawers, doorknobs, and counters were all placed at a convenient height, and the fact that the home was built all on one level eliminated the need to install an elevator. The ramps that allowed access to the house proper and to the greenhouse blended into the scenery to the point that it was easy to forget they were even there. The greenhouse had been the sole addition he'd made to the property, employing a trio of contractors to keep its secrets safeguarded.

Those secrets were contained in a smaller section built into the far rear of the greenhouse, undetectable from the outside and concealed behind what appeared to be a solid wall on the inside. Only two people in the world knew of its existence. He was the first, and the second had been told only because, should anything happen to Lutayne, his instructions were to destroy the secret room's contents at all costs.

Lutayne had never fully understood why he'd kept the mementos of the years he had otherwise sought to forget. Perhaps as a reminder, maybe as punishment, potentially out of the practical concern he might somehow need the contents of that secret chamber for reasons other than their original intent. Tooele Army Depot in Tooele County, Utah, where he'd spent a big portion of his life, had once contained the means to wipe out the entire world's population many times over, the audacity of that notion exceeded only by the reality of it. All of those contents were gone now, destroyed under his supervision on the eve of his secret lab being shut down forever.

Except for one.

He blamed fate for the one item in Tooele's deadly inventory that remained unaccounted for. That thought spurred Lutayne to check his watch. As usual, he'd lost all track of time. Today was the day his monthly package, stuffed with press clippings the sender had flagged, was due to arrive via FedEx. The clippings mostly covered strange and inexplicable happenings, almost all of them involving mass deaths that had not been adequately explained or were clearly being covered up. Lutayne still preferred actual newspaper clippings, but there were always several printouts contained in the box as well, since so many newspapers were operating on a digital-only model these days.

Lutayne wheeled himself from his sanctuary, along the flagstone path and back to his house. Instead of circling all the way around the front, he wheeled himself through the more easily accessible side entrance and then made his way to the front door. Opening it, he saw a simple, plainly wrapped box sitting on his porch, in the spot where those who had someone to welcome would have set out a welcome mat.

Lutayne retrieved the box, rested it on his lap, and rolled on toward the kitchen, where he set the box on the table and fetched a knife to split it open. Peeling the top side of the box back revealed a swell of contents, the usual mix of printouts and actual press clippings cut neatly from the issues that had originally contained them. A typical month's worth of materials, given that nothing inexplicable was too small to ignore, given the potential of what might have been to blame. Lutayne eased all the contents from the box and set about reviewing them in his typically thorough, pragmatic fashion.

He was halfway through the pile when a headline from a physical newspaper froze him between breaths: "Officials Seek Cause of Poisoning Deaths of Local High School Students."

He was no stranger to such headlines, most bearing simple, tragic explanations. But, for reasons he could neither explain nor comprehend, this one felt different from the moment Lutayne glimpsed it. Just a feeling, a nagging sense of unease that left his hands quivering as he clutched the tear sheet tightly. He read on, his fear growing with each word, sentence, and paragraph, as if . . .

As if what he had been fearing for five years now had finally come to pass.

He continued reading, eager for more details, hoping against hope that his greatest concerns had not been realized. But the more he read, the more he knew his original instinct had been correct, knew in his heart and his mind that the most dangerous and deadly relic from his past had been recovered at last. Somebody had it, and that somebody had used it. A test maybe? An accident? What else could account for the circumstances surrounding the deaths of these students from a Baltimore, Maryland high school?

Unprecedented precautions had followed the shutdown of Lutayne's work, all the product of his genius and expertise transported to Utah to be disposed of. Except for one shipment, a shipment that had never made it to its destination after being separated from its lead and trail vehicles in a violent storm. No trace of that shipment had ever been found. Even the soldiers assigned to the truck itself had been lost with it.

The mystery had haunted him since the shuttering of his lab, stealing a measure of his sleep every single night for five years now. The fear that the contents of that final Red Dog run was gone but hardly lost was always at the forefront of his mind.

Lutayne wheeled himself across the kitchen to a utility drawer and from inside it lifted a satellite phone, his only means of communicating with the outside world. It had been so long since he'd used it, he had to remind himself how to turn the phone on. He was relieved when it powered up immediately.

"You know who this is?" he said, when the call was answered.

"Did you get the box?"

"I'll take that as a yes."

"Unusual for you to call."

"Then you should know the reason."

Silence filled the other end of the line, Lutayne picturing the man on the other end processing the ramifications of what he'd just said.

"I do," the man said finally.

"I need to see you."

"I can be there the day after tomorrow."

"Not soon enough," Lutayne told him.

"Make it twenty-four hours."

"Make it twelve," Lutayne said, with the semblance of an order. "And you need to bring something with you."

PART TWO

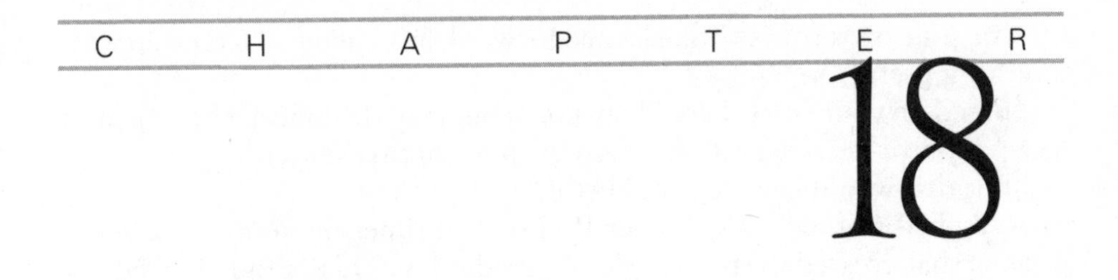

CHAPTER 18

BALTIMORE, MARYLAND

"What's this going to cost me?" Xander Peel had asked her the night before.

"Breakfast tomorrow morning," Kelly had told him.

And now she sat waiting for him at a table at the quirky Papermoon Diner on West Twenty-Ninth Street, a mile from her apartment. It wasn't hard to spot Peel when he entered. The man knew how to make an appearance, with movie star looks straight out of Central Casting for the modern G-man. But today, she noticed, as he steered toward her table, he looked ruffled and nervous, eyes swimming about anxiously when he took the seat across from her, pressed up against the wall.

"You look like you got as much sleep last night as I did," Peel greeted, in his silky-smooth voice.

"I was too excited, after we made this date for breakfast."

He flashed his adolescent-like smirk, born of a self-confidence many would have found distasteful but that Kelly accepted as Peel being Peel. "Is that what this is? A date?"

Kelly slid the orange hospital bracelet, now tucked into a Ziploc bag, across the table. "And I made this whole thing up just to see you."

That smirk again, even wider. "Wouldn't be the first time."

The Papermoon was a bright, colorful, and airy spot that Kelly loved, in spite of the fact that it carried too many memories of her years with the Baltimore Police Department. At times, it felt like eating in a kind of counterculture art gallery, with walls adorned with paintings that changed as they were either sold or the artist put them on display somewhere else. It was modern or outsider art mostly, rich, vibrant, and bursting with life, unlike the series of mannequins interspersed on the restaurant floor, which even at second glance appeared to be scantily clad customers.

Peel snatched up the plastic bag so fast it was like watching a magician make an object disappear.

"Thank you. For this and the phone call."

Kelly gestured toward that trio of scantily covered mannequins. "The first time I came here, I almost arrested one of them. For streaking."

"A mannequin?"

"Imagine my surprise." She leaned forward, just enough. "Come up with anything useful, X?"

"Based on your story, I could say no. I could say the bracelet belonged to a seventy-five-year-old retiree who was in for hernia surgery."

"But that would be a lie, wouldn't it?"

Kelly had worked with Xander Peel several times on homicide investigations that crossed over into federal jurisdiction. He not only looked the part, he also played it very well, as solid an FBI agent as she'd ever encountered, who took nothing for granted. An excellent operative who excelled at interrogations, thanks to his uncanny ability to establish a rapport with suspects, which led them to give up far more than they'd intended.

"Name Philip Rappaport mean anything to you, Kel?" he asked her.

Kelly remembered the initials PR. So the hospital bracelet didn't belong to the woman from the Capitol lawn bench at all; it must have belonged to her husband, the shooter.

"Not a thing," she told Peel. "Should it?"

"No." Peel tapped his own wrist. "Those are the initials of the owner of this hospital bracelet. And not just any hospital, either. Baltimore Behavioral Health."

"A psychiatric hospital," Kelly noted.

"We're not having this conversation, right?"

Kelly ran a finger along her closed lips.

"Treatment at Baltimore Behavioral Health is also covered by the Veterans Administration, since their mental health facilities are few and far between." Peel eased a piece of paper from his pocket. It had been folded in quarters, but he didn't open it up. "Are you leveling with me here, Kel?"

"I called you, didn't I? I just gave you what might be a piece of vital evidence from the Capitol shooting yesterday, and I explained exactly how I'd come by it. What else do you want?"

"Whatever you're leaving out."

"Why would you think I was leaving something out?" Kelly shot back, trying not to sound defensive.

"Because Philip Rappaport was the Capitol steps shooter." Peel paused just long enough to let his point sink in. "And I think you knew that."

"Suspected, maybe. But I thought the hospital bracelet belonged to that woman, and that's the truth."

"The woman you let slip away."

Kelly sighed. "Not my most shining of moments."

Peel finally straightened out the printout he'd pulled from his pocket. Kelly could see it was a picture of a woman, even before he handed it to her.

"Recognize her, Kel?"

She held the picture in both hands, regarding the face of the woman who'd disappeared in a daze from the Capitol grounds the day before, scattering the contents of her handbag everywhere. She nodded and handed it back.

"Her name is Jean Rappaport. Turns out, we'd already managed to ID her husband from someone who served with him in the army and the National Guard, a guy who caught his face on CNN."

"Wait. If he was army or National Guard, his prints would have popped up."

"So you'd think."

"They didn't?"

Peel shook his head. "And it wasn't a glitch, either. Rappaport wasn't in the system, because somebody erased him."

He waited for that to settle.

"Could have been done inadvertently," Peel continued. "Somebody hits the wrong key or something."

"But you don't think so."

"I don't need to think anything, Kel."

"Since when?"

"Since it's not my case."

"Why would someone wipe the fact that Philip Rappaport was in the army from the database?"

"Stop," Peel said firmly.

"What?"

"I know how that mind of yours works. You're looking for something to make sense of this, to make the pieces all fall together. Somehow, Philip Rappaport's service in the army was erased."

"Don't forget the fact that it also turns out he spent time in a psychiatric hospital."

"We don't know what he was in for," Peel reminded her, "and we don't know if it had any connection to his time in the military."

"You mean the time that was wiped off the books?"

Peel regarded the menu for the first time. A server came and filled both their coffee cups. Kelly ordered the sausage, egg, and cheese on whole wheat toast, hoping she could force herself to eat it. Peel opted for the Bananas Foster French Toast, which drew a raised eyebrow from Kelly.

"What?" he asked her.

"I thought you avoided sugar."

"Except when I'm amped up, and I'm amped up this morning."

"You pass the word to HQ?"

Peel sipped his black coffee and nodded. "Took it to my boss in the Baltimore field office and let him run it up the chain. He said he'd keep me in the loop. Said there might be a commendation in my future."

"Congratulations. How'd you explain me?"

"I didn't. I told the boss I had an anonymous source."

"Smart move, under the circumstances."

Xander Peel looked about the restaurant, as if seeing it for the first time. "Wasn't this a popular spot for your old squad?"

"It still is. Every time I come in here, I hope to run into one of them, let them see they knocked me down, but not out."

"You think they give a shit?"

"Not at all."

Peel leaned forward across the table and lowered his voice. "You know, you never gave me the whole skivvy on what went down."

"You never asked."

"I'm asking now, Kel."

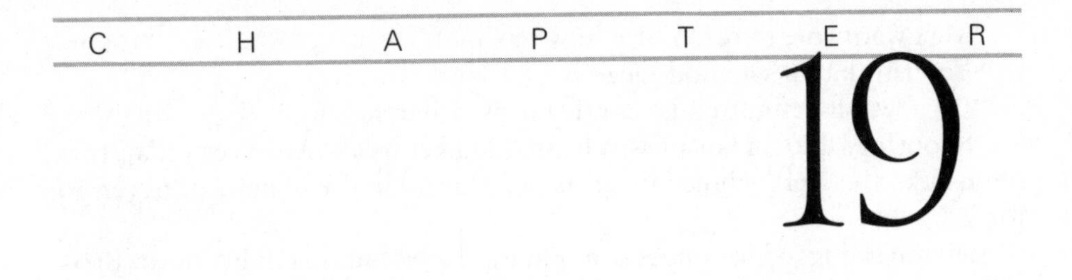

CHAPTER 19

WASHINGTON, DC

Brixton's wake-up call at six a.m. came courtesy of Mackensie Smith.

"I can't believe you didn't call me, Robert."

"I knew Flo would tell Annabel and Annabel would tell you. It was a long day, Mac. I'm sorry I didn't check in," Brixton said. "One of the longest days of my life. It feels like my lunch with Alexandra was last week, instead of yesterday. I never even had the chance to report to you on that."

"How'd it go?"

"I'll tell you over coffee. Peet's?" Brixton posed, referring to the coffee shop that was just two blocks from the offices of Mac's firm in the Warner Building.

"Where else?"

Flo Combes was literally waiting by the door of their Arlington, Virginia, apartment when Brixton pulled it open the night before, throwing herself into his arms.

"Robert!"

"Easy, babe," he said, trying to sound a lot more flippant and casual than he felt, as they separated. "We've only been apart since breakfast."

"Poor Max, Robert. Oh, my God . . ."

"He's fine—at least as well as can be expected."

"You should have called me from Bethesda."

"I was coming straight home."

She hugged him again. Brixton could feel her trembling, heard her sniffling as she held back her tears. He waited for her to pull away on her own.

"How is he?"

"He saved a friend's life. I learned this morning that the kid's going to pull through."

Flo's eyes widened at that. "But is he . . ."

"He seems fine right now. The shock hasn't worn off yet. Once it does, I'd expect him to show signs of trauma. Kids are good at hiding that, bottle it all inside until it becomes the cause of real problems."

"Post-traumatic stress disorder," Flo nodded knowingly. "So what are you going to do about it?"

"Max wants me to teach him how to shoot."

"You think that's a good idea?"

"It's a way for him to take control back. Like therapy."

"Shooting," Flo said dismissively, shaking her head. "After yesterday, that seems like the worst choice imaginable. Margot and Ezekiel will never go for it."

Brixton shrugged in concession. Flo was right, but that didn't mean Brixton wasn't, too. Then again, the sound of gunshots, even on a firing range, might be all it took to trigger for Max flashbacks to the Capitol steps. So he would keep his grandson's request to learn how to shoot on the back burner until the time was right.

As was his custom, the night before, Brixton had walked the six blocks from the Metro stop to the Arlington, Virginia, apartment he shared with his now fiancée, having upgraded to a three-bedroom on a higher floor. Real estate values and apartment rental costs hinged on many things, not least of which was distance from the nearest Metro station. Inside a block was the benchmark, while more than five threatened to render a building irrelevant. Nobody who was anybody had to walk that far. But Brixton had been struggling financially for a stretch, around the time he proposed to Flo, and a one-bedroom was the best he could do.

Exo Apartments was just over a half mile from the station, and he'd learned to make the best use of side streets to cover that distance in the shortest possible walk. The gleaming apartment tower featured an array of luxuries he never took advantage of—like the yoga lawn, pool and grill area, rooftop deck, and community garden. But Flo took advantage of all of it, ultimately preferring this place to the original apartment they'd shared in the heart of DC.

"You want something to eat, Robert?" Flo asked him.

Brixton had no appetite. "Thanks, babe, but I'll pass."

"I called Annabel. She said she'd bring Mac up to speed. But that was a long time ago. You should call him."

"It's too late."

"No, it's not. And Mac's probably called you fifteen times."

"Try twenty."

Flo looked down, then up again. "I should have been there with you. In Bethesda."

"Next time," Brixton said, before catching himself. "You know what I mean."

"No next times, Robert, God willing. And you've got that look."

"What look is that?"

"The one I call 'unfinished business.' Something you'd like to talk about but don't want to betray a confidence—something like that."

"Let's go to bed. I'll tell you in the morning."

WASHINGTON, DC

Mac preferred Peet's Coffee over Starbucks, and pretty much everywhere else near the Warner Building, for that matter; claimed he'd never had a bad cup there. Brixton had never once seen Mac drink anything but black, regular, the roast itself irrelevant. No lattes, frappes, or anything else that had to be mixed, blended, stirred, or shaken.

Peet's was forever jammed, but Mac always seemed able to snare a seat when needed. Brixton didn't think a place like this would take reservations, but if they were going to make an exception for anyone, it would be Mackensie Smith.

Mac was already working his way through the first of what would likely be two black coffees when Brixton entered. Brixton stuck out his hand as he reached the table, only to be swallowed by Mac in the tightest hug his friend had ever given him.

"Why are you a magnet for this kind of thing, Robert?" he asked, after finally letting go. "It's like violence is drawn to you."

"You mean to the people I love. I don't have to tell you about loss, Mac. You've experienced more than your share."

Mac nodded and sat back down, watching Brixton take the other chair as if he were studying him. "At least this time it comes with a happy ending."

"Not for seven of my grandson's classmates at Gilman. Make that eight," Brixton quickly corrected.

"You're right. I'm sorry. Terrible choice of words. Tell me what's on your mind."

"I've got an awful lot on my mind right now, Mac."

"I mean what you really wanted to discuss with me, other than my newfound daughter. It's written all over your face, Robert. I know that look because I've seen it before."

"It's something Max told me," he told Mac, recalling what the boy had said after they'd both managed to eat something the night before. "He thinks he saw a second shooter."

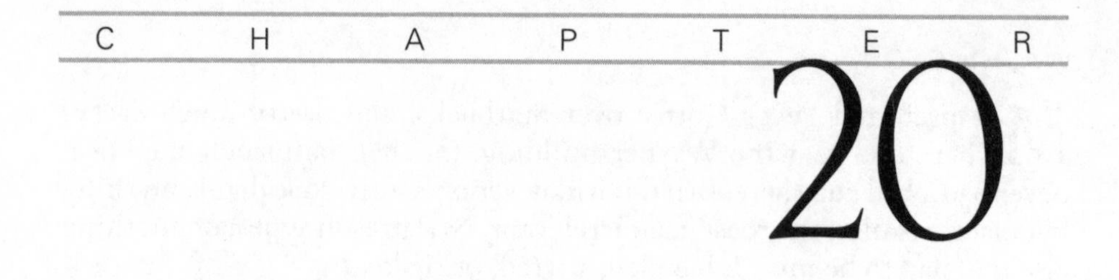

BALTIMORE, MARYLAND

It had been the worst experience of Kelly Loftus's life, the first time she'd experienced true betrayal and injustice.

Peel listened from the other side of the table, stoic and silent, to let Kelly tell it her own way.

TWENTY-TWO MONTHS AGO

Kelly was working the overnight shift out of Robbery-Homicide on the night in question. The call had come in that uniforms had responded to a domestic violence call too late, with tragic consequences. They'd forced their way into the home of Nathaniel Brown when they heard screams and no one responded to their pounding. The high-pitched wails were coming from children watching their father hover over the body of their mother.

It was later determined that Brown was performing CPR on his wife, who'd suffered an epileptic seizure. One of the children had called 9-1-1, the boy's panicked utterances all but indistinguishable in the recordings that would later become a key element in determining what had gone wrong. The 9-1-1 operator falsely interpreted the ranting to mean a domestic assault was in progress and dispatched two vehicles and four officers to respond.

Because of his kids' screaming and his own focused efforts on resuscitating his nonresponsive wife, Brown never heard the pounding on the door. He thought his home was being broken into. So he had grabbed a knife that his wife, Lakeasha, had been using to cut fruit when she was stricken by the seizure. The officers drew their weapons but managed to subdue Brown without discharging them. Up until this point, those officers could not be faulted for their response, and they continued to assess the scene as one where a domestic assault had taken place. And when it was further determined that Lakeasha was dead—murdered, by all accounts, in full view of the couple's children—they arrested Brown on suspicion of murder.

He tearfully and desperately tried to explain what had happened, but the officers paid his protestations no heed. Though handcuffed, he bull-rushed the ranking officer, a sergeant, and was violently subdued and placed in a choke hold.

Kelly arrived while the choke hold was still being applied and ordered the ranking officer to back off. When he failed to comply, she repeated the order, and when that attempt at deescalating the situation failed as well, she drew her firearm and ordered the officer to back down. Two of the other officers drew their weapons, aiming not at their fellow uniform but at Kelly. She had already radioed for additional backup, but she knew it wouldn't arrive in time to help defuse the now truly dangerous standoff. By then, Nathaniel Brown had gone limp in the ranking officer's choke hold and Kelly was certain he was near death. She had no idea of the true circumstances at that point, but it didn't matter. Choke holds had been outlawed in Baltimore city, and even with the mistaken report from the 9-1-1 call center and a potential murder victim lying on the floor, this was a serious breach of department protocol.

Finally, Kelly pretended to relent by easing one hand into the air while the other returned her pistol to the holster clipped to her belt. As the other officers were holstering their weapons as well, Kelly pounced on the ranking one. He had her by five inches and a hundred pounds, but Kelly was an ex-Marine who had been trained for just such a scenario, and she'd put it to use numerous times with the military police. She slammed the ranking officer in the throat and forcibly separated him from the suspect, who, as she feared, was unresponsive. As she began applying CPR to Nathaniel Brown, as he had been doing to his wife when the officers burst in, she saw the ranking officer was gasping for breath. She feared she might have ruptured his windpipe with a blow born of adrenaline.

Both the ranking officer and Nathaniel Brown would ultimately survive. Brown recovered quickly, but the officer ended up leaving the force on full disability. The police union sued on his behalf, and Kelly found herself both under investigation and a pariah in the department for violating the "blue code" of never intervening against a fellow officer. Even when the facts became clear and she was fully exonerated by a review board, it was clear she could no longer serve with the BPD. The officer she had injured was long tenured and was popular as one of the department's chief mentors for uniforms new to the streets. The fact that he had been only seconds from killing an innocent man did nothing to mitigate the cancerous response to Kelly's intervention. She had ended the career of a fellow cop and, prior to that, had drawn her weapon on him.

Against that backdrop, the truth ceased to have any meaning. The only facts that mattered had nothing to do with actual events, and her complete exoneration did nothing to dispel that. It wouldn't have hurt as much if Kelly hadn't genuinely loved her work as the city's youngest female homicide detective ever, and an African American one to boot. She came to realize the level to which that had ruffled feathers when she'd been selected over a host of white male applicants for the same position. Never mind that she'd won the job strictly on merit.

In the end, the truth was what Kelly had hung her hat on. Her actions had prevented those three kids from losing their father, as well as their mother, in a matter of minutes. Police officers had been deemed heroes for less, while Kelly found herself decried as a reckless, overly ambitious cop who'd scored a "political" job, thanks to the color of her skin, and was on a fast track to an administrative slot with the higher-ups at BPD headquarters at 601 East Fayette Street.

Those higher-ups understood how politically explosive and potentially damaging the whole situation was, and they intervened quickly to seek to mitigate matters by finding an acceptable resolution. Initially, the only such resolution, for Kelly, was to see this all the way through and let the truth prevail. But truth, in this case, had little to do with justice, not when departmental politics had reared its ugly head. On the one hand, she knew her actions had been proper and justified. On the other, she would spend the rest of her career in the BPD as an outcast, shunned by all and loathed by many, those who supported her afraid to do so openly for fear of suffering similar ostracism. The blue wall, as the inner world of cops was known, had plenty of cracks, but it stood strong and sturdy when it came to situations like this.

The chief himself put the Capitol Police option offer on the table. It promised more money, less burnout and, as the chief insisted, could prove a stepping-stone back into police work, or something comparable in federal law enforcement. Kelly didn't bother telling him her already realized dream was being stripped away from her, that nothing else was a suitable alternative. Why bother? While self-serving to both him and the department, everything he said about her current situation was accurate. And once she accepted the inevitability of her departure from the BPD and of giving up her shield as a homicide detective, she had to acknowledge that her options were slight, the United States Capitol Police likely being the best of them, under the circumstances.

It was all arranged in a means and manner Kelly neither understood nor sought to learn about. She had no desire to understand how political wheels spun and were greased. The chief's assistant called her with the date and time for an interview she knew was wholly perfunctory; the position was already hers, because the fix was in and it came with no scandal, no reproach, and no backlash on the department. She wouldn't be commenting or responding to anything relating to the incident that had ended her career as a real cop, and she resolved to throw herself wholeheartedly into her new role with the Capitol Police Protective Services department.

She underwent a rigorous three-month training course, alongside fledgling Secret Service agents, to master the tools of her new trade. Some of those had already been covered at the Police Academy and at Quantico, where, years before, she'd signed up for several sessions to better position herself for promotion through the detective ranks.

Kelly actually found the rigors of Protective Services to be fresh and stimulating at first. The problem was everything was about watching and waiting, learning to see what others couldn't, in time to stop an attack, attempted assassination, or bombing. She missed the charge of putting together a homicide case, finding the evidence to identify a perp and put him, her, or them behind bars. She genuinely believed in the good she had been doing, bringing justice to the victim and giving the family a sense of closure. The means were definable and the ends rewarding.

The difference in serving with the Capitol Police Protective Services division was the lack of ends and the inability to find closure beyond the end of each shift. There was nothing to investigate, no case to close, and she didn't feel cut out for it; the fit just wasn't right. The passion with which she attacked each case as a homicide detective had come to define her existence. She didn't mind taking her work home, obsessing over it, living with the victims in her mind. It provided her with purpose and a measuring stick with which to define her life.

Kelly had been unable to muster even a facsimile of that passion with the Capitol Police. Every day was generally the same, only the location varying, if the Speaker of the House was on the move. She wasn't part of the travel detail that accompanied the Speaker home to provide protection for her there, which meant intervals where she was loaned out to other protectees as a fill-in or supplemental when the threat assessment level was raised. She came to look at Protective Services as a stepping-stone to find her way back into homicide in another city.

THE PRESENT

Like going forward in reverse," she told Xander Peel, concluding her story.

"You really got screwed, didn't you?" he commented.

"Yup."

"Ever consider the Bureau?"

Kelly nodded. "The question being, would they consider me, under the circumstances?"

Peel nodded grudgingly. "Right. Probably better to let the dust settle."

"How do you think they'd view my Baltimore experience?"

"Depends on who's viewing it. Anywhere between 'Not a team player' and 'Straight shooter who goes by the book.' And I've got some clout now," he said, "thanks to you. Maybe some favors I can call in."

"You really think I'd have a shot?"

"I think you deserve one, Kel."

"That's not what I asked you. The Bureau isn't known for taking on reclamation projects."

"Coming straight from Baltimore, maybe. But coming from the Protective Services division of the Capitol Police, well, that's something else again. And if the right people at HQ happen to find out about the assistance you lent to the shooting on the Capitol steps . . ." Peel let his voice drift off, his intent clear.

"I'd appreciate that, X. In the meantime—"

"Why is there always a meantime?"

"Can you keep me in the loop?"

Peel's eyes flashed concern. "You don't have an Off switch, Kel. You need to stay clear of this."

"That a warning?"

"Just some friendly advice. Focus on rebuilding your career with Protective Services and don't make the kind of waves that could capsize your future."

"Nice metaphor."

"You bring the rest of what you recovered yesterday from the handbag belonging to the woman who must be Rappaport's wife?"

"Widow," Kelly corrected, reaching down for the brown shopping bag she'd placed on the floor beneath the chair, just short of her feet.

She had flattened the bag and doubled it over around forty different pieces spilled from Jean Rappaport's leaky handbag. Kelly had placed each one in a separate, sealed Ziploc bag. She had no idea what the FBI might be able to glean from the innocuous materials ranging from shopping lists to drugstore receipts, but it felt good to pass the bag on to an eager Xander Peel. It left her with the same feeling she got when working a homicide case back in her former life.

"This everything?" he wanted to know, tucking the bag on his lap.

"Yes," Kelly said, even though she'd left one thing out.

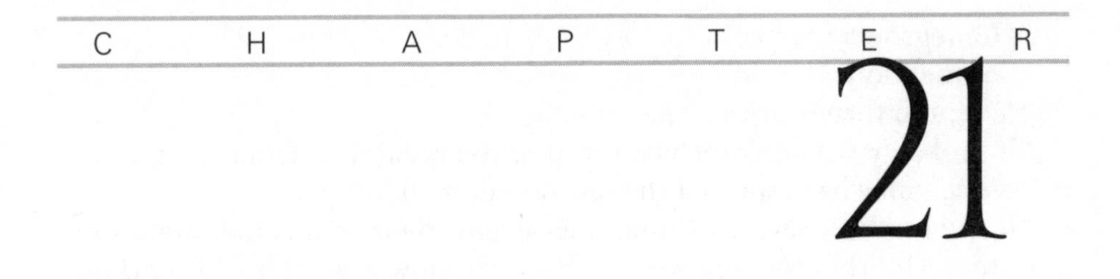

CHAPTER 21

WASHINGTON, DC

Brixton let Mac ponder the possibility of a second shooter while he went up to the counter to get himself a light roast. The condiment bar hadn't reopened yet, so he included cream and sugar in his order. The server asked him how many of each, but he wasn't sure and just said regular.

Mackensie Smith looked almost ready for a refill by the time Brixton got back to the table. He could see Mac weighing the implications of Max believing he'd spotted a second shooter, running them through his mind at the speed of a supercomputer.

"He asked me if I'd look into it, check things out. I think he's afraid to be wrong," Brixton said, retaking his chair just as another customer was moving to snatch it.

Mac made sure the guy was out of earshot before responding. "So who do you think he takes after?"

"Who can we talk to discreetly, on the down low? Max says he a spotted a man well off from where the shooting was concentrated. He thought the man was holding a gun, too."

"And firing it?"

"He's not sure. It was just a glimpse, right after he lunged over a boy who'd been shot, and stopped the bleeding. That boy had just watched his twin brother die, and now he's going to live. Thanks to my grandson."

"I'll ask again, who do you think he takes after?" Mac said, but he was smiling this time.

"I'm no hero, Mac."

"Tell that to all the people whose lives you've saved."

"There's one I couldn't save, and that's the only one that matters."

Brixton didn't elaborate further; he didn't have to, given that Mac had suffered the loss of a child as well.

"Let's get back to this potential second shooter," Mac said. "It sounds like he was positioned to shoot those fleeing in his direction."

"That was my thought, too."

Mac's eyes were flashing again. "Means we'd be looking at a coordinated attack, as opposed to a more random one. A lone gunman is normally acting on emotion or obsession with a cause. A pair of gunmen signals enemy action. Terrorism?" Mac posed softly, as if reluctant to say the word out loud.

"Homegrown maybe."

"So what do you need?"

"Access to the security camera footage."

"It probably wouldn't include the area you're talking about, where Max believes he may have spotted the second gunman."

"It might. Max says he thinks the second shooter was holding a long gun, too. And that footage would definitely show the angle of fire. If he's right, a portion of the victims may have rushed straight into the second shooter's line of fire, something that footage would reveal."

Mac nodded grudgingly. "All the same, that's a big ask for me, Robert."

"I don't want to put you under any—"

"Stop," Mac interrupted. "I guess I should have said that I need to figure out *who* to ask. That footage is likely being disseminated frame by frame as we sit here and sip our coffee. Anyone who dares leak it to the press . . ."

"You're not the press."

"You get the idea."

"So you'll try, right?"

Mac drained the rest of his coffee, staring into the depths of the cardboard cup as if to see if there were a message at the bottom. "I've never let you down, Robert, the reason for that being that you've never let me down. Give me a few hours and look for a video file to show up in your email inbox. It'll be a link to a sharing service that can't be traced. It won't come from me, and neither of us will ever know the identity of whoever sent it."

"Works for me." Brixton stopped there, ready to change the subject. "You haven't asked me about my lunch with Alexandra yesterday."

"I figured you had enough on your mind."

"She's your daughter, Mac. It was like sitting across from a younger version of you."

"Well, she is female."

"There is that. But otherwise . . ."

Brixton let his comment dangle, waiting to see where Mackensie Smith took this next.

"DNA test, Robert?"

"Would you need one to tell you I'm your best friend?"

"Of course not."

"Same thing here, Mac. I've only met two people in my entire life with eyes that color."

"You noticed."

"Surprised?"

"Not at all. It's why I didn't mention anything about that. I wanted you to see for yourself, tell me if I was crazy."

"You're not crazy."

He watched Mac take a deep breath, looking uncharacteristically placid and content, two adjectives that were seldom used in conjunction with a high-powered Washington attorney. "What did you think of Alex?"

"The truth?"

"The truth."

"I think she could be president someday."

"So you must not have liked her."

The two men shared a smile.

"Care to elaborate?" Mac resumed.

"If our lunch had been a job interview, I would have hired her on the spot."

"For what?"

"Anything, pretty much. She's poised, confident, and smart as a whip. Oh, and did I mention beautiful?"

Mac smiled again. "She must get that from her mother."

"What were you thinking, taking up with a socialite anyway?" Brixton asked him.

"I wasn't; the booze did the thinking for me."

"I know the feeling."

"It's hardly an exclusive club, Robert."

Brixton let that settle between them. "So what now, Mac?"

"As in making Alexandra a part of the family?"

Brixton nodded.

"I was going to take things slow, but 'slow' isn't in Annabel's vocabulary. She says I need to make up for lost time. Priority one. Instant and immediate."

"She's got a point."

"That's why I married her." Mac started to continue, stopped, then started again. "Do you believe in second chances?"

"I'm living proof they exist, Mac. But it's up to us to take advantage of them."

It was hardly sage advice, but Brixton could tell from Mac's expression that it was exactly what he needed to hear. Affirmation of something he desperately wanted to believe but couldn't quite convince himself of.

"Losing my wife and son," Mac started, groping for the right words. "I . . . I almost asked you to help me avenge their deaths, kill the drunk who got off with a slap on the wrist. Even though it was a while after the fact."

"What stopped you?"

"I knew you would have done it yourself. I knew you'd never let me get involved."

"True enough," Brixton conceded.

"I still think about it, Robert. Once in a while, I look the piece of shit up, just to see what he's up to, if fate has made him pay for his sins in a way I never did."

"And?"

"He's serving twenty-five to life for another DUI, death resulting. A whole family in a minivan this time. You see my point?"

Brixton was going to say no, when Mac continued without any prompting.

"That maybe I should have asked you, after all."

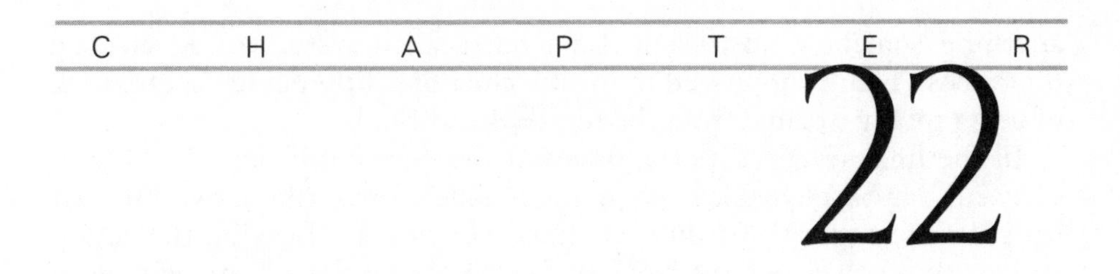

CHAPTER 22

AURORA, COLORADO

Dr. Efram Lutayne was waiting by the window when the car rumbled up the unpaved road leading to his property. He'd wheeled himself over when the sensors layered under the roadbed at the turnoff a mile away sent an alarm screaming through his house to alert him that someone was coming. The two-lane that led to the unmarked turnoff was the only way to access the private road that brought this man here at sporadic intervals. Lutayne's groceries and supplies were delivered as needed by a single, trusted establishment in the center of Aurora, but he never once met whoever left them on the front porch. And it had been three months since the driver of the approaching car had last visited—Lutayne's last true contact with the outside world.

The younger man who had shipped the press clippings was driving a dark-colored dirt-and-dust-riddled sedan that must have been a rental picked up at the airport. He emerged from the driver's seat in clothes wrinkled by the flight, and he stretched before starting up the walk to the house, gravel crunching under his shoes. The man was empty-handed, which surprised and disappointed Lutayne, given his final instructions.

Hadn't he been clear enough?

Lutayne yanked open the door before he reached it and rolled his chair out to greet the visitor. The younger man stooped and hugged him as tightly as the wheelchair would allow. Lutayne barely returned the hug; he had too much on his mind to make time for affection.

"Dad," the younger man said.

"Effie," Lutayne greeted.

He was the only person who ever called Efram Lutayne Jr. by that name. In fact, to the rest of the world, his son was E. Davis Lutayne, with the "Junior" left out. Certified public accountant, according to his business cards. Lutayne had seen very little of his son in the years he'd been stationed at Tooele Army Depot in Utah, where he was prohibited from leaving the base, except in the rarest of instances, and not allowed any visitors. The base had been a self-contained world, the PX store stocking everything anyone could need and capable of ordering, within twenty-four hours, anything somehow unstocked. Lutayne recalled a story of an electric toothbrush being choppered in for the chief of a different lab, a rare perk of being totally isolated from the rest of the world.

In the final seven years the base was in operation, from late 2009 to early 2017, Lutayne had left the premises a mere three times, twice to visit his sick wife and a third time to attend her funeral. Leaving the young Effie with relatives was the hardest thing he'd ever done in his life, made easier only by the fact that he'd had no choice. He would be in Utah for as long as he was required to stay, because that's what he'd signed up for when he was solicited to join the most secret lab constructed since Los Alamos and the Manhattan Project. He told himself it was a great honor, told himself his country needed him, told himself this was validation he was the best in the world at what he did: growing the most lethal poisons the world had ever known, in the same way he now grew orchids. Creating vast stockpiles of toxins that could wipe out the world a hundred times over.

His work represented the pinnacle of research undertaken after it became abundantly clear that nuclear weapons would never be employed by a nation-state again. Different means were now required to inflict mass destruction, and Lutayne had been placed in charge of an operation that stretched far beyond traditional bio- and chemical warfare. His work wasn't about killing tens or hundreds or even thousands of people.

His work was about killing millions. *Hundreds* of millions, even.

He had to admit that shutting down the base had saddened him, his very purpose in life stolen. In the absence of human interaction and emotional support, he had bonded with the fodder of his work in the same way he more recently had with his orchids. Lutayne had traded one form of isolation for another, finding solace in the secret, reinforced area of the greenhouse when the orchids proved to be not enough. He had left Utah with seeds secretly in his possession, not many but enough, unable to destroy the last remnants of his work after the final products were all destroyed.

Except for one: the shipment that had inexplicably vanished forever.

"You didn't suspect anything yourself?" Lutayne asked his son, wheeling himself back inside and waiting for Effie to follow before closing the door behind them.

"I didn't know what I was looking at, really. My computer did most of the work. I just did the printing."

"Wait," Lutayne said, trying to get straight what his son had just said. "You used a *computer*? You left a digital trail?"

Effie brushed him off. "Relax, Dad. I'm good at this. I know how to hide my trail."

"Not from these people."

"Well, it's too late now, anyway. And we've got other fish to fry, don't we?"

"Yes," Lutayne said. "We do."

Lutayne expressed considerable reservations over the fact that his son had transferred all the materials he'd requested onto a thumb drive, which he pulled from a pocket. Effie had brushed him off again, snickering.

"Relax, Dad, I got this covered."

"Relax? You don't know how these people work."

"What people?"

"I dropped off the grid so they wouldn't be able to find me. You start looking for certain things on a computer, they notice, Effie. How many times do I have to tell you that?"

His son didn't look convinced or concerned. "All I searched for were those geothermal mapping grids, like you told me, covering the six hundred and fifty or so miles between Tooele County, Utah, and Umatilla, Oregon."

"I don't need the whole distance, just—"

Effie cut him off. "I know, Dad. You only needed the final stretch, the last hundred miles."

Because that was the last checkpoint at which the final Red Dog run, headed to the Chemical Agent Disposal Facility at Umatilla, had checked in before vanishing during the final leg of its journey. They weren't scheduled to check in again until they reached Umatilla, which suggested that whatever had befallen the truck and its two-man crew had happened within that grid. As soon as they realized they'd lost the tanker, the lead and following vehicles, with their two four-man security teams, doubled back and split up to check every road the truck might have accidentally turned onto.

The fact that they found not a trace of the truck or its crew led to a massive search operation that stretched into months but produced nothing. Not a single clue as to what might have befallen the missing truck. No skid marks, no indication of an ambush, nothing whatsoever suggesting foul play. It was as if the tanker had simply dropped off the face of the earth. As impossible as that sounded, Lutayne took it as a positive sign that in the months and years that followed, there had been absolutely nothing to suggest hostile action. He still trembled when he considered how the contents of that tanker could be used to inflict mass casualties on a level the world had never seen before. Indeed, if someone had arranged an ambush to steal those contents, the world would have known about it a long time ago, almost for sure, and certainly by now.

"There are two sets of topographical maps on this for that hundred-mile stretch, yes?" Lutayne asked his son.

Effie nodded. "Just as you requested. One set dating back a year and the other only a few days. You're looking for alterations in the landscape, aren't you? Evidence of disturbed ground; digging, excavating—that sort of stuff."

Lutayne hadn't bothered, and didn't bother now, to elaborate further. Whatever had befallen the final Red Dog run, it had never been recovered, despite all the men and resources that had been brought to bear. They'd had all the information about the shipment, back then, that he had now, and they had still come up with nothing, despite expending the unlimited resources of the United States government in the recovery efforts.

"They would have done everything we're doing, right?" his son asked, as if reading his mind.

Lutayne nodded. "Yes. But they weren't looking for variations, however subtle, in the landscape."

"You think somebody found the tanker, don't you? You think its contents are what poisoned those kids in Baltimore."

"I'm hoping I'm wrong."

"Why don't we see what that flash drive can tell us, Dad."

Effie showed his father how to view on his computer the topographical maps he'd been able to locate, which were superimposed over one another to make it easier to spot changes in the ground topography. He also instructed his father on how to place them side by side, if he preferred that angle instead.

Lutayne saw that his son had already divided the maps into individual grids of approximately five square miles, twenty different "slides," to use the old-fashioned term with which he was more comfortable. And Effie was right: superimposing the most recent overhead satellite shot over one from a year ago provided an entirely different perspective.

"Do you have any idea how much time I've spent studying these maps over the past five years, looking for something I kept missing? Any clue, any anomaly. But there was never anything."

"Dad?

"What?"

Effie's answer was to gesture with his eyes toward the screen.

"Right. Sorry. I got carried away." Lutayne returned his attention to the screen. "This offers a whole different perspective, like nothing I've ever looked at before."

His son nodded. "That's the geothermal satellite mapping. It's not a new technology, but a whole bunch of refinements have been made recently, thanks to virtual reality. The general principle for our purposes is that when ground areas are disturbed—dug out, replaned, et cetera—it produces a heat signature that can persist for a considerable time. We're talking about a variance of as little as a degree or two, plenty to be read by a geothermal mapping satellite using this VR software. That's why you asked for this kind of mapping on top of the regular, isn't it, Dad? Because you think maybe the truck was buried."

"It dropped off the face of the earth. If there's a better explanation for that, I'd like to hear it."

Lutayne watched his son wet his lips—once, then again, and then a third time. Since he was a little boy, this had been a sign that he was thinking.

"Are you listening, because I think I may have it," Effie said. "You're aware, of course, that this region is a prime area for the formation of sinkholes."

"It was one of the first things we considered, in fact. But there was no sign of one, so we settled on hostile action and went to the equivalent of DEFCON five in our world, because that seemed like the only alternative."

"You had satellites back then, too, Dad. Did they spot anything? Anything at all?"

"Not through that storm. They couldn't. We were proceeding along two different tracks: that the truck strayed off its route because it was hijacked, or that one of the crew members was in league with the hijackers and was heading to a specific rendezvous point."

"Any hint of either member of the crew ever surfacing again?"

Lutayne shook his head. "We checked and kept checking. For months. Nothing ever came of anything we tried. And the more time that passed without us hearing anything about the tanker's contents, the more we were able to breathe easier, figuring that whatever had happened, those contents wouldn't be harming anyone, if they hadn't already."

"And then you read this month's press clippings, and singled out the mass poisoning at that high school in Baltimore."

"The indications, the cluster of them alone, was enough to make me fear the worst."

"But you're not sure, Dad. There's no way you could be."

"I wrote the algorithm you've been using to isolate potential hot spots every month. This one carried the highest degree of probability of any you've brought me in five years."

"Prob-a-*bility*," Effie repeated, drawing out the syllables to better make his point. "Not certainty."

"No, but there is the fact that all seven of those kids from that Baltimore high school died within twenty-four hours of each other. The term 'respiratory distress' was used, a strong indication in itself. And it's not just what the article and the follow-ups mentioned; it's what they didn't mention."

"Survivors?" Effie mused.

"In which case," Lutayne said, nodding, "we'd be looking at a one hundred percent mortality rate of those exposed."

"Somebody . . . what, Dad? Testing the waters? Experimenting?"

Lutayne shrugged. "I don't know. I'm as lost as that damn truck itself."

Effie gestured again toward the computer screen. "Then let's see if we can find it."

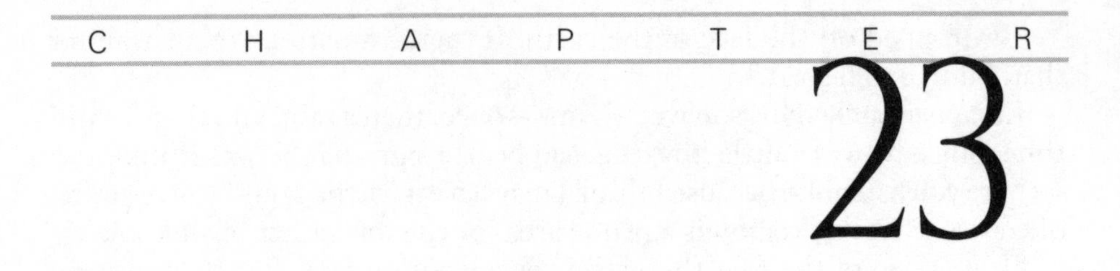

CHAPTER 23

SHIAWASSEE COUNTY, MICHIGAN

All right," said Jack "Bull" Dozier, rapping a gavel dramatically down on a podium set up at the front of the packed meeting hall. "Let's get this party started."

The crowd assembled before him hooted and cheered, and Dozier let them have their fun. True to his nickname, he was a bull of a man, with a rangy beard that seemed to flow from his chin to his chest, while skipping his virtually nonexistent neck. He had a roundish head dominated by bulbous cheeks that made his face look like an overinflated basketball. His complexion was ruddy and pocked by acne scars beneath his stubble-laced head. Same hairstyle he'd been wearing, the evening's guest of honor knew, since he'd been drummed out of the army on a dishonorable discharge for an attitude that saw him fail basic training his first three times. He'd finally passed, only to last all of four weeks before being told to pack his bags, just before he was supposed to deploy.

That made him Deacon Frank Wilhyte's kind of guy, a man who took no shit and wasn't afraid to get his hands dirty. The kind of man he'd be needing, big-time, when zero hour came in a mere few months, and, more importantly, the kind of man who needed Deacon Frank.

"You've all heard of our distinguished guest, so I won't bore you with a long introduction," Dozier resumed, the crowd having gone quiet. "Suffice it to say he is a man who shares our vision that this country is FUBR. For those of you who don't know what that stands for, it's 'fucked-up beyond recognition,' and Deacon Frank Wilhyte is just the man to unfuck it."

Dozier waited for the new wave of hooting, cheering, and clapping to subside before he resumed.

"He's a man who talks the talk we talk and walks the walk we walk. He's the absolute real deal and he's going to deliver the change this country needs if it's going to survive. But to do that, he's going to need us. So I ask, are you with me?"

"Yes!" the crowd shouted back.

"Are you with me?" Dozier yelled back at them, louder.

"*Yes!*"

"Are you with me?" Louder still.

"*YESSS!*"

"So, ladies with the balls to join us and gentlemen, please give a hearty Michigan welcome to Deacon . . . Frank . . . Wilhyte!"

The crowd leaped to its collective feet with a thunderous roar, as Deacon Frank approached the podium, their cheers making his ears pop. He recognized a whole bunch seated in the front row, but besides them and Bull Dozier, he knew not a single one. Nor did he have to.

Because they knew him. And what was coming had drawn them here to this American Legion Hall, reopened recently after being long shuttered by COVID-19. The boards remained plastered over the windows. Those coming had been alerted to park a few blocks away, on the dark side streets populated by closed businesses and by others hanging on by a thread. The power still worked, but the building lacked air-conditioning and the old building's poor ventilation had turned it into a petri dish of stale sweat, hair oil, and rank work clothes. Deacon Frank looked out over the crowd as they cheered him and saw a smattering of sheriff's uniforms mixed among the crowd. The real law of this country, elected by their fellows to serve communities instead of being appointed by politicians. Men with badges pinned to their chests, who knew how their neighbors thought and considered protecting them against the intrusion of that which they neither wanted nor needed in their lives to be paramount in the job description.

Deacon Frank knew the sight of them well, because such uniforms were a regular sight at his daddy's revival meetings. Local lawmen mixing with the locals they served. It didn't get any more American than that.

The Reverend Rand Atlas Wilhyte had never bothered with something as pedantic or pointless as divinity school. He'd just followed his own daddy's footsteps into the world of preaching, moving those footsteps through the mud and muck of tent revival meetings, where congregants would pack themselves in through air that felt like soup. Sit themselves down on folding chairs that would sink into the mud, where rain had softened the ground. As a boy, Deacon Frank remembered the fattest ones would sink in the deepest. He'd watch them practically disappear from his sight line while his daddy ranted and raved about sin and following the gospel, as designated deacons passed around the collection baskets, gathering reams of crumpled bills his daddy's flock could hardly afford to part with.

Those collection baskets had been a precursor to the sponsors who lined up to fill the Reverend Rand Atlas Wilhyte's coffers once he became one of the earliest, and most successful, televangelists. He was also one of the first to build his own megachurch, a pioneer in that respect, too. His only child, Frank, had been homeschooled his whole life by his mother, Mrs. Rand Atlas Wilhyte, who was called that to the point that Deacon Frank hadn't learned her real first name until he was twelve years old.

"This country is sick." He spoke into the microphone once the cheering finally died down, channeling his daddy's best sermons. "This country is hurting. We've got ourselves two choices in that regard. One is to watch it die."

A smattering of *No*s filtered through the crowd when Deacon Frank paused briefly.

"The other is give it the CPR it so desperately needs."

The assembled crowd leaped to its feet hard enough to make the floor tremble beneath Deacon Frank's feet. Deacon wasn't his first name. That came when young Frank Wilhyte, though still little, was deemed old enough to participate in his daddy's prayer meetings. Reverend Rand, as he was called by those who hung on his every word while their fingers peeled fresh bills from their billfolds or handbags, proclaimed his boy a deacon in the Church of the Faithful, and from that day forward he became Deacon Frank.

He remembered looking up the specifics of a deacon's duties at one point. He wasn't sure when or how anymore, but he recalled that during the mass, the deacon's responsibilities included assisting the priest, proclaiming the gospel, announcing the General Intercessions, and distributing Communion. Deacons were also known to preach the homily.

Deacon Frank didn't know what all that was at the time, and he had come to believe that a deacon's responsibilities were to stand by his father as little more than a prop. He was also responsible for manning the collection basket at the doorway or tent flap, to grab added bills from givers or to snare the first ones from guilty stragglers on their way out so they could drive home with a clear conscience, no longer risking the wrath of God. Thinking back on those times, he couldn't help but wonder if his father had ever even conceived of him reaching the heights he had, having abandoned televangelism and religion altogether in favor of a higher cause and more noble pursuit.

And he felt like his father now, felt his fire and fury only toward a purpose rooted beyond money, since Reverend Rand had left his son a boatload upon his untimely passing, after a mugger had shot him in the head when he wouldn't fork over his wallet. Deacon Frank was twenty-three at the time. The wallet had never been found. But his father's murder had set the stage for the cause of saving the country, paving the way for the new America.

Now that God himself, or some other higher power, had given him the means.

"We can all be saviors, we can all be heroes, because this country needs its share of both. They may have us outgunned, they may have us outmanned, but they don't know what's coming and how many are sure to jump to our side when the time comes."

Murmurs coughed up through the crowd, and Deacon Frank waited for them to subside before he continued.

"We've tried prayer, haven't we? But it hasn't worked, and we let ourselves believe that God wasn't listening. So we wallowed in our failure and our pity, not realizing He was waiting, waiting for us to act. He's done listening, because He's as frustrated as we are about how things have gone so wrong in this great nation. The blessing being that it's not too late, that we still have time to set things right, to get America back on the tracks it had been riding on until a whole bunch of folks hijacked the train and drove it off the rails."

Deacon Frank gazed over a sea of nodding heads, picturing this scene repeated a thousand times with crowds just like this. This particular assembly of local militias had spawned the likes of Timothy McVeigh, and some of the older members, he'd heard, still boasted of the fact that they came up with the money for the deadly truck bomb McVeigh had ignited in Oklahoma City.

"It's coming, friends. Oh, it's coming, all right. We've got the means now. And when we pull the cord on a cannon the size of Lake Michigan, I need you with me."

The applause started to ripple, but this time Deacon Frank rolled right over it.

"I need you standing by my side when the dying starts and the chaos begins. I need you holding your spot on the wall to defend what used to make this country great, that nobody seems to remember anymore. They got it all twisted around and backward. They need to be shown the way, and when the time is right, I need you to take them by the hand and lead them. I need you to fill the holes. I need you to stand ready."

The crowd leaped to its collective feet once more. Deacon Frank's eardrums felt like somebody had taken a sledgehammer to them. He glanced behind him to see Bull Dozier and the other leaders cheering and clapping the loudest of all. And in that moment Deacon Frank understood his father's reverie as he preached, understood that it was about far more than the money his faithful pressed into his grasp, because it was the souls he held in his hand that truly mattered.

But all the Reverend Rand Atlas Wilhyte's work and travels—this night and that, this town and that—came to nothing more than individual exploits that didn't add up to any whole at all. There was nothing beyond the people he could charm with deceptive intent and the piles of money that could be equated with devotion. No ends, just means. Deacon Frank, on the other hand, was all about those ends. No way his father could have ever conceived of him reaching the heights he had, never mind the even greater ones that were coming by his own hand.

He moved out from behind the podium, moving about the crowd, his voice bellowing without need for amplification.

"We can be mice or we can be men," he said to the crowd, which had gone dead quiet. "And we've been mice for too long. Give us our six packs and our sitcoms and our sick leave and they thought that would be enough to keep us happy, keep us numbed to the pain all around us. We made that pain a part of ourselves, and you know where it hurt the most?"

Deacon Frank tapped his chest.

"Right here. They thought they'd broken our hearts, broken us. But we fooled them, didn't we? And now we're gonna make them eat their words and their deeds. Before long, they'll be begging us to step in, 'cause they won't have anywhere else to turn. The wall they've built to keep us out is high, the wall is thick, the wall is wide. I say it's time to blow straight through that wall, friends. And I promise you this, as I stand here tonight: I promise you're gonna love the sight you see on the other side of that wall. I know you've heard this kind of thing before, but you haven't heard it from me.

"Because a lot of people are going to die, a whole lot, and we're going to be the ones digging their graves."

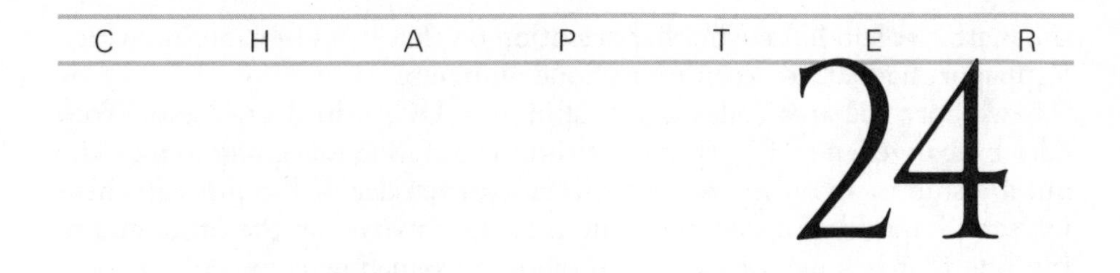

CHAPTER 24

BALTIMORE, MARYLAND

Kelly Loftus hadn't given Xander Peel everything she'd managed to salvage from the handbag belonging to the woman who Peel had identified as Jean Rappaport, wife of the mass shooter from the Capitol steps the day before. She'd held back a single scrap of paper that held something she couldn't let herself give up: phone numbers, almost certainly scrawled by Philip Rappaport, given that the handwriting was a close match to the note she'd tried to reconstruct. The single unlined sheet of paper containing those phone numbers somehow ended up getting stuffed in Jean's handbag, likely at the same time she had recovered the note he'd left for her.

You don't have an Off switch.

Xander Peel's warning to her, a warning she continued to disregard. Kelly was acting as if this was her case, when nothing could be further from the truth. Yet something was stopping her from letting go, like an itch she couldn't quite scratch. She hadn't been involved in an active investigation in the nearly two years since the incident that had effectively ended her career as a detective. That had become like a drug for her, and she needed her fix. She was committing yet another gross act of misconduct and insubordination by not turning the phone numbers over, thereby denying the federal authorities potentially vital clues in their investigation. She kept telling herself she would turn them over soon, make up some excuse to Xander Peel that these had found their way between their couch cushions or something.

Second-guessing her actions made Kelly reflect on her career in Baltimore, and she was starting to consider some truths she had avoided since her dismissal, like the fact that her dismissal wasn't related to that single incident—well, it was, per se, but the fact that no one in the department had rallied to her defense was something that continued to claw at her. What she saw as being professional had likely been viewed by others as obsessive and compulsive. She was a pit bull when it came to pursuing all of her cases, leaving nothing to chance and expecting the same from her fellow officers, who were made to look bad by comparison. And their response had been to bide their time until the right opportunity came, ultimately served up on a silver platter by Kelly herself.

She realized her mind had been wandering, and she snapped it back to the matter at hand: focusing her attention on that sheet of paper on which Rappaport had jotted down four phone numbers.

Two bore 202 area codes for Washington, DC, a third a 646 New York City exchange, and a fourth was Baltimore: 301. She was going to look the numbers up in an online reverse directory, then decided to just call them instead. Something inside her wanted to hear a voice on the other end of the line that belonged to a person who was somehow connected to this, though she couldn't explain why that was.

After activating an app that made it impossible to ID her number, Kelly tried the number with the 301 Baltimore area code.

"Hello," a recorded voice greeted, *"and thank you for calling Baltimore Mulighet High School. If you need information about—"*

Kelly hung up before the recording got any further. She was familiar with the school, both because of its location within the city proper and, even more, seven students had died there under mysterious circumstances around a month back. Moving on from that in her mind, Kelly tried the first number on her list for Washington, DC, and got an entirely different result.

"Senator Byron Fitch's office."

"Sorry," Kelly said, through the surprise that had forced her mouth to drop. "I dialed the wrong number."

Fitch was the junior senator from Maryland, an independent who was fond of supporting crazed conspiracies and had eked out a victory in a special election a few years back, in which turnout didn't even reach twenty-five percent.

Kelly realized she was still wearing the light jacket she'd donned to meet Xander Peel, and she pulled it off, feeling suddenly warm. Next, she dialed the second 202 phone number. It rang once.

"Hello, you've reached the Washington office of the Centers for Disease Control and Prevention. If you know your party's extension and would like to—"

Kelly terminated the call, ever so glad she'd used her masking app, even as she was totally baffled.

Why would Philip Rappaport have called the CDC? And, for that matter, why had he called the offices of Byron Fitch, junior senator from his home state of Maryland, and that high school in Baltimore?

The fourth and final number had a 646 area code for New York. Kelly dialed it and counted the rings all the way to eight before a canned message repeated the number she'd dialed, followed by *"At the tone, please leave a message."*

Kelly tried looking up the number in the reverse directory but drew a blank, indicating that it was likely a cell number, since the database left out a great portion of those. So Rappaport had called Senator Byron Fitch, the CDC in Washington, a high school in Baltimore, and a number that led nowhere, a cell phone exchange registered in New York. There had to be a connection between all the calls, though without knowing when the calls had actually been placed, she had no convenient means of uncovering it.

Before Kelly could further ponder where all this was leading, her phone rang, startling her. A number she didn't recognize appeared in her caller ID.

She answered the phone anyway, her hand a bit unsteady.

"Hello?"

"Forget to tell me something at breakfast?" greeted the voice of Xander Peel.

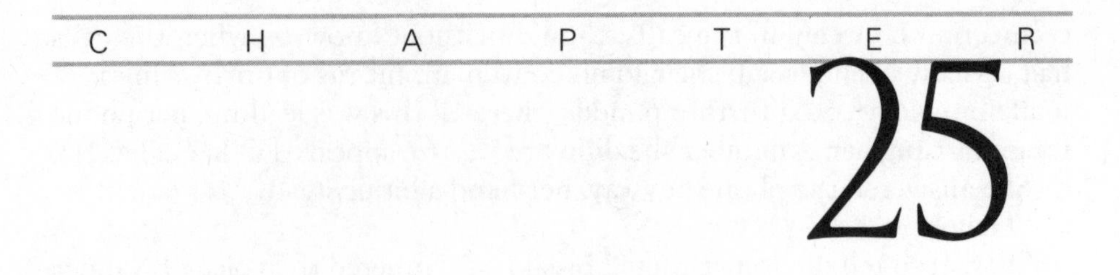

CHAPTER 25

WASHINGTON, DC

Brixton returned to his apartment, instead of accompanying Mac back to the firm's offices in the Warner Building. He needed to be alone with his thoughts, to continue considering the ramifications of his grandson's claim that he'd caught a glimpse of a second shooter brandishing a long gun. He resisted the temptation to stop by Flo's clothing boutique, her original shop, which she'd later supplemented with a second location in Manhattan. Sales in Manhattan had been brisk until the blight of COVID-19 struck, but like much of the city, sales had shown no sign of recovering anytime soon. Fortunately, her lease was up for renewal, allowing Flo a graceful exit. She'd relocated the inventory from the Manhattan store down here, where the retail business had recovered much faster.

The months they'd been apart had served to cement their relationship. It had survived the crisis of Brixton's emotional and professional decline, only to emerge stronger now that they'd found each other once more. He'd come to realize, with great relief, that Flo had never stopped loving him. She'd moved up to New York to lend Brixton the space he needed to find himself again, never intending to make the first move to reconcile, but ready and waiting for him to make it.

Oddly, it had been his thwarting of yet another terrorist bombing that had set Brixton on the road to pulling himself out of the hole he'd fallen into, offering him redemption at long last. He was, at heart, transactional, needing a mission, a purpose, to define him. Sitting in an office all day, either chasing work or waiting for Mac to dump it on his desk, had dulled his edge and robbed him of his center, which had been restored in the wake of his stopping a second bomber, after losing his daughter to the first.

Those torturous days had ended with him riding that horse-drawn carriage illegally down the Fifth Avenue bus lane, after which he had proposed to Flo outside her Manhattan boutique. He was picturing that scene in his mind again when his phone indicated an incoming email.

Mackensie Smith's contacts proved to be better than ever. How else could Mac have managed to produce a massive number of MP4 video files that contained all the security camera footage capturing the Capitol steps in the midst of the mass shooting, coupled with cell phone video recordings that the FBI, running lead on the investigation, had managed to pull together? Brixton had no idea from which source Mac had gotten the footage, or what favor he needed to call in to get it, only that his friend had provided the means by which Brixton could ascertain whether his grandson's claim of spotting a second shooter had any validity.

Even now, a day after the shooting, specialists would be combing through the same footage, inspecting it frame by frame at times. They'd want a real-time, second-by-second chronology of everything that transpired so as not to miss any clue or leave anything to chance. If there was evidence of a second shooter, they surely would have found it by now and would be racing to determine that shooter's identity.

For his part, Brixton needed to know whether the incident had been part of a conspiracy, instead of a single gunman acting alone. It was a classic intelligence maneuver, in which a motivated individual was recruited as essentially a fall guy. Some operative cleverly placed to spur him into doing a deed that would surely result in his death, rendering him a patsy to cover up the part played by the true organizers of the plot.

Brixton downloaded the files and scrolled through a host of different video clips, all labeled by number. There were dozens of them, which was not entirely surprising, given the number of security cameras offering angles of the Capitol's east steps, along with a comparable number of amateur cell phone videos.

He couldn't help but wonder how many of those there would have been had the Kennedy assassination happened today. Brixton tried to imagine a thousand Zapruder films battling for the airwaves across cable news stations. Hell, he mused, there would be enough footage to start a whole new station totally dedicated to running all those videos in a constant loop.

He'd been reviewing the recordings for an hour when he came upon the first cell phone video offering glimpses of the far side of the steps, where Max had told Brixton he'd glimpsed that second shooter. But the footage was choppy, shot by someone with a cell phone while he or she had been fleeing.

It did, though, seem to capture a lone figure standing in the general area where Max said he'd spotted the second shooter. Though otherwise indiscernible, the mere fact that the figure was motionless suggested plenty in itself. Why wouldn't he, or she, also be running away from the fray—or toward it, in the event the figure was a first responder of some sort?

Another hour and two iced teas into his work, Brixton found a snippet of coverage from a video camera that must have been dropped by someone fleeing the scene. A few frames caught what appeared to be the same still figure as the one caught by the cell phone video.

Brixton extracted a magnifying glass from his top desk drawer and used it to more closely examine the most complete shot of the figure that the off-angled camera had caught. The figure was definitely holding something high up, around shoulder level, aimed at the steps. Brixton felt something grasp his insides and twist, as he realized that not only might Max have been right but also no one else viewing the footage may have noticed this, since they wouldn't have been looking for what he was. Try as he might, though, his efforts to determine what the figure was holding failed at every turn.

Brixton was barely halfway through all the footage contained in the files, but he reviewed the rest quickly, just to see if any may have contained a similar angle that revealed more of the figure. When it didn't, he knew his best chance lay with taking the footage in question to a contact of his who specialized in the kind of technology that could isolate and enhance that lone motionless figure in a manner infinitely better than what he could do with his computer's limited offerings.

He transferred the contents of Mac's file onto a flash drive. Figuring he had better call his best friend with an update, he was reaching for his phone when it started ringing. The caller ID said it was Mac himself. Brixton had a nagging feeling something was wrong, so much so that he had to clear his throat and take a deep breath to steady himself.

"Mac?"

"Robert!"

Mackensie Smith's tone was enough to tell Brixton that his sense of foreboding was justified.

"What is it?"

"Robert, it's . . . it's Alexandra," Mac barely managed, his voice cracking.

Brixton waited for him to continue.

"She's been hospitalized at Walter Reed. They called me because she added me to her contact list in the event of an . . . you know."

"All too well."

"They won't tell me anything else, nothing at all."

"I'll meet you there, Mac."

"I'm already on my way."

"Mac?"

It was too late, Brixton realized. Mac had already hung up.

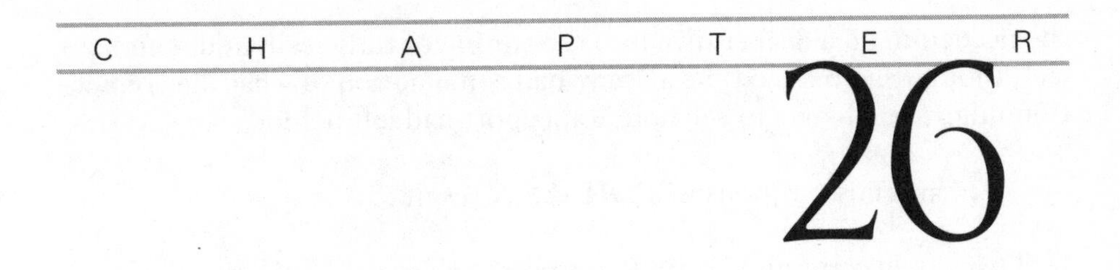

CHAPTER 26

BALTIMORE, MARYLAND

What's this number, X?" Kelly said to Special Agent Xander Peel.

"My office at the Baltimore field office. More likely to get a response than when 'FBI' appears in somebody's caller ID."

Kelly swallowed hard, worried that Peel had somehow figured out that she hadn't been totally forthcoming with him and had held back those phone numbers from Jean Rappaport's handbag.

"I need to put a BOLO out on Jean Rappaport, based on everything you told me," Peel said, using the acronym for "Be on the lookout." "But you never gave me the details of the direction she headed off in, Kel."

She breathed a sigh of relief before recounting the specific path she had followed while recovering as much of the contents of Jean Rappaport's handbag as she could, ending with the fact that Jean likely had boarded a Maryland Transit Administration bus at a stop on Independence Avenue.

"Any idea which direction it was headed in, which route?" Peel asked her.

Kelly admitted that she hadn't bothered to follow that up, had been too engaged with salvaging those contents and with cursing herself for losing the woman in the first place.

"But the bus must have departed just before I got there," Kelly told Xander Peel. "That would be somewhere between three fifteen and three thirty. I think they come by every fifteen minutes or so in both directions, both sides of the street. The pattern of the scattered items that fell from her handbag tells me she boarded a bus on the north side of the street. That would be the general direction in which I'd look, X."

"We've got an agent stationed at the Rappaport home outside of Baltimore, in case she returns. In the meantime, we're going to flash her picture around to the local hotels and motels, starting with the lower-end ones that would be more in the woman's price range, heading east from the Capitol."

Peel hesitated, and Kelly waited for him to go on, instead of picking up again herself.

"If you had to run this by the numbers," he resumed, "what do you think it would add up to?"

Kelly knew she couldn't let on anything about Philip Rappaport's calls to Senator Byron Fitch and the Washington office of the CDC. She knew she needed to do a deeper dive into the timing of those calls and their subject, though she realized she already had some notion of what the connection might be, thanks to the note Rappaport had left behind.

> . . . and now millions will **DIE AS A** result . . .

That would certainly explain Rappaport's call to the CDC, which implied that however those millions were going to die involved something the expertise of the Centers for Disease Control might help decipher. Might that also explain the connection to the Baltimore city high school where seven students had been exposed to some poison that killed them over a month ago? She had the sense that things were starting to fall together, though there was still nothing to suggest any kind of a motive for Rappaport shooting up the east steps of the Capitol.

"I don't think Rappaport just showed up at the Capitol and started shooting, X," Kelly finally said, uttering the whole truth for a change. "I think he had a target in mind, which makes no sense, since he shot up those kids first. Unless, for some reason, they were the target."

"Maybe just one of them," Peel ventured. "We're doing a deeper dive into their families, looking for some connection with Rappaport just in case."

"And?"

"It's early."

"In other words, you've found nothing so far."

"I'll let you know when we do, Kel."

"You mean 'if,' don't you?"

The phone call completed, Kelly moved to her laptop to give the reconstructed note Philip Rappaport must have left for his wife, Jean, a fresh look, to see if anything she'd learned since compiling it might help to fill in some of the blanks.

> ____________ wish there had been another way, wish this
> hadn't been forced upon me by ____________ beyond
> ____________ only I had known that ________________
> do not seek this but nor do I shun my duties before the
> eyes of ________________ I know you'll never forgive
> me __________ the pain ____________ was another
> way ____________ my fault . . . failed to heed my warnings
> no matter how much I tried to . . . ________________
> ____________ the fate that r ______ suf ____________
> not survive this, nor do I deserve ____________ because no
> one else deserves to d ____________ . . . and now millions
> will **DIE AS A** result . . . can no longer live with my . . . hate

me ___________ time you read this ___________
Sena ___________ I can only ___________ loving
hus ___________

Kelly had forgotten about the "Sena" mention in the note, with a capital *S*. Assuming "Sena" finished with "tor," this could only have referred to Byron Fitch, the senator whom Philip Rappaport had at least tried to contact. And whatever that call had been about had merited mention in what amounted to a suicide note.

Kelly knew she didn't have a lot of options at this point, having reached a dead end when it came to further avenues to pursue. Unable to help herself, though, Kelly thought of one last road she could take. It would likely lead nowhere, but she had to try. She'd come this far, after all, so where was the harm in launching one last Hail Mary?

Kelly lifted the scrap of paper containing that 646 phone number and dialed it again, prepared to leave a message this time.

"Hi," she began after the beep, forming her lie as she went along, "this is Kelly Loftus of the Capitol Police. We have reason to believe you may have some knowledge of the perpetrator of yesterday's shooting at the Capitol Building. If you could call me back at . . ."

Mere seconds after she'd hung up, her phone started buzzing. The sound and vibration startled Kelly, and at first she thought the person on the other end of the 646 exchange was already calling her back. Instead, the number she now recognized as Xander Peel's office lit up in her caller ID.

"Miss me already?" she greeted, doing her best to keep her tone light.

"You know the Metro Points Hotel?" Peel said.

"Yes. It's located on Annapolis Road in New Carrollton. I didn't know our relationship had reached that level, X."

"Not yet, anyway" Peel said, unable to resist the opportunity. "I'm on my way there now, Kel. We found Jean Rappaport."

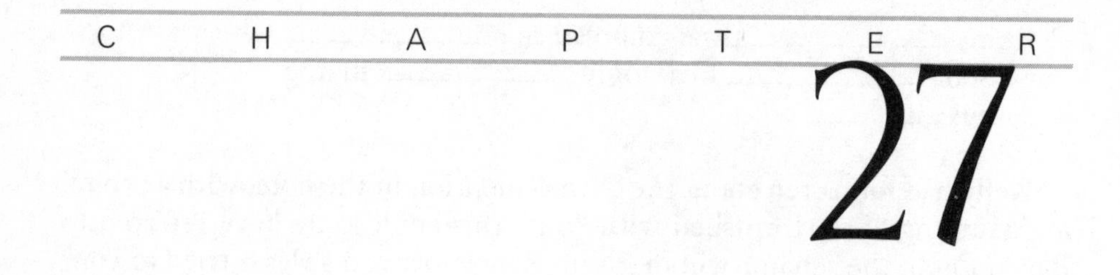

CHAPTER 27

BETHESDA, MARYLAND

Brixton found Mackensie Smith standing by a wall-length piece of glass at the entrance to the Walter Reed emergency room. He figured that Alexandra had been brought here because she was a government employee, though it could also have been that whatever had led to her being rushed to the hospital was something the center was more equipped to deal with.

"Robert!" Mac said, hugging him tightly as soon as he was through the sliding door.

Brixton waited for his friend to separate, felt him trembling.

"What have you learned so far?" he asked. Mac was still holding him at the shoulders.

"Not very much at all, beyond the fact that she was brought in with a fellow worker from the CDC—her supervisor, by all accounts. They're working on both of them back there," Mac said, gesturing toward a set of sliding glass double doors with NO ADMITTANCE stenciled across them, just beyond the waiting room sitting area. "There's been a lot of activity, people coming and going." He seemed on the verge of breaking down. "It doesn't look good, Robert. It looks very, very bad."

"And they haven't told you anything?"

"Not a thing. A pair of DC Metro cops are back there, too. I saw one come out to move his vehicle. He wouldn't tell me anything, either. Told me he wasn't at liberty."

"Those words?"

Mac nodded. "Verbatim."

"You know anyone in authority at the hospital?"

"I know people in authority at every hospital in the area, *except* Walter Reed. You know the damn military bureaucracy."

"I do. Tell me what you do know, Mac."

"Whatever led to Alexandra and her supervisor being rushed here happened at the CDC offices in Washington."

"An attack of some kind?"

Mac shrugged. "I haven't a clue, Robert." He shook his head. "Did she say anything at lunch to you yesterday about being in some kind of trouble, that feeling I told you I had?"

Brixton hated betraying Alexandra's confidence, but he felt the circumstances called for it. "You were right, Mac."

"You forget to mention that, after you told me how well the two of you got along?" Mac asked him, sounding as annoyed as he was anxious.

"I got the feeling she was in over her head with something. She was going to get back to me with more."

"That's it?"

"We'd known each other for all of an hour, Mac."

Brixton ran part of his conversation with Alexandra through his mind.

Because I could use your help. Your advice, anyway. I'm involved in something that's a little out of my element. Maybe more than a little.

"She didn't say anything was wrong, Mac," he said, after repeating those words as well as he could remember them. "Only that she had gotten involved in something and wanted to know if I could help her."

"Because something was wrong."

"Mac—"

"No, Robert," Mac said shortly, cutting him off. "It's this damn town. It eats its young, corrupts anything it touches. I don't know how I've lasted here so long."

"You can't blame Washington for this. Not yet anyway."

"Did Alexandra mention anything specific?"

Brixton searched his memory again for her exact wording, searching for something that might provide an answer to Mac's question.

The receptionist put one of those crackpot calls through to me. You know, low person on the totem pole and all that sort of shit.

But she must have had reason to believe this call was different. . . . What can you tell me about it, Alex? . . .

Like I said, Uncle Robert, the receptionist put the call through, and I listened to the caller issue some wildly outlandish claims that were so crazy they actually made a degree of sense.

Brixton summarized that for Mac as well as he could. His friend's displeasure was worn on his face like a mask.

"That's all? Did anything Alexandra said suggest she may have been in danger?"

"She doesn't seem like the kind of person who gets scared—or scared off—easily," Brixton told Mac, careful to use the present tense. "I got the sense that whatever she's looking into, she's on her own."

"So maybe she was getting too close to something. You know the drill."

"All too well. But there's no way we can be sure whatever it was had anything to do with what happened. We haven't got a shred of proof of that. Whatever landed her and her boss here might involve something else entirely, or turn out to be an accident."

Mac snickered, not buying that in the slightest. "Who was the detective who didn't believe in coincidence, Robert?"

"Sherlock Holmes."

"You agree with him?"

"He's fiction, Mac."

"I'm not sure it matters in this town anymore, because everything's made up, everything's a con. There was a time when things made sense, when there were rules people played by instead of making up their own." Mac shook his head. "I swear, I don't even recognize this city anymore."

Just then the sliding doors beyond NO ADMITTANCE whooshed open and a doctor wearing layers of PPE clothing emerged, stripping off his mask and face shield as he approached Mac. Brixton figured it was likely post-COVID protocol, but the protective gear could have been donned for an entirely different reason.

"Mr. Smith?" he said, grinding his feet to a stop.

Mac leaped to his feet. "How is she? How's my daughter?"

"You're the young woman's father, then."

"Please," Mac implored him, "tell me how she is."

"It was touch and go at first, but we managed to get her stabilized. Do you have any idea what she ingested, Mr. Smith?"

"Ingested?"

"Your daughter was poisoned."

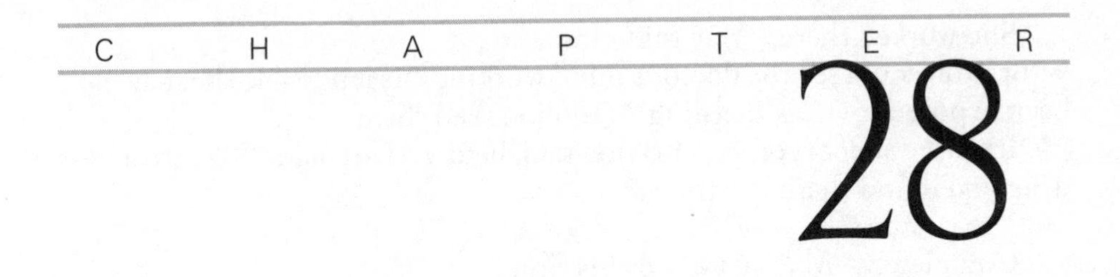

CHAPTER 28

BETHESDA, MARYLAND

Mac looked toward Brixton, then back at the doctor, whose name tag read "Dr. James Toolin."

"With what?" Mac asked.

"We've been unable to identify the toxin at this point. Was she depressed? Was she having any behavioral issues?"

"What's that have to do with anything?"

Toolin's expression answered Mac's question for him.

"You think she poisoned *herself*? As in *suicide*?"

"It's a possibility we must consider, Mr. Smith."

"Well, she didn't poison herself. This wasn't a suicide attempt."

Brixton could tell the doctor wasn't convinced of that. "What about the second victim who was brought in, too?" he asked Toolin.

"Are you a relative?"

"No."

"Then I'm afraid I can't share—"

Brixton flashed his State Department ID from his days with SITQUAL, featuring the outdated design. "Yes, you can."

"Unfortunately, he didn't make it."

"Was he poisoned, too?"

Toolin nodded. "All indications point to that, yes."

"Same toxin?"

"Since we haven't been able to identify it yet, we can't be sure."

"And this happened at the CDC's office in Washington."

"That's where they were brought in here from," the doctor acknowledged, still hedging on the details.

"So it must be where they were poisoned," Brixton noted.

"That has not been definitively confirmed yet."

"Can I see my daughter?" Mac asked, moving between the doctor and Brixton.

"She's breathing on her own, Mr. Smith, but comatose."

"Can I see her?" Mac asked louder.

Toolin nodded but made no move to lead Mac through those sliding glass doors. "As was just raised, she and the victim who was DOA were brought in from the CDC."

"She worked there," Mac told him.

Brixton could see the doctor's mind working. "Is it possible she may have been exposed to . . . something?" Toolin asked them.

"It's just a support office," Brixton said, before Mac could. "The strongest drug you'll find there is aspirin."

"You're sure?"

"Completely," Mac answered this time.

"I thought as much," Toolin nodded. "But I just wanted to be sure. Let me take you back there so you can see your daughter." Toolin watched Mac's eyes move to Brixton. "Family only, Mr. Smith."

Mac nodded, shaking his head as his eyes moistened. "Family," he repeated, no doubt thinking of a daughter he'd known for barely a week being in peril.

He looked toward Brixton.

"I haven't called Annabel, Robert."

"I'll take care of it, Mac."

"I didn't know what to tell her."

"I'll take care of it," Brixton repeated, certain that Mac hadn't heard him the first time. "And Mac," he continued, drawing closer, so the doctor wouldn't hear what he said.

"What?" Mac asked him.

"I'll explain later."

Brixton called Mac's second wife, Annabel, as requested, getting her voicemail and asking her to call him as soon as possible, trying to keep all semblance of panic and worry out of his voice.

While waiting for her to call back, and for Mac to reemerge through those glass doors, Brixton busied himself by further reviewing the substance of that part of their conversation that had dealt with whatever unpleasantness in which Alexandra had found herself involved.

Like I said, Uncle Robert, the receptionist put the call through, and I listened to the caller issue some wildly outlandish claims that were so crazy they actually made a degree of sense.

And that scared you?

Terrified me, would be a more accurate way to put it, if they were true.

So you followed the claims up.

And I think there might be something to them.

This time, instead of continuing the replay in his mind, he stopped to consider her words. He'd forgotten Alexandra had said "Terrified me," until now. It had seemed a touch too dramatic, and until this moment Brixton had thought she might have been exaggerating. But something had scared her, and now she was hospitalized.

Had this been Atlanta, Brixton knew there could be multiple explanations for being exposed to something toxic. But Capitol Hill's version of the

CDC was just a paper office with no more potential toxins present than in Mac's law offices in the Warner Building. That made one explanation rise significantly above any others: someone had tried to kill Alexandra.

She clearly knew more than she had told him over lunch, and Brixton cursed himself for not pushing her harder. She had needed him, had said as much, and he had let her down.

If this turns out to be true, Uncle Robert, time is our biggest problem.

Brixton's phone rang, "ANNABEL SMITH" lighting up in the Caller ID.

"What's wrong, Robert?" she greeted him.

"It's Alexandra Parks, Annabel. I'm at Walter Reed with Mac . . ."

Brixton heard the glass doors leading back to the hospital's trauma center whoosh back open and looked that way to find Mackensie Smith emerging, glassy-eyed and clearly shaken. He met Mac halfway across the floor, his eyes asking the question for him, which Mac promptly answered.

"They haven't been able to treat her for any specific toxin in her system, because they haven't been able to identify what poisoned her and killed her coworker."

"Do they have any notion as to how they ingested the poison?"

"Not a clue. My God, Robert, Alexandra's coworker was still in the bed next to her. They hadn't even removed his body yet." Mac squeezed his hands together to still their shaking. "I wasn't even allowed into the room. All I could do was look at her through the glass. I wanted to squeeze her hand. I wanted her to know I was there."

Brixton squeezed his friend's shoulder, not bothering to search for words when he knew nothing he could say would make him feel better. He wanted to ask about witnesses present in the CDC offices at the time, wanted to know what they had to say, wanted to know what any security cameras might have revealed. But Mac wouldn't know any of that, so he held his tongue.

"Before you ask, Robert, I asked if they could turn Alexandra's cell phone over to me, but they said it was evidence at this point and needed to be turned over to the police."

"I spoke to Annabel, Mac."

"What'd you tell her?"

"What little we know so far."

"Somebody tried to kill my daughter a week after I met her for the first time . . ."

Brixton nodded. "I took the liberty of adding something else: that we're going to find whoever did it."

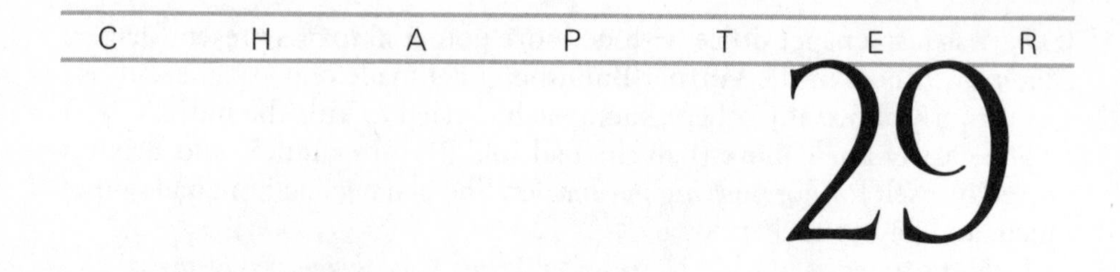

CHAPTER 29

AURORA, COLORADO

They'd been at it for hours now, going over the same material, the same maps, the same overhead satellite shots time and time again, comparing the topography of the highlighted grid over the years. The oldest series of shots was from just before the truck had seemingly vanished into thin air. The latest overhead photos were not even a week old. Lutayne's security clearance still allowed him access to the same satellite feed database, which stored potential locations of hidden weapons sites all over the world.

He had hoped that whatever it was those satellites keyed on might reveal some anomaly all the previous mapping he'd seen had somehow missed. The improvements in technology, though, had done nothing to designate a hot spot or blip that could be indicative of the missing truck's ultimate resting place or of any disturbance at ground level.

Lutayne had joined the initial search five years ago and for weeks had remained with the retrieval crews in the area between the truck's final reported location and its destination in Oregon. That area had been divided into grids, which were then searched meticulously and then searched again. Not a single square yard, foot, or inch was spared, because the crews had no idea where they might find the clue, any clue, they desperately needed. But after nearly three months, the crews hadn't turned up a thing. Not a thrown lug nut, not a smear of paint, not a torn fragment of tire rubber, not a single shard of windshield glass—nothing.

With one exception, his son pointed out, as they viewed an overhead satellite shot for the hundredth-plus time.

"What does that look like to you?" Effie asked, pointing toward an irregular splotch of black amid the landscape.

"I'd say a pond or small lake. Why?"

"Because," Effie started, leaving it there as his fingers danced across the keyboard, bringing up a shot of the same general area from five years before, prior to the final Red Dog run. "Notice anything different?"

Lutayne squinted from behind his glasses. "Not really."

"There's no body of water there in this shot, Dad."

Lutayne squinted again. "It looks the same to me."

"That's because this overhead must have been taken after or during a storm, accounting for the darkness occupying the same general size and scope. But you can tell by the variances in shading that it's actually just sodden ground. You're looking at groundwater, Dad."

Lutayne felt a prick of excitement, as if the solution to the mystery that had plagued him for five years was about to be revealed.

"Describe the general composition of the ground in these parts," his son said.

"Bedrock, shale, limestone, and clay. Some combination thereof."

Effie nodded. "I remember you telling me your first thought was that a massive sinkhole had swallowed the tanker."

"A cover-collapse sinkhole, specifically, and the most dramatic of the brand. The surface area above the bedrock in this instance is mostly clay. But since the clay is sturdy, arches form as it slowly spalls into the cavities. This arch continues to support the surface ground until it becomes so thin that it collapses into the cavern below, swallowing up everything above it." Lutayne enjoyed having his son hanging on his every word. "But there was no telltale depression," he continued, "and the geological surveys we did revealed none of the signs that such a depression had filled itself in."

"You mean with soil."

"Yes."

"I think you missed something, Dad. Did you consider the possibility of a dissolution sinkhole instead?"

"I remember the term, but that's all."

"Dissolution sinkholes are the result of there not being much ground cover, like vegetation, over the bedrock. Water slips through preexisting holes in the bedrock and begins to circulate through the bedrock. A depression in the ground forms, and if the bedrock layers beneath are sturdy enough or there's enough debris blocking the flow of water, the sinkhole stops deepening. Which could result in the formation of something like . . ." Effie paused for effect here, pointing at the screen where an overhead shot of what appeared to be a pond was still projected. "That."

"You're saying . . ." Lutayne started, stopping to let his son continue the thought.

"That it's possible the truck was captured in a massive sinkhole, the ground first swallowing and then burying it. But then the rains that night, coupled with runoff following the natural slope of the land, created a body of water that, for all intents and purposes, looked like it had been there forever."

"A sound theory," Lutayne complimented, "except for the fact that we had divers explore every body of water along the route—including that one, I'm sure."

"Except the truck wouldn't have been hidden under the water, Dad. It would have been under the sediment and surface area that formed the base on which the water has rested ever since."

Lutayne considered his son's words, feeling suddenly numb. Much of the experience of the search over those long weeks had been lost in his memory. But he was virtually certain no mention had ever been made that dive teams had explored what lay beneath the bottoms of all the bodies of water they had searched. He wasn't even sure they had the kind of equipment needed to dig under water, which was more like drilling.

Something they had missed . . . something that had never been considered for five years . . .

"It offers the perfect explanation for why you never found the truck in the immediate aftermath of its disappearance, and how it's remained hidden for so long. We need to have a look at what's under that pond, Dad," Effie concluded. "Or . . ."

"Or what?"

"You could report your suspicions to the proper parties."

"They don't exist anymore," Lutayne told his son. "And even if they did, contacting them would require exposure. There's a reason why I've spent the last five years hiding out here so they'd never find me."

"I know, Dad, but—"

"There are no buts, Effie. In the world I used to live in, you're either an asset or a liability. I was an asset; I'm not anymore."

A puzzled look crossed his son's face. "The years I've been sending you stuff, you never once told me exactly what it was you were looking for. I think it's time, Dad."

Lutayne nodded, knowing the time had come to share his greatest secrets. "Why don't I show you, instead?" he asked Effie.

PART THREE

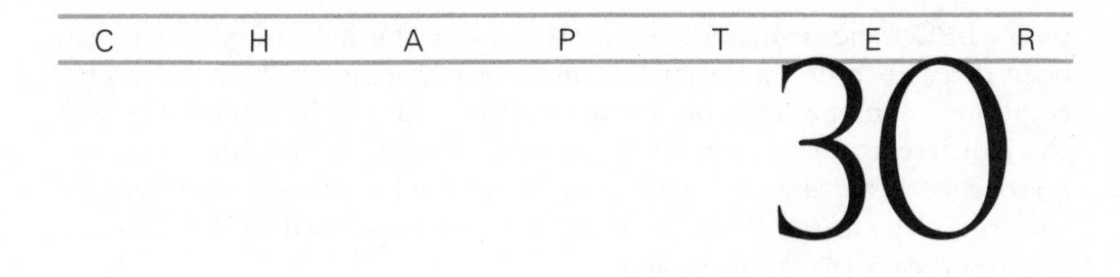

CHAPTER 30

NEW CARROLLTON, MARYLAND

"Put these on when we get to the room," Xander Peel said, handing Kelly a pair of plastic booties and evidence gloves outside the Metro Points Hotel, where they'd arranged to meet so Peel could escort her to the fourth-floor room where Jean Rappaport's body had been found.

From what he'd already told her, Kelly knew that one of the hotel's maid staff had made the discovery upon entering the room, two hours past the hotel's noon checkout time. The front desk had called the room several times to inquire about why Rappaport had yet to check out, but they had failed to alert the housekeeping staff of the anomaly. The maid had found her lying on her back atop the bedcovers.

"We've already recovered an empty prescription bottle for an antidepressant or something," Peel explained, as they entered the lobby and headed to the elevator. "In her husband's name."

"Makes sense, given that he has a history of mental illness. It also could suggest that Philip Rappaport had been off his meds, which might help explain his becoming a mass murderer."

Peel nodded as they stepped into an open and empty cab. "We're looking at a suicide here, Kel, plain and simple."

"It's never plain and simple," Kelly said, the former homicide detective in her talking.

"True enough. You bring your Capitol Police ID?"

Kelly pulled a lanyard from her pocket and looped it over her head, so her Capitol Police credentials dangled at chest level. "How do you plan on explaining my presence?"

"I'm hoping nobody asks. Because of the connection to the shooter, the Bureau has taken lead, but there are still locals involved and about, so you'll have plenty of company."

"Nobody from Capitol Police, then."

Peel shook his head. "Not their jurisdiction."

"Thanks for the heads-up, X, and for letting me join the party."

"Hey, you helped me out. Quid pro quo, right?"

The Metro Points Hotel was an aging property that had been around seemingly forever, its freshly renovated exterior belying the fact that much of its interior was in various states of disrepair. It was one of the locales used by the BPD to house material witnesses to violent crimes whose safety had been threatened or compromised, and stories abounded about its shoddy conditions. On one occasion, Kelly recalled, a witness had to be relocated three different times before finding a room with electricity, hot water, and no roaches. It was the kind of property that would ultimately be either gutted or leveled entirely to make room for a new hotel with all the bells and whistles the Metro Points lacked.

Its location off the beaten path from the prime Washington sights and tourist attractions had long made the hotel a popular choice for budget-savvy travelers, both business and leisure. But it had suffered badly in the age of critical customer reviews, many of which warned travelers off at all costs. Kelly couldn't imagine what it must be like to own a business today, particularly in the restaurant or hospitality industry, where success depended to a large extent on the whims of customers and anyone with a keyboard could be a critic.

"Strange, isn't it?" Kelly asked Peel, when the elevator door slid open on the fourth floor.

"What?"

"That the bottle of pills stayed in her handbag, while so much of the contents fell out."

"You're saying she'd still be alive otherwise. Maybe. But not for long, Kel. Swallowing the whole bottle shows she was determined to do the deed."

She fell in stride slightly behind Xander Peel as they moved toward Jean Rappaport's room, the basic model, which went for around a hundred bucks a night, a pittance in the DC Metro area. The police rate was somewhere around half that, in large part because protected witnesses were often lodged for multiple nights and, in some cases, even had police officers occupying the rooms on either side of them.

Crime scene techs from the FBI's Washington field office were already at work on the room and around the body of Jean Rappaport when Kelly and Peel reached the room. She watched them going over the room with a fine-tooth comb to make sure they didn't miss anything, even though suicide had already been determined to be the most likely cause of death. Kelly slipped on her booties and then donned her evidence gloves before accompanying Peel inside. She was careful to keep her distance so as not to draw attention from the other three agents who were watching as the crime techs worked. There was also a pair of uniformed New Carrollton police officers posted outside the door. One of them gave her a strange glance, likely recognizing her from a case she had worked in these parts for Baltimore Homicide.

This must have been one of the hotel's more recently renovated rooms. The carpet still smelled new, and a flat-screen television peeked out from a credenza that lacked the telltale signs of wear and age and came complete with a card on the desk area for how to connect to the hotel Wi-Fi.

Kelly figured Jean Rappaport hadn't bothered with that—or even with the television, for that matter. Having failed to reach the Capitol in time to stop her husband, she had come to the Metro Points Hotel for one purpose and one purpose only. A man Kelly took to be the coroner was performing a cursory examination of the body, checking the temperature and lividity levels to best determine the time of death, which Kelly guessed wasn't long after Jean Rappaport had checked in yesterday.

In contrast to the victims in scores of violent deaths Kelly had investigated, Rappaport looked reposed, serene, like she was taking a nap. It was easy to picture her waking up in the middle of the coroner's examination to find her room cluttered with technicians and law enforcement officials.

"Case closed," Peel said to her.

"This part of it, anyway. I never should have let her out of my sight. She's dead now because I screwed up."

Peel shrugged. "You couldn't have possibly known who she was when you saw her sitting on that bench, Kel. Don't beat yourself up over it."

"What would you be doing?"

"Beating myself up over it."

Kelly realized that two more FBI agents, in matching dark suits, had entered the room, their focus trained more on her than on Peel. He nodded their way, stiffening, something all wrong about his expression.

"These are Special Agents Vickers and Webb, Kel," he said. "They need to talk to you."

"Need to talk to me?" she repeated, as the agents advanced toward her.

The reason for the agents' presence was written all over Peel's pained expression. "I'm sorry."

"You sold me out?"

"You held back information in a federal investigation, and I know you're holding back more."

Kelly looked him in the eye, as the agents came up on either side of her. "What are friends for, right?"

"You didn't leave me any choice."

"Don't sweat it. I'm used to being betrayed."

"You betrayed yourself, Kel. First with the BPD and now with the Capitol Police. I'm doing you a favor."

"Oh, is that what they call it?"

Kelly felt the agents take hold of her by the arms.

"See you around, X."

"You'll thank me for this someday."

"Fat chance," she said, as the agents started to lead her from the room.

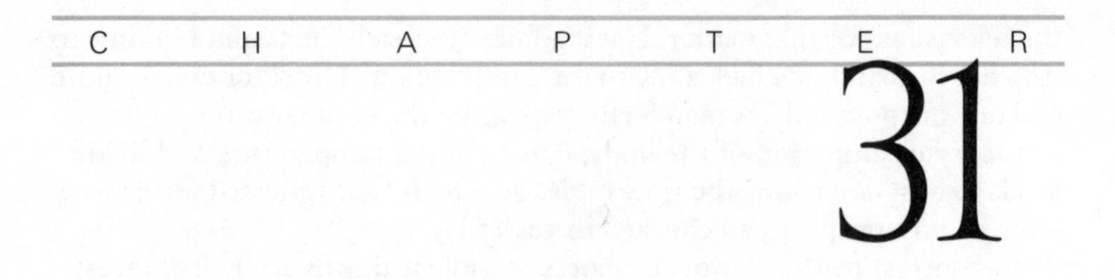

WASHINGTON, DC

Before heading over to the Warner Building, Brixton and Mac made a stop on the seventh floor in a gleaming steel-and-glass office building on F Street Northwest. Mac had driven to Walter Reed, not wanting to waste a precious second under such dire circumstances, which meant they now had to find a place to park. Ultimately, they opted to risk a significant fine to leave Mac's BMW in a No Parking spot, still a block away from the building.

"I should have stayed at the hospital," Mac said, as they climbed out. "In case Alexandra wakes up—I mean, *when* she wakes up."

"How many times have you told me how important it is to stay active? To not sit around, accomplishing nothing?"

"I said that?"

Brixton nodded. "The exact words."

That seemed to ease Mac's guilt, at least a little. "So what's next? They should give out beepers, like they do in restaurants—the things that light up and start flashing when your table's ready. When there's news to report, it starts vibrating."

"Not a bad idea, actually."

"Do I know this gentleman?" Mac asked him, once they'd started for the building.

"You know his work. He's the absolute best when it comes to finding something where there's nothing to find."

"You're talking about that looped footage from the Capitol, captured during the shooting, that I sent you," Mac realized. "I was wondering why you didn't say anything more about that second shooter your grandson thought he saw."

"First off, you've had other things on your mind, and second, there's nothing to say. Yet."

"And that's why we're here," Mac said.

Moments later, they entered the building, signed in as guests at the reception counter, and rode an elevator alone to the seventh floor. The door slid open, diagonally across from Compu-Tech, a computer repair outlet that doubled as something else entirely.

"A contact of yours?" Mac posed.

Brixton nodded, leading the way to the Compu-Tech entrance. "From back in my days with SITQUAL, when he was CIA. If Max was right about there being a second shooter off to the side of the Capitol steps, then Jesus Arriaga will find him."

"Cuban?"

"A grandchild of the revolution, you might say. His grandparents on both sides came over in the 1960s with his parents. His mother and father actually knew each other from back there. Jesus worked the South American desk for the CIA, as a data analyst, until he figured he'd take his talents elsewhere. He's helped me out a whole bunch of times, Mac, and a few of them have been on the firm's dime."

"I don't recall seeing his name, or Compu-Tech's, anywhere in your vouchers."

"Figure of speech. It doesn't work that way with us."

Mac nodded knowingly, as they reached the glass door entrance to Compu-Tech and pressed the buzzer, per the instructions posted there. "That's right, the code of special operators. Don't tell me: he owes you a favor."

"A whole bunch. And I owe him about the same. We don't keep tallies."

"And who's counting, among friends?"

A louder buzzer sounded and the glass door opened with a *click*. Brixton moved up to the reception counter, which was manned by a young man who looked like a college student.

"The boss in?" Brixton asked him.

A spark of recognition flashed in the kid's eyes. "He's not expecting you, but you can go right on back," he said, with the slightest of smirks, touching a Bluetooth device cupped around his ear. "I'll tell him you're here."

"So your friend decided to retire on Capitol Hill?" Mac asked, as Brixton led the way to Jesus Arriaga's office.

"'Retire' is the wrong term. He's moved on to life's second act—on Capitol Hill. Because that's where the business is."

"And the money."

"There's that, too."

Arriaga emerged from his glassed-in office just before Brixton and Mac reached it. He looked tan and fit as ever, exactly the same as the first time his and Brixton's paths had crossed, in the Balkans, ten years ago.

"My man!" Arriaga beamed, greeting Brixton with a warm bro hug while shaking his hand at the same time. "Que pasa, amigo?"

"I need your help with something."

"Why else would you be here?" Arriaga held open his door and bid them to enter. "Right this way."

Brixton handed him the flash drive as soon as they were inside, making sure to block the maneuver from any prying eyes that might have been peering in through the glass.

"Words or pictures, amigo?"

"A video, and you never watched it."

"What flash drive?"

"Right."

"So what is it I never watched?"

Brixton laid it out for him in concise fashion. Arriaga's interest was grabbed by his first mention of the Capitol steps shooting.

"No *mierda*?"

"No shit," Brixton acknowledged, nodding.

"Guess you're keeping busy."

"This one kind of fell into my lap. My grandson was on those steps, Jesus."

Arriaga's expression tightened. "Lo siento."

"Nothing to be sorry about, unless you don't find that second shooter."

Arriaga grinned broadly, showcasing twin rows of gleaming white teeth. "Hey, amigo, if I'd been around in 1963, we'd know the truth about Kennedy."

What now, Robert?" Mac asked, once they were back in the car that, miraculously, was still there, and with no ticket squeezed beneath a windshield wiper.

"I make a phone call to someone who can get us the data records from Alexandra's cell phone."

Mac nodded, needing no further elaboration, as Brixton dialed a number manually. "Should you be using your cell phone?"

"He won't pick up, otherwise. The professor never answers a call from a number he doesn't recognize."

Mac nodded, knowing enough about the man Brixton was calling not to press matters further.

"Hello, Robert," a voice answered.

"How are your pigeons, Professor?"

"On diets, in the hope some of them will fly off. I've been leaving the cage doors opened, but there are more about every day."

Brixton considered the occasions he'd visited him, during which he'd been feeding the birds on his apartment rooftop. "How are you with cell phone dumps?"

"A bit below my pay grade, but for you, I'll make an exception," the professor said, not pushing Brixton for more, just as Brixton would not have pressed him. "You have the number?"

Brixton recited it from the contacts in his phone, having plugged in the number during his lunch with Alexandra the day before.

"Anything else I should know?"

"The phone belongs to Mackensie Smith's daughter," Brixton said, looking at Mac.

"I didn't know your friend had a daughter."

"Neither did he, until recently."

"I'll jump on this right now."

"Thank you, Professor."

"Happy to help. Who knows, I might need a good lawyer myself someday."

Brixton didn't bother asking him what for.

"I'll email you the results as soon as they're in hand. Same box?"

"Yes," Brixton told him, referring to a secret, untraceable email address he'd kept active after leaving SITQUAL, so secret his former employers were clueless that he still had it.

"Okay, then. I'll call you once I'm done. And Robert?"

"Yes?"

"Be careful."

"Who said I was in danger?"

"You did, when you called me."

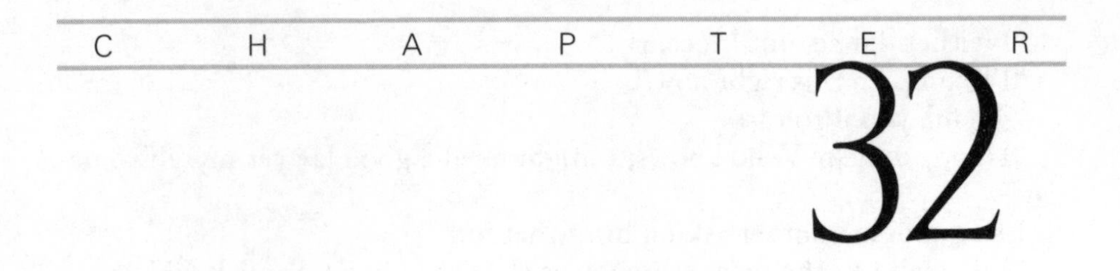

CHAPTER 32

WASHINGTON, DC

"How long's this going to take?" Mac asked Brixton, while waiting on hold with Walter Reed yet again, after they were inside his office with the door closed.

"Knowing the professor, you'll still be on hold with the hospital when he gets back to me."

"Thanks for doing this, Robert, using a contact like this professor of yours. I know you can't make too many withdrawals from that bank."

"People like him, and Arriaga, don't keep score. I told you that. It doesn't work that way."

Mac looked at him strangely. "There's a part of you, your life, I'm never going to fully understand, isn't there?"

"You don't want to, Mac. The people I've met along the way prefer the shadows."

"Sometimes I think you prefer them, too, Robert."

Brixton didn't bother to nod. "The shadows are simpler. Never having to worry about the why, only the what, who, and when. Life's a lot simpler when there's nothing before you but the immediate mission. Men like the professor and Jesus Arriaga never saw the things, or did the things, I did, but I never would have survived without them. And that goes for a whole lot of others just like me."

Mac held a hand up to indicate that the right person at Walter Reed was finally on the line. Brixton listened to him speak sparingly, watched him listen with interest but not trepidation. Mac finally looked back up, after ending the call.

"They're telling me Alexandra's stable, whatever that means."

"It means she's out of immediate danger, that whatever they're doing is keeping her alive."

Mac looked down, then up again. "Can I ask you if . . ."

"No," Brixton answered, when Mac's voice trailed off. "I never used poison. I was a door-kicker, Mac. Smash-and-grab nighttime raids in body armor and night vision. No poison-tipped umbrellas."

"You miss it, don't you?"

"It's like I just told you. I miss the simplicity."

Brixton's phone rang.

"That was fast," he greeted the professor, not bothering to ask him why he'd called instead of texted.

"You didn't tell me this phone number had already been flagged."

"Because I didn't know," Brixton said, glad in that moment that Mac couldn't hear the other end of the conversation.

"Somebody dumped the phone's contents. I mean, made them disappear, including the number itself. Somebody from our circles, Robert. Somebody good."

"Uh-oh."

"Don't worry," the professor told him, "because I'm better. They went by the book, wiping the stored contents from the cloud."

"That doesn't sound good."

"Good thing I wrote the book, then. I sent the contents to that usual email drop, no trail left to either of us."

"Of course not."

"Whoever's behind this is serious, Robert. Looks like you've poked another hornet's nest."

"It's becoming a bit of a habit."

"Good thing I double as an exterminator. I'll be waiting for your next call."

Brixton used Mac's computer to access his email drop box.

"Who could have dumped the contents of Alexandra's phone, Robert?" Mac asked him, while they waited for the spinning ball on the screen to stop, indicating access had been granted.

"You know the answer to that as well as I do."

Mac shrugged, sighing. "You hear about these things happening, but you don't pay a lot of attention until it happens to someone close to you."

"Don't focus on the who; focus on the why."

"Okay," Mac said, leaving the door open for Brixton to continue.

"Either whatever Alexandra was following up was flagged because it was classified or . . ."

"I'm listening, Robert."

"Someone made it disappear because she was getting too close to something."

"Someone powerful, then. No shortage there, in this city."

"There is when it comes to getting personal phone records dumped, Mac. That's a whole other level of power reserved for a select few."

Mac nodded. "I'm not going to end up with men in black knocking on my door in the dead of night, am I, Robert?"

"The drop is completely untraceable. And those men in black aren't in the habit of knocking. Trust me."

"I do. But you still haven't told me what your professor friend said."

"Let's see what he came up with first, Mac."

"It's bad, isn't it?"

"Alexandra apparently ran afoul of the wrong people."

"In government or out?"

"Still to be determined," Brixton said.

He found the file containing the stored contents of Alexandra's phone, which the professor had somehow recovered from the cloud, and downloaded it to Mac's desktop. Understandably, it was huge, and the machine took its time creating the file.

"We'll wipe this from your computer once we've reviewed the contents," he told Mac, anxiety still claiming his expression.

The machine dinged, signaling the download of the folder was complete. Seated behind Mac's desk, Brixton opened it and saw both text files and an assortment of MP3s. The huge volume of the phone's contents, lots of gigabytes, accounted for the slow download speed. The professor was nothing if not thorough, and Brixton had failed to be specific about what to include. As a result, the file included every single one of Alexandra's emails and text messages; songs downloaded to her Apple Music app; a slew of voicemails, both stored and deleted; her contacts, listed alphabetically; her call log; and a bunch of apps Alexandra used for both work and play.

"Wow," Mac said, suddenly behind him, having noted the huge amount of material.

For some reason, Brixton positioned himself to block the screen. "We need to work the timeline."

"We don't know the timeline, Robert."

"Whatever Alexandra had become involved in was relatively recent—that was the impression I got at lunch yesterday."

"A week, two maybe?"

"The attack," Brixton noted, referring to the poisoning that had killed Alexandra's coworker, "is what we need to key off of. That means we start from the most recent emails, texts, and calls and work backward."

They decided to work together, even though dividing the duties would have speeded up the review process. That was Brixton's idea, since he did not totally trust Mac's capacity to be sufficiently objective about what he was seeing, under the circumstances. Mac had already told his assistant to not put any calls through, and all his appointments for the day had already been moved in the wake of learning that Alexandra was being rushed to Walter Reed. And about devotion to the company—the assistant was still here and would remain, as was her custom, until Mac was out the door for the night.

They started with emails and texts, though nothing of note surfaced after an hour spent reviewing both, going day by day.

"All routine," Mac noted. "Unless we're missing something."

The anomaly felt strange to Brixton, given what Alexandra had told him at lunch.

"She could have created an email account she only accessed via the Web. We'll need to check her internet browsing history as well."

Mac sighed. "Looks like we'll be ordering in dinner." He checked his watch. "Time to call the hospital again," he added, moving aside to do so.

While Mac waited for the proper party at Walter Reed to be summoned, Brixton moved on to Alexandra's voicemails, plugging in a set of earbuds so as not to disturb Mac, and keeping him from potentially hearing a personal message at the same time. Starting with this morning, he worked backward through them in order, combing through the first dozen without finding a single thing of note besides one from the office of Senator Byron Fitch, which stood out only because he'd been on the Capitol steps when the shooting erupted.

"Ms. Parks, this is Senator Fitch's office, returning your call."

Short and sweet and likely connected to a briefing the senator had been party to in Alexandra's primary duties at the CDC's Washington office. Four more voicemail messages not worth noting followed, leaving him only one left: a message that, according to the time stamp, must have been received around the time Alexandra was being rushed to the hospital or had already arrived there. There was a brief pause, followed by a scratchy female voice, as if the connection was less than perfect.

"Hi, this is Kelly Loftus of the Capitol Police. We have reason to believe you may have some knowledge of the perpetrator of yesterday's shooting at the Capitol Building. If you could call me back at . . ."

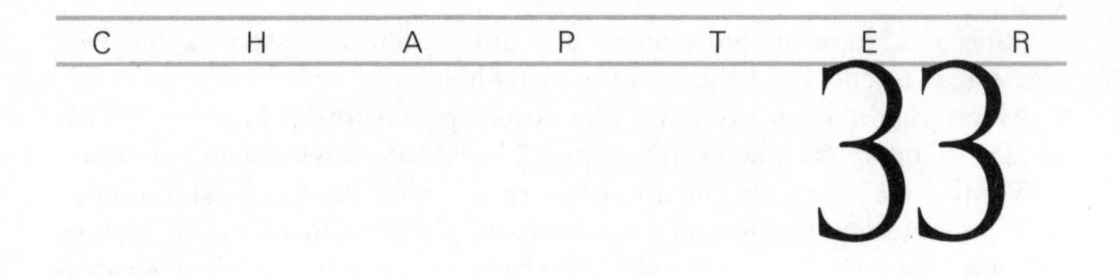

AURORA, COLORADO

Sorry, Dad," Effie said, when the wheelchair snagged in a rut and nearly toppled Lutayne from the seat.

"Good thing you drive a car better than this chair," Lutayne quipped. "Otherwise, who'd make sure I got my press clippings?"

Lutayne liked the feeling of his son pushing his wheelchair toward the greenhouse, the moment of levity breaking the silence that had persisted since Effie had posed his theory about a dissolution sinkhole. The fact that the final Red Dog run might have been right there under the searchers' proverbial noses all this time made both no sense and all the sense in the world. Occam's razor, after all, postulated that the simplest explanation was normally correct, and the conclusion that his son had reached more than followed that dictum. The missing truck hadn't vanished into the ether, been appropriated by space aliens, or slipped through some cosmic rip in the space-time continuum. The whole time the search crews had scoured roughly a hundred-square-mile grid, the truck might well have been right below them.

Divers had indeed searched what they had taken for a pond, without result. Reflecting on that, Lutayne figured the truck might well have sunk into the same silt that was coughed up when the sinkhole opened. That would explain why none of the seismic sensors rigged to find anomalies below the surface of the ground and water had picked up the truck. Likewise, it would not have been registered by heat sensors, because a combination of the silt and water entombing it would have chilled its exterior to camouflage any heat signature. It all made perfect sense, everything coming full circle. What better time for Lutayne to introduce his son to what he'd been hiding almost since the day he'd begun his new life in Aurora, thanks to those seeds he'd smuggled out of Tooele Army Depot.

The years I've been sending you stuff, you never once told me exactly what it was you were looking for. I think it's time, Dad.

Why don't I show you, instead?

And that's what Lutayne was doing now. He was about to share his greatest secrets, because his son deserved that much for potentially solving a mystery that had eluded him, and the entire military apparatus, for five years. Those secrets encompassed the sum total of all his work in Utah. It was one thing to be party to destroying the deadly treasures he had lovingly nurtured from seedlings, creating hybrid versions of some of nature's already deadliest killers; it was quite another to let the product of his labors vanish forever. So he'd pocketed seeds and put them aside for a moment like this. Six sets of a dozen each, so small he could have closed his fist around the lot of them.

In those last moments before the base was finally shuttered, Lutayne feared he'd be searched by the soldiers wearing uniforms that lacked the markings of any branch of the military. He had always welcomed their presence for making him feel safe from attack, realizing only in those last hours that they were there as much to keep Lutayne prisoner as to protect him. It was a twisted dichotomy that made sense only in the world he had inhabited for far too long.

Effie used his father's key to open the greenhouse door, sniffing at the luxurious scent of the variously colored orchids arranged in neat rows before him.

"Am I missing something here?" his son asked, having seen his father's spectacular collection on every visit.

Lutayne rolled himself past Effie and into the greenhouse. "Yes, and you're supposed to. Follow me."

Lutayne wheeled his chair toward the far wall. From the outside, the greenhouse appeared to be a slab of a building dominated by glass, with solid walls on either side. The camouflage was so effective that no one could possibly suspect the existence of a second, smaller, windowless chamber, fed entirely by artificial light, in which the contents were grown hydroponically.

He reached the rear wall, felt for the slot that was indistinguishable from the rest of the planking, and pressed a button as soon as his fingers located it. Instantly, a section of that rear wall opened like a giant elevator, revealing a secondary greenhouse lined by flowering plants encased in thin, sheer plastic.

"Here, put this on," Lutayne said, twisting enough to hand his son an N95 mask.

Effie donned it, knowing better than to ask any questions at this point, since the answers to them would soon be forthcoming.

Lutayne looped his own N95 mask behind his ears and made sure the seal was tight enough to protect him. Air humidifiers and recirculators hummed, maintaining the perfect temperature and humidity levels for growing the hybrids he had genetically created during a lifetime of work. Some of the flowers before him were every bit as beautiful as the orchids in the greenhouse beyond, but it was a fatal beauty, because these flowers produced some of the deadliest toxins ever known to man.

Efram Lutayne had taken the most poisonous flowers on the planet and subjected them to genetic enhancements that multiplied their toxicity by between one thousand and ten thousand times.

Effie couldn't believe his eyes. "How long . . . how long . . . " he stammered, unable to push his thoughts forward, having a general concept of what he was looking at.

"Since I came here and had the greenhouse built," Lutayne confessed.

He'd been worried the whole time about being caught with the pilfered seeds on his person, his heart hammering over whether the expected search might reveal them. But he was never searched; one of the benefits of living in a wheelchair.

"What am I looking at exactly?" Effie finally managed.

Lutayne wheeled himself forward, leading his son onward. He stopped at a plant that vaguely resembled a dandelion, except that its flowers were white and more closely bunched.

"This is water hemlock," he told his son, "generally considered to be the most violently toxic plant in North America. It's a wildflower infused with a poison known as cicutoxin, concentrated mostly in its petals. Anyone who has the misfortune of consuming it is as likely to die as to suffer a variety of symptoms that would otherwise make them wish they had."

Not waiting for Effie to comment, Lutayne rolled on to the next plantings in line.

"Deadly nightshade," he announced, indicating a dull green, leafy plant rich in dark berries about the size and consistency of cherries. "According to legend, Macbeth's soldiers poisoned the invading Danes with wine made from this sweet fruit. It's native to the wooded or waste areas in central and southern Eurasia and contains atropine and scopolamine in its stems, leaves, berries, and roots. It causes paralysis in the involuntary muscles of the body, including the heart. Mere physical contact with the leaves may cause skin irritation."

Next, Lutayne came to another leafy plant, with small white flower stems. It didn't look like very much at all.

"White snakeroot," he said, picking up on his narration. "Contains a toxic alcohol called tremetol. The danger with snakeroot lies in the fact people can be poisoned by drinking the milk of cows that may feed on it when grazing. So it presented an entirely different op—"

Lutayne thought he'd stopped himself just in time, but Effie's glare told him he hadn't.

"Opportunity," his son completed for him. "That's what you were going to say. An opportunity to, what, kill by poisoning livestock, which would then be ingested into the targets somebody wants dead? That's what all this was about, right? Targets."

"In theory."

"What about practice?"

Instead of responding, Lutayne wheeled himself on to another leafy set of green plants that shed brown, seedlike beans.

"Castor beans?" Effie guessed.

Lutayne nodded, grateful to be spared another explanation. "The source of ricin," he said instead. "Under normal circumstances, it would take the contents of eight or so of these beans to kill an average-sized man."

Effie gazed about the secret chamber. "None of this is normal."

Lutayne ignored his son's insinuation. "We liquefied an immensely concentrated version of the ricin so a single droplet would be fatal."

Effie shook his head, more in amazement than disdain. "Which of your concoctions was in that tanker, Dad?"

"We're getting to that. First," he continued, wheeling himself to the next set of plantings, "meet the rosary pea, also known as jequirity beans. The seeds contain abrin, an extremely deadly ribosome-inhibiting protein. They're native to tropical areas and are often used in jewelry and prayer rosaries. While the seeds are not poisonous if intact, seeds that are scratched, broken, or chewed can be lethal. It only takes three micrograms of abrin to kill an adult, less than the amount of poison in one seed, and it is said that numerous jewelry makers have been made ill or died after accidentally pricking their fingers while working with the seeds. Like ricin, abrin prevents protein synthesis within cells and can cause organ failure within four days, in the wild."

"And what about in your lab?"

Again, Lutayne didn't hold back, risking his son's disapproval. "A few hours, but not on a mass scale. This was meant to be used in a more targeted fashion."

"As in assassinations."

Lutayne nodded.

"But the contents of your lost truck, that was all about killing on a mass scale."

Instead of nodding again, Lutayne rolled his chair on to the final stop, a grouping of pinkish-white flowers every bit as beautiful as the multicolored orchids in the greater greenhouse beyond.

"Oleander, containing the deadliest toxin of any plant in existence. All parts of the oleander plant are deadly, thanks to lethal cardiac glycosides known as oleandrin and neriine. If eaten, oleander can cause vomiting, diarrhea, erratic pulse, seizures, coma, and death. Indeed, the toxins in oleander are so strong that people have become ill after eating honey made by bees that pollinated the flowers."

"But fatalities from oleander poisoning are exceedingly rare," Effie noted. "The plant hardly qualifies as a weapon of mass destruction."

"Until we increased its toxicity on the level of twenty thousand times through a combination of selective breeding and genetic enhancement. Exposure to the glycosides contained in the plants we created attacked the respiratory system en route to short-circuiting the central nervous system, leading to catastrophic organ failure within twenty-four hours."

"You sound proud, Dad."

"I was. I am. I'm not going to deny that."

Effie was shaking his head. "You could kill thousands, tens of thousands."

"Millions, actually," Lutayne corrected.

"How much of your creation was actually produced?"

"Well, because every part of oleander, from stem to sap, is poisonous, we were able to grind the plants into a liquid, combined with active agents of simple alcohol and a form of clear grape juice. Milky white in color, exposure to as little as a drop to two would be almost certainly fatal."

"How much, Dad?" Effie pushed him.

"That tanker was carrying fifteen thousand gallons."

Effie swallowed hard. "That's a lot of drops. How were you planning on deploying it?"

"I wasn't planning on deploying it at all."

"No," Effie said derisively. "You left that task to others."

"And many options were considered, yes. Everything from contaminating foodstuffs, pills, candy, baked goods—pretty much anything."

"What was the anticipated fatality rate?"

"Theoretically?"

Effie nodded. "Theoretically."

"Ninety-eight percent."

"And you lost *fifteen thousand gallons* of the stuff."

"I never stopped looking for it, Effie. That's why you're here."

Effie scratched at his head. Lutayne could see his hand was trembling.

"I'm not trying to defend myself, or my actions."

"You should be, Dad. My God, what you were doing . . . What you've done . . ." His eyes fell back on the pinkish-white flowers, whose beauty belied their deadliness. "This is monstrous, utterly monstrous."

"Explaining why I've kept watch so meticulously," Lutayne said defensively. "The whole purpose behind those monthly newspaper drops. Waiting. Watching. To make sure the world stayed safe from my creation."

"Those high school kids who were poisoned in Baltimore . . ."

Lutayne nodded. "The toxin that killed them was never identified. But the cause of death in seven cases was respiratory distress, followed by a complete breakdown of the central nervous system. That was all I needed to read to fear someone may have found the missing tanker. That article was what I've been dreading for over five years now."

"Dreading or hoping for, Dad?"

"Weapons like this are never meant to be used, Effie, any more than nuclear bombs."

"But atomic bombs were used once, weren't they? And you're not talking about the massive destruction and desolation they leave behind; you're talking about a perfect killing machine with a nearly one hundred percent fatality rate."

"That's why we need to find out if someone got to the White Death ahead of us."

"White Death," Effie repeated. "That's what you called it . . ."

"Because that's what it was."

Lutayne heard something rattle in that moment, followed by the quick, heavy thump of footsteps, which drew his gaze to the open sliding door of his secret chamber. In that moment, a half dozen armed figures wearing black tactical gear stormed inside, peeling away from a smaller figure who was sporting a Panama hat that matched his wrinkled khaki-colored suit.

"Nice to finally meet you, Dr. Lutayne."

Lutayne had reflexively moved his wheelchair in front of Effie to shield his son. The government must have finally found him by following Effie to his off-the-grid lair. He cursed himself, not so much for his stupidity in summoning his son but for not anticipating the danger to which it had exposed Effie. After five years, he'd let himself believe they weren't looking for him anymore, that he'd slipped off everyone's radar, thanks to the revolving door of government service. Could be there wasn't a single person left in Washington who knew him as the Poison Master, a riff on the term "puppet master."

"Who are you?" he asked the man, who had the most nondescript features he'd ever laid eyes on.

"Call me Panama," the man said, tipping his hat for effect. "Not my real name, but what I've been calling myself for, oh, about a year now. I've kind of taken to it."

Lutayne continued to stare at him. Effie was standing stiff and scared behind the wheelchair.

"Interestingly enough," Panama continued, "you and I are on the same page, Dr. Lutayne, and we need to be on the same plane ASAP. Another of my men is already packing a bag for you."

"Where are we going?"

"Oregon, Doctor. Umatilla."

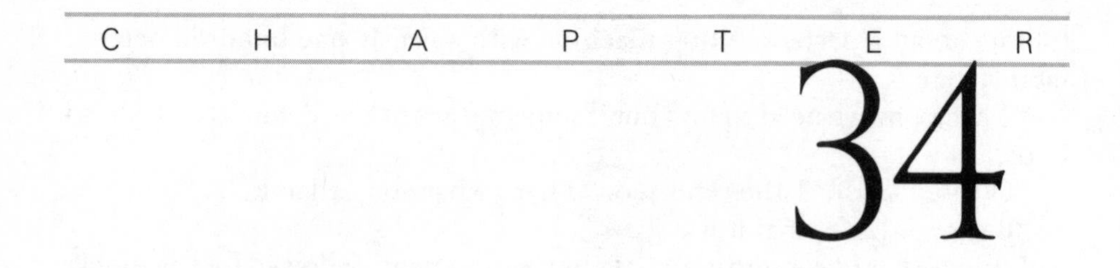

CHAPTER 34

BALTIMORE, MARYLAND

Kelly was still shaking when she got home from the Metro Points Hotel, both unsettled and miserable over being dressed down by a pair of FBI special agents, who had interrogated her for hours before ultimately letting her go without an arrest.

Just like the officials who'd summarily ended her police career in Baltimore.

It was getting to be a habit, though it was considerably different this time. After all, the incident that had unceremoniously ended her career as a homicide detective hadn't been her doing—or, more accurately, it had been the result of her doing the right thing. That was in stark contrast to what had happened this time, where her own actions had caught the attention of the FBI in the absolute wrong way. Kelly didn't even blame Xander Peel for violating her trust; after all, she'd tried to use him for her own gains in the first place.

What did you expect to accomplish?

A question she had asked herself, with no satisfactory answer. Why didn't she just collect the trail of contents from Jean Rappaport's handbag and turn them over to the appropriate parties? Explain her part in this and be done with it. Instead, she'd seen a puzzle, a mystery she could solve.

Out of spite for the forces that had ended her career as a detective?

Maybe.

To prove to herself she still had it, and to prove them wrong in the process?

More likely.

Because she hated the day-to-day, mind-numbing routine of working Protective Services for the Capitol Police?

Most likely. But probably some combination of all three.

Kelly opened up a kitchen cabinet and took out the Jack Daniel's bottle she'd barely touched since she bought it, way back when she was still on the force. She hated the taste of the stuff, really, but it had been her father's preferred poison and that made it hers as well. Her father had been a cop, too, a uniform his entire career. He'd been killed in the midst of a routine traffic stop gone bad. Ask any cop about traffic stops, and you'll hear universally that they're the most dangerous part of the job. Homicide detectives spent their careers around death and murderers, but she couldn't name one who'd ever been killed in the line of duty.

But homicide cops never did traffic stops.

Kelly had been just a kid at the time her father had been shot and left to bleed out on the side of the road. The shooter was a coked-up gangbanger who literally forgot he was driving his own car and not the stolen one he'd dropped off at a chop shop earlier in the night. Her dad pulled him over for a busted taillight and the guy stuck a gun out the window and started firing before her dad could even say "License and registration, please." He got caught the next day and was doing two consecutive life terms, though Kelly had heard his sentence had been commuted to a single one, without possibility of parole. He only had one life, so she found that fair.

Joe Loftus had never seen his daughter become a cop, which meant he'd also not been around to witness the inglorious end to the career of the youngest woman in Baltimore history to ever make detective—and this was *any* woman, not just a Black woman. And he wasn't around now to watch her make a different kind of history. So when she drank, it was Jack Daniel's, even though she hated the taste and the hangover.

She pulled down a short, squat rocks glass that had come in the same package as the sour mash whiskey and poured in just enough to fill the glass after she had added ice. Drinking it cold dulled the taste a bit and made it easier to swallow. She took a big gulp, nearly gagging as the Jack left a trail of fire down her throat.

Right now, Kelly's plans for the future amounted to drinking as much whiskey as she could to dull what she was feeling and pass out. She wasn't looking forward to the hangover, but she wasn't really looking forward to anything, at this point. She fully expected the next call she received to be from the offices of the Capitol Police, informing her of an indefinite suspension, since a hearing would be required to fire her for cause. Kelly thought about just resigning, to save them the bother.

Then the phone rang. Kelly decided not to ignore it, saw no sense in putting off the inevitable. Just answered her cell without even bothering to check the caller ID.

"Is this Kelly Loftus?" an unfamiliar male voice asked her.

"Who's this?" she asked.

"My name is Robert Brixton. I'm a private investigator working with a Washington attorney whose daughter was attacked this morning."

"What does that have to do with me?"

"You called her right around the time she was being rushed to the hospital."

Suddenly, Kelly forgot all about the Jack Daniel's. Her throat no longer burned.

"Wait a minute. You say she was *attacked*?" She recovered her thinking, started to process what this man was saying, through the haze the whiskey was already forming. "Wait, is this that New York number, a six-four-six exchange?"

"I think we should meet, Detective."

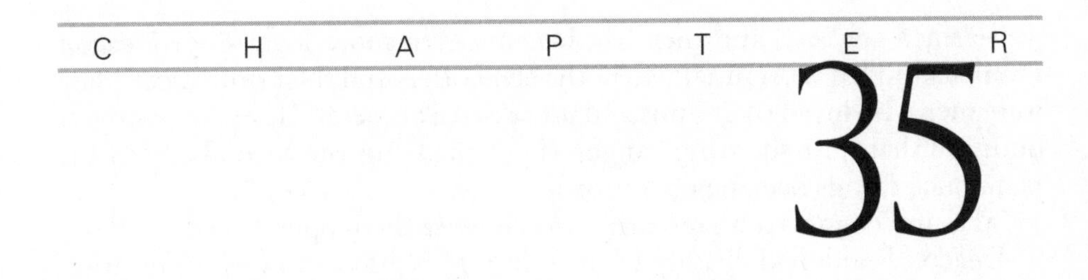

CHAPTER 35

OLDTOWN, MARYLAND

"Get your ass down here!" Deacon Frank Wilhyte said from the bottom of the stairs. "You hear me, boy?" He could hear his son rummaging around, but the boy was showing no signs of appearing from the room where he'd been confined as punishment for more than a month, since his charter high school in Baltimore had been closed indefinitely.

Like his father, Deacon Frank had only a single child, also a son. He'd named him Daniel for the biblical connotations, because Jeremiah seemed a bit much. The boy was absolutely prohibited from going online, but his father had found evidence that he had done so, when he got back from Michigan, and now Daniel had to be called on the carpet for that. His own father, the Reverend Rand Atlas Wilhyte, had taken the belt to him more times than he could count, often more out of spite than punishment, telling his son that it was for his own good, so the pain would register with him if he even contemplated doing something wrong.

Deacon Frank wondered if his father had ever even conceived of him reaching the heights he had, having abandoned televangelism and religion altogether in favor of a higher cause and nobler pursuit. How his collective efforts in organizing like-minded groups all over the country had made him wealthy behind his imagining, had paid for the two thousand acres on which were located his sprawling mansion, built to look like an ancient cathedral, and thriving dairy farm. He'd chosen Oldtown as his base of operations because it boasted a rare isolation, given that it was so close to the seat of government power in Washington, DC. Deacon Frank knew he needed to be near power, to absorb it almost like osmosis, until that power was his.

Oldtown had been founded in the eighteenth century as Opessa's Town, or Shawanese Old Town because it had been the site of a Shawnee Native America village years before. It had started as no more than a trading post along an old Indian trail between the Cumberland Narrows mountain pass and the Monongahela River valley. In later years, the explanatory prefix was dropped from the name and the place became known simply as Oldtown.

Now it was Deacon Frank's seat of power, a power soon to be realized, thanks to his ability to command the disparate groups of the nation's militia movements. Combined, they offered him upward of a hundred thousand well-armed soldiers, and they had become even more loyal since Deacon Frank had added substantially to both their coffers and their ordnance. They were men who loved their guns and possessed a desperate desire to use them on more than just shooting ranges. They made up the second cog of his plan, once things became operational.

The first cog was a weapon that would *make* them operational.

Deacon Frank had already been training his efforts toward unification of the nation's militias when the weapon in question fell into his lap. His daddy would have said it was all God's work, part of His plan more than of Deacon Frank's, and in this case he wouldn't have bothered arguing with the Reverend Rand, because that fateful day was finally drawing closer.

That is, until his son had almost destroyed everything, all his plans.

"Don't make me come up there and get you!" he shouted up the curving stairway of his mansion's east wing, toward his son's bedroom.

He heard the door finally open.

"What'd I do now?" Daniel yelled down at him.

"Don't take that tone with me, boy!"

"Jeez," Deacon Frank heard his son say, just loud enough for him to hear.

He appeared at the top of the stairs wearing the same ragged sweatpants and T-shirt he'd been wearing for days. Even from the foot of the stairs, Deacon Frank could almost smell the rank musk rising off him.

He waited for Daniel to begin his descent, clambering down the stairs, each step a thumping effort, a labor in itself.

"Take off your shirt," Deacon Frank ordered when they were eye to eye. His son was as tall as he was but thin, with arms as thin as toothpicks.

"Why?"

Deacon Frank slapped him across the face. "Because I said so."

Tears welled up in the boy's eyes as he stared at his father in shock. "What the fu—"

Deacon Frank slammed him again and ripped the raggedy T-shirt off him, feasting in the sound of the fabric tearing. Daniel was sobbing, whimpering, muttering "Dad, Dad, Dad" and "Don't, don't, don't," the words sometimes strung together.

Then he bent his son over the back of his chair so he was facing an antique mirror hanging from a foyer wall, father and son captured in the reflection. The boy's face was beet red, and the tears streaming down his face filled Deacon Frank not with guilt or compassion but with affirmation and certainty of purpose. He hadn't beaten his son for the transgression that had nearly derailed his life's mission, but this was different, because the boy had disobeyed a direct order that was part of his punishment.

He held his son down with one hand while the other stripped his belt from its loops and folded it over.

"I didn't punish you like I should have for the damage you did. That's on me. But you stuck it in my face. You think I don't know you been on the Web, doing whatever you do when you think nobody's looking? Well, boy, I was looking. And now you're going to look at yourself in that mirror while you pay for what you've done."

With that, Deacon Frank cracked the belt across his son's back, watched the skin pucker and darken into a purplish welt. He hadn't heard that sound since the last time Reverend Rand Atlas Wilhyte punished him, for no good reason at all. It had been a test, he realized now, to see how much he could take, proving to him that he could take a lot more than he thought. His daddy had been teaching him a lesson, and that lesson had brought him here to Oldtown and to a power that was even greater for the country's lack of recognition of it. That made him think Daniel's transgression had been his fault, for not setting the boy right before he went wrong, and today he aimed to make up for that.

"Tell me you're sorry, boy."

"I'm sorry!" Daniel screeched.

"Not good enough."

And he lashed the belt across his back, drawing a second purplish welt.

"Try again."

"I'm sorry!"

Thwack!

"Not good enough."

"I'm sor-ry!"

Thwack!

"Like you mean it, boy."

Thwack!

Daniel was bawling now, both nostrils heaving snot that rained down on the Persian carpet that could have paid for the boy's entire college education.

"I'm so goddamn sorry I messed up!" the boy managed between heaves. "Forgive me, please forgive me. I thought I was doing right, 'cause of what they did to me. I thought you'd be proud of me."

Those words made Deacon Frank stop his next lash in midflight. Making the Reverend Rand Atlas Wilhyte proud was all he'd ever cared about as a boy, but he'd never managed it. The closest he came was a smile when the collection basket overflowed with bills. But even that was balanced by the counterweight of his father's disdain when he ripped a half-empty collection basket from his grasp. Daniel speaking those words struck a chord in him, reached him in a place he didn't think was there anymore. He spun his son around and held him by the chin in a beefy hand, belt stretched to its full length again, dangling by his side.

"Get yourself upstairs and bring me whatever device you used to get on the Web. I'm going to grab a hammer so I can watch you smash it. We clear?"

Daniel sniffled, nodded.

"Then get going."

He watched his son thump up the stairs, the sweatpants hanging off his narrow hips.

"Hurry!" Deacon Frank yelled to him, even though the boy was going as fast as he could.

He felt a buzzing and thought it was a high from the sense of fulfillment that came from properly disciplining his son. If he'd done this earlier, if he'd been tougher on him, then maybe Daniel never would have created the mess that he had.

Deacon Frank realized the buzzing was coming from the cell phone tucked in his pocket, and he jerked it to his ear just before the buzzing stopped. There was no number in the caller ID, but he knew who it was anyway.

"How's your day going, my friend?" Deacon Frank greeted.

"We need to talk," said Senator Byron Fitch.

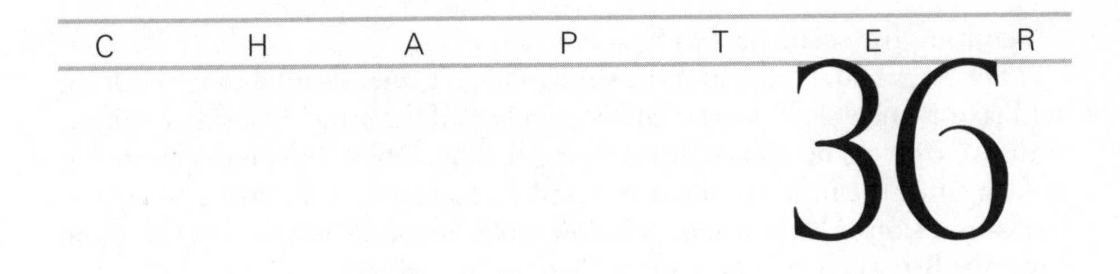

WASHINGTON, DC

"We don't even know who this woman is," Mac was saying.

"I confirmed she's Capitol Police, but working out of Protective Services," Brixton told him.

"Since when do they conduct investigations?"

"They don't."

"So she called Alexandra . . . Why?"

"That's what we're going to find out, Mac."

"What else?"

"Kelly Loftus was a Baltimore homicide detective before coming to the Capitol Police."

"An unusual transition."

"I haven't had time to do a deeper dive."

"You should handle this alone, Robert. I need to get back to Walter Reed. Annabel's already there. I can't bear being away from Alex any longer."

Brixton didn't bother saying he was glad for Mac's decision, but he was. Meeting alone with former homicide detective Kelly Loftus was much more to his liking; the whole nature of one-on-one meetings in general was, especially since his own background in law enforcement created common ground between them. That said, they also had something even more vital in common: Alexandra Parks.

"The source of my interest?" Kelly Loftus asked Brixton, after they exchanged pleasantries inside Einstein Bros. Bagels, on street level in Union Station's eastside shopping concourse.

They'd made arrangements to meet at five p.m. sharp, the height of rush hour, when the station was certain to be packed and they'd be less likely to draw any attention from strollers emerging or heading to trains and concerned only with where they were headed. Brixton had shown up at four thirty to scout the immediate surroundings, and he spotted a lone African American woman sipping coffee from a cup emblazoned with the Einstein Bros. logo. From his position thirty feet away and slightly to the right, Brixton could see the steam rising off it. That was enough to tell him the coffee was black, typical for a cop. In addition, the woman's eyes didn't stay fixed on anything for too long.

Scouting the scene, just as he was.

Their eyes hadn't met, and the woman hadn't even seemed to notice him, but Brixton knew she'd registered his presence all the same. Instead of waiting until five o'clock, he approached the bagel shop, which featured a cluster of tables against the inside of the store window, and more just outside, along the concourse. Loftus had chosen a window table, farthest from the entrance, the same one Brixton would have taken, had he arrived first.

Drawing closer, he noted her long legs and firmly toned upper body, showcased by a tight-fitting shirt that showed the lines of her triceps. She looked like an athlete—soccer more than tennis—and Brixton guessed she was a runner too, or had been at one point. Long-distance instead of sprint.

"Ms. Loftus?" he posed, approaching from the side, to remain out of her sight line for as long as possible.

"Clumsy approach, Mr. Brixton," she said, turning in her chair to face him. "I watched you the whole way."

"Maybe I wanted you to see me coming."

"Did you?"

"No."

He sat down across from her. They started to speak at the same thought, Brixton starting the thought Loftus ended up finishing.

"I should grab a coffee . . ."

"Because someone with nothing in front of them stands out. You've done this sort of thing before," Loftus said to him.

"Once or twice."

"You said you were a private investigator."

"I was a cop in another life, though I wasn't cut out for the flashy world of the homicide detective, like you."

"You checked me out."

"Just as I'm sure you did the same."

Loftus nodded. "Baltimore PD forgot to deactivate my password after they canned me. Robert Brixton," she narrated from memory, "street cop in both Georgia and Washington, DC, before taking your talents to SITQUAL, which at the time served as the security arm of the State Department. Currently employed as a licensed international private investigator with an office at the Mackensie Smith and Associates law firm. Divorced with two daughters, one deceased. Currently engaged."

"Guess that password's still serving you well, Detective."

"It's not 'detective' anymore, Mr. Brixton. And what's a licensed international private investigator do, anyway?"

"The same thing a private investigator does, only internationally."

"Very funny."

"It's true. Does require a bit of additional expertise, though."

Loftus nodded. Brixton watched her size him up. "Which I'm sure you learned during your time with SITQUAL."

"I made my share of contacts," Brixton affirmed.

"Wish I could say the same."

"You left the force on bad terms."

Loftus laid her cup down on the table, the steam rising into a steady mist between them. The two of them took turns surveying the passengers scurrying down the concourse, checking for overly watchful eyes.

"That show up in your research, Brixton?" she asked him, taking easily to addressing him by his last name.

"I guessed. And you're the first homicide cop turned Capitol police officer I've ever heard of."

"Protective Services division."

"Why'd you call Alexandra Parks, Loftus?" Brixton asked, returning the favor of address.

"I didn't. I called a phone number. I didn't know who it belonged to until you returned the message." Loftus hesitated, started to reach for her coffee again, then changed her mind. "You said she was attacked."

Brixton nodded. "Hospitalized, as we speak. You mentioned I have an office at Mackensie Smith's law firm."

She nodded back.

"That's her father."

Loftus's eyes tightened their focus, like a person searching for the next piece to add to a jigsaw puzzle.

"How'd you get her number?" Brixton continued.

"Long story. You've got the floor. Why don't you keep it?"

"Did you know Alexandra Parks works for the Centers for Disease Control here in Washington?"

"No, but another of the numbers I had was for their offices on Capitol Hill."

Brixton recalled Alexandra telling him how she took one of the many "crackpot" calls the CDC received on a daily basis, and he wondered if there might be a connection here.

"Where did these numbers come from, Loftus?" he asked the woman seated across from him.

"Like I said, long story with a sad ending."

"You didn't mention the sad ending before."

"I seem to attract them," Loftus said, leaving it there.

"So you came across these numbers. The CDC, where Alexandra Parks works, and her personal cell phone number. Any others I should know about?"

"Two."

"Care to elaborate?"

Loftus started to raise her coffee again. "After you tell me more about the attack that hospitalized Alexandra Parks."

"She was poisoned."

"Sound's like something the Russians would do."

"It wasn't the Russians, in this case. She was in over her head, working on something that scared the hell out of her."

"And you know this because . . ."

"She told me, and the suggestion was more than confirmed in the wake of the attack that nearly killed her."

"How?"

"Her phone records were made to disappear."

Loftus didn't look bothered by that. "I worked cases all the time where cell phone records disappeared."

"As in erased by a suspect or person of interest, but ultimately recoverable. In this case, those records vanished. As in ceased to exist. As in gone forever."

"Then how did you access them?"

"Let's say I've got a friend who specializes in the impossible."

"Can I meet him, Brixton?"

"You don't want to." Brixton leaned slightly forward. "Now it's your turn. Tell me those other two phone numbers."

"I can only put a firm name to one of them: Senator Byron Fitch of Maryland."

Brixton felt his heart skip a beat. "Looks like we've got something else in common, Loftus."

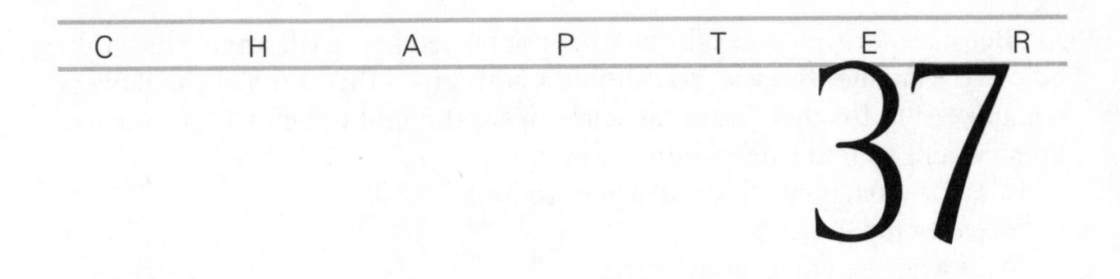

CHAPTER 37

UMATILLA, OREGON

"We need to get started at the site right away," Panama said, when their private jet landed at the Eastern Oregon Regional Airport.

Not named for a senator, congressman, or local dignitary, just Eastern Oregon.

"I don't have to tell you, we don't have any time to spare, Dr. Lutayne. You know the stakes here even better than I do."

Effie hadn't been allowed to accompany them, or to return home, either. In fact, he was currently confined to his father's residence, watched by two of the big men in tactical gear who Panama had left behind to make sure he stayed where he was.

"And I have a crew at the site now, already prepping," Panama continued.

"What kind of crew?"

"I imagine it's similar in many respects to yours five years ago, after the tanker went missing. Difference being we know exactly where to look now, don't we?"

"You had my house bugged."

"Within weeks of you settling in back in Colorado, going on five years ago. But I wasn't involved back then. Your work didn't reach my radar until relatively recently, and I'm going to hazard a guess that you know what brought me to Aurora today."

Lutayne nodded, as the private jet continued to taxi toward the terminal, which had grown from a speck to a splotch in the gleaming afternoon sun. It was two p.m., here in Oregon. "The poisoning of those students at that high school in Maryland."

"Seven dying in less than twenty-four hours. Not a single survivor. Obviously, we follow the same algorithms, just as you follow those newspaper clippings, sent to you by your son on a monthly basis, either hard copies or printouts off the internet."

"You opened the boxes."

"Well, not me personally, but yes, guilty as charged."

"Why do I think you planted cameras in my house, too?"

"Because we did, Dr. Lutayne. I suspected this day would come—no, I more than suspected it. I *knew* it would come. It was inevitable."

"Why?"

"Because nothing as deadly as what got buried in the silt under that sinkhole ever vanishes forever. You should know, given that some of the flowers you harvested for their toxic capacities were thought to be extinct. But you knew where to find them, didn't you?"

Lutayne shrugged. "I knew where to look."

"Exactly my point."

"And who are you exactly, Panama?"

The jet came to a sudden stop, jolting both of them forward. The four commandos who'd accompanied him never even flinched.

"You mean, my real name?"

"More like what you do."

"In the circles I travel in, Dr. Lutayne, what you do *is* who you are. I don't have a specific title or job, really. String any three letters in the alphabet together and you're bound to come up with one of the many organizations that populate Washington, my particular distinction being that I work for none of them and all of them at the same time."

"That doesn't make any sense."

"What in Washington does? Normally, my job is to make connections, determine where information should be routed. With all the various three-letter organizations, and otherwise, staking out their own territories, somebody needs to know which is best suited to handle what."

"So, what, you're like a referee?"

"Well, I don't have a whistle. Nor do I have a rank, a badge, a position, a portfolio—nothing like that. This country is surrounded by walls that are just as invisible as the one that never got built along the Mexican border. Cracks form in those walls and get bigger with time. I man that wall and live in those cracks, Dr. Lutayne, because that's where the greatest dangers to this country lie, with what comes in through those cracks, with who we don't pay attention to until it's too late, until they've done something that forces them out. And by then the damage has been done. Oklahoma City, nine eleven, those were the most dramatic and well known, but there are others, more than I can count. You don't know about them because I or somebody else who lives in the cracks stopped them. Because my job is to keep whatever or whoever gets into those cracks from getting through. And that's what I plan to do here."

"You think somebody has the White Death."

Lutayne had the sense that Panama was studying him, the way Lutayne studied his lab animal test subjects.

"And how'd you go about creating it, Dr. Lutayne?"

"You want to breed a bigger dog, you mate the largest female with the largest male. Flowers mate, too, and we kept genetically enhancing and crossbreeding the plantings that produced the highest toxicity. Nearly a thousand generations of oleander over more than a decade to create the toxin that became the White Death."

"Like those souvenirs you're growing in that extension of your greenhouse, Doctor?"

"Offspring. Just in case."

"Just in case *what*?"

"That they're needed again. You're talking about my life's work, my entire legacy," he told Panama. "It's not easy to give that up—something I'm sure you know."

"My only legacy is the country's survival, Doctor, at the hands of what gets past my wall. And your creation left a trail that led somebody through the cracks in that wall, straight to Umatilla."

"What do you expect to find when we get there?"

"Nothing," Panama told him. "And that's the problem."

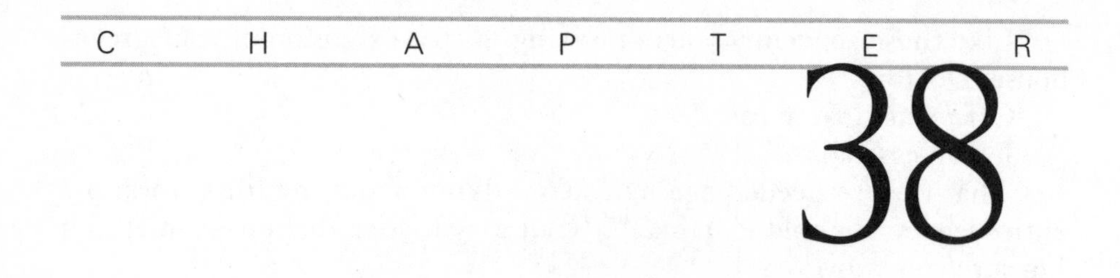

CHAPTER 38

WASHINGTON, DC

Senator Byron Fitch," Loftus said.

Brixton nodded. "Alexandra Parks, the poisoning victim, had placed several calls to his office. And how exactly did you come across that one, Fitch's office number, and the number for Alexandra Parks's cell?"

Loftus laid it all out for Robert Brixton in blow-by-blow fashion, starting with spotting a woman seated on a park bench on the Capitol lawn. Brixton stopped her occasionally, wanting to keep all the facts and the chronology straight.

There was something about Kelly Loftus that made him feel comfortable in her presence. Maybe it was the fact that they both were outsiders, playing by their own rules instead of those the system tried to impose upon them. Brixton thought about his unceremonious departures as a cop in both Georgia and Washington, DC. He'd ruffled feathers, went off on his own, just as Loftus had as a homicide detective and now with the Capitol Police. It explained why he'd thrived with SITQUAL and, later, in the world of international private investigations. In neither did he have to account for his actions, provided the results were successful. In SITQUAL, that meant the State Department official with whose life he'd been entrusted got back safe and sound, often because those who'd targeted him or her had been eliminated. As a private investigator, he was accountable only to his clients, most notably Mackensie Smith, whose firm made up for the lack of lobbying efforts with a robust international practice that kept Brixton busy.

"Her name was Jean Rappaport," Loftus told him, after describing her efforts to retrieve the trail of contents from the woman's handbag. "Her husband's name was Philip. I assume you recognize it by now."

Brixton stiffened. "My grandson was on those steps. School trip."

Loftus swallowed hard. "How bad?"

"He's fine, physically anyway."

"And otherwise?"

"He takes after me," Brixton told her.

"Taking it in stride then."

"For now. He thinks he spotted a second shooter."

"You believe him?"

"He saved a classmate's life, Loftus. So, yes, I believe him." Brixton paused long enough to hold her stare. "So how'd you go from following a trail of a leaky handbag to calling the CDC?"

"I didn't turn over everything I found; in fact, I didn't turn over any of it, not at first. And when I finally met up with an FBI contact I thought was a friend, I held some things back."

"Don't tell me . . . phone numbers."

"Apparently I don't have to tell you."

Brixton let her comment settle, an excuse to study her closer. She had a smooth face and eyes set a bit too close to each other, which dominated her expression, just like Flo. They each wore their hair short, were both tall, lithe, and athletic. They might have been twins, sisters anyway, save for Kelly Loftus's darker complexion.

Brixton's thoughts spun in a different direction. "Senator Fitch was on the Capitol steps when the shooting started, standing maybe five feet away from my grandson."

"And this Alexandra—What was her last name?"

"Parks."

"This Alexandra Parks called him, and so did the shooter, Philip Rappaport."

"Anything else you can bring to the party?"

Brixton watched Loftus's eyes widen and her mouth drop.

"Oh my God," she uttered.

"What is it, Loftus?"

"There was another number Rappaport called, a high school in Baltimore."

Brixton held his stare on her, waiting for what came next.

"Baltimore Mulighet High School, where seven kids died last month. They were poisoned."

Brixton felt himself lean backward, as if the motion was involuntary. "How?"

"It was never identified. What about the poison that nearly killed your friend's daughter?"

"No identification, either, at least not yet. And it killed a supervisor she was meeting with at the time."

"You mind explaining the connection to me?"

"You mean besides Philip Rappaport and Senator Byron Fitch? Would if I could, Loftus. The most obvious one would be Rappaport himself. He calls up the CDC's Washington offices, not realizing all the heavy lifting happens in Atlanta," Brixton continued, recalling Alexandra's explanation of those "crackpot" calls. "Alexandra Parks takes his call and finds his claims valid enough to do some follow-up."

"And then she gets poisoned, just like those kids."

Brixton's phone rang.

"Got something for me?" he greeted, recognizing the number as Jesus Arriaga's.

"It's not what you asked for, amigo, but I got something, all right."

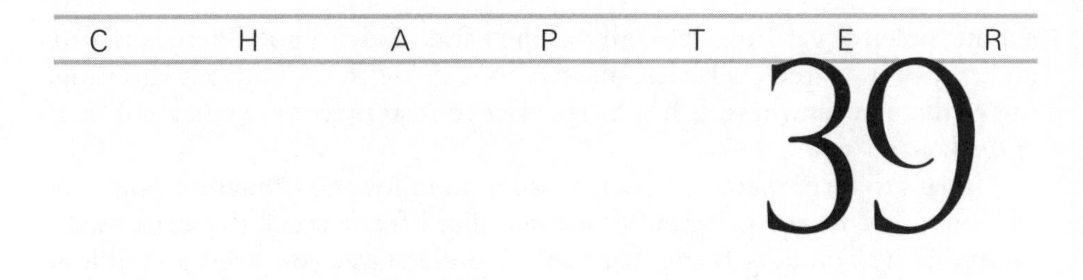

CHAPTER 39

UMATILLA, OREGON

Night had fallen by the time things were up and ready to go at the site in question, fifteen miles from the airport. Panama's men had to help Lutayne out of the car and into his wheelchair, just as they had to carry him up and down the foldout stairs to the private jet, since neither airport had boasted a ramp.

Night may have fallen, but the scene was daylight bright, thanks to the bevy of powerful construction lights, multiple arrays of bulbs on each, that cut through the darkness with umpteen-million candlepower. A couple of teams could have played football under so much light. The bulk of it was concentrated in the area of the shiny patch of darkness that Lutayne had originally taken for a pond but that his son had called a dissolution sinkhole. He shivered at the mere thought that the final Red Dog run had met its fate in this very spot, where it had remained for the five years since.

To explore that possibility, even likelihood, a host of scuba divers, equipped to the gills, was staging in various parts of the black water. For all his genius in many areas, Lutayne's spatial sense had always been inferior. He wasn't good at judging distances or spacing by eye. This pond looked to be spherical in shape—oblong, to be more accurate—wider than it was long. He estimated, roughly, that at its widest the pond stretched maybe a hundred and fifty yards. Studying it further under the spill of bright light, he adjusted his estimate to closer to two hundred yards, with its length as a whole measuring maybe half that.

"None of our seismic, geological, or temperature sensors have indicated there's anything down there at all," Panama reported. "As you can see, I was not to be deterred, even when the initial dive survey turned up nothing."

"You sent men down there?" Lutayne asked.

"It's not like they have to worry about sharks in these waters, Doctor. Even a robotic submersible wasn't able to find anything."

Lutayne again surveyed the area, running his gaze over as impressive an assembly of men and machines as he'd ever witnessed. In addition to security personnel, an army of divers, and trucks bearing their equipment and those daylight-bright construction lights, there were three robotic submersibles of varying sizes, all prepped and ready to go. There was also an array of high-tech vehicles, massive in scale, with appendages shooting out of them everywhere. They looked like monsters from a remake of *War of the Worlds.*

"It pays to be prepared," Panama told him, following Lutayne's gaze. "At this point, we have equipment that can either lift the truck from the water or drain the contents from that tank. I understand you used a stainless steel tank reinforced with a layer of tungsten, which accounted for the slow speeds the truck had to travel at but would take a century or so to degrade. I studied the schematics, in case the need arose to detach the tanker from the rest of the apparatus and crane it up."

"You said that would be too dangerous, that it might cause the tank to rupture."

"Like I said, it pays to be prepared. In a perfect world, divers would be able to thread hosing through one of the fill valves and suck the contents into one of those waiting tankers you've taken an interest in."

"That is, if the White Death is still there."

"There is that, yes," Panama affirmed.

"So you weren't getting anywhere with your divers and equipment," Lutayne summed up for himself. "What'd you do then?"

"Called in better divers and equipment," Panama said. "Both arrived just before we did."

And that's when a sudden commotion a hundred feet away, on the ink-black shoreline glowing in the spill of the floodlights, drew their attention.

The shoreline was a wheelchair user's nightmare, strewn with ruts, soft spots, and rocky patches that challenged Lutayne every inch of the way. Panama had taken off at a sprint, leaving him to fend for himself.

Lutayne got to the source of the commotion to find that a trio of divers had shed their drained tanks in favor of fresh ones, ignoring the protestations that they'd already been under for too long a duration.

"Tell that to the guy on our team who hasn't surfaced yet," one of them said.

"He's a navy diver," another followed. "Best trained in the world. If he isn't up here, it's because something got him down there."

"So . . . what?" Lutayne heard another voice whine. "Now we've got a sea monster to worry about?"

Just then, something broke the surface near the middle of the pond. The night went dead quiet, save for the steady hum of the nearby generators. Lutayne's first thought was that it was the body of the missing diver, but he dismissed the thought when the shape began swimming toward shore, visible as a ripple of approaching currents.

The figure, encased in a black wet suit gleaming in the spill of the floodlights, staggered into the shallows, where two of his fellow divers assisted him the rest of the way, supporting him under each arm. They eased him down and he crumpled just a few feet from where Lutayne had found a level patch of ground for his wheelchair.

"I found it," the man said, between labored breaths.

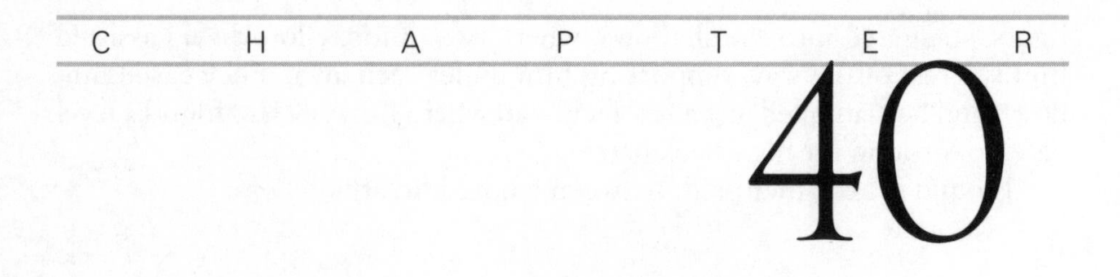

CHAPTER 40

OLDTOWN, MARYLAND

Deacon Frank met Byron Fitch out by the main gate, directly beneath the Atlas Dairy Farm sign, as soon as his guards alerted him about the senator's arrival.

"Let's take a walk," he greeted, when he saw Fitch leaning against his gleaming SUV. "One of my men will bring your car up."

Fitch looked through the darkness that hung beneath one of the biggest moons Deacon Frank had ever seen. "Who takes a walk when it's dark?"

"You and me tonight, Senator. I've never shown you around the farm, how the milk gets made. I figure this is as good a time as any. We can rehash old times."

"Speaking of which, you mind if I ask you a question, Deacon Frank?"

"Ask away."

"If your father was such a cruel son of a bitch—a genuine bastard, according to what you've told me—why'd you name your farm after him?"

"To keep him close enough to see that I came out just fine in spite of him, to make sure that sticks in his craw. Now, how about that walk, Senator?"

The "old times" to which Deacon Frank referred had started two years previously, with a phone call. He had met his home state senator a couple times before, the two of them speaking just enough to know they had plenty in common.

"We need to meet," Fitch told him in that phone call. "Have a sit-down about something that's in our mutual interests."

"If you're going to twist my arm for money, you could do that over the phone. Better yet, send me an email."

"Nothing in writing, Deacon Frank. Nothing that can ever come back to bite us."

"I need to hear a bit more than that, Senator. Like what's this about, at least in general?"

"Power."

"You've got my attention."

Senator Byron Fitch had come out to the farm the next day.

"You ever milk a cow, Senator?"

Fitch hadn't looked pleased by the prospect. "Don't you have machines for that now?"

"Machines don't help me get the measure of a man. You got something to say, I want to see what you can do first."

Deacon Frank brought Fitch out to the barn where schoolkids came on field trips to witness the workings of a real live dairy farm. Different priority when he sat the senator down on a stool and showed him the basics.

"Normally, we'd have to secure the cow's head first so she can't wander off. But given that we're inside a stall, we can skip that and move right to the milking."

He handed Fitch a damp rag.

"First thing, I want you to clean her udder."

Fitch regarded the bulging sack on the animal's underside, his expression crinkling. "There a point to this, Deacon Frank?"

"You bet, Senator: to get a full day's supply of calcium and vitamin D."

Fitch eased off the stool and swiped at the cow's udder with the damp rag, tossing it to the side as he retook the stool. "Happy?"

"Thrilled." And with that, he handed the man from Washington a tube of a gel-like compound. "Next you need to lubricate the teat you're going to be pulling on."

"Come on," Fitch protested.

"You want to do business with me, you need to prove yourself, like a rite of passage."

Deacon Frank waited.

Senator Byron Fitch finally swabbed the lubricant into place.

Deacon Frank positioned the bucket properly. "All you need to do now is pull downward on the base of the teat and squeeze the milk out into the bucket. Think you can handle that all on your own?"

Fitch's response was to follow Deacon Frank's instructions, flashing him an occasional look of disdain.

"Squeeze too hard and you may get kicked in the teeth, Senator."

Fitch started squeezing, not too hard. He was a rawboned man with sun-scorched, leathery skin from his roots working the docks as a longshoreman. He'd never been afraid to get his hands dirty.

"How'd you like to kick this country in the teeth, Deacon Frank?"

"I guess it depends on how hard you're talking."

"Hard enough to knock the teeth out. Get what both of us want."

"How do you know what I want?"

"You may not be a preacher man like your father," the senator told him, "but I've got an inkling of the kind of groups you're fond of supporting."

"Do you now?"

Fitch nodded. "We've got some mutual friends, Deacon Frank."

"I've never supported a Democrat in my life."

"I'm an independent."

"I never supported one of those either."

Speaking of teeth, that was when the senator flashed a pearly white smile that was the product of enough dental work for five people. "I use politics like a Halloween costume. I keep it on, you never see the real person underneath. I don't plan on doing that until I'm in the White House, if you get my drift."

Deacon Frank had nodded, getting the point. "And what you're here about can help you get there. Am I reading the cards right?"

"Along with one wild card: you, Deacon Frank. A man came to see me. Used to be in the army, assigned to security for a facility in Utah that was about as secret as it gets."

"*Was?*"

"Ever hear of the Tooele Army Depot in Tooele County, Utah?"

"I barely ever heard of Utah. It wasn't on my preacher daddy's tour list, with all those Mormons."

"Well, according to this soldier, they developed some badass shit there before a certain section of the base, devoted to research and development, was shut down five years ago."

"So why am I standing here teaching you how to milk a cow, Senator? How is it that this badass shit, as you call it, can help you make your bed in the White House?"

"Before the base got shuttered, all that badass shit got sent to another facility in Oregon for disposal. Make it like none of the stuff ever existed in the first place."

That got Deacon Frank's attention. "You're talking about biowarfare agents."

The senator nodded. "I am indeed. And not just any old biowarfare agents, either. These were something special."

"Why bother telling me if all those agents have been disposed of, all done and gone?"

"Because one of them went missing in transit, and this soldier I mentioned has a pretty good idea where to find it."

Downwind from the scent of manure mixed with freshly cut grass, Deacon Frank remembered the senator describing how he'd milked that guilt-ridden soldier for all he was worth, employing far more skill than he used when he'd milked his first cow. The soldier claimed he wasn't able to sleep because of the nightmares that had resurfaced over something he called the "white death," which had vanished into nowhere. Couldn't live with himself, keeping that secret anymore, ended up hospitalized in some nuthouse as a result. So he'd come to his home state senator to do something about it. Finish the job of flushing the white death down some proverbial toilet, which is what was supposed to happen when it reached Umatilla, Oregon—before it disappeared off the face of the earth.

How much of this shit are we talking about, Senator?

Enough to set this country right. Enough to get us back on the track we belong on. Get rid of the people standing in our way. Make me president and make you something even bigger.

And by "get rid of," you mean . . .

Yes, I do, Deacon Frank.

There's an awful lot of them.

That won't be a problem.

But now they had a problem.

Deacon Frank swung his gaze about the sprawling property, which had the look of a national park, with all the greenery that looked carved out of a pristine forest. Indeed, this land had all been forest at one point, and Deacon Frank had painstakingly constructed his mansion so as to disturb the vegetation as minimally as possible. The natural beauty was why he had fallen in love with this stretch of property, so he wanted to preserve as much of it as he could. He also believed it was why his farm produced the best milk in the region. He had the trophies to prove it.

Deacon Frank also wanted no part of bringing the senator to the main house, where he would be in close proximity to Daniel. He'd applied salve to the wounds left on his son's back by the belt lashes, and had then dressed them in gauze and adhesive tape. Daniel had moaned and sobbed through the whole process. Deacon Frank was not of a mind to kowtow to modern-day norms and rules, whether written or unwritten, like the ones that said you couldn't punish your children anymore. In his mind, the very notion of a parent being charged with child abuse for keeping his kid in line was the height of absurdity, and he felt nothing but loathing for the segment of the population that was driving such practices.

In other words, the segment of the population that was destroying this country, letting it rot from the inside out. Deacon Frank had no problem with progress. Progress had made him rich beyond his wildest imagination, even though he'd inherited the vast bulk of his wealth from the Reverend Rand Atlas Wilhyte. His father's fortune had paid for this spread and for his mission in life, which had seen Deacon Frank traveling the country for years now, building an army for purposes yet unrevealed, as if he were stirred by what his father might call divine intervention. Now that purpose had revealed itself, and the army he had cultivated in the dark basements and rank meeting halls was about to be mobilized toward the higher purpose to which Reverend Rand had claimed to aspire but had never realized.

"Come on, Senator, enjoy the fresh air," Deacon Frank picked up. "It's a beautiful night."

Fitch's expression wrinkled. "Smells like shit. And if you don't mind, I don't want to be stepping in any shit. I've already got plenty to clean off my shoes, thanks to all I've been dealing with. I almost got killed yesterday, in case you didn't know."

"You told me the whole story. I think I know. And maybe you should stop by during the day sometime."

"Too easy to be spotted in your company. No offense."

"Then maybe you should have gone to somebody else to help get you elected president."

"That's the point. We can't let anyone see us together."

"Press doesn't pay much attention to me."

"Wish I could say the same, Deacon Frank. And we don't want anyone casting aspersions on what they might view as my trying to influence those tax problems you've got."

"I'm being looked into for tax evasion, like everybody else with more than two dollars to his name."

"You don't think you're on the FBI's radar? All these visits you've been paying to the faithful and all. Stirring up a pot boiling with the likes of the Proud Boys, the Oath Keepers, and the Boogaloo Boys."

"I prefer to call it getting them prepared for what's coming."

"The Bureau might call that domestic terrorism, Deacon Frank. You think there weren't informants in those meeting halls, listening?"

"We'll be flipping the switch long before they get anywhere with whatever those informants have to say. Lighten up, Senator. I took care of that little problem for you, didn't I?"

He watched Fitch ease closer, until there was only the scent of cow shit between them.

"Not really, Deacon Frank, because that pain-in-the-ass bitch is still alive."

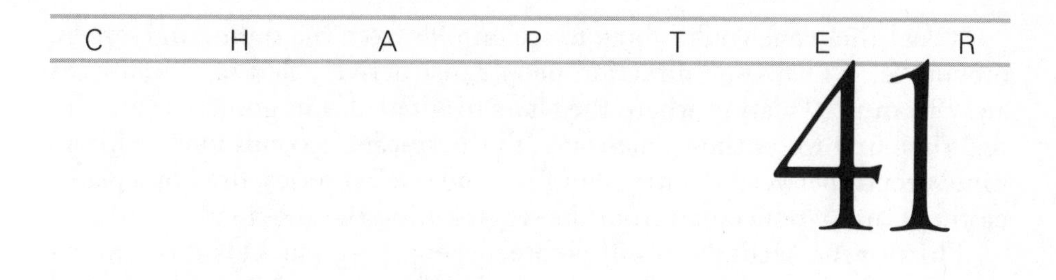

CHAPTER 41

WASHINGTON, DC

Is she one of us, Robert?" Arriaga asked, after Brixton and Kelly Loftus had been ushered back to his office at just past eight o'clock, escorted by the same assistant, who looked all of fifteen years old.

"Close enough," Brixton told him, casting Loftus a wink.

"How so?"

"Detective Loftus bucks the system, doesn't do what she's told, and is fond of taking matters into her own hands."

That drew a smile from Arriaga directed toward Loftus. "That more than fills the bill." Then, to Brixton, "She's one of us."

"What was it, exactly, the two of you did?" Kelly asked them.

"A topic for another day," Arriaga told her. "Today's topic is more pressing."

Brixton noted he looked a bit anxious and unsettled compared with their previous meeting that morning. There were three separate twenty-seven-inch computer monitors atop Arriaga's L-shaped desk, which was otherwise unoccupied except for a single keyboard. One keyboard for three monitors didn't make a lot of sense to Brixton, but technology had never been his thing. He found himself calling his grandson every time his screen froze or some other calamity struck him from cyberspace.

Brixton and Loftus took the chairs on either side of Arriaga, who was positioned in the center, directly before his keyboard. His fingers danced across the letters and numbers and all three screens sprang to life.

"Okay, here's what I did. I took all the assembled footage—security camera and cell phone—divided the scene into three grids, and created a loop to string the best available angles together in a constant flow, to utilize the optimum views of what you need to see."

Need, Brixton noted. Not *want*. A curious choice of words, perhaps in keeping with the source of whatever had left Arriaga unsettled.

"In other words," Arriaga elaborated, not sure either of them grasped his explanation, "I turned a disjointed series of videos into a single montage. Like watching a movie."

"Happy or sad ending?" Brixton asked him.

"That remains to be seen, doesn't it?" Arriaga came back.

He worked his keyboard again to bring all three screens to life and then froze the action to allow for further explanation.

"Okay, the scene you're about to see unfolds from the right-hand screen, moving left. That's the direction people instinctively fled in, because it's away from the location where the shots originated. I'm going to run it in real time first to set the framework. It's thirty-nine seconds long—thirty-nine seconds between the first shot fired and the last series, fired by a plain-clothes Capitol policeman from the steps, killing the shooter."

Thirty-nine seconds to kill eighteen people—eight kids now among them—and to wound another twenty. Brixton figured Rappaport must have been using an extended magazine. He could have also duct-taped two of them together to allow for an easy swap when the first mag was drained, but a National Guardsman approaching the Capitol steps with a "jungle mag," as that was called, would have attracted attention. At least, it should have, and Brixton recalled no mention of its use in all the news reporting.

Brixton and Loftus watched the video unfold from their chairs, both flinching and gnashing their teeth. Brixton felt his stomach quiver and then turn while following the carnage in real time, particularly the opening salvo, which had blown some of his grandson's classmates backward and tore the legs out from under them. He caught a glimpse of Max lunging atop that wounded boy's frame, while the other students, and the chaperones, fled. His eyes teared up at his grandson's bravery.

They fled to the left, as Jesus Arriaga had indicated, leaving the right-hand screen for the center one, the *rat-tat-tat* of the assault rifle fire seeming to trail them the whole way, felling other victims instead of the students from the Gilman School who appeared to be the intended targets. Brixton should have been relieved that more kids hadn't been shot to death, but instead he fixated on those whose lives had been cut down for no reason other than where they were standing at the worst possible time.

As the action moved to the screen on the left-hand side of his desk, Arriaga manually widened the shot from behind his keyboard and then froze it. The counter on his screen read 00:39.

"What do you see, Robert?" Arriaga asked him.

The image, captured at the very edge of the screen, wasn't sharp enough for Brixton to be sure, but he had a pretty good idea.

"The second shooter," he said, referring to the claim made by his grandson.

"He was a shooter, all right, just of a different kind."

As Brixton tried to make sense of that, Arriaga enlarged and enhanced the picture of the figure Max had taken for a second gunman. Except that the man was holding a camera with a long telephoto lens instead of a weapon. Hard to tell if he was a professional or an amateur photographer; Brixton guessed amateur, since there was no press badge dangling from his neck. Easy to tell, though, how in a desperate, fleeting glimpse from so far away, Max could have taken his camera for a rifle.

Brixton looked from the third screen to Arriaga. "Okay. I get that this is what you meant when you told me it's not what I asked for . . ."

"Right as rain, amigo."

"But you also said you found *something*."

Arriaga's gaze fixed on Loftus and lingered. "How much do you trust the former detective here?"

"You need me to ask me that, after I brought her with me?"

"I'm going to take that to mean you must be well acquainted."

"For the last few hours, anyway," Loftus offered.

Arriaga grinned, not taking her comment seriously. Both Loftus and Brixton let it go.

"Now on to that *something*," Arriaga picked up, working his keyboard again. "I'm going to slow the footage down a bit so you can follow what you need to see."

With that, all three screens returned to their starting frames. Striking a final key spot-shadowed a figure standing among the kids on the right-hand screen.

"Senator Byron Fitch," Brixton said, recognizing him, and stealing a glance at Loftus. "My grandson told me he and a local congressman, one of the dead as it turns out, were out there posing for pictures with the kids."

"Okay," Arriaga resumed. "I'm going to highlight him in red so you can follow what you need to see. Here we go . . ."

Watching the scene unfold in slow motion was even more painful for Brixton, revealing just how close Max had come to becoming a victim instead of a hero. Brixton literally couldn't breathe for a few moments, watching two of the kids nearest Senator Byron Fitch felled by the shooter's automatic fire. Brixton then watched as Fitch, shadowed in red, rushed away to the left, moving onto the center screen after a few agonizing seconds that left more bodies falling in his wake.

"You see the something?" Arriaga asked him, as the footage continued to unspool in slow motion. His voice rang with pride over what he'd managed to uncover.

More bodies toppled around Fitch as Rappaport shifted his fire along the same line, from right to left, his bullet trail tracing the direction in which the kids were fleeing. But his fire seemed to be ignoring their flight, homing in on a different target instead.

"Holy shit," Kelly Loftus gasped, realizing the truth at the same moment Brixton did.

"Holy shit is right," Brixton managed.

"That's an understatement, bro," said Arriaga, "since Senator Byron Fitch was the shooter's real target."

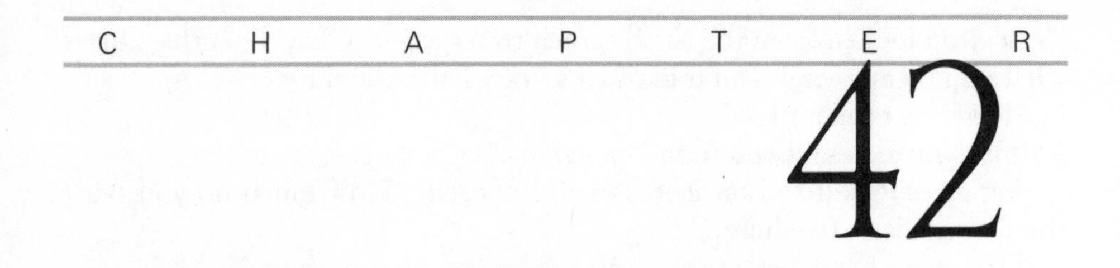

CHAPTER 42

OLDTOWN, MARYLAND

"Come again?" Deacon Frank said to Fitch, caught off guard by the news that his target had survived.

"You heard me. She's still alive. You killed a supervisor of hers who didn't know shit. They were in his office at the time."

Deacon Frank reflected on how the scientists working out of the secret lab he'd spent a boatload constructing to their specifications had provided the few drops he needed to solve the problem. According to a team he had scoping the CDC's Washington offices, the center regularly had coffee, snacks, and sandwiches sent up from a bistro in the lobby. On the morning in question, the order had the female target's name on it—just the opportunity they'd been waiting for.

"You want to explain to me how she's still alive?" Fitch asked him.

"Something went wrong."

"Tell me something I don't know, like how everything went to hell."

"The toxin could have been inhaled or absorbed through drinking the coffee. Could be the woman didn't drink it but her supervisor did. Could be she was too far away to inhale enough of the particles, molecules, droplets, or whatever you want to call them, to kill her." Deacon Frank hesitated. "She anybody?"

"Daughter of a rich, recently deceased socialite in New York, from what I've been able to learn."

"The dead can't hurt us, Senator. And neither can this young woman who was sniffing around, anymore."

Deacon Frank was glad that the night disguised at least a measure of his annoyance, worn as a scowl. He started on again without telling Fitch to follow. Typical politician, scared of his own shadow while pretending to be tough and unyielding. Then he heard the rapid thump of footsteps, the senator hurrying to catch up, as they continued the long loop around the fenced-in grazing fields where his cows roamed. The grass was moist and his work boots skittered across it. Deacon Frank wondered how long it would be before Fitch started complaining about his feet getting wet through his dress shoes.

"The shooter didn't just fire off bullets."

"No?"

"He also fired off phone calls to anyone he thought might listen. We know he called me and the woman from the CDC, at the very least, and who knows how many more."

"So whatever he had to say died with him, Senator. There's no disputing that."

"There isn't? You don't think somebody who might not have listened to him at first might find themselves curious, now that he showed up at the Capitol with an assault rifle?"

Fitch took off his shoes and wiped the soles of his feet on his corduroy slacks, hoping to dry them. Then he kicked at some of the wildflowers Deacon Frank had fallen in love with the very first time he saw this property. Sights like that convinced him this was home, so much beauty amid a country that was rotting at its core, rooted in the ugliness of its soul. What better place to base his movement's efforts? Of course, those efforts would have been mere annoyances and mostly ineffectual if not for the contents of that tanker truck recovered in Oregon eleven months back.

With the information provided by Senator Byron Fitch in hand, Deacon Frank had brought in a crack geological team and offered to triple their fee if their efforts at finding the missing truck were successful. It took two months before the geologists got the hit they were looking for and summoned a whole salvage team to Umatilla. At that point, the problem became one of logistics: how to get the contents of that tanker out of the water and not die in the process.

Toward that end, the original plans to raise the whole truck from the water in which it was entombed were scrapped when engineers insisted that the structural integrity of the truck and tanker, after four years buried under water and silt, wouldn't survive the effort of lifting it to the surface. They were certain it would break apart. So the various teams he'd assembled came up with a safer plan to suck the contents of the tanker out through one of the flow valves, always under cover of darkness or clouds to avoid the prying eyes of satellites.

Sure, he had paid those teams exorbitantly well, but they'd been chosen because the members had ties to his movement, which meant they could be trusted. Deacon Frank would have bet every dollar he'd inherited from Reverend Rand Atlas Wilhyte that his background checks and security efforts had forestalled any infiltration by the FBI here in Oldtown. Sure, the groups he was involved with may have been on the Bureau's radar, but they had thousands of groups on that same radar and lacked the manpower to pursue each one with the same commitment.

"You want to tell me again how we got ourselves into this mess?" he heard Senator Byron Fitch saying, the words lifting him from his reflections on the past.

Deacon Frank realized that Fitch had moved into the moonlight, the odd spray of light casting his complexion in a gray tone. "It's not a mess, just an inconvenience."

"Really? That's what you'd call this? 'An inconvenience'? That stunt your boy pulled damn near got me killed yesterday," Fitch said, stopping as Deacon Frank nodded to one of his security teams, which was patrolling the property on an ATV, the two of them caught briefly in the spill of its headlights.

Deacon Frank looked back at Fitch, feeling his heart race a bit but managing to avoid comment on what the senator had just said. "And you said you'd take care of the inconvenience," he noted instead.

"I did," Senator Byron Fitch told him. "Except the stuff I couldn't."

"Maybe I made a mistake, telling you the truth after Rappaport came to you complaining."

"He knew what killed those kids. He knew I'd been lying to him all along. He made that much plain."

Deacon Frank stopped just short of a wide shaft of moonlight that reminded him of the old sodium vapors that used to illuminate roadways before LEDs came along. "Then maybe it's a good thing he showed up at the Capitol, shooting up a storm, because now he's dead and out of our hair. Think about it, Senator."

"I have been. We still don't know who else he talked to, besides me and that woman from the CDC."

"He wouldn't have shot up those steps if anybody else had listened to him," Deacon Frank noted. "He was trying to take you out as a matter of last recourse."

"Lucky me."

"Don't complain; you're still alive. And if you want to think about people dying, think back to the days when kids practiced hiding under their school desks in case the nukes started flying."

"That's a bit before my time, Deacon Frank."

"Picture it, then. Picture a hundred million Americans dead in a day."

The senator's mouth dropped. He cocked his head to the side and shook it, as if trying to shed the water left by an ocean swim. "Did I just hear you right?"

"You did."

"We can kill a hundred million people?"

Deacon Frank nodded again. "Probably more. Too many variables to provide a firm estimate. We still have a lot of logistics to work out, the delivery mechanism being first and foremost."

"That's what I wanted to ask you about, the delivery mechanism. We any closer to nailing something down?"

"Almost there, Senator. My people are working around the clock. I should have news for you soon."

Byron Fitch suddenly seemed to be enjoying the night air, stench of cow manure or not. He took a deep breath, seeming to suck in the world. "What are things going to look like, once it's done?"

"A hell of a lot better than they do now. I can promise you that much," Deacon Frank told him.

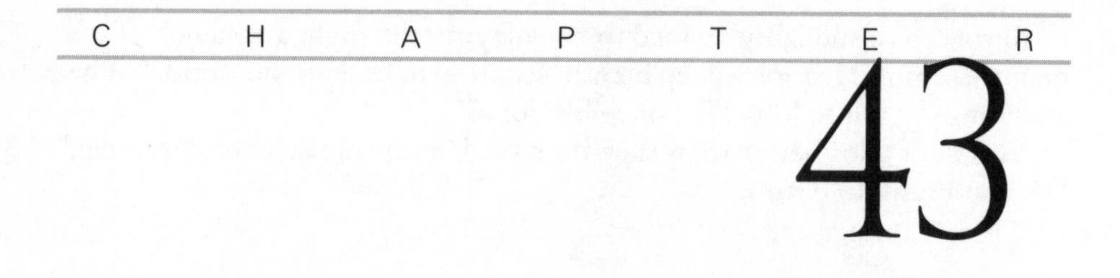

CHAPTER 43

UMATILLA, OREGON

Lutayne listened as the navy diver who'd just clawed his way to the surface explained finding the final Red Dog run entirely entombed in the silt, and only because he'd sunk into the black ooze and gotten stuck. Something must have gone wrong with his communicator, because no one heard him trying to summon help. In the end, the only thing that had saved his life was coming to rest on what must have been the top of the tanker, amid the same silt that had snared the truck in its grasp five years previously.

Lutayne knew enough about geology to know that wasn't really accurate. Since the sinkhole had formed *around* the Red Dog run rig, the process of sinking deeper would have occurred over time, until it must have finally come to rest atop a ledge of bedrock or shale, maybe limestone. Being totally buried beneath not only cold waters but also all that insulating silt would indeed have cloaked the truck's existence from all manner of direct-view and technological means to uncover its presence. The mystery that had plagued and haunted him for so long may have been solved, but Lutayne felt no manner of relief or satisfaction, since Panama had suggested that somebody had beaten them here.

"You come upon any signs that someone else found that truck before you did?" Panama asked the navy diver, just as Lutayne formed that thought.

"Have you been listening to what I went through down there?" the man snapped back.

Panama just looked at him. Lutayne couldn't see his eyes, but they must have gone colder than the water's frigid temperatures.

"No," the navy diver said, his tone a mix between subservient and apologetic. "No signs."

The trio of robotic submersibles took things from there. Lutayne watched them being lowered into the water by hoists rigged onto the backs of truck beds, monitored by their remote operators like the machines were their offspring.

"Here's what's going to happen," Panama explained to Lutayne. "We're going to send the underwater rovers down to clear away enough of the silt to snap some pictures, see what we can see."

Lutayne sat back and watched the process continue, as all three of the submersibles disappeared beneath the dark surface. Long a fan of horror movies and books, he imagined something beneath those dark waters blasting toward the cameras before the operators' monitors went dark. This, though, was a horror movie unfolding before him in real life, and the only monster lurking in the water below was the one he'd created in those Utah labs. And, like Dr. Frankenstein himself, he'd fallen in love with his own creation.

Panama had one of his men wheel Lutayne's chair across the rugged, uneven terrain. Negotiating the stairs of a trailer rig that held the operational controls for the submersibles proved impossible, so the man carried Lutayne up the stairs, while another man, who might have been his twin, toted the wheelchair. It wasn't going to be easy to negotiate the narrow single aisle that ran the trailer's length, leaving Lutayne looking for a spot to anchor himself without getting in anyone's way.

Panama joined the party a few moments later and helped Lutayne find a position with a view of the centrally placed and largest monitor, which showed three different perspectives, accounting for each of the submersibles.

"Okay," said Panama, who was still wearing his namesake hat. "Let's get this show going." Then he turned to Lutayne. "Something we haven't been able to ascertain, Doctor: the truck's specifications."

"We started with a standard tanker truck," Lutayne told not just Panama but also everyone crammed into the trailer. "Double as opposed to triple axel. No connecting cables to interchange the rigging. Singular construction, with the tank itself permanently mounted behind the cab."

"For better maneuverability," Panama nodded. "And security."

"We added Kevlar insulation to the interior of the tank and an extra layer of tungsten, which could resist a rocket attack."

"You did a good job of hiding all that, Doctor. We couldn't find a single picture or schematic in all the archived records."

"That was the point."

Lutayne realized Panama was referring to him as "doctor" as a way of explaining his presence here to the others gathered in the trailer. And judging by the way they deferred to Panama, it wasn't hard to figure who was in charge of this "show," as he'd called it.

"There were three separate chambers inside the tanker," Lutayne resumed. "On the chance one became compromised, the other two would remain intact. Single spigot, though, with control valves for each of the three."

"Everything by the numbers, in other words."

"We took every precaution possible."

Panama looked toward the screen featuring the three perspectives of the submersibles that had been lowered into the water. "Apparently that wasn't enough, Doctor."

Only the very topmost portion of the tanker poked up from its tomb of silt, the steel still shiny in the spill of the Rover One's piercing trio of exterior lights. Lutayne clung to the hope that both he and Panama were wrong about the poisonings at that Maryland high school, that maybe it hadn't been the White Death at all, despite all the indications otherwise. As the three submersibles continued to survey various aspects of the buried tanker, he waited for the news that the contents, fifteen thousand gallons of the White Death he'd created, were still inside.

Initial surveys by the rovers indicated that the truck was intact, its structural integrity not compromised. In the pictures being relayed from areas where the rovers managed to clear the silt away at least temporarily, Lutayne discerned not even a single dent or ding, as if the rig had just slipped peacefully into this dark abyss.

Clearing the cab revealed the bodies of both the driver and a second officer, riding shotgun, both remarkably preserved by five years of cold and pressure. They looked like mummified wax figures or something a taxidermist might fashion, especially their sightless eyes, which looked more like glass orbs wedged into the sockets. For some reason, the same could not be said for their uniforms, which had thinned, peeled away, and degraded over time, looking almost translucent in some places and completely missing in others.

"Initial pressure tests aren't conclusive," Panama told Lutayne, referring to the rovers' attempt to ascertain whether the White Death remained in the three-chambered tank. "But there are worrisome indications."

"Indications," Lutayne repeated.

"We're getting identical readings from two of the chambers, and an entirely different set from the third."

"The third being the rearmost chamber."

Panama nodded. "Lucky guess?"

"The rig looks like it settled on a backward list, so the rearmost chamber would be lower than the other two. That means gravity would be working against whoever showed up before us."

"Or maybe ten thousand gallons of your concoction was all they needed, Doctor," Panama said caustically, as if this whole thing was his fault.

And, at the end of the day, Lutayne supposed it was.

"What's next?"

"Magnetic resonance testing. Going on as we speak, along with an inspection of the remainder of the rig to make sure the contents didn't just spill out from some fissure the structural inspection didn't reveal."

"What about the two men up front?"

"What about them, Doctor?"

"They have families," was all Lutayne said in response.

"They don't exist, no more than this rig does. We never found it or them. Sorry."

Lutayne watched over the next several minutes as the product of the magnetic resonance testing appeared on screen. Remarkably, he found himself looking at a perfect image of the tanker, lined with grids the computer extrapolation had created. The first chamber to appear in full was that rearmost one, which was sitting on a downward tilt.

All the grids on the screen were colored in, indicating that the White Death stored in that chamber, at least, was intact.

Lutayne breathed easier, waited for the image of the next chamber to fill in comparable fashion.

It didn't.

Then the third chamber.

It didn't, either.

Nearly total confirmation that two of the three chambers had indeed been emptied by whoever had gotten there ahead of them. This was further confirmed by the kind of scratches and markings that gave clear indication that someone had opened the valve.

"Any way to tell when they were here?" Lutayne asked, breaking the silence that had settled over those squeezed into the trailer.

Panama shook his head. "Not definitively, from what I've been told. And before you ask, I've reviewed satellite imagery going back as far as it exists to look for activity in this area. Nothing, Doctor. Ordinarily, that would provide some hope we're dealing with a perforation here, cracks in the two empty chambers, and your White Death has sunk harmlessly to the center of the earth."

Lutayne didn't like the way Panama said "your," making him wonder if he had been invited here to take the fall for this, instead of just offering knowledge and assistance.

"Ordinarily," Panama repeated. "But in this case, it's far more likely that whoever emptied those front two chambers did so under considerable cloud cover the satellite imagery wouldn't be able to penetrate."

"In other words, they knew exactly what they were doing."

Panama nodded. "Then it's a good thing I do, too. Ready to take another plane ride, Doctor?"

"Where to?" Lutayne asked him.

"The East Coast—Maryland. Where this whole thing started, at that high school in Baltimore."

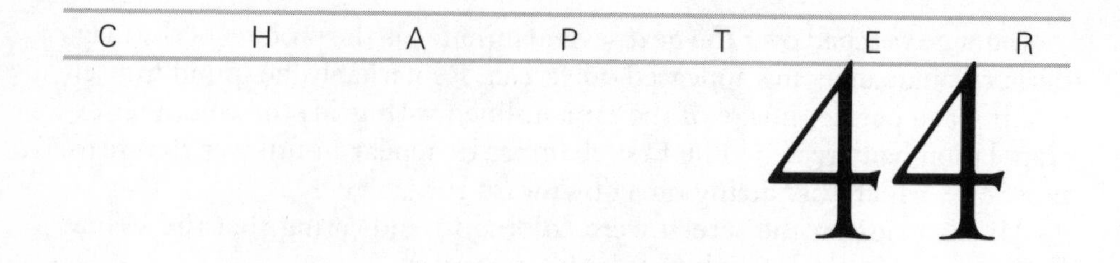

CHAPTER 44

WASHINGTON, DC

Something I forgot to tell you," Kelly Loftus said to Brixton from across the table at the Hamilton, a restaurant located just down the street from Jesus Arriaga's Compu-Tech office. "The FBI initially had trouble ID'ing Philip Rappaport. Turned out his file had been pulled by the military."

"'Pulled' as in redacted, or as in made to disappear?"

"Made to disappear. What's that mean?"

"That Rappaport worked on something beyond secret—beyond top secret, too."

"The development of this poison maybe?"

"That would be my first thought."

Loftus nodded. "Okay, so we know Philip Rappaport called Fitch's office. And that the contact occurred in the aftermath of the poisonings at that school."

"He was there for the development, so he recognized what had happened, knew the poison was responsible for the death of those kids, which meant it was operational."

"Wait . . . You're saying that somebody used the poison to *murder* them?"

Now it was Brixton who nodded. "I'm saying it's possible, even likely."

"And when Fitch's response to his claims didn't satisfy him, what, he shoots up the Capitol steps, just to take him out?"

Another nod from Loftus, but weaker and less sure. "It's thin, sure. But we know Rappaport had psychological issues, know he was on meds he wasn't taking, by all accounts. That could have pushed him over the edge."

"Like you said," Brixton acknowledged. "It makes sense."

"You don't sound so convinced."

"It's too neat. In my experience, things are never this neat."

"You were a cop."

Brixton's turn to nod. "Right here in DC, after a stint in Georgia," he said, repeating what Loftus already knew.

"Then you should know, from that experience anyway, that when you show up at a murder scene and somebody's covered in blood, they're the killer."

"My other experience indicates otherwise."

"Sorry," Loftus told him. "I can't relate."

"You'd be good at it, Kelly. It's right up your alley."

"Why?"

"Because the rules don't matter as much."

"Since I'm not good at following them, you mean."

"From what I've seen about you," Brixton started, letting his thought trail off there.

"You've known me all of four hours."

"Five, now. Speaking of which, we should order. When was the last time you ate?"

"I don't remember."

"Me either," said Brixton.

They'd chosen the Hamilton because of its late-night menu in the upstairs bar. There was a live music space on a lower, basement-level floor that had recently reopened, and they could feel and hear some of the guitar riffs and drumrolls through the floor, which felt as if it was vibrating in rhythm with the music. Brixton and Loftus ordered a trio of appetizers to make up for the dinner they'd never gotten around to eating.

"Let's get back to Senator Fitch," Brixton said.

He was thinking of another of the voicemails from Alexandra Parks's phone, which the professor had pulled off the cloud.

"This is Senator Fitch's office, returning your call."

So she must have acted upon whatever suspicions Philip Rappaport had expressed to her about the poisonings, after not getting the results he'd hoped for from Fitch. Alexandra had impressed Brixton as the kind of person who didn't go through the motions. There must have been something that Rappaport had said that raised enough flags for her to contact a sitting United States senator. Then again, the call she made, and the subsequent return voicemail she received, could have been about something else entirely, something more directly related to her mundane duties for the CDC's Washington office.

Which led Brixton's thinking to veer in a different direction that he wasn't ready to share with Kelly Loftus. He interrupted their reflections on the case to ease his phone from his pocket.

"I need to make a call," he said, hitting the contact labeled "MAC," without bothering to leave the table, and waited for him to answer. "You still at the hospital?"

"Annabel just went to grab some coffee, maybe a snack."

"Any updates?"

Mac sighed deeply, his voice hoarse from exhaustion and all the anxiety. Vigils spent in a hospital waiting room tended to have that effect.

"Alexandra remains in stable condition. That's good news in its own right. You know what they say about the first twenty-four hours."

"Sure, but I didn't know it applied to poisonings."

"I think it applies to everything that brings you to the emergency room in critical condition."

"What about the poison? Has toxicology been able to identify it yet?"

Brixton heard Mac sigh again. "They isolated *something* in her blood, but they haven't been able to identify it yet. Would you believe they sent it to the Centers for Disease Control in Atlanta, of all places? Talk about irony."

"It's not a disease, though."

"No, Robert, but the CDC has the foremost experts anywhere, on everything, on speed dial. They'll know who to call."

Mac tried to clear the hoarseness from his voice but failed.

"What else?" he resumed. "You calling this late tells me there's something else."

"Jesus Arriaga found something on that compilation of recordings of the shooting on the Capitol steps, just not what we were expecting," Brixton said, going on to explain the revelation produced by Arriaga stringing the recordings together.

"So no second shooter, but a confirmed target for the shooter."

"I wouldn't say confirmed, Mac, but the indications are there, and strong. Not saying it would hold up in court."

"Depends on the lawyer," Mackensie Smith quipped.

It was true. Brixton had seen enough of Mac in a courtroom to know he could make something out of nothing, and everything out of little more than that.

"Assume Alexandra's poisoning was no accident, Mac."

"I've been assuming that from the beginning."

"The return call from Byron Fitch's office came in the morning I met Alexandra for lunch."

"So, prior to the shooting." Mac hesitated, tried to clear his throat again. "You think she was looking into something, based on what Rappaport told her about Fitch. Then Rappaport tries to kill him, and the next day Alexandra is poisoned."

"There's something else," Brixton said, a new thought striking him. "Seven kids who were poisoned to death at a Baltimore high school—sound familiar?"

"Of course, but I'd forgotten all about it."

"According to everything I've read, the poison that killed them was never positively identified. Does *that* sound familiar?"

Mac didn't respond immediately, processing what Brixton had just said. Brixton gave him all the time he needed.

"Who's running the investigation in Maryland?" Mac wondered finally.

"Local PD. No FBI involvement, because there's no clear evidence of a crime. They're still looking at this as a tragic accident, and the school's been closed ever since, because the going assumption is that something in the building poisoned the victims. They're not going to open up again until the source of the toxin, poison, or whatever you want to call it is identified."

"You want me to have the toxin they isolated in Alexandra's blood compared to the poison that killed those kids?"

Brixton nodded, even though Mac couldn't see him. "Also unidentified. You can see where I'm going with this. Alexandra was following up the poisoning of these kids and then she got poisoned herself. I'm just connecting the dots."

"But who poisons *kids*?"

"Somebody with a reason to, just like they had a reason to poison Alexandra."

"Let me see what I can do," Mac said, his voice weak and strained.

"No, Mac."

"No?"

"In all the years we've been friends, I've never once heard you say 'Let me see what I can do.' Because your approach is to go out and get it done. There's a reason why you're one of the best trial lawyers in the capital. No one wants to face you because they know what they're up against."

Brixton could visualize Mac cracking a smile in the hospital waiting room.

"Okay, you've convinced me, Robert. They've moved Alexandra to the ICU, and what you said about the poisoning, this connection, makes me wonder if . . ."

"The answer's yes," Brixton said when Mac's voice trailed off.

"I didn't finish the question."

"You wanted to know if we should put a guard on the ICU."

"And?"

Brixton let himself smile. "Let me see what I can do."

"Very funny."

"I'll have somebody over there within an hour, Mac."

Brixton noticed Kelly Loftus checking her phone when he ended the call, her expression taut with worry.

"What is it?" he asked her.

"Email from my Capitol Police captain. Apparently, the chief wants to see me tomorrow morning."

"What time?"

"Nine a.m. sharp. Why?"

Brixton already had his phone out again. "I'm calling Mac back."

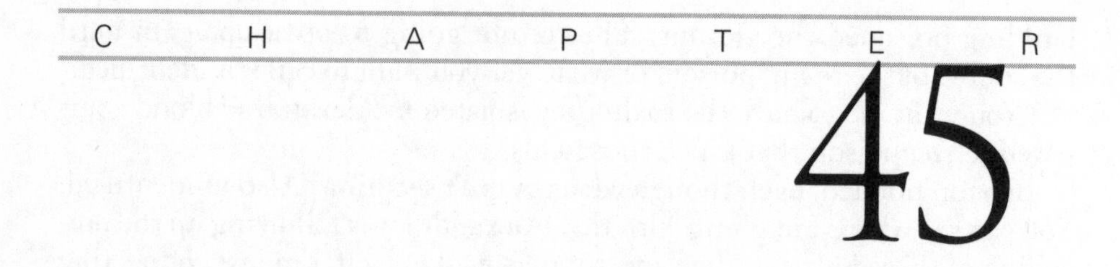

CHAPTER 45

OLDTOWN, MARYLAND

Deacon Frank was glad when Byron Fitch finally took his leave, waving at him as he pulled off in his car. Needing some time to think, he opted to continue on the stroll he'd started with the senator, hoping to clear his head.

Daniel might have the worst case of ADHD on the planet, but he'd always been a savant when it came to science. Deacon Frank remembered buying him chemistry sets for Christmas from the time the boy was five years old, and Daniel always blew through the whole collection of experiments in less than a week. Deacon Frank had taken him to visit the lab a while back, to indulge the kid's passion. He should have known what the boy was up to when a wide-eyed Daniel kept peppering the scientists with questions Deacon Frank couldn't grasp—and he understood the answers even less. That must have been when he somehow lifted enough of the White Death to do the deed that had landed them in this mess.

"We're different sides of the same coin, Deacon Frank," Fitch had told him once, explaining their alliance. "You can be heads, I'll be tails. Because we both got the world fooled. You with all your foundations and charity work, a secular saint, and me with my political leanings."

Deacon Frank knew that Senator Byron Fitch had learned long ago that politics was like a costume ball: you dressed up any way you wanted, except people didn't know it was a costume. Conservatives didn't get elected to the senate in Maryland, which was fine, since Fitch hadn't started out as one. A faux fierce independent streak had defined much of his career, independence defined as what suited his best interests at the time. Fitch found being an independent to be the ideal way to launch his brand, allowing him to be all things to all lobbyists before supporting the causes advanced by those who most lined his pockets. His move to the conservative side of the spectrum had been born of opportunity as opposed to ideals. Indeed, Byron Fitch had been blessed with the one trait certain to propel him to the heights of power: he believed in nothing.

But Fitch had a nose for those who could advance his personal cause. The presidency had been on his radar long before his first encounter with Deacon Frank Wilhyte made achieving it a real possibility. Each enabled the other, and both knew that patience was more than a virtue; it was a strategy. It was one thing, though, to boast of a plan to alter the country's DNA forever, quite another to actually bring it to pass.

It was all talk until the White Death came into the picture. Fitch had seen the polls, and more importantly, the internals behind them. Bottom line was a hard fifteen to twenty percent, maybe as much as thirty percent, of the country was ready for another civil war, ready to throw everything up in the air and let the chips fall where they may. Fitch may not have spoken the language of that hard fifteen to twenty percent, but Deacon Frank did.

His youth spent on the Bible-thumping circuit had left him attuned to those who loved spending an evening under a tent, in a folding chair, sinking into ground covered with mud left by a storm that morning. Deacon Frank could weasel money out of the poor lot with a coy smile, his collection basket a harbinger of the message he would someday spread in return. Traversing the country with the Reverend Rand Atlas Wilhyte had imbued him with a deep understanding of how far someone would go for something they believed. He saw that in his father's devoted flock, who would line up in monsoon-like thunderstorms or hundred-degree-plus heat for hours to get a cherished seat at one of Reverend Rand's revival meetings. Celebration after celebration of lives well lived on the part of a loyal following of men wearing clothes that carried the rank odor of yesterday's sweat. They'd drop their last twenty dollars for the week in Deacon Frank's collection basket on the way out of the tent because he'd made them feel good, and that was better than eating.

Deacon Frank had studied their eyes and learned how to read them. It was a skill that became the driving force in his ascent to power in a movement that had started out as a loose amalgamation of militia and separatist groups, of men—and women—who hated the new America that had left them behind. And as the years passed, those tents became dingy, rank basements and stuffy meeting halls that smelled of Old Spice. It was there that he listened more than he spoke, listened to men talk of their dreams long dead and the hatred they felt for those they blamed for the deaths. He knew he was sitting on a powder keg that was ready to blow at any moment. The problem was there were hundreds, even thousands, of these powder kegs. The boom each made would be barely loud enough to hear outside the cellar or hall. A kidnapping here, a break-in there, torching a temple or a Black church—none of it amounted to very much at all.

Draw those powder kegs into the same circle, unite them under an umbrella of fear and loathing, and the world could change. Strength in numbers became geometric in growth, the collective finding an efficacy individual groups could never hope to muster.

His movement, *the* Movement, was born in those basements and meeting halls, like that shuttered Knights of Columbus hall in Michigan, as Deacon Frank crisscrossed the country, much like his father had—and on his dead daddy's dime no less. He never wondered if the Reverend Rand Atlas Wilhyte would have approved, even been proud of him, because he didn't care. He didn't cry at his daddy's funeral because he'd learned all he could from him and grasped how rich he was about to become at the tender age of twenty-two. The heir apparent who gave it all up and let it die, turning his father's minions into the seeds that had now sprouted into something big and wonderful.

Early on, his father had grasped the importance of first mailing lists and then email lists. That's how the invite listservs to revival meetings were built. That's how his outwardly pious daddy became a millionaire a hundred times over, thanks to ten dollars here and twenty dollars there, much of it in cash. Cash coming into headquarters on a daily basis to be counted by a literal army of hands in a room the size of a basketball court. Deacon Frank saw all that cash not just as accumulated tens and twenties but also in terms of the sheer number of bills. Each addition to the pile was another potential devoted member of the Movement he would go on to build, affirmation for his work in advance.

On the day of Reverend Rand's death, that name, address, and phone number listserv crossed the four million mark. Many, if not most, members were elderly or infirm, sometimes both. They were not soldiers themselves in the war he saw coming, but they had friends and neighbors and children. Each bill, check, or credit card number was viewed as a potential application.

And as Deacon Frank's own years on the road went by, the powder kegs coalesced and learned to coexist, reassured by the notion that they couldn't accomplish anything worth a shit alone, and finding solace and strength in the swelling numbers Deacon Frank brought to the table. The attack on the Capitol Building—the insurrection or whatever you wanted to call it—was a dry run. A test case to see if the powder kegs would back up their words with actions. Deacon Frank had been pleased more than satisfied, but the experience had revealed to him something was missing: a fuse. A fuse that could ignite the singular powder keg and unleash its true power and potential. And then fate, God, or maybe the Reverend Rand Atlas Wilhyte had delivered him that fuse, from heaven itself: the White Death. Ten thousand gallons of the deadliest toxin ever known to man.

PART FOUR

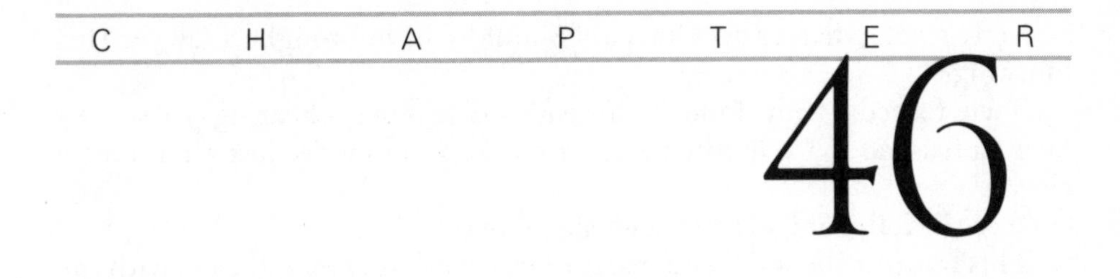

CHAPTER 46

WASHINGTON, DC

"Go right on up, Officer Loftus," said the uniformed receptionist at the front desk of Capitol Police headquarters. "The chief's expecting you."

"Thanks," Kelly told her, having arrived an hour earlier.

She'd used the D Street entrance of the United States Capitol Police headquarters, a beige-toned concrete and granite building between Stanton Park and the Supreme Court of the United States, and was standing there when it officially opened for business at eight a.m.

The chief's name was Thomas Boyle and he had a reputation for being an apolitical straight shooter who'd come to the Capitol Police from Providence, Rhode Island, where he'd risen to the role of public safety commissioner. Before moving to Providence, he'd spent his entire career in law enforcement, working his way up the ranks in the Massachusetts State Police, where he had specialized in the ongoing violence associated with the internecine struggles between clashing Irish and Italian crime families. Boyle had cut his teeth doing battle with both the murderous elements of the infamous Winter Hill Gang and the more traditional Angiulo mob.

After emerging from the elevator on the fifth floor, she was escorted by Chief Boyle's assistant straight into his office, where she found her supervisor, Captain Slattery, standing on one side of the seated Boyle, and a man she didn't recognize standing on the other side.

A single chair had been placed directly before the director's desk, which Boyle offered her with a polite "Good morning, Officer Loftus. Please take a seat."

Kelly did, not liking the messaging of this at all. Her seated, being forced to look up toward the three men looming over her. Director Boyle noticed her gaze wandering to the man in the suit, standing to his left.

"This is our legal counsel, Louis Craven."

The lack of explanation for Craven's presence was confirmation in itself that this meeting was going to go even worse than she'd expected.

"We've reviewed the notes from your interview with the FBI yesterday," Boyle continued, "and there are several issues we'd like to gain some clarity on."

Kelly's gaze drifted to Craven. "Should I have brought a lawyer this morning?"

Boyle forced a thin smile. "This isn't a disciplinary hearing per se, Officer Loftus, so that's hardly necessary. Like I said, we're just after a little clarity."

"I see," Kelly said, even though she didn't.

This was just the way her departure from the BPD had started, with the chief and others just wanting a "little clarity." It's like these people were reading from the same script.

"Can we assume everything you told the FBI in your interview yesterday was truthful?" Boyle asked her.

"Yes," Kelly answered immediately, not equivocating.

Boyle nonetheless glanced toward Craven, the lawyer, in an unspoken gesture for him take over.

"Can we also assume then," Craven started, in a nasally voice that made Kelly think his nose was stuffed up, "that you left nothing out?"

"I don't know what you mean, Mr. Craven."

"That there might have been areas you didn't touch on, that weren't necessarily raised by the agents' questions."

"Could you be more specific?"

Craven nodded. "Focusing on the contents of the handbag belonging to the woman you failed to report . . ."

Craven kept speaking, but Kelly fixated on his use of the phrase "failed to report." She wondered if he was laying a trap, asking a question he already knew the answer to, which meant her failure to provide it would be incriminating in itself. A classic interrogation maneuver she had used herself on several occasions.

With criminals, which made her think that was the way she was being viewed today.

"If perhaps you neglected to mention anything else you may have recovered, that may have slipped your mind. Is that possible?" the lawyer finished.

"Is *what* possible?" Kelly asked, having lost too many of his words to be sure of what he was asking.

Craven looked annoyed at having to repeat himself, one side of his mouth tilting upward in the beginnings of a snarl. Then Chief Boyle jumped in ahead of him.

"We have reason to believe you haven't shared everything you've learned, or are in possession of, with us."

"On what grounds?" she asked.

Boyle and Craven locked glances, Craven taking the floor back. "Some notes to that effect from the FBI agents who interviewed you."

"Don't you mean 'interrogated'?" Kelly heard herself ask, the words emerging before she could snatch them back.

"That depends on whether you're a suspect or not."

"Are you a suspect, Officer?" Boyle picked up from there.

Kelly cursed herself for walking straight into their trap. She should have known better, having set any number of comparable ones herself over the three years she'd worked homicide. You walk into a hornet's nest, expect to get stung.

"Because there is the matter of some anomalies in your cell phone records."

Kelly felt suddenly overheated, her breath coming in shallow heaves she found hard to disguise. Whatever came out of her mouth next, she knew, would push her past the point of no return. She tried to remain silent, but Craven's half snarl framed her mind, a fitting complement to Boyle's sententious sneer.

"Would you like to detail those calls to us, all made in the general aftermath of the Capitol shooting?" Craven asked her.

She knew he was referring to her calls to Baltimore Mulighet High School, Senator Byron Fitch, the Centers for Disease Control in Washington, and the personal cell of someone at the CDC she now knew to be Alexandra Parks. All four phone numbers scrawled by Philip Rappaport on a scrap of paper she'd never turned over.

Kelly looked toward Captain Slattery, who was standing still, silent, and stoic. She was hoping for some manner of support, but none came.

"You can see our problem, Officer Loftus," Chief Boyle resumed. "In fact—"

The door burst open, freezing him midsentence. A tall, rangy man with a thick crop of graying hair barged his way into the chief's office, with Boyle's assistant helplessly trailing him.

"I assume you had a warrant to check those phone records," the man shot out, his words striking her interrogators like bullets. "Because otherwise . . ."

He glanced down toward Kelly in her chair, then back at Boyle and the men standing on either side of him.

"My name is Mackensie Smith. You may have heard of me, you may not have; I really don't care. All you need to know is that I am Officer Loftus's attorney and your interview with her has just ended."

Mackensie Smith. Brixton's friend, Kelly remembered.

She watched Smith lock gazes with Craven, two gunfighters waiting to see who was going to draw first.

"Did you advise my client of her rights, Counselor?"

"We are in the midst of an investigation," Chief Boyle said, again jumping in before Craven had a chance to respond. "Officer Loftus is neither a suspect nor a person of interest. Our interview with her was strictly internal."

Kelly could see the air go out of Craven as fast as a balloon that had just been popped. She could also see the man Brixton had called "Mac" fail to suppress all of the smile he was fighting back.

"Then I'm sure you're aware that under the law enforcement statutes the Capitol Police operates under, you have no right to any means of search and seizure. I believe that includes cell phone records, doesn't it, Mr. Craven?"

Craven swallowed hard.

"I'll take that as a yes, and I'll take my client with me. Should you wish to speak with her further, all contact should go through me." Smith's eyes moved to Craven again. "Mr. Craven has my number. Thank you, gentlemen."

Kelly didn't realize she'd risen to her feet until Mackensie Smith took her lightly by the elbow to steer her for the door.

"Robert sent you," she said, after they'd brushed past Chief Boyle's assistant.

"Indeed he did. And he's waiting for you downstairs."

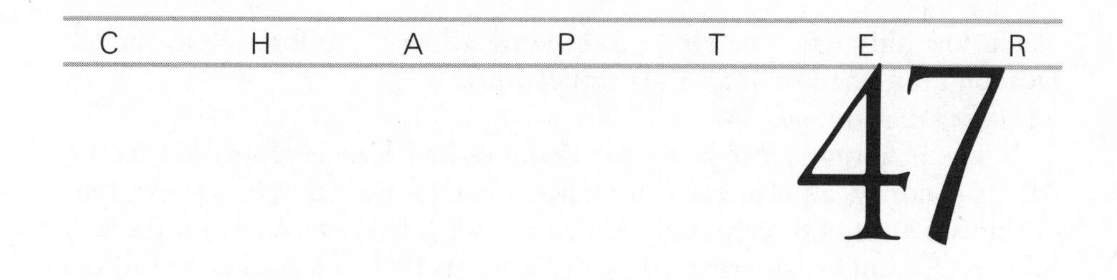

CHAPTER 47

BALTIMORE, MARYLAND

I'm afraid we've encountered a problem, sir."

Deacon Frank looked at the man wearing a white lab coat and glasses, glad he'd closed the door to the lab's single enclosed office. Visions of dollar signs danced through his head as he considered what he was paying Professor Leonard Cutlow to run what he privately called his White Death operation. Of course, you could scratch "Professor" as a title, since drunken behavior and improper sexual advances aimed at his former college students had ended Cutlow's careers in both academia and research. His loss had become Deacon Frank's gain, given that defrocked academics don't have a lot of career options. He'd been glad to pull Cutlow off the scrap heap.

"Problem?"

"More of a setback, you might say."

"What do *you* say, Doc?"

Deacon Frank called him that because "Doctor" was included on his business card. Not the medical kind, of course.

"That we're going to need some more time to get things right."

"You told me you were almost there. On the verge of being ready to go, you said."

"That was before we encountered the setback. That young woman who ended up in a coma should be dead. That was enough to tell us the airborne delivery mechanism we've committed ourselves to appears to have a faster deterioration rate and a significantly smaller zone of spread."

Deacon Frank felt a surge of heat prick the nerve endings on his arms, making it feel like the hairs were standing up. "Faster deterioration rate," he repeated, his voice picking up steam. "Smaller zone of spread. I thought I was paying you to take that kind of shit off the board."

"It's just a delay, Mr. Wilhyte."

"Deacon Frank. I told you to call me Deacon Frank. And how long is this delay going to last?"

Cutlow swallowed hard. "It's impossible to say. A few weeks, a month. Two maybe."

"How about six, how about nine, how about a whole goddamn year? I mean, that's possible, isn't it?"

Cutlow didn't answer him, not looking all that comfortable in the lab Deacon Frank had built to his specifications.

Hiding in plain sight.

It was a notion Deacon Frank Wilhyte had learned from his father. All that money, all that cash, funneled through the church coffers. Tens of thousands of both crisp bills, harvested fresh from an ATM on the way to a service, and cash crinkled from being stuffed in a pocket or billfold or being returned as change at some fast-food outlet. Sometimes the bills held the scent of whoever had dropped them in, rank perspiration or stale perfume, hair oil or something like dried mud. With all that money, sometimes stretching into the millions at week's end, when mail contributions were added, you'd think Reverend Rand would have commandeered Fort Knox for the counting and storage.

Instead, it all took place in nothing more than the basement of the mansion, which Deacon Frank's mother hadn't left a single time in the nine years between his father's death and her own. She'd been a shut-in, confined to ten thousand square feet of luxury, including her own pool, movie theater, and spa. When Deacon Frank built his own spread in Oldtown, he'd insisted that the square footage be exactly the same as the one his father had paid for with cash. Not a single foot more, suggesting he was trying to better his famous father, or a single foot less, suggesting on the contrary that he was inferior to him.

Deacon Frank, similarly, had originally planned to construct the lab he needed, in the wake of acquiring the White Death, either on his considerable Oldtown property or beneath it, in the sprawling basement, which was constructed with iron and rebar-reinforced ultra-high-strength PFC concrete, further enhanced by incorporating steel fibers. He'd built it with a survivalist's eye toward being able to live out a nuclear war in the abstract, or the civil war that was now coming in reality.

At his behest.

He was never anything more than an errand boy, a prop, for his famous father, never entrusted with anything beyond smiling while holding the collection basket in hand, a role extending into his teens and even twenties. The Reverend Rand Atlas Wilhyte had never entertained any serious discussions regarding improving his son's station. The lack of such positioning had grated on Deacon Frank as he grew older, the source of both embarrassment and malcontent. He grew to hate the services for the degradation they served upon him as a glorified usher in the church of his father, with little more responsibility than he'd enjoyed as a little boy.

Reverend Rand had preached of a fire and fury that was coming, though it never came. An ever-looming apocalypse out of which only the strong of heart and faith would survive.

Join me and be saved! Join me and walk through the meadows of a new Baby-

lon fit to our own making. Walk with me, my brothers and sisters! Walk with me with a place by my side.

Such a place, of course, came with a price that escalated higher and higher, even as the apocalypse was delayed time and time again.

Walk by my side, as we await the raging fires to consume this evil world. Walk by my side and know not when that time will come and that we will be tested and teased to make sure we are committed. Know that your faith is secure, your hand clasped in mine. I am your guide. I am your shepherd. And when the time comes we will watch the raging of the fires together.

And the Book of Revelation . . . Reverend Rand Atlas Wilhyte loved quoting from the Book of Revelation.

"Then I saw a new heaven and a new earth, for the first heaven and the first earth had passed away, and the sea was no more. And I saw the holy city, new Jerusalem, coming down out of heaven from God, prepared as a bride adorned for her husband. And I heard a loud voice from the throne saying, 'Behold, the dwelling place of God is with man. He will dwell with them, and they will be his people, and God himself will be with them as their God. He will wipe away every tear from their eyes, and death shall be no more, neither shall there be mourning, nor crying, nor pain anymore, for the former things have passed away.' And he who was seated on the throne said, 'Behold, I am making all things new.' Also he said, 'Write this down, for these words are trustworthy and true.'"

Except they weren't. Far from it.

"But the day of the Lord will come like a thief, and then the heavens will pass away with a roar, and the heavenly bodies will be burned up and dissolved, and the earth and the works that are done on it will be exposed."

Except they weren't, despite all the assurances.

"And the devil that deceived them was cast into the lake of fire and brimstone, where the beast and the false prophet are, and shall be tormented day and night for ever and ever."

Except they weren't, not ever.

Deacon Frank had watched and listened, struck by his father's capacity for twisting the hearts and minds of his followers to his own design, for a world that never came. But what if it had? What would the Reverend Rand have done with the millions who hung on his every word?

Watching from his assigned station in the role of glorified usher, the dutiful son Deacon Frank seethed and simmered at his father's ability to get the audience to buy what he was selling. It made him realize how much their empty, vapid lives could be filled with promises of blood washing over the land. What did they care? The land belonged to the bank or the landlord. They were forever a payment behind, forever facing foreclosure, but never fearing it, because Reverend Rand had told him that all manner of floods and plagues would wash it all away under the pounding hooves of the four horsemen.

But my horse is faster. My horse is kept on by my faith in God. We are all His soldiers in this war, and there is room for all in the saddle that will bring us to the future. So climb up behind me, my brothers and sisters, climb up and let us ride toward a better tomorrow.

A tomorrow forever promised, but which never came.

Until now.

What better way to show his father that his hands were worthy of holding far more than just the collection basket? But now this . . . a "setback," as Leonard Cutlow had put it.

Deacon Frank had purchased a warehouse building on Aisquith Street in Baltimore. The location was set far off from the city center, nestled among comparable industrial structures, the kind of businesses where workers showed up by eight a.m. and left by five p.m. without ever paying attention to their surroundings. The facade of the rough, rust-colored concrete finish still read "Pride Master Service Inc.," a gesture meant to give the impression that the building was the same as it had always been. There were a few parking spaces in the front, striped perpendicular to the building, but the bulk of parking was located in the back, where it would draw no attention from passing drivers.

The double glass-doored entrance hadn't been switched out, either. Except now those glass doors permitted entry into a secured portico, where only a combination of the proper key code and a thumbprint scan allowed access to what lay beyond, in the laboratory built precisely to Dr. Cutlow's expert specifications. That hadn't been even twelve months ago, but it felt like twelve years, so agonizing was the wait to see his plans come to fruition, his creation of a legacy of which the Reverend Rand Atlas Wilhyte could only dream. The 7,500 square feet, with a comparable amount contained in a basement, had been turned into a research lab that would have made the biggest biotech firm in the world proud. It was still a tight squeeze, with all the workstations, storage areas, ventilation systems, vacuum chambers, electron microscopes, and plenty of other equipment Deacon Frank wouldn't have been able to identify even with an owner's manual. He had delivered samples of the White Death whenever Cutlow had requested them for his ongoing development of potential delivery systems, but the good doctor had never laid eyes on the entire reserves, which for obvious reasons were stored elsewhere.

"Talk to me about this setback, Doc," he said to Cutlow, his body temperature rising toward the red. "How can we minimize this delay you're talking about?"

"The White Death doesn't behave like anything I've ever encountered before."

"This coming from a man who cut his teeth at the bioweapons lab at Fort Detrick, right here in Maryland."

"Where our job was to envision and create, not expand on someone else's work product."

"Is that what you call it?"

"This is an incredibly complex compound, thanks to its organic elements."

"You mean because it was derived from a flower."

Cutlow nodded. "And like a flower, its composition is altered by the environment. Light, temperature, air composition. The alterations are subtle but enough to reduce the compound's efficacy and its levels of toxicity. We reached the final stage of testing with flying colors, only to encounter inexplicable variances in the results, once it was employed outside of the lab."

"Inexplicable, and yet you're explaining them to me now."

"That woman should have died, Deacon Frank. The fact that she didn't indicates the toxin doesn't behave outside the lab the same way it does inside the lab."

"Because of these alterations. Environmental factors."

"We thought we had accounted for them. We were mistaken. I believe what we're looking at here is a work in progress. That original lab at Tooele Army Depot was shuttered before it became a finished product."

That was something Deacon Frank hadn't expected. After all, who goes through all the trouble of transporting fifteen thousand gallons of something unfinished a thousand miles just to dispose of it? Why not just pour it down a drain?

"So what's the plan, Doc? Give me the plan."

Cutlow shrugged his bony shoulders. "Short of modifying the timetable—"

"A nonstarter."

"All I can tell you is that it's open-ended, absent knowledge from someone who's worked with the White Death directly and has gained a working knowledge of its operational capabilities."

Open-ended . . .

The term echoed in Deacon Frank's head. He wanted to snap the man's scrawny neck with his bare hands, in which case he'd have to replace the pissant. Then a thought struck him, absurd in its obviousness.

"Someone who's worked with it," he repeated.

Cutlow nodded. "If you could find someone with that experience . . ."

"I just might be able to do that, Doc," Deacon Frank told him.

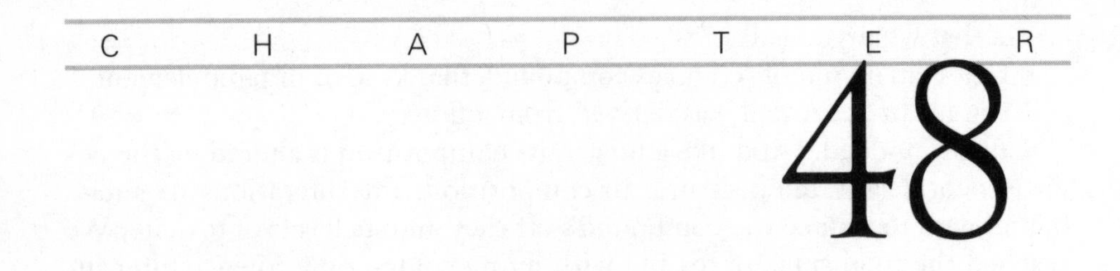

CHAPTER 48

BALTIMORE, MARYLAND

Brixton was leaning against his ten-year-old BMW when Kelly Loftus emerged from Capitol Police headquarters alongside Mac.

"Thanks, Brixton," she said to him, her eyes more grateful than her tone.

"What are friends for, Loftus? And it's Mac you should thank."

"Only because you haven't gotten a bill from me yet," Mac said, managing a smile.

"What's the latest?" Brixton asked him.

"Good news on Alexandra," Mac reported. "She's been moved to a private room. I left Annabel with her. Her vitals all continue to be stable, and however they're treating her, it's showing results in declining toxicity rates in her blood."

"A toxin they haven't been able to identify."

Mac's expression sobered. "There's another possibility, Robert."

"That they have managed to identify the toxin and aren't sharing the results."

"The labs at Walter Reed would have passed the results of their tests up the toxicological food chain, and someone at the top wants to keep this buried. And there's more, to the point you just made. You asked me to check if whatever poisoned Alexandra is the same toxin that killed those high school kids in Baltimore."

"I remember."

"Well, my contacts drew a blank. They informed me that the seven kids were rushed to three different Baltimore-area hospitals."

"And?" Brixton prompted.

"There is no 'and,' Robert. My contacts weren't able to find a single medical record on those victims in the records of any of the three hospitals. And there's more: the autopsy report on Alexandra's supervisor. They were in his office when both took sick. He passed out first. Alexandra was calling nine-one-one when she collapsed."

"Those seven kids all died within twenty-four hours of each other," Brixton said, pointing out the obvious discrepancy.

"You didn't let me finish, Robert. I was going to tell you about the man's autopsy results."

"What about them?"

"They don't exist either. Not in the system for anyone to access, including me, and I can access anything."

"They were brought in to Walter Reed together, though, weren't they?"

Mac's expression tightened in anxiety mixed with fear. "Apparently not. I saved the best for last. There's no record of Alexandra's supervisor ever being treated in the ER, even though I saw him covered up on the bed next to her when they first took me back there."

Brixton considered the ramifications of that. "Maybe we should add a second guard to watch over Alexandra."

Mac nodded. "I'll leave selection to you."

They had locked stares at that point, Brixton waiting for Mac to continue.

"You need to get to the bottom of this, Robert," Mac said, leaving it there.

Brixton turned his gaze back to Kelly Loftus. "You ready to go to work?"

She nodded and he swung back toward Mackensie Smith.

"We're going to need another favor, Mac," Brixton said to him.

CHAPTER 49

BALTIMORE, MARYLAND

The name of the school, Mr. Cleese," Brixton said, standing before the desk of the principal of the high school that all seven students who'd died of poisoning had attended. "Where's it come from?"

He and Loftus had come to Baltimore Mulighet High School as soon as Mac had completed the arrangements for the favor Brixton had requested. Jefferson Cleese was wearing a typical school-day suit, even though the building was otherwise vacant, having been shuttered indefinitely. The last five weeks had clearly taken their toll, showing in the nervous jitter of his fingers and the uncertain bent of his gaze. It was the gaze of a man who no longer trusted what he was seeing. Cleese told them his first name was Jefferson, but he went by Jeff.

"*Mulighet* is Norwegian for 'opportunity,'" he said. "Nationality of the donor behind its construction. Hence our name: Baltimore Mulighet High School."

Brixton watched Kelly Loftus lean forward as gracefully as she did everything else, steadying the notepad in her lap. She held the pad the same way she had when conducting interviews for a homicide case just a few miles from the school's location, at 1300 West Thirty-Sixth Street.

"We were founded as a part of an initiative to consolidate large school sizes into smaller learning environments," Cleese continued, sad irony creeping into his voice. "Seven students smaller now."

He seemed to catch himself, moving in closer to the desk, which was empty save for a computer that wasn't turned on, as if that would make the two EPA officials give him a pass on the tone of his words.

"I'm sorry. That was uncalled for."

"But it's the truth," Brixton said. "Isn't it? And the truth is what we're here to find."

"The Environmental Protection Agency has already weighed in," Cleese told them both. "Scoured every inch of this school from basement to rooftop and didn't find any toxins. Not even asbestos, lead in the paint, or any of the other usual suspects. But here we are, still closed, with me the only one allowed access to the building."

"That's why we're here," Loftus interjected. "To get you up and running again, once our final report has been issued."

A faint flicker of home gleamed in Cleese's eyes. He was so glad to welcome a fresh investigative team to the school that he hadn't questioned their credentials or called the EPA to confirm their assignment. Not that it would have mattered, since the identifications Mackensie Smith had provided extended beyond their laminated IDs to include the rigors of a follow-up call to the agency. It paid to have a best friend who was among the most connected lawyers in the city, who possessed a trail of favors owed that ran from one side of Capitol Hill to the other.

Brixton thought about what Mac must have been going through, nearly losing the daughter he had just found. That fact alone had invigorated him with a fresh resolve to help Brixton's—and now Kelly Loftus's—efforts in any way he could, given the clear connection between the death of the seven students from Mulighet and something Alexandra Parks had been following up.

Until she and her supervisor had been poisoned, too.

"Those poor kids weren't poisoned at this school," Cleese insisted to Brixton.

"It's the only thing they had in common," Brixton noted.

Cleese shook his head slowly. "No, it wasn't."

"You're aware of another?" Loftus prompted.

He shook his head again. "But there has to be one. When you called, after all this time, I thought—I hoped—you had found it."

The investigative reports Mac had been able to produce for them, from the EPA and from other agencies involved in the investigation, had confirmed both the lack of another link between the seven students who had perished and that the school itself had tested clean in all respects. Mulighet was housed in a four-story brick building that had once held a public high school, before declining enrollment in the city had led to its shutdown. The Mulighet Group, which was behind this and several dozen other charter schools across the country, had invested heavily in a total renovation, focusing on technology, open spaces, and something they called pod classrooms. The eight hundred students affected by its closure had already been placed in other high schools. Originally, this had been done as a temporary safety precaution, but these measures soon became permanent when it was clear that parents had no intention of letting their children ever return to this building.

"The victims died within less than twenty-four hours of each other," Brixton advanced. "That means they must have been exposed to the toxin in the same time frame, or very close. And this building is the only place all of them can be accounted for at the same time, at any point within that time frame."

"Yes," Cleese said, nodding. "But no one can say for certain when they were poisoned. And there was never anything evidentiary linking whatever poisoned them to this building, as the EPA is well aware, since you conducted the tests."

"Did Homicide ever participate in the investigation?" Loftus asked him, jumping in.

Cleese looked confused by her question. "BPD did, but Homicide?" He shook his head again. "They were never here. Why would they be?"

"It never occurred to anyone conducting the investigation that the victims might have been targeted?"

"Did it occur to anyone? Yes. Did it lead anywhere? No, absolutely not." Cleese paused long enough to pass his gaze from Loftus to Brixton and back again. "The FBI looked into the possibility and then dismissed it because it went nowhere."

"But the seven victims did have classes together," Brixton reminded him.

"One class," Cleese corrected. "And that was physical education, with fifty more of their classmates. And before you ask the question, the answer's yes: the other forty-three were all interviewed before that part of the investigation was closed."

"You think the investigation missed something?" Brixton posed.

"I'm sure it did."

"And that's why we're here," Loftus jumped in. "To figure out what it was they missed. Two sets of fresh eyes and ears."

"You want to speak to the other kids in that physical education class again?"

"No," said Brixton. "We want to speak to the families of the victims."

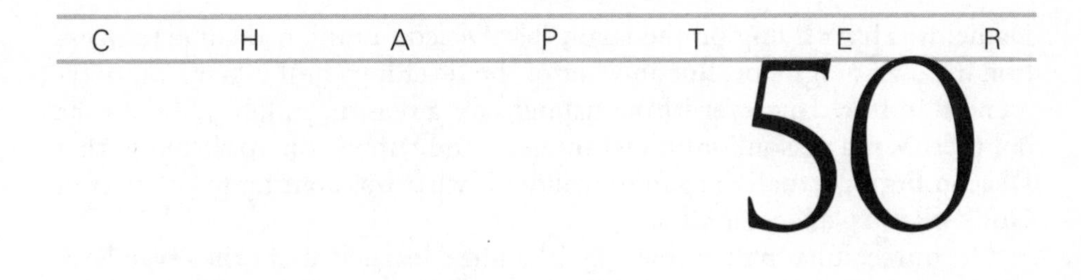

CHAPTER 50

OLDTOWN, MARYLAND

Daniel wasn't in his room when Deacon Frank got home. He had somehow had a feeling about what he was going to see when he unlocked the boy's door, a general sense of unease that felt like someone was dragging a nail head down his spine.

The boy had left the window open behind him, after he climbed out and shinnied down a nearby tree. No easy task to manage. He must have grabbed hold of the gutter in order to hoist himself from the window and onto a branch big enough to support his weight, risking a thirty-foot fall in the process.

The sight of that open window filled Deacon Frank with an immediate sense of dread; his initial fear was that Daniel had up and run away. But he took considerable comfort in the fact that his son had nowhere else to go except back to his mother, which would be a nonstarter and result only in the boy's prompt return. A quick check of the boy's closet and drawers revealed he hadn't packed anything, and the last bit of reassurance Deacon Frank needed was the sight of Daniel's iPhone on his night table. What teenage boy goes anywhere without his phone?

Deacon Frank had a pretty good idea where the boy had gone. He stopped to grab something from his own suite of rooms on the second floor before heading back outside. He found Daniel, as expected, sitting on the bank of the pond that filled several acres of the property, serving as a retention pool to catch runoff from the worst of the storms to hit the area and as a source of water for his livestock. The boy was tossing rocks, watching one dapple the water before repeating the process with the next. He'd worn only baggy jeans in the shape of Hefty bags for a while, and then skinny ones that clung to his skin like paint. Today's were somewhere in the middle. Deacon Frank was glad to see him out of the sweatpants he'd spent the last month in.

After he'd split from the boy's mother, she'd moved Daniel in with her at the penthouse apartment she'd purchased by forging Deacon Frank's signature on the mortgage papers. But Deacon Frank got the last laugh, after threatening to press charges if she fought him for sole custody. It wasn't that he wanted to raise Daniel himself so much as that he detested losing of any kind. It was maybe a week after the divorce had been finalized, when

Daniel was back living on the farm, that Deacon Frank had come to question his own judgment. But another of the teachings he'd taken from Reverend Rand was that everything happens for a reason, and, boy, did it turn out there was a reason for him winning custody of his son, to the point that Deacon Frank actually began to wonder if what was coming wasn't part of God's divine plan, after all.

Of course, it hadn't felt that way when he'd learned about the seven boys who were poisoned to death at the Baltimore charter high school that his wife had insisted Daniel attend because she resented people of privilege even more than she hated them—never bothering to realize that she'd become one. Deacon Frank remembered the frantic email that had come in from the school's principal, pretty much figuring out exactly what had transpired as soon as he read it. To his credit, when confronted, Daniel had owned up to what he'd done. Deacon Frank had no choice but to punish the boy, lest he think his actions were justified, even though, upon further reflection, they were. Men who take shit end up eating it, his daddy was fond of saying, and Deacon Frank was the living embodiment of that, having taken so much shit from Reverend Rand that the taste still hung in his mouth.

Deacon Frank had spent his life trying to avoid becoming his father, and look where that had gotten him. He never should have taken a belt to the boy, he had become just another bully, had pushed the boy to murder. It felt like his own father had possessed him in those moments, dictating his actions, as if to remind Deacon Frank that "dead and gone" didn't mean gone at all. Wanting to get the last laugh.

Deacon Frank had tried to integrate the boy into his world, just as Reverend Rand had brought Deacon Frank into his. He'd even enjoyed toting Daniel to meetings when he was a baby, bouncing the boy about on his knee while he and the others discussed plans for an America that would fit their dreams, not those of the raucous, rancorous, despicable lot that had risen up and stolen the country right out from under them. He was sick and tired of the protests, this or that life mattering more than others, people who claimed righteous indignation at the treatment of their fellow man just to give them an excuse to bellow into a bullhorn while wearing a shirt with a catchy slogan.

When Daniel was a toddler, Deacon Frank would sit on the plank stairs in the grungy basement, where the principals of the Movement met amid must, mildew, and the stench of stale sweat that hung in the air like a cloud. When Daniel hit elementary school, Deacon Frank had sent him to a special summer camp for children of the Movement, where the order of the day wasn't baseball or arts and crafts but guns and survival training. Daniel had washed out badly. Couldn't shoot for a lick and once set himself on fire while trying to spark some twigs into flame—with some lighter fluid secretly added to the mix.

The boy had been an embarrassment to him ever since. If Daniel had been delivered by Amazon instead of the stork, Deacon Frank would have boxed him back up and slapped the return label in place. And yet, in insane counterpoint, murdering seven of his classmates had actually served to bring the boy into his good graces, made Deacon Frank realize the depth of the boy's capacity to strike back, to lash out, to refuse to remain the victim, a human punching bag. The apple, indeed, didn't fall far from the tree, and for the first time he could remember, he found himself proud that Daniel was his son.

Out by the pond, Daniel heard him coming and cocked his gaze backward, his thin, knobby shoulders stiffening before he turned back to the water. Not acknowledging his father at all when Deacon Frank took a seat on the bank of the pond next to him and shoveled some more stones Daniel's way to restock his dwindling pile. The angle prevented the boy from seeing what Deacon Frank had lifted from a lockbox in one of the drawers in his suite, and which now was tucked low along his far hip.

"You're pissed at me," Deacon Frank started, letting the words find themselves. "I get that, and I don't blame you."

Daniel was wearing a baggy white T-shirt, thin enough for Deacon Frank to spot the contours of the welts the belt lashes had left the other day. Deacon Frank had made sure to sit an arm's length away, so his son wouldn't need to fear he was about to be beaten again.

"Sometimes I get carried away, son. Sometimes I let my temper get the better of me, same way my own daddy let it get the better of him."

He could see his son snicker at the cliché, maybe believing it was too convenient to be true. Deacon Frank decided it was time.

With that, he ducked a hand toward his far hip and eased the Springfield Model 1911 .45-caliber pistol from his belt, laid it on the ridge of grass between him and his son.

Daniel regarded it, eyes gaping before they moved to his father questioningly.

"This was my daddy's pistol, and his daddy's before him. Reverend Rand had issues, all right, and when he beat me, it wasn't about making it so I'd do better. It was because he enjoyed it. He beat me because he could, because where else was I going to go, and my weakness made him feel strong."

Daniel was half looking at him, and Deacon Frank made sure the boy heard him take a deep breath.

"I made a mistake the other day, son. I had a lapse. That's what happens when I lose my temper, this lapse where I turn into my father. He never beat me again after he gave me this gun, maybe 'cause he figured I'd use it on him if he did. But I was in my twenties by then, and he'd given up on the belt by then anyway."

Daniel let his eyes wander back to the black steel of the old pistol, then met his father's gaze fully for the first time since Deacon Frank had sat down next to him.

"I didn't bring it out here to pass it along today, son. I brought it out here to tell you I once killed a man with it."

The boy's gaze locked with Deacon Frank's.

"I'm telling you something I've never told another soul, not even one. It wasn't self-defense, just something that had to be done. It had to be done and I did it, but I haven't fired that gun since, and I haven't had anything I've done claw at me the way killing that man did—until I took the belt to you the other day. I think it was the Reverend Rand. It felt like he was inside me, guiding my hand, but it was me who pulled the trigger, of my own volition. But he was in my head the whole time and I hated myself for it. I thought the shooting would end all that, but instead it—"

Deacon Frank cut himself off, about to reveal too much to his own son, who was suddenly looking at him wide-eyed, hanging on his every word for the first time, maybe, since he'd read Daniel biblical bedtime tales from a series called Read Aloud Bible Stories.

"I'm telling you this," he resumed, starting on a different track, "because I don't want you to hate me the way I hated my father. That's why I'm telling you something I've never told another soul. And now I need you to do the same for me, man to man."

The boy looked at him like he didn't know what to make of that, listening to words that didn't seem right, coming out of his father's mouth. Deacon Frank thought he might have nodded. He wasn't sure, but at least Daniel hadn't turned away.

"We need to talk about those kids from your school," he said to his son. "You need to tell me how you did it."

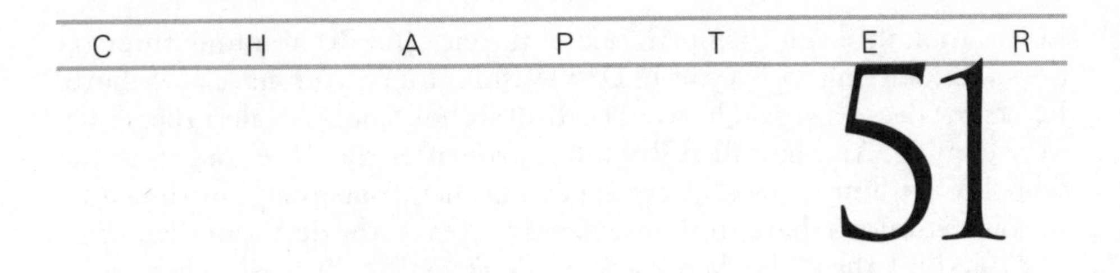

CHAPTER 51

BALTIMORE, MARYLAND

We want to speak to the families of the victims.

"Sorry I sprang that upon you," Brixton said to Kelly Loftus outside the Baltimore Mulighet High School, as they walked back to his car.

"I was already thinking the same thing. Once a cop, always a cop, as they say."

"You still are a cop, Kelly."

"I'm waiting for a call from the Capitol Police informing me I've been suspended."

"I'm talking about up here," Brixton said, tapping his head. "Same thing with me, though it's been a while since I was involved in a traditional investigation."

"You call this traditional?"

Brixton nodded. "Compared to what I did for SITQUAL and have been doing since, in the private sector. Standard interviewing, in the hope of finding what everyone else missed."

"A lot of high-level Washington creds included in that 'everyone else,' Brixton."

"The fix was in on this," he told her. "You heard Mac say there still isn't a definitive answer on whether the same toxin that poisoned Alexandra killed those seven kids."

"That doesn't sound possible."

"Because it isn't. What is possible is that truth is being buried by the same parties who don't want the toxin identified."

"I didn't deal with a lot of conspiracies as a homicide detective," Loftus told him.

"I have. And just because you can't see them doesn't mean they're not there."

She thought for a moment, looking up and down when they reached Brixton's car. "You really think the FBI and everyone else looking into the death of these seven kids *missed* something?"

"I'm sure of it."

Upon learning that one of the seven families that had lost a son to the poisoning had left the area, Brixton and Loftus divvied up the families of the remaining six victims, three each, divided by location clusters.

Loftus took three on the north side of the city and Brixton took three on the south, starting with a pair in Fort Washington, a working-class suburb. Jefferson Cleese had said he would call all six households to alert them they were coming. And he called Brixton shortly after they'd set out from the school to let him know all were expecting them, apparently intrigued by the opportunity to have fresh investigative eyes on the deaths of their sons.

"You think these kids were targeted, don't you?" Loftus asked him, as he drove to her apartment so she could pick up her car. "You don't think there was anything accidental about this at all."

"No more than there was with Mac's daughter."

"Why?"

"Throw seven stones up into the air and they're going to almost surely land on a relatively equal mix of males and females."

"So the fact that the victims were all male . . ."

"They were targeted."

"And you don't think our investigative predecessors wouldn't have considered that?" Loftus challenged.

"They may not be as jaded as I am, seeing conspiracies everywhere because I know they're there."

"Speaking of jaded, what about the other piece of this, Brixton?"

"Senator Byron Fitch?"

Loftus nodded.

"Alexandra Parks was poisoned twenty-four hours after reaching out to his office," Brixton reminded. "Following up on whatever Rappaport told her."

"Of course," Loftus noted, "we can't be sure that what your friend's daughter had contacted Fitch about had anything to do with the poisoning deaths."

"Don't forget that, according to what we saw in that video feed assemblage, Fitch was Rappaport's intended target."

Loftus sighed. "And he ended up killing eight more kids in the process."

"Now we need to find out why."

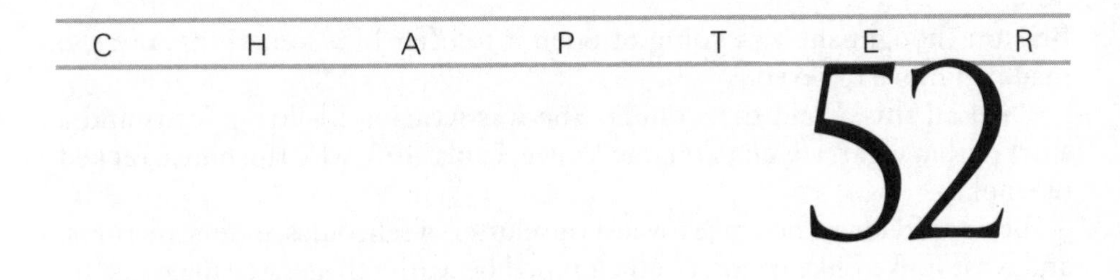

BALTIMORE, MARYLAND

Brixton dropped Kelly Loftus off at her apartment and headed to the first name on his list: a family named Jamison who lived in northwest Baltimore. He hated going under false pretenses into a household that was still grieving over the tragic loss of a child. But he took solace in the fact that his lie would be well worth it if he was able to find the truth that would provide all of these families with closure. Not much of a rationale for the deception he was about to commit, but it made for his only justification.

The family Brixton would be seeing first had lost their son Cal, the first of the seven victims to die of the poisoning in that twenty-four period. What he had no idea about was when the kids had actually been exposed. A day before? A week? A month?

"I'm Robert Brixton, Mrs. Jamison," he greeted the late Cal's mother, Emma, when she opened the door.

It was a modest two-story home badly in need of a paint job, the lawn and landscaping both with a do-it-yourself quality. Typical of this working-class neighborhood; any student attending Mulighet would likely be on scholarship, given the low-five-figure tuition.

"You're EPA, right? The school principal told me to expect you and a woman."

Brixton flashed the ID Mac had provided. "My partner's currently interviewing another family."

Emma Jamison still hadn't opened the door to invite him in. "So you got some answers for me?"

"Questions first."

The door closed a slight bit. "Like the others. Where'd that get them?"

"Is your husband home, Mrs. Jamison?"

"Yup—at the motel he now calls that. Losing your son isn't good for holding on to a marriage that was already falling apart."

She finally opened the door.

"We can talk in the kitchen, Mr. . . ."

"Brixton, ma'am."

He followed her to the kitchen, hovering near a table with a red and white checkerboard tablecloth, while Emma Jamison lingered by the refrigerator.

Brixton thought she was going to open it to offer him something, but she made no move to do so.

"See all this?" said the woman. She was wearing ill-fitting jeans and a shirt with a cigarette burn on one sleeve, explaining why the house reeked of smoke.

Brixton followed her gaze toward the clutter of schedules, letters, pictures, and what looked like coupons, all clumped beneath refrigerator magnets.

"This is all Cal, kind of like a final collage to remember him by," the woman continued. "I'm never going to touch it, not a damn thing. If the fridge breaks, I'll keep the door. If I move, I'll take the whole fridge with me. See this?" she said, pointing to a postcard-size coupon for what must have been a local coffee shop. "This place is crazy popular with the kids. They all go there. But Cal told me I could have this coupon because he doesn't drink coffee. It was the last thing he ever stuck to the fridge, the final piece of his collage."

Brixton gave up waiting for Emma Jamison to invite him to sit down. He took out his phone.

"Do you mind if I record this conversation, Mrs. Jamison?"

"Knock yourself out."

Brixton held the phone between them. "I apologize for the intrusion."

"You got questions for me, go ahead."

"Did you notice anything unusual about Cal in the day or so prior to his being rushed to the hospital?"

The woman shook her head. "Business as usual."

"Did he make mention of anything unusual that had happened, out of the ordinary?"

She frowned. "He's a teenage boy. What do you think?"

"So, nothing?"

"Nothing."

"He didn't say anything about eating or drinking something different? Unusual again, maybe?"

Jamison almost smiled. "I'm a lousy cook, Mr. Brixton. Anything he could eat outside this house was considered a step in the right direction. But unusual?" She shook her head. "No."

Brixton looked toward the refrigerator, the last weeks of a boy's life arranged in scattered fashion before him.

"These are the same questions I've already answered like a hundred times," his mother said. "Ask me something different. Better yet, *tell* me something different."

"Did Cal have any enemies, Mrs. Jamison?"

"Come again?"

"Anyone who may have wanted to do him harm."

"As in poison him to death?" she shot back, shaking her head.

Brixton let his statement stand.

"You, the EPA, think he was *murdered*? Well, that's a new one."

"That's why I raised it. Reading the reports of the other authorities you spoke with, the only time all seven victims were together in the general time frame was gym class the day before they were all rushed to the hospital. Is that your understanding?"

"Since you read those reports, you already know it is."

"So, to the best of your knowledge, that is in fact the case?"

"Well . . ."

Brixton waited for Emma Jamison to continue.

"He stopped at the same coffee place that coupon on the fridge came from, after school. I assumed that's where he got it. I guess the other kids could all have been there."

"You told this to the other investigators, Mrs. Jamison?"

"I may have. There were so many of you, I honestly don't remember what I told to who, or how many times. Maybe, maybe not."

"Cal had no visitors the afternoon or evening before he was hospitalized?"

"It was Friday night. He was supposed to go to the mall, the movies, but then he got sick, ended up in the hospital. Two hours later he was dead." Emma Jamison took a step toward Brixton. "You think somebody murdered my son. That's why you're here, isn't it?"

Brixton let his face go somber with the grimness he was feeling at invading this woman's space, at giving her false hope. "It's the one factor that hasn't been explored yet."

Jamison shook her head, her expression tilted in derision aimed at him. "So who kills seven high school boys, Mr. Brixton? You got some notion as to that?"

Brixton's gaze wandered back to the refrigerator door, to the last of a boy's life, held up by magnets. "Not yet."

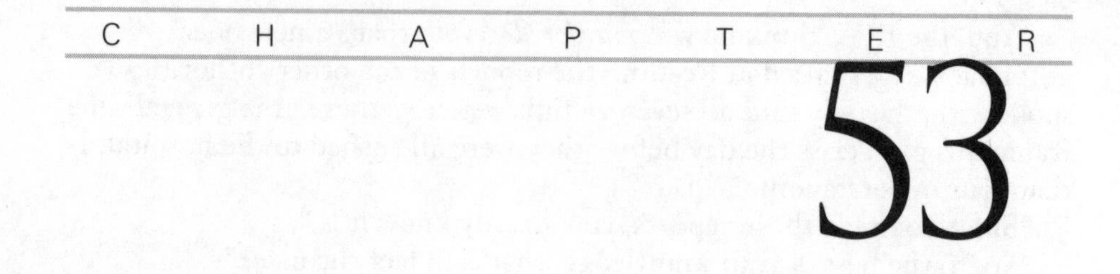

CHAPTER 53

OLDTOWN, MARYLAND

Daniel looked away again, maybe pretending Deacon Frank wasn't there watching his chest expand and contract rapidly in concert with his suddenly shallow breathing. As quickly as he'd had his son, he'd lost him again. First time he'd raised the matter again since the original conversation in which he'd confronted Daniel.

"You never told Mom, did you?" the boy asked, his voice cracking slightly.

"She doesn't suspect a thing. The only reason I got the notion and made you own up was because of the way those boys died."

Deacon Frank started to stretch his hand out to touch his son's shoulder, then pulled it back.

"Tell me about those boys, son," Deacon Frank said, dialing it back a notch. "How they treated you, why you did this."

Daniel took in a big breath and let it out slowly. "Assholes. Every day—it never let up. The school claimed to have a no-tolerance policy toward bullying. What a crock of shit."

Deacon Frank nodded, trying to recall another time when his son had used such an expletive in his presence. All the more reason to let it go today instead of smacking him upside the head the way the Reverend Rand Atlas Wilhyte would have done. He flinched, just thinking about the jarring *thwack* of impact.

"They hurt you," Deacon Frank said, in what had started out as a question.

"Not physically, not much anyway. They knew what to avoid. It was always open to interpretation—that's what the vice principal said."

"You reported this?"

It was Daniel's turn to nod. "For all the good it did."

"But not to me. You didn't say anything to me."

Daniel looked as if he was about to laugh. "What would you have done, Dad?"

"I suppose I would've told you to handle it by yourself. Be a man, all that sort of shit."

And just as he'd wondered whether his son had ever used that word before in his presence, he knew it was the first time he had used it in the presence of his son.

"And I did," the boy said simply. "I didn't have a choice anymore, it had gotten so bad."

Deacon Frank looked at the young man seated on the grass next to him and realized he didn't have even an inkling about who he was. This was what despising his own father had come to, full circle: he had become Reverend Rand. Or maybe he'd always been.

"You took matters into your own hands," Deacon Frank said to his son.

A nod.

"Just like I did with this forty-five here."

Another nod.

"You didn't have a choice either, like you said. You'd burned through all your options."

"I knew you'd tell me to handle it by myself, so that's what I did. Handled it."

"You clipped some of the poison when I brought you to see the lab. That's what happened, wasn't it?"

The boy was looking out at the pond again, fiddling with another rock from the pile he'd made, but not picking it up. He nodded without meeting his father's gaze.

"Yeah," he said, barely loud enough to hear.

Deacon Frank looked over at his son again, recalling the day he'd brought Daniel to his secret lab the way other dads tote their kids off to baseball games, never imagining the chain of events that visit would set off. He remembered the questions the boy had posed to Leonard Cutlow, who was clearly impressed by the boy's intellect and amazed by his grasp of chemistry. It was like they were having a conversation in an entirely different language, and Deacon Frank had been struck by a glimmer of pride in his son for the first time since he started walking and talking. He'd never suspected a goddamn thing.

"You know what makes a man strong, son?" he asked Daniel.

The boy cast him a sidelong glance and shook his head.

"Knowing he's got his enemies beat. Knowing no matter what they got going for them, he's got the upper hand. You know what makes a man smart?"

The same sidelong glance, accompanied by another shake of the head.

"Not using that upper hand until all other available options have been exhausted. Having the choice is what gives you the power. Exercising that choice risks losing it. How much you clip from the lab, son?" he asked without missing a beat, hoping to catch Daniel off guard.

"A vial. There wasn't much in it. I didn't think anyone would miss it."

In point of fact, nobody had, but Deacon Frank didn't want to dwell on that.

"You knew you had those boys beat at that point. And when they pushed you right up to the edge, you pushed back. I get that. What I don't get is—"

"Did you like it?" Daniel interrupted.

"Like what?"

"Killing that man. Did you enjoy it?"

Deacon Frank never considered anything but the truth for an answer. "You bet I did, all things considered. The man had it coming to him."

"Those kids did, too. I knew they were going to die. I knew I was killing them, and I was . . . I was . . ."

"Say it, son."

"Excited! I was excited! I only wish . . ."

"What?" Deacon Frank prompted when Daniel's voice trailed off again.

"Nothing," the boy said, under his breath.

"You ever feel bad about what you did? You know, regrets?"

"You have to be right there to shoot a person. You get to watch him die."

"True enough, I suppose."

Daniel looked as if his father had made his point for him. "That's what I regret—not getting to watch them die. I'll bet it was bad."

"There's no good way to die, son."

"Some are worse than others, and this was bad. They must've suffered, Dad. I'm glad they suffered."

Deacon Frank felt something like a heat flash rising from his core, a warm blanket that coated his insides with a feeling he couldn't identify because he'd never experienced it before, at least not in a very long time, when he'd been a different man. When Daniel took his first step, uttered his first word.

He realized he really was *proud* of his son, truly proud of him for killing the boys who'd tormented and tortured him, who'd turned his life into a living hell. Deacon Frank reached all the way out this time and squeezed Daniel's shoulder in as big a display of fatherly affection as he'd ever managed, getting to the point he'd come out here to make.

"And now, thanks to you, plenty more are going to suffer too, son."

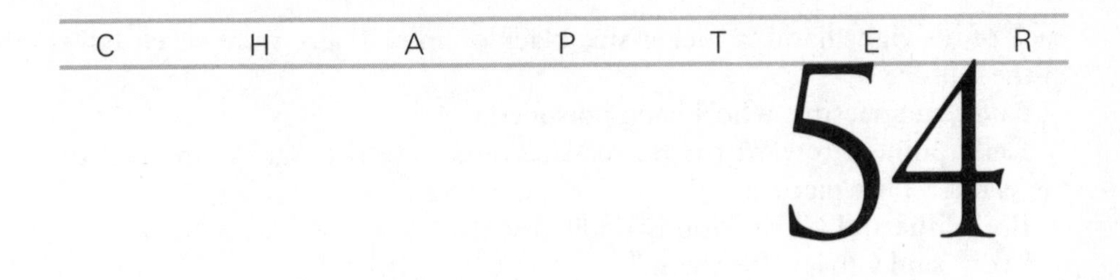

CHAPTER 54

RUXTON, MARYLAND

Kelly felt back in her element, almost as if she'd never left. The first home she visited was in the tony suburb of Ruxton, north of Baltimore, where she'd meet Chris and Julia Moody. They'd turned their living room into a shrine for their late son, Jared, to which Kelly had a front-row seat from an armchair facing the couple seated on the couch, holding hands.

Pictures of their son dominated the room—blown up, mounted, and displayed on easels. Residue of the memorial service and funeral. What to do with all the oversize impressions of the boy they had lost, exaggerating him in death? Kelly found herself staring at Jared wherever she turned, like he was a fourth person in the room.

"There's really nothing more we can say," said Chris.

"If you've read the reports, you've already seen it all," Julia added.

"We have reason to believe the original investigators missed something," Kelly told them.

"Why?"

"Because we've been unable to isolate the source of the poisoning. Five weeks and still nothing." She hesitated, met both their gazes in turn. "You called the agency repeatedly for three weeks. Then you stopped. . . . Nothing for the last two weeks."

"We gave up," Julia conceded.

Chris's turn. "It felt like we had to move on."

Kelly's eyes went to one of the movie-size posters hanging on the wall directly over the couple, showing fifteen-year-old Jared in football regalia after scoring a touchdown. So much for moving on.

"When was that taken?" she asked.

"Last fall, about a year ago now." From Chris.

"State championship." From Julia.

"*District* championship," her husband corrected.

Julia shot him a look. "What's it matter now?"

Kelly was focused on the back of the boy's hand, which was smooth and unmarred in the football picture. Then she remembered something she'd spotted on the most recent picture of him, which had been taken on a camping trip with friends the weekend before he died. In that second photo, she had noticed what she'd originally taken to be a birthmark on the back of his right hand, a nickel-size black dimple. There were seven boys in the picture.

And seven victims who'd been poisoned.

Kelly pointed toward the poster-size rendering that sat on an easel to her right. "That picture . . ."

Both Julia and Chris Moody nodded sadly.

"Yes," said Chris. "It's them."

"Seven of the eight who were inseparable since they were little boys," added Julia.

Chris squeezed his wife's hand. "Friends forever."

"Would you mind if I gave it a closer look?"

"Please," the Moodys said in unison.

Kelly rose and moved to the picture, having spotted what looked like shadows. The picture showed the seven boys with arms draped over one another's shoulders. Smiling, happy, not a care in the world, with no idea what the next week would bring. The backs of five of their right hands were plainly visible, including Jared Moody's.

And all of them had an identical black nickel-size dimple.

"You mentioned an eighth friend," Kelly said, without turning back toward Chris and Julia Moody, unable to lift her eyes from the blowup.

"Yes," she heard Julia say. "He was the one who took the picture, the only one of them who's still alive."

The survivor's right hand wasn't visible in the picture, leaving Kelly unable to discern whether he had a similar mark, which clearly was not a dimple. Both Chris and Julia professed that they had never noticed the mark on their son before—nor, they claimed, had any of the other investigative bodies with whom they'd spoken previously. Julia gave Kelly the phone number of the only boy in the camping group who'd survived, and printed out an eight-by-eleven version of the enlarged picture, which had been lifted off Facebook or Instagram.

Kelly had an idea she was onto something, but she had no idea what. The black dimple-like marks commanded all of her attention during the drive to the next home on her list, where she found no one home—at least, no one answering the door. She thought she heard sounds inside, glimpsed what could have been a flicker of movement through a bay window to the right of the door. When further ringing of the doorbell produced no results, though, she headed back to her car, stealing glances toward the house to see if anyone was peeking out a window or peeling back the sheer curtain that covered a vertical pane of glass to the right of the door, above a mail slot.

The next victim on her list, Lloyd Betts Jr., was the lone African American in the group and had lived in a sprawling home in a neighborhood comprised of mini-manses, as they were known. In stark contrast to the Moody home, there were only a few pictures of Lloyd in evidence, one a posed solo shot of him in his football uniform, kneeling, with his right hand resting on his knee. Kelly looked closer.

No black dimple-like mark.

She compared that with the printout Julia Moody had made for her, which she showed to the boy's parents, Victor and Lacy.

"No idea," said Victor.

"I never even noticed," Lacy followed.

"Did anyone else notice, any of the other investigators you spoke with?"

They shook their heads.

"You think . . ." Victor started, leaving it there.

"I don't know," Kelly answered, honestly. "Maybe."

The couple looked at each other, eyes widening, something that passed for hope passing between them.

"What do you know about the one boy who survived?"

"He came back from the camping trip sick," Lacy told her. "He missed school, wasn't there all week, including the day they . . ."

Kelly locked in on that. A boy who had returned from the camping trip and survived. Maybe because he hadn't been in school.

"We thought this might help you," Victor was saying.

He was holding a shoebox in his outstretched hands. Kelly could see that the top read "LLOYD'S STUFF." She took it from his grasp, feeling the rough patches of the duct tape that was holding the cardboard edges together.

"There's a dozen more of these in his closet," Lacy told her. "This is the most recent, his latest stuff. The other people who came weren't interested in it. We thought you might be, this fresh look you're giving things and all."

Kelly placed the box in her lap, intending to take it with her to placate the woman, as much as anything else. Nonetheless, she was intrigued.

"So no one else has inspected the contents?" she wondered.

Victor shook his head. "Like my wife said, they didn't even open it."

"You'll bring it back, though, right?" Lacy asked her, in what sounded like a plea.

"Of course," Kelly said, her thinking still fixed on those black dimple-like marks from the camping trip photo.

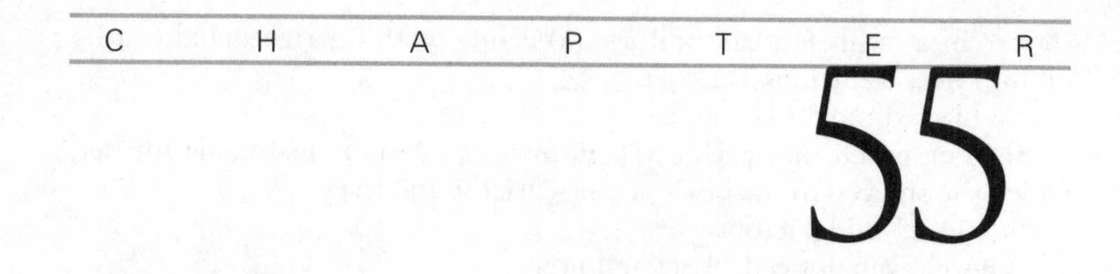

CHAPTER 55

OLDTOWN, MARYLAND

Daniel was looking at Deacon Frank with his head tilted slightly to the side, unsure of where this was going.

"You remember me telling you about how I came to be called 'Deacon' Frank, son? How I used to help my father out at his services?"

The boy nodded. "You collected the money."

"I wanted to help, be a part of things. A part of his life, his work. Now I want you to be a part of my life, my work."

Daniel didn't look away. He held Deacon Frank's gaze, looking as surprised as he was willing to reveal. Deacon Frank thought maybe he'd underestimated his son—the gumption it took to steal that vial from the lab, risking his father's wrath, the way Deacon Frank had risked Reverend Rand's that time he clipped three twenties from the collection basket to buy some music tapes he didn't want his father to know about.

Thirty years ago.

He was known as Deacon Frank even back then, and on this particular Saturday he was lost between the headphones of his Walkman, the contents of one of those just-purchased cassette tapes strumming in his head. His father was waiting in his room in the big house—the family home, when they weren't on the road—sitting on the edge of Deacon Frank's bed with that look in his eyes.

Deacon Frank had known that look from the time he was eight years old, seated off to the side at the first service where Reverend Rand had let him participate. It was the look he flashed when a stray dog pranced into the tent jam-packed with the faithful, the dog distracting row after row of his flock, stealing their attention from him, which likely had the effect of making them not dip their hands as deep into their pockets, handbags, or billfolds as they normally would. Deacon Frank spotted the mangy mutt from his perch near the front but forced his eyes off it, out of fear of roiling his father on the first day he'd gained the appointed duty of manning the collection basket at one of the tent's exit flaps.

The Reverend Rand Atlas Wilhyte's eyes held that look when the dog made its way to the makeshift altar. Deacon Frank watched his father force a hand downward to pet the mutt—and be greeted with a growl.

"Must be a nonbeliever," he quipped into the microphone, his smile looking like part of a Halloween costume somebody had stitched onto his face.

The dog hung around overnight, ready to enjoy the next day's repeat performance. Deacon Frank played fetch with it for a time and fed the dog some scraps of food pocketed (literally) at the free congregant breakfast the Reverend Rand hosted prior to the next day's service. The boy was even working up the courage to ask his father if they could keep him.

Then he saw one of the men who set up the traveling tent and chairs, and then doubled as service security, walking with a heavily weighted trash bag slung over his shoulder. He knew what was inside even before he caught the gleam in his father's eyes—the exact opposite of the glare he now fixed on his teenage son from the boy's bedside.

Deacon Frank plucked the headphones from his head and watched his father stand up, seeming to block all the light out as he loomed over him.

"Something you want to tell me, son?"

The words wouldn't come at first, and when they finally did, Deacon Frank still had to pry them from his mouth.

"I'm sorry, Dad."

"Sorry for what?"

Deacon Frank glimpsed his father stealing a glance at the Walkman clipped to his belt and knew in that moment there was no sense lying. Reverend Rand already knew the answer to the question he'd just posed, just like he always did.

"I was going to pay it back," the boy managed, unable to push the whine from his voice.

"Pay *what* back?"

"The money."

"What money?"

"The money I stole."

"From where?"

"The collection basket."

"The Lord's money, then. You stole from the Lord."

Deacon Frank swallowed hard. "I was going to pay it back, I swear."

"You swear to God?"

A nod.

"Why should He believe you're not lying to Him, after you stole from Him?"

Reverend Rand took a single step forward, still seeming to block all of the room's light. "Why do you test me like this?"

"Dad?"

His father grabbed his arm and dragged him into the bathroom. He'd never felt so light, so weak, his father's strength making him feel like he weighed all of ten pounds. His father's strength was born of years lifting tent poles and hoisting them into place, since before Deacon Frank was born.

Reverend Rand closed the door behind them and turned on the hot water. "If I were a good father, I'd take an ax to your hand to teach you a proper lesson."

Satisfied the water was hot enough, a light mist of steam rising from where it pooled slightly over the drain, his father lifted the rod that fastened the sink stopper in place.

The water rose rapidly, bleeding more of that steam.

"The belt is what you get when you cross me. But crossing God? That deserves a more potent punishment, son."

Father and son standing there together, watching the steaming water rise.

"Dad . . ."

"If I was worth my salt, I'd take that ax to you instead."

The mirror was misting up now, hiding the view of the glinting madness in Reverend Rand's eyes and the terror bursting in Deacon Frank's.

"I won't do it again, Dad, I swear!"

"You swear to God?"

"I swear to God!"

"Except He don't believe you, boy."

And with that, Reverend Rand Atlas Wilhyte plunged his son's hand into the water.

Deacon Frank looked at his hand, half expecting it to be still puckered and blistering, even though the pain was long gone and plastic surgery had erased all but a small portion of the scarring. He didn't remember how long his father had held it under the scalding water; maybe a second, maybe a minute. He remembered thrashing, the water kicked up and spattering both of them. He could feel its scorching heat through his shirt, the pain so bad it felt like he'd forgotten how to breathe.

Deacon Frank's son, all joints and skin, with no muscle to speak of, was about the same size he'd been that day. Looking at him now, Daniel looked even frailer, his hips so narrow that even a belt barely held his pants up.

"Your grandfather, who you never had the fortune to meet, taught me that you never ask a question you don't already know the answer to. Because what you don't know makes you weak, and you never want to appear weak. It didn't matter to him what he didn't know, since he figured he knew enough. In his mind, being strong was always better than being smart, because the strong people brought in the money so the smart ones could figure out what to do with it."

Daniel was still looking at him, though it was clear from his gaze he wasn't grasping the point of Deacon Frank's words.

"Thing being, your grandfather was wrong," Deacon Frank resumed. "Because being strong allows you to be smart enough to know what you don't know. That was your grandfather's greatest sin: he thought he knew everything, at least everything he needed to. I find myself wondering a lot what his final thoughts were, after he'd been shot and knew he was dying."

"I read somewhere it was a robbery, some asshole who thought he was carrying all that cash on him," Daniel said.

His son's words made Deacon Frank realize this was the first time they'd ever discussed the boy's grandfather, beyond the mention of his name.

"Yeah, that was it," he said.

Daniel's doe eyes widened. He suddenly looked older, a kid on the cusp of adulthood, instead of a little boy.

"I want to help you, Dad."

Deacon Frank laid his hand on the boy's shoulder and let it stay there this time. "I'm glad, son."

"We'll be doing good, setting the world right."

"That's the plan, starting with you telling me a story, just like I used to tell you stories from the side of your bed when you were a little boy."

"Dad?"

"The story of how exactly you killed those kids from your school."

CHAPTER 56

BALTIMORE, MARYLAND

Mr. Brixton?"

Jack Frankel sat in a front porch swing next to his husband, Vic, adjacent to Brixton's matching wooden chair. They had been together for fifteen years and were among the first gay couples to marry when it became legal in Maryland on January 1, 2013. A surrogate had carried their son, Sam, into the world fifteen years earlier, and he was the oldest of the victims to be claimed by the poisoning that struck Baltimore Mulighet High School. He had repeated his freshman year following a transfer that both his fathers had called a group decision.

The men weren't of a mind to dwell on their son's death, wanting instead to tell Brixton about his life. But Brixton was having trouble paying attention, not because of lack of interest or time but because of how their words brought both his daughter Janet and his grandson, Max, to mind, one lost to the same kind of senseless, mindless violence that had nearly claimed the other three days ago. Brixton had suffered through post-traumatic stress disorder enough over the years to recognize the symptoms popping up again—a mild case, as such things went, but he knew that with PTSD there was really no such thing as a "mild case."

He found himself listless and only pretending to listen, every story out of either Jack's or Vic's mouth deepening the pain of the daughter he had lost and the grandson he almost had. For some reason, he felt the near loss of Max more than the actual loss of Janet. The passage of time was largely to blame there, but it was also a matter of how the deaths of these seven boys, who were about the same age as Max, magnified how close the shooter's bullets had come to killing him. He kept replaying in his mind, on a constant loop, the video compilation Jesus Arriaga had assembled. Up until now, he'd been able to suppress it when focusing on the investigation. For some reason, though, Jack and Vic Frankel's words about their own son merged his tortured psyche with the rational part of his thinking to the point where he couldn't focus on what the two men were saying.

Until he latched on to something Vic said, as the porch swing rocked back and forth, coughing out a slight creak at maddeningly regular intervals.

"... funny smell to it, that's what he said."

That jolted Brixton back alert upon the cushioned chair that matched the one on the swing. "I'm sorry, could you repeat that please?"

Vic looked annoyed by the need to, then ran a hand through his neat but thinning hair, which was set over a highly arched forehead that matched Jack's. "I was talking about football practice the Monday after the camping trip. The team had a bye that Saturday, then it was back to work on Monday. He said his uniform smelled funny."

"Just him?"

"The other kids noticed it too," Jack elaborated.

"Same kids as the camping trip?"

"Some, for sure. Maybe all, except the one who came back sick. You asked us to think of something we hadn't told the others who interviewed us."

"We didn't even think about the uniform thing at that point," Vic added.

"Did you call anyone to report what you'd remembered?"

Vic and Jack both shook their heads.

"It didn't seem important enough," Jack said.

Brixton found himself leaning forward, believing he might be onto something. "You wouldn't still have his uniform, would you?" he asked Sam's fathers.

They both shook their heads.

"Sorry," Jack said.

"Nothing to be sorry about," Brixton told them, rising from the chair. "I'm sure it's still at the school."

"Number thirteen," Vic told him. "Sam's favorite number."

"Mine, too."

The two men slid off the porch swing and stilled its rocking.

"You'll let us know?" Jack posed.

"Either way," Brixton said, more assuredly than he'd meant to.

They didn't have the uniform, which meant it would still be at school, perhaps in the boy's gym locker.

Brixton should have called it a day right then. But there was one more family on his list of three, and he didn't want to put off speaking with them until tomorrow.

Unfortunately, not only did they have nothing to contribute to the investigation but also he was of no mind to listen. He was more interested in speaking again with Baltimore Mulighet High School principal Jefferson Cleese and was waiting for Cleese to call him back to address the issue of those football uniforms. Good thing he was recording the conversation in Donna and Donald Nugent's den, because he certainly wouldn't be able to remember any of it.

He didn't remember ending the conversation with the Nugents or stopping the recording or saying his good-byes. One minute he was in their den and the next he was sitting in his car with his hands squeezing the steering wheel, until his phone rang. He recognized the number but didn't remember the owner.

"Hello?"

"Mr. Brixton, this is Jefferson Cleese. I got your message. What can I do for you?"

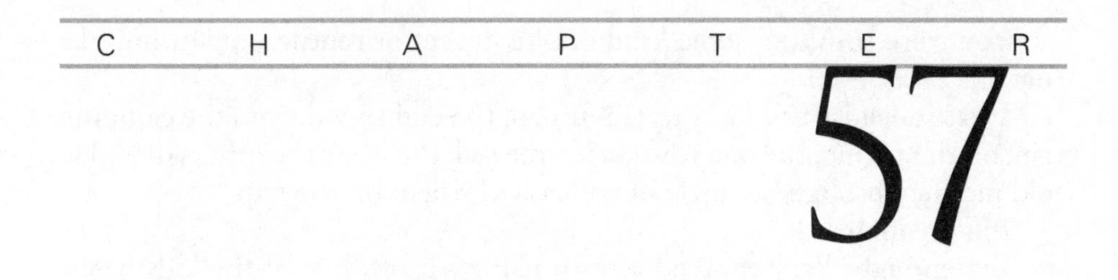

CHAPTER 57

BALTIMORE, MARYLAND

So, these football uniforms," Kelly Loftus prompted, from the other side of the table at the Cat's Eye Pub on Thames Street between South Broadway and South Ann Street.

Brixton looked about the club, which was among Baltimore's top live music venues, specializing in blues. "Tell me why we're meeting here again?"

Loftus tilted her frothy mug of beer, ale, or something in that family. "Because it's the only place in town that serves Paddington's on tap—that's the 'Cream of Manchester,' for the less educated."

He sipped his Diet Coke served in the same mug. "Count me among them."

"Come on, Brixton, live a little."

"I lived too much for a while. Kind of lost track of myself. And people don't come to places like this to find themselves, Loftus."

"Yeah? You may feel differently if we're still here when the music starts."

He checked his watch, found it was closing in on six o'clock, and he was a lot hungrier than he was thirsty. "Past my bedtime."

She'd brought a shoebox labeled "LLOYD'S STUFF" in with her and had been in the process of reviewing its contents when he joined her at the table. She left it sitting between them on the table, like a centerpiece. The silver duct tape looked shiny in the spill of the bar's overhead lighting.

"You know this city well, Loftus."

"I used to like it a lot more than I do now."

"This place, or Baltimore?"

"This place didn't destroy my career."

Brixton let the remark lie and took another sip from his Diet Coke.

"So this football uniform thing . . ." he heard Kelly Loftus continue.

"A dead end. The school principal didn't know what I was talking about, which gave me hope that there was a contamination issue or something, until the principal got back to me after speaking with the football coach. Turns out there was a problem with the dye on the team's practice jerseys. Unpleasant, but hardly deadly."

Loftus nodded knowingly, able to match Brixton's disappointment with her own. "Sounds like those marks on the back of the victims' hands when they came home from that camping trip."

"You were thinking some kind of bite, insect or reptile, something like that."

"I was indeed, until I got Kyle Nunzio, the eighth kid from the camping trip, on the phone, the one who was home sick the week the others died. He told me they brought a bottle of vodka with them on the trip."

"Big or small?"

"Big enough, Brixton. And after finishing it off, one of the kids broke out a cigar. The plan was to smoke it, but then they ended up burning the back of their right hands with it. You know, like a ritual."

"I've got a grandson about the same age, remember? So I kind of know about rites of passage."

"Any burn marks on the back of your hands?" Loftus asked him.

Brixton flashed them for her to see. "What about you?"

"Do tattoos count?"

"No."

"Good, because I wouldn't be able to show you mine, anyway."

Tonight's band was setting up on a stage that had been traveled by the best blues bands Baltimore had to offer, along with the occasional one with a national profile. A trio of balding guys with ponytails was lugging their own equipment in from a van parked out back. Brixton enjoyed watching one of them erecting a drum set in a way that reminded him of the Tinkertoys he played with as a boy.

He took another sip of his Diet Coke, treating it like the scotch he'd once favored. "So where does that leave us?"

Loftus shrugged. "Back at square one, but at least not needing to lie to any more grieving families."

"I take it you weren't crazy about that either."

Loftus took the top off the shoebox and rifled through it in cursory fashion. "Last thing that family had of their son, with stuff from right up until the last day he was alive. What was I thinking, taking it with me?"

"That you might find something important inside, Loftus."

"Well, I didn't. But at least I made sure to put the contents back exactly as they were."

"This kid—Lloyd—was he some kind of collector?"

"More like he was a hoarder. His parents told me there were a dozen more of these boxes in his closet, crammed with old report cards, tests, receipts. A lot of nothing, in other words."

"Not nothing to the kid."

"Like this," Loftus said, fishing out a laminated cardboard square about the size of a postcard, some kind of coupon.

Brixton did a double take. "Wait a minute . . ." he said. "I saw the same thing on the Jamison kid's refrigerator, under a magnet." He gave the coupon another look. It promised half off on the bearer's next beverage of any brand or size—like money in the pocket for a high school student. "Same exact thing."

Loftus regarded it again, as if seeing it for the first time. "It's a coupon, Brixton."

"It's a connection, at least between two of the boys. Don't be jealous because you didn't make it."

"Luck of the draw. And as I recall, you didn't make detective until you hung out your own shingle."

"Stick around and you may learn something."

"I was always taught to respect my elders."

"Ouch."

She looked around the Cat's Eye in dramatic fashion. "People at the other tables probably think I must be your daughter."

Brixton shook his head. "You're much too pretty for them to make that connection."

Loftus leaned back. "If I didn't know better, I'd say you were flirting."

"But you do know better. And if I wasn't engaged, I might be—if I wasn't an elder."

Loftus studied the coupon card again. "I know this place. Never been inside, but it's right down the street from the school."

"Let's call the other families. See if they remember their sons getting one of these, too."

It turned out only Donna and Donald Nugent—the last couple Brixton saw, and had almost forgotten already—distinctly remembered their son bringing the coupon home, because it was sticking out the top of his backpack.

"They remember when?" Loftus asked Brixton.

"The day before their son died."

There was a clanging from the stage area; the drummer had dropped one of his cymbals.

"That makes three of seven, Brixton," Loftus noted.

"Three that we know of."

Brixton already had Principal Cleese's phone number keyed up. He watched Loftus's reaction through the duration of their brief call.

"Cleese never gave permission for this coffee place to distribute coupons on school grounds," he reported, leaving the phone atop the table.

"Doesn't mean it didn't happen," Loftus noted, holding the card between them. "Or they could have gotten the coupons somewhere else."

Brixton pushed his chair backward and started to stand up. "Let's find out."

C H A P T E R

58

BALTIMORE, MARYLAND

Where'd you get this?" the manager of Common Ground Coffee, whose name tag read "Dave," asked them, when they arrived minutes before the nine o'clock closing time.

They faced him from the other side of the counter. The cardboard coupon was now in a plastic evidence sleeve.

"It's part of an active investigation," Brixton told him.

"Can I see your IDs again?"

Brixton and Loftus held their EPA ID wallets up closer and longer.

"You know, around here, you can buy any IDs you want."

"And I'm sure there's a ton of people out there looking to impersonate Environmental Protection Agency investigators."

"I'm just saying."

"Then say what we were asking you about," she told him, in full cop mode. "Unless you want us to give this establishment a once-over. Would shutting it down due to code violations be enough to establish our bona fides?"

Dave gave the coupon another look through the plastic. A second plastic evidence pouch contained the coupon they'd retrieved at the Jamison home, after the victim's mother reluctantly pried it off her refrigerator. Good thing Loftus had an ample supply of these pouches and sleeves left over from her days as a homicide detective, a number of which she'd never removed from her car. Force of habit.

"We don't do coupons very often," he told the two of them. "And when we do, they look nothing like this. They're almost all sent via email, with a bar code kids scan from their phones."

"So no distribution at Baltimore Mulighet High School," Loftus prompted him.

He handed her back the evidence pouch. "You want to reach high school kids, you do it on the Web. Hard copies are so yesterday."

"Like the Beatles song," Brixton noted.

Dave looked at him as if he had no idea what he was talking about. "Huh?

Jefferson Cleese's phone went straight to voicemail all six times Brixton tried it. They didn't have a home address for him, but Loftus was able to find it in a city database for which she still had the password. They drove over there, trying not to speculate on whether something, or someone, had stopped him from answering his phone.

When Cleese finally responded to Brixton's repeated ringing of the doorbell and banging on the door, they breathed easier. Cleese, in pajamas and a bathrobe, asked them in, closed the door, and listened to them explain, right there in the foyer of the modest home, what they'd learned and what they needed to do next.

"This is going to have to wait until tomorrow morning," he told them.

"It can't," said Loftus.

"It'll have to," Cleese reiterated. "Because another one of your inspection teams is giving the building a fresh once-over. Don't you people talk to each other?"

Cleese was already waiting outside the school when Brixton and Loftus got there early the next morning, well ahead of the coming inspection.

"I don't really understand what it is the two of you are looking for," he said, leading them into the building. "You never told me last night."

In the dimly lit lobby, Brixton and Loftus took turns explaining again their suspicions about the Common Ground Coffee coupons that hadn't been produced by Common Ground Coffee at all. Because at least three of the seven deceased sophomores nonetheless had such coupons in their possession, Brixton explained, they needed to ascertain whether that might be the missing link between the victims.

"The only explanation for how Kyle Nunzio survived is that he wasn't exposed," Brixton said in conclusion.

Cleese didn't look like he was getting it. "But exposed to *what*? I mean, that's been the question all along, hasn't it?"

"That's why we need to open up the boy's locker," said Loftus.

The long row of sophomore lockers ran the length of an entire hallway. They were the full-size variety, of the style that could be found in any high school in the country: number at the top, combination locks, and louvers cut out of both top and bottom to provide ventilation. The lockers were a rich blue color that looked relatively new, suggesting this was one of the upgrades the owners of Mulighet had made upon taking over the building.

Brixton couldn't help but notice that those louvers could easily accommodate a cardboard coupon the size of the one from Lloyd's box and the Jamison boy's fridge. Kyle Nunzio had come home sick from that camping trip and hadn't been in school the entire week leading up to the death of his classmates.

"I hate violating a young man's privacy this way," Cleese noted, fitting a master key into a slot tailored for it.

"Even if it helps solve the deaths of his best friends?" Loftus challenged.

They both watched Cleese twist the key to the right, pop the latch, and jerk the thin metal locker door open.

And watched a cardboard coupon, identical to the others, fall to the floor.

Loftus donned evidence gloves this time, before slipping the coupon into an evidence pouch.

"You don't—" Cleese managed, veering away midthought. "You think these coupon cards are how the victims were *poisoned*?"

"We'll leave that to the experts to determine," Loftus told him.

"But as long as we're here," Brixton picked up, "why don't we check some more of the lockers?"

They ended up opening every locker along the sophomore row, including the lockers belonging to the seven boys who'd perished from the poison, which were marked with yellow crime scene tape. He avoided close scrutiny of the contents, other than to confirm the obvious: that none of the seven contained the red coupon cards for Common Ground Coffee.

Neither did any of the rest of the lockers in the row, to which Brixton gave far more scrutiny. Had the cards been slipped through the louvers of all these lockers, those coupons would still be contained in at least several. The only thing Brixton could conclude from this was that only the seven poisoning victims had found the cards in their lockers—and that the number would have been eight, had Kyle Nunzio not been out sick.

"You're saying this was intentional," Cleese said, his voice cracking, reaching that conclusion all on his own. "You're saying those seven kids were *murdered*."

Brixton jumped in quickly. "We're not saying that at all."

"We're not saying anything," Loftus added.

"Except this," from Brixton. "The only thing the seven victims, and the boy who survived, had in common, as far as school goes, was football and PE class."

"That means," started Loftus, "that we need to talk to the football coach and the gym teacher in question."

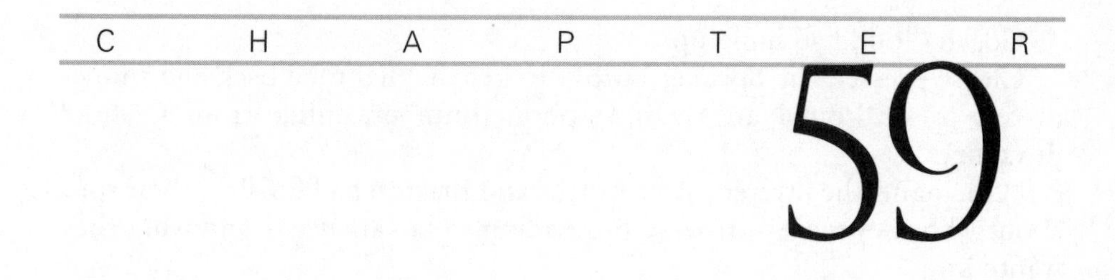

CHAPTER 59

BALTIMORE, MARYLAND

Brixton asked Jefferson Cleese to remain present for the duration of the phone calls to both head football coach Chris Good and Nan Marino, the physical education teacher who'd had all seven victims, plus the one survivor, in one of her classes.

"I don't even know what you're asking me," Good snapped at them over the speaker, clearly perturbed at whatever this conversation was insinuating.

"This is Robert Brixton again, Coach Good. And all we're asking if you remember anything about the behavior of the boys in question."

"What do you mean by 'behavior'?"

"Badgering, bullying, singling another kid out," Loftus answered him.

"Giving him reason to *kill* them?"

"One step at a time, Coach."

"You know, we had two girls on the team this year: kicker and one of our backup quarterbacks."

"Actually, I didn't," Loftus told him.

"Different world, isn't it?"

"Not for the seven kids who died," Brixton noted sharply.

"You know we're talking about freshmen here, people," said Coach Good. "Who exactly do you think they bullied, badgered, or singled out?"

"That's what we're asking you, Coach," Brixton told him.

"And the answer's nobody," Good insisted, his tone brusque and dismissive. "I run a tight ship. No hazing, not even any running laps for punishment. A trainer present at every single practice, and mandatory water breaks. You hear what I'm saying?"

"You run a tight ship," Loftus answered.

"We're a team. I don't tolerate any abusive behavior or anything else that may detract from that. Our seniors lead by example. Even all our preseason captain's practices are taped, as a precaution, since there are no adults present. You hear what I'm saying?"

"One more time, Coach," began Brixton. "Can you think of anyone those eight sophomores may have—"

Click.

Coach Good had hung up.

Cleese pressed the Speaker button to get the dial tone back and immediately pressed out Nan Marino's phone number, pulled from a school directory.

"Oh, man," she uttered, after Loftus and Brixton had finished their spiel about who they were—or were pretending to be, anyway—and what they wanted.

They waited for her to continue.

"I should have reported it. I thought about it but decided not to, because in my experience it only makes things worse."

"Could you please elaborate, Ms. Marino?" Loftus said toward the phone's speaker.

"They were good kids, you need to know that. But sometimes good kids do bad things."

"And what bad things did these seven kids do?"

"Eight," she corrected. "I told them to knock it off a hundred times, and it usually worked . . . for a while. Then it would start up again. I threatened to knock their grades down a notch and thought that would do the trick, but . . ."

"Ms. Marino?" Loftus prompted.

"They were picking on this boy in gym class. Singling him out and generally making his life miserable. It started because he couldn't throw a football. I mean, it *was* kind of pathetic."

Loftus and Brixton exchanged a glance, of one mind about the gym teacher's reaction.

"Who was the kid they bullied?"

"I didn't use that term."

"Would you prefer *abusing*, ma'am?" Loftus snapped, in full cop mode again. "Choose your own word for it."

"Daniel Wilhyte. That's the boy's name. Wait . . ." Nan Marino picked up again, after a pause. "Why would the EPA care about this?"

"Ma'am, I'm going to need you to keep this conversation between us. I'm going to need you not to share it with anyone, under any circumstances. Is that clear?"

"I suppose."

"Yes or no, Ms. Marino?"

The woman sighed over the speaker. "Yes."

"Thank you for your help, ma'am," Loftus said, and she ended the call, cutting off some further explanation Marino had sprung into.

Brixton looked toward Jefferson Cleese. "You know this kid—Daniel Wilhyte?"

The principal nodded. "Sad case. One of those boys who's like a human pin cushion."

"What's that mean exactly?" Loftus asked him.

"He seemed to attract abuse. And no matter how many times the school stepped in to put a stop to it, it only got worse. We tried making examples of some of the worst offenders, but like I said, it only got worse."

"And would the seven poisoning victims be among those 'worst offenders'?" Brixton asked him.

"I believe there were some reports that mentioned them and the Nunzio boy. It's a long list." The color drained from Cleese's face. "Surely, you don't think . . ."

His voice trailed off. He either saw no need to complete his thought or was not able to.

"Here's what we think," Loftus interjected, before Brixton could respond. "Seven of your students died from being exposed to some kind of toxin. That toxin remains unidentified, and the one thing the victims have in common, besides football and that camping trip, was that physical education class where they made another student's life a living hell."

Cleese nodded, his expression empty, maybe not processing all the ramifications involved. "Those fake coupon cards," he managed. "You think that this boy, Daniel Wilhyte . . ."

His voice drifted again, another thought left unfinished.

"That's what we need to find out, Mr. Cleese," Brixton told him. "And we're going to need your help."

Cleese looked from Brixton to Loftus, then back to Brixton. "What can I do?"

"Let's start with the school security tapes from the day the victims were stricken."

It took a while for Cleese to get the footage keyed to the proper point.

"I haven't had to do this much," he offered.

"That's a good thing," Loftus told him.

"Got it," Cleese said, waiting for the two of them to move into viewing position before he started the tape.

Ten minutes later, Cleese froze the tape at the point identified as precisely 7:03 in the morning on the Thursday prior to the day all seven victims had died. "That's him, all right. That's Daniel Wilhyte."

The frozen picture showed a rail-thin boy wearing ill-fitting jeans that sagged on his hips. He was slipping a red coupon with all the markings and logos of Common Ground Coffee through the louvered opening of one of the boys' lockers. In less than two minutes, Wilhyte managed to repeat the process with seven other lockers.

"How is it nobody noticed this before?" Loftus wondered.

"Maybe they did," Brixton told her, "but they weren't looking for the same thing we were here. Whoever reviewed these tapes before us might have fast-forwarded right past this section."

"It was him, wasn't it?" Cleese asked, his voice cracking. "Daniel Wilhyte was responsible for the deaths of those seven students."

"You can't share this with anyone, Mr. Cleese," Brixton warned him.

"But it exonerates the school. We'd be able to reopen."

"Not yet," Loftus added.

"Why? What else do you need?"

Loftus leaned in closer to him. "Everything you can tell us about Daniel Wilhyte."

"I, er, I don't know the extent to which I can help you. There are confidentiality issues here, channels I have to go through."

"How badly do you want to get your school opened again, Mr. Cleese?" Brixton said.

"Well, I just don't know—"

"Sir," Loftus said, raising her voice several octaves. "Here's what I know: I know that seven of your students are dead and your school is now closed as a direct result of that, and could be facing a wrecking ball. We're the EPA, sir. We can help you. We can turn this whole thing around."

"Whatever you tell us will be kept in the strictest of confidence," Brixton promised. "What we need most at this point is just this boy's contact information, where we can find him."

Cleese moved behind his computer. "Let me see what I can do."

They sat in Brixton's BMW in silence for a time, after closing the doors behind them. The plastic evidence pouches, three of them now, rested on the center console, each displaying an identical fake coupon for Common Ground Coffee.

"I'm scared, Robert."

He turned toward her from the driver's seat.

"There's a term for a toxin that infects through the skin," Loftus continued.

"Transdermal," Brixton elaborated.

"You really know your shit when it comes to this kind of thing, don't you?"

He shrugged. "I've got a friend."

"A bullied boy poisons his abusers . . . Not so far-fetched, is it?"

"Only the part about him happening to have access to a transdermal poison with a one hundred percent kill ratio."

"Kill ratio," Loftus repeated. "Nice term. SITQUAL?"

"More or less."

"So where does Senator Byron Fitch fit into all this? Why did Philip Rappaport shoot up the Capitol steps trying to kill him?"

"It all starts with the poison, Loftus. It isn't something this kid could have whipped up with his chemistry set. He went seven for seven, and they all died within twenty-four hours."

"Scary stuff."

"More than scary. It's either a dream scenario or a nightmare, depending on your perspective."

"What do you think Daniel Wilhyte's perspective was?"

"That's what we need to find out."

"We're on the clock here, Brixton," Loftus said, an edge of anxiety creeping into her voice. "We were exposed, remember? We both touched cardboard coupons that killed two of the kids."

"Transdermal poisons have a short life span. Whatever killed those kids might be a whole lot different, but it wouldn't still be toxic after more than five weeks."

"You sure about that?"

Brixton shrugged. "We're still alive, aren't we?"

"For now."

"I'm thinking we could use some help, Loftus."

"From who?"

Brixton held her gaze. "Like I said, I've got a friend."

New York?" Loftus asked him, after he told her where they were headed.

"Nice day for a drive," Brixton told her.

"And who's this friend?"

"Long story," he said, not able to come up with a quick response to describe the professor.

"Good thing it's a long drive."

They reached Brixton's car and climbed in, closing their doors behind them.

"We're getting close, aren't we, Brixton?"

"I believe we are, Loftus."

He drove off, never noticing the man snapping pictures from the front seat of an Amazon delivery van across the street.

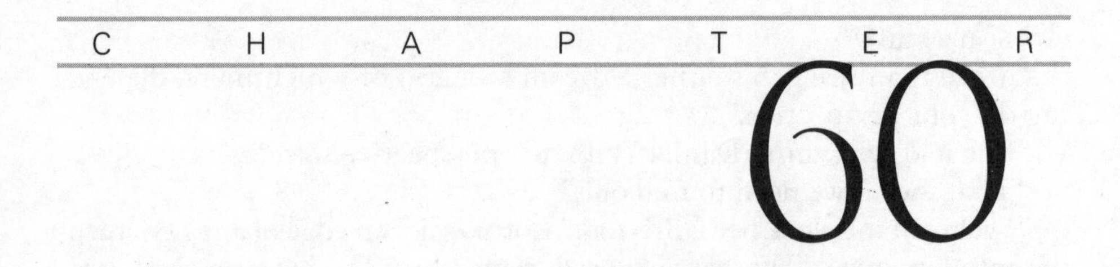

CHAPTER 60

BALTIMORE, MARYLAND

We've got a problem," Deacon Frank heard Senator Byron Fitch tell him through the cell phone, which he had pressed tight against his ear because of the voices rising from the table.

"Hold on a sec," he said, rising from his chair and moving away.

Deacon Frank had no idea what anybody was talking about anyway. He'd hired the four best scientists with biowarfare backgrounds that money could buy, for whom the dollar signs overrode any compunction, guilt, or sense of disloyalty on their part. Like Leonard Cutlow, they'd all cut their teeth at Fort Detrick in Frederick, Maryland, home to the U.S. Army Medical Research and Matériel Command (USAMRMC) as well as the Army Medical Research Institute of Infectious Diseases (USAMRIID). Fancy terms for being experts at figuring out how to kill large numbers of people in the shortest period of time possible, using biological agents. They also were men whose careers had come to bad ends for reasons they considered blatantly unjust, giving them just the kind of ax to grind against the government that Deacon Frank needed.

He had built this lab to their specifications, no expense spared. Deacon Frank didn't know jack shit about the reasons for all the excess spending on designs and materials; these were so far over his head they might as well have been on Mars. All he needed to know was that these geniuses could take the White Death Byron Fitch had dropped in his lap and weaponize it to the benefit of the senator, Deacon Frank himself, and ultimately the whole damn United States of America.

Which weren't all that united anymore, and soon never would be again. At least, that was the plan, or had been, until his geniuses had encountered problem after problem, setback after setback, this or that holding everything up. Always an excuse for why things weren't moving faster.

Hey, Deacon Frank reminded himself, even God took six days to create the world.

Listening to them evaluate how Daniel had pulled off his feat had made Deacon Frank feel as dumb as a rock. It was like being in a Zoom meeting with a bad internet connection and only getting every other word. Deacon Frank perked up at hearing terms and phrases like "death rates," "skin penetration levels," "commutability," "super-heating," "super-cooling." Not that he grasped the entire context of what these geniuses were saying.

His son was sitting among them, holding court and holding his own. How he had turned a small vial of the White Death he'd pilfered from this very lab into a poison capable of killing on contact. How he'd laminated the coupons he'd created on his printer and mixed in a few drops while it cooled. Deacon Frank listened as Daniel explained using a tiny paintbrush he once used for painting his monster models to cover as much of the cards as possible. Maybe a half dozen drops per card. Eight targets with seven victims claimed, the eighth surviving only because he wasn't in school to claim the coupon slipped into his locker. That put the kill rate at one hundred percent, unheard of even for a sample size this small.

In other words, his son Daniel had picked up the ball these brilliant bozos had dropped.

If those few drops could claim seven victims in such rapid fashion, what could ten thousand gallons do? Deacon Frank wasn't any better at math than he was at science, so he couldn't even begin to calculate how many that amount of the White Death could kill. He'd always envisioned killer clouds of the stuff, or figuring out how to make it an unlisted ingredient of tomato sauce, breakfast cereal, or maybe cough syrup. But the team he'd assembled and paid way beyond top dollar was having trouble making anything work on a consistent basis. Besides, what Daniel had come up with was better than all of them. Hundreds of years of experience between the lot of these geniuses and it took a fifteen-year-old boy to carry their water, do the heavy lifting for them.

"Okay," he said, now far enough away from the table. "I can talk now. What's this problem?"

"I just sent you some pictures," the senator told him. "Let me know when you get them."

His phone buzzed once, and then again. Deacon Frank opened his texts and clicked on the first of the two pictures.

"Okay, got them. Who am I looking at?"

"A man and a woman—"

"I figured that out all by myself."

"Let me finish. The woman's name is Kelly Loftus. We haven't ID'd the man yet."

"Okay, Senator, who's Kelly Loftus?"

"Capitol cop who's been poking her nose where it doesn't belong."

Deacon Frank felt a flutter in his stomach. "Meaning, our business?"

"She and the unidentified guy have stumbled upon some stuff that could lead them to us," Fitch told him. "It's still a long shot, and they're nowhere near close right now, but I'd be lying if I didn't say it was a serious concern."

"You're a politician. You lie for a living."

"Not to you, Deacon Frank. Not with what we've got going between us."

Deacon Frank sneaked a gaze back toward the table, where his son was still holding court, schooling these experts who always wore loafers because they probably couldn't tie their own shoes.

"What about this guy the woman's with. He a long shot, too?"

"That's what we're trying to find out."

"I'm all for that. I'm assuming you still got eyes on Loftus and whoever the man is."

"As we speak, Deacon Frank."

"How serious a problem you think we're looking at here?"

"On a scale of one to ten, I'd give it a five, pending identification of the man. I'm running his picture through the government database as we speak. Expecting a hit any moment."

"I'll handle things from there, Senator. Everything we're doing here comes with a risk. And we both knew there'd be bumps on the road, maybe lots of them."

Deacon Frank heard a beep, indicating that Fitch had just received a message of some kind.

"Not this big," he heard the senator say, his voice ringed with concern. "We just ID'd the man in the picture."

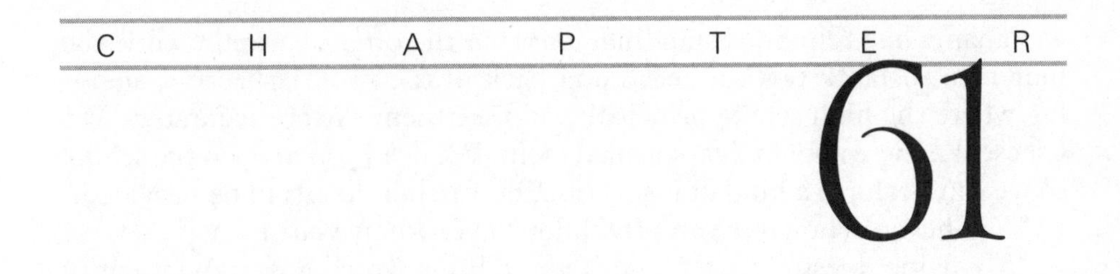

CHAPTER 61

BALTIMORE, MARYLAND

Efram Lutayne hung back in his wheelchair as Panama kept ringing the home's doorbell. The four men who'd flown across the country with them enclosed him in a ring like coiled springs ready to pop. Finally the front door jerked open, revealing a man wearing suit pants and a tie loosened a few notches beneath his neck.

"What the hell?" The man rapidly scanned the figures aligned before him, no idea what was going on. "Who are you people?"

"Truly sorry to disturb you, Mr. Cleese. I just need a few minutes of your time," Panama greeted him.

"I'm busy. Wait. How did you know my name?"

"Why don't we go inside?"

Lutayne sat in his wheelchair, well behind everyone else in the living room of the Baltimore Mulighet High School principal. First time in five years he'd been away from his home in Aurora. He'd learned to revel in silence over the years, taking in the sights of the nearby Rockies, the way the sun framed their peaks in an amber glow while sinking behind them. The fresh smells of Rocky Mountain juniper, bigtooth maple trees, and bristlecone pine, all of which grew wild on his property and formed a smorgasbord of scents.

He missed the sights, missed the silence, but it was the change in scents, away from his property, that bothered him the most, setting his insides aquiver and leaving him squirming for comfort in his chair. There were too many smells, clashing in their unfamiliarity, all of them unpleasant. Humans grow accustomed to scents to the point that they ignore the ones that have grown commonplace. In Lutayne's case, being in one place for so long had left his nervous system intolerant of what he was being exposed to here. The air, perfectly normal for men like this high school principal, smelled revolting to him. His nose reacted the way it would respond to roadkill steaming on the side of a highway or to opening a refrigerator to the stench of rotting food.

"You're here about the poisoned kids, aren't you?" the principal asked from behind an armchair he'd rested his hands upon. He had tightened his tie for reasons Lutayne couldn't fathom.

Panama had remained standing, ignoring the offer of a chair, while the four men in black tactical gear hung back in the room's shadows, standing where the high school principal could see them. "More accurately, Mr. Cleese, I'm here about *what* poisoned them. We need you to open the school so we can perform a kind of inspection, no further details to be provided."

"You haven't shown me any ID. I don't even know your name."

"My name doesn't matter, and if you tell me which government entity would make you most comfortable, I'll produce their ID with my name on it. I have quite a collection."

Cleese shifted uncomfortably. "You sent them, didn't you?"

"Sent who?"

"The man and woman. They said they were from the EPA, had the IDs to prove it, but, I don't know, they didn't seem like EPA to me."

"No? What did they seem like?"

"Cops, or FBI agents maybe. You should talk to them. I think they found what you're all looking for."

Lutayne watched Panama move a chair directly in front of the high school principal and sit down. "Tell me more about this man and woman."

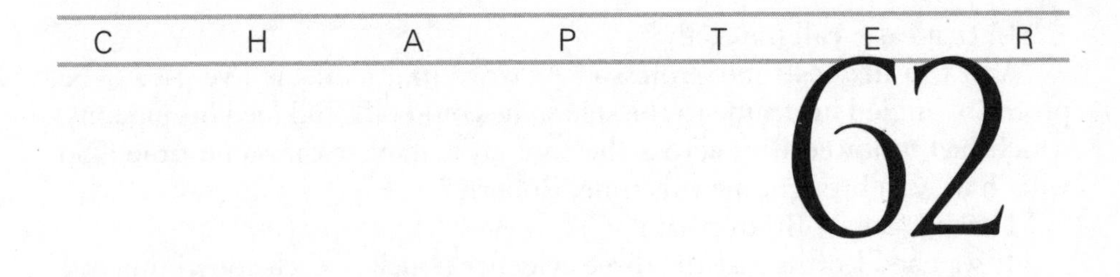

CHAPTER 62

NEW YORK CITY

I've been expecting you, Robert," the professor said, not bothering to turn around when Brixton led Loftus through the heavy steel door on the rooftop.

He was in the process of feeding his pigeons at what must have been the birds' dinner hour, six p.m. sharp. Everything for the professor was order. Order was his life.

Along with death.

That was how Brixton knew this man. Not a name, a firm background, or even a nationality. He knew there may be some military experience in the man's background, likely in the blackest of ops. Not as the man carrying out the assignment but as the maker of the device designed to do the deed. How to get at people who were unreachable, that had been the professor's specialty—and might still be, for all Brixton knew. He was an enigma, a puzzle, a contradiction, to the point that Brixton had heard the professor being referred to as something else entirely: Dr. Death.

There were targets impervious to the efforts of even the Navy SEALs or Delta Force, targets so well hidden or guarded that ordinary commando raids would never succeed. In some cases, the target might be accessible but other determining factors had ruled out a strike, execution, or assassination. Sometimes people had to die with no indication left to suggest it had been murder. And when that was the case, men who worked in the black arts of government came to the professor.

The professor finally turned from tossing bird feed to his pigeons. This was the first time Brixton had ever seen the lot of them wandering free of their cages. The professor's beard and scraggly hair, which dropped well beneath his shoulders, were both longer and grayer than when Brixton had seen him last.

The professor spotted Loftus and regarded her curiously. "Since I don't believe you'd bring your lovely fiancée to meet me . . ."

"This is Kelly Loftus, formerly a homicide detective with the Baltimore PD, now attached to the Capitol Police Protective Services unit."

"Not anymore," Loftus corrected.

"Don't fret, Ms. Loftus," the professor consoled. "I've learned to judge success by the number of enemies I've made."

"In that case, call me Kelly."

"And you may call me Professor. As close to a name as I've got." The professor angled his frame to the side so he could talk and feed his pigeons, which had followed him across the roof en masse, at the same time. "So what have you brought me this time, Robert?"

"I wish I knew," Brixton said.

He watched Loftus ease the three evidence pouches, each containing one of the fake coupons for Common Ground Coffee, from her bag and hand them to the professor.

He held them by the edges, at arm's distance, as if he didn't trust the plastic. "Why do I think these aren't stocking stuffers?"

"We think they're murder weapons," Brixton said, still stiff from a drive north littered with traffic jams that stretched for miles. "We think they were treated with some kind of transdermal poison."

"You've captured my attention, Robert. And I believe I'm already familiar with the victims: high school students from Baltimore. Is my supposition correct?"

"It is indeed," Brixton told him.

He didn't bother asking the professor to elaborate. Instead, in concise fashion, he briefed him on what he and Loftus were looking into, keeping the focus on the seven high school sophomores who'd been poisoned and the eighth who had been spared that fate only because he was home sick that week.

"Within twenty-four hours, you say?" the professor noted, an edge of concern atypical of him creeping into his voice.

Brixton nodded. "By all accounts, yes."

"And a one hundred percent morality rate."

Another nod. "Again, by all accounts."

The professor's eyes flashed, as if that had struck a chord in him. That same edge of concern moved from his voice to his expression.

"In which case, we are standing in very rarefied air, Robert, and I don't mean because we're on a rooftop."

He handed Brixton the bag of the bird feed he'd set down by his feet. "Why don't you finish feeding my birds while I give these stocking stuffers a closer look?"

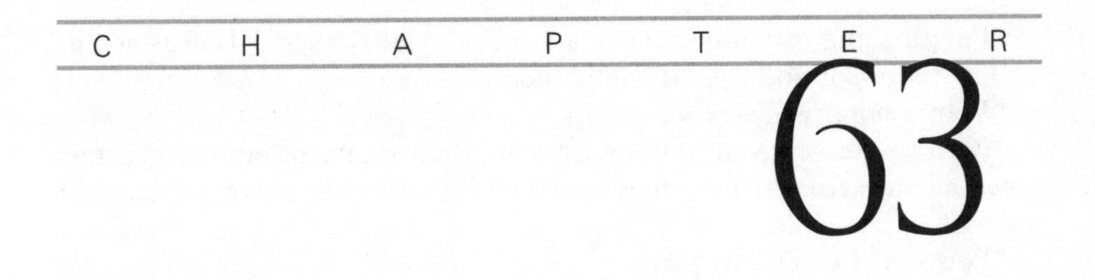

NEW YORK CITY

The professor reemerged just under an hour later. The color had washed out of his face and he seemed a bit unsteady on his feet.

"Do you believe in ghosts, Robert?"

"I never gave it much thought."

"Because we're dealing with one here, a compound that's been literally raised from the dead." The professor looked toward Loftus, as if wondering whether he could trust her with what he was about to say. "Ever heard of the Tooele Army Depot in Tooele County, Utah?" he asked Brixton.

"Vaguely."

"Which perfectly describes the work conducted there. On the surface, the base serves as a resting place for war reserve and training ammunition. The depot stores, issues, receives, renovates, modifies, maintains, and demilitarizes conventional munitions. The depot also serves as the national inventory control point for ammunition for particular equipment, developing, fabricating, modifying, storing, and distributing such equipment as requisitioned."

"On the surface," Brixton repeated, waiting for the professor to get to the point.

"The base also contains the Deseret Chemical Depot and the Tooele Chemical Agent Disposal Facility, with both in operation until 2012, when the last of the chemical weapons stockpile was supposedly destroyed."

"Uh-oh," Brixton said, feeling Loftus, at his side, growing tenser and tenser by the moment.

"Uh-oh, indeed. The work of one scientist remained ongoing, a scientist who was as much a botanist as he was a bio and chemical weapons specialist. The powers that be back then agreed to let his work continue, after substantial lobbying by the Pentagon, arguing that it was too vital, too effective, to be summarily suspended and arbitrarily disposed of."

"Define *effective*," Loftus requested.

The professor turned to Brixton, smiling tightly. "She doesn't know our world, does she, Robert?"

"She's learning—the hard way, unfortunately." Brixton turned to Loftus, about to dispense her next lesson. "*Effective* could refer to any number of things, mostly kill ratio."

"I'm guessing one hundred percent would qualify there," Loftus noted.

The professor nodded. "It would indeed."

"Why a botanist?" she wondered.

"Because he believed, quite correctly, that nature offers the greatest potential on earth when it comes to unlocking the deadly power of chemical toxins."

"Poisons," Loftus advanced.

"Get back to those ghosts, Professor," Brixton urged.

"So this plant expert, and lover, whose name is insignificant at this point, goes right on about his business, developing and refining toxins that are, for all intents and purposes, the perfect weapon. Some, of course, were more effective than others, and one was downright terrifyingly efficient—and that's coming from someone who doesn't scare easily, if at all. This botanist gave it a name, not just a numerical label: the White Death."

Brixton remained silent, giving the professor as much time as he needed to continue on his own. He realized Loftus was squeezing his arm.

"There were other concoctions he came up with," the professor resumed, "but nothing like the White Death, since there'd never been a toxin like the White Death."

"Because of that one hundred percent mortality rate," Brixton interjected.

"Close enough to it, anyway. Everyone except for a select few believed the Deseret Chemical Depot had been shut down in toto. Then 2016 happened."

"A new administration," Loftus elaborated.

"The outgoing administration didn't trust the new one, and didn't dare leave a weapon as deadly as the White Death behind for them to make use of, so all of our botanist's research and development was suspended and all of his amassed stockpiles destroyed. By then, though, the Tooele Chemical Agent Disposal Facility had been shut down, necessitating transport of the stockpiles to a comparable base in Umatilla, Oregon, to be done away with. Six separate trips, always at night, in a guarded convoy called Red Dog runs. The White Death was the last one to make the trip."

"Don't tell me," Brixton broke in. "It never made it."

"Disappeared," the professor acknowledged. "As in dropped off the face of the earth. I remember the night in question like it was yesterday." He looked toward Loftus. "You see, Detective, I am often consulted in such emergencies by any number of officials aware of my existence. They consider me their personal nine-one-one on such occasions, and a call from one of them is never a good thing. Calls from *all* of them makes for a very bad thing indeed."

The professor stopped to let his point sink in, then started in again.

"The search went on for months, with no results. It had to be conducted without the new administration catching wind of what had happened, on the chance, even likelihood, the White Death would be recovered and that administration would have a shiny new toy to play with. I don't have to tell you, such a thing needed to be avoided at all costs."

"No," said Brixton, "you don't."

"But that's not the point. The point is there were plenty of sighs of relief when no evidence surfaced of the White Death's deployment over the ensuing weeks and months, once the search had finally been suspended. There was no choice but to accept its loss as one of those inexplicable anomalies that occur from time to time and leave even folks like me, who are geared for such eventualities, scratching our heads. The White Death, it seemed, was gone forever, and that was all that mattered."

"Except . . ."

The professor seemed to be speaking to both of them now. "That assessment has now been proven wrong. I've confirmed traces of the White Death on all three of those coupon cards. Not enough anymore, mind you, to cause damage or death, but enough microscopic residue to positively identify. So the good news is that neither of you has anything to fear if you came into contact with the cards."

By his side, Brixton heard Loftus utter an audible sigh of relief. "What's the bad news, Professor?"

"There are still fifteen thousand gallons unaccounted for."

Loftus did a double take. "How much of this stuff would have been required to kill whoever came into contact with those coupon cards initially?"

"Three or four drops would likely do the trick. I can't be sure, given that the residue has degraded so badly in the five weeks since it was deployed."

Brixton wasn't sure he'd heard that right. "Did you say *three or four drops*?"

The professor nodded. "We're talking about a toxin that attacks the respiratory system and ultimately shuts down the entire central nervous system, using the body's cells to replicate itself in incredibly efficient and rapid fashion. The White Death's only weakness, if you want to call it that, is the fact that its potency dilutes in water. Not exposure to something like rain so much as total immersion. That would rule out the toxin being deployed to poison water systems. Other than that single exception . . ." He finished his statement with a shrug.

"*Deployed.* That's twice you used that term," Loftus noted. "You know we're talking about high school students, right?"

The professor nodded casually. "Only for now."

Brixton was still trying to figure out how many drops went into fifteen thousand gallons of the deadliest poison ever created by man. "What about the delivery mechanism, those fake coffee coupons?"

"Paper is normally an unpredictable delivery mechanism for toxins that are absorbed transdermally—through the skin. The game changer in this case was that the poison, however many drops of the White Death, must have been incorporated into the laminate." The professor turned his focus on Brixton alone. "Whoever killed those seven kids knew exactly what they were doing, Robert. If I didn't know better, I'd say it could only be the botanist himself."

"What makes you think it's not?"

"Because he makes me look like a social butterfly, by comparison. He's been hiding out, dropped completely off the grid, hiding from the past as well as the future. It wasn't him; you can be assured of that."

"You know what you're saying."

The professor nodded. "That the White Death didn't disappear forever. It's back, and somebody's got it."

PART FIVE

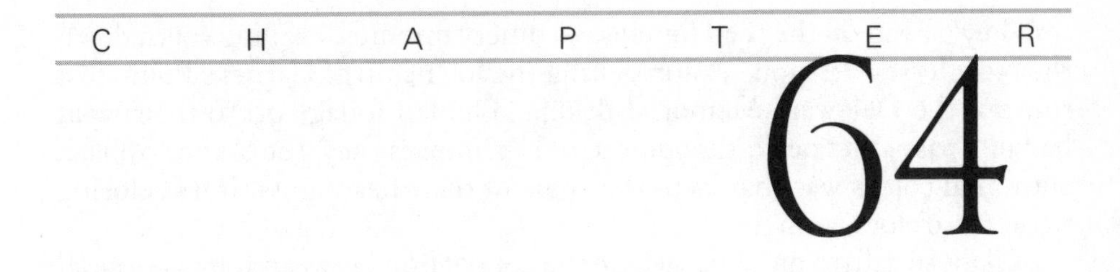

CHAPTER 64

CARNEYS POINT TOWNSHIP, NEW JERSEY

The early part of the ride back home was spent in silence, which was finally broken by Loftus when she popped awake from a nap, as if something had roused her from her slumber.

"Here's what I don't get," she said, clearing the sleep from her voice. "My involvement in this all goes back to the shooting on the Capitol steps, Philip Rappaport gunning down everyone in his sights in an attempt to kill Senator Byron Fitch. We know Rappaport called Fitch's office. We know something had pissed him off big-time, but we have no idea what. What's the connection? We also know Rappaport was struggling with mental illness, but that doesn't explain the man mowing down everyone in his path, kids included, to get to his target."

"I'm thinking more about that bullied kid, Daniel Wilhyte, who had plenty of reason to get back at those football players."

"By killing them with the deadliest poison ever known to man? What sense does that make?"

"None, until we figure out how he, or somebody else, got his hands on the stuff, not to mention having the wherewithal to figure out how to laminate those fake coupons so the poison would kill anyone who touched them, at least for a time."

"How long, Brixton? That's one of the things even your genius we just left couldn't figure out."

"Just because he didn't tell us, Loftus, doesn't mean he didn't know. The professor told us everything we needed to hear, and nothing more."

"So you think he knows more?"

"I'm sure of it."

"But you didn't press him."

Brixton smiled, glanced at Loftus in the passenger seat. "It's a very strange world we operate in."

"You and me?"

"Me and the professor. I press him on this, next time I call he doesn't answer. It's like a code."

"More like a fraternity. Men like you need the professor's resources to do what you do."

"*Did*," Brixton corrected.

They'd been on the road for close to ninety minutes, heading south down the New Jersey Turnpike, approaching the township of Carneys Point, just short of the Delaware Memorial Bridge. The fall foliage off to their right had just passed its peak, though the only glimpses they got of the still rich autumnal colors was thanks to the angle of their headlights. It was closing in on ten o'clock at night.

"Okay, so talk to me about where the connection between Rappaport and Fitch fits into all this."

Brixton focused on the road ahead. "Run the numbers for me."

"Rappaport called the CDC offices in Washington and ended up with the personal cell phone number of your friend's daughter, who ended up in the hospital, almost certainly poisoned by the White Death, as were those seven sophomores from Mulighet High School. How's that, for starters?"

"Fine," Brixton acknowledged. "Except it didn't take Alexandra twenty-four hours to end up in a coma and her supervisor to die. So what are we looking at? Same poison with a different delivery mechanism utilized?"

"A question better posed to your friend the professor. But you're right about Rappaport. There's got to be something that connects him not only to the White Death but also to Senator Fitch. Otherwise, none of this makes any sense at all."

Brixton saw Loftus take her phone from her shoulder bag.

"Before I nodded off," she explained, "I tried googling the name Wilhyte. It sounded familiar, and it turns out the kid's father is the son of one of the country's original televangelists, the Reverend Rand Atlas Wilhyte. Ever heard of him?"

"No."

"Well, his son's name rang a bell because of an investigation the Maryland attorney general has been conducting into alleged tax fraud. He calls himself Deacon Frank Wilhyte, owner of one of the state's largest dairy farms."

"That's not his name?"

"Frank is. The 'Deacon' comes from collecting money at his father's services. Part of what the state's looking into him for is funneling money to right-wing extremist groups."

"In Maryland?"

"Across the whole country. Been going on for years. You see all the heavy firepower those militia groups aren't shy about displaying; now you know where it all comes from. I heard there's one group out West, Idaho maybe, that has tanks and refurbished Cobra gunships hidden away for the revolution."

"More like the second civil war."

"There's that, too. Makes you think, doesn't it, Brixton?"

Brixton turned to meet her gaze briefly, before Loftus resumed.

"What if it's Deacon Frank Wilhyte who found those missing fifteen thousand gallons of the White Death? His bullied son uses it to kill his tormenters, while his father's prepping to supply militias from coast to coast with the stuff."

"Whoa . . ."

"Yeah, that was my thought, too."

"Here's mine," Brixton picked up. "How does a dairy farmer find the same missing truck the military spent months looking for and came up empty, despite their unlimited resources?"

"Okay," Loftus conceded. "That's where the story breaks down."

"We need to find if there's a connection between Wilhyte and Fitch. If it's there, maybe we've got something. If it's not . . ."

Brixton's voice trailed off when he spotted flashing lights cutting through the night ahead of them.

CHAPTER 65

CARNEYS POINT TOWNSHIP, NEW JERSEY

Kelly watched the glow of those lights, which seemed to splash across the wooded area off the road's shoulder, beyond the embankment. Looked like some kind of emergency construction job; the road narrowed to a single lane maybe a half mile up.

"Just what we needed," she sighed.

"Gives you a chance to nod off again."

"Fat chance of that happening. Speaking of which, why don't we switch off? I drive, you rest."

"Sounds good to me," Brixton said, slowing his BMW to a crawl and then a stop behind a dozen cars crawling one at a time through a maze of rerouted roadway.

If nothing else, the late hour had kept the traffic to a minimum. Finally, they snailed up to a New Jersey state policeman handling traffic duties.

Brixton rolled down his window. "What's going on, Officer?"

"Just be patient, sir."

"I am. I was just wondering what the problem was."

Kelly could feel Brixton tense. She had noticed the state policeman's trigger restraint was unsnapped and glimpsed Brixton's hand ducking to the door latch an instant before he slammed the door hard into the cop's hip and groin area. Impact resounded with a thud, followed by a sound like air fleeing a balloon, as the cop doubled over.

Brixton launched the door into him again, cracking him in the skull this time and pitching him backward onto the roadbed.

"Out!" he ordered her. "Now!"

Kelly had her gun drawn by the time she lurched out the passenger side. She saw Brixton was brandishing his as well. Figures rushed them out of the blinding light dead ahead. She'd drawn her gun a handful of times as a cop and had fired it once, missing. Her tactical experience was thus limited to cardboard targets popping up on combat shooting ranges.

She felt Brixton grasp her arm and draw her toward the guardrail as gunshots pinged the night, muzzle flashes flaring out of the brightness ahead. The windshield exploded. Both front tires popped. Light clangs sounded as bullets pockmarked the BMW's hood.

"Come on!"

"How'd you know?" she managed, as they pushed themselves over the guardrail together.

"Man was carrying a SIG. New Jersey state cops carry Glock nineteens now."

They scampered down the steep embankment toward the edge of the woods that bordered the turnpike. The air sizzled and hissed with bullets whizzing past them. Kelly was struggling to breathe. Brixton returned fire, his shots coming in such rapid succession that it sounded like a continuous stream, as he tried to hold the enemy at bay.

Most cops spend their entire careers without experiencing a single gunfight, much less one like this. Kelly's whole body felt locked up solid, still holding fast to her Glock 22, the same standard issue sidearm she'd carried with the BPD. She was raising it to fire, following Brixton's lead, when he dragged her into the cover of the woods.

"How . . . how . . . how," she kept starting, unable to go on.

"I don't know," Brixton answered, still pulling her on. "Maybe they were watching us, or the professor."

"Who, Brixton? *Who?*"

He didn't answer her. He was more concerned with the footsteps thrashing through the low brush of the woods, closing in on them from everywhere at once. The woods dipped into a narrow, crevice-like gully, wet with runoff from the nearby Delaware River. It felt freezing, as Kelly sank low into the muck behind the cover the ledge of the gully offered.

"Aim and fire only to the left!" Brixton ordered. "Don't look right! Stay left!"

She said something, but he unleashed a fresh round of fire that drowned out the words, the gunshots continuing to hammer her eardrums even after his pistol's slide locked open and Brixton jammed in a fresh magazine.

"How ma—"

"One more after this. You?"

Kelly shook her head. She could see Brixton's eyes flashing at that, as he weighed the ramifications. Cops liked to think they're tough, but when it came to real experience, they hardly measured up against those like him, who'd spent some measure of their lives getting shot at and shooting back. It was the kind of gunfighter mentality that was unhealthy for the police to let loose on the country's streets, in stark contrast to the kind of hostile environments in which men like Brixton operated. It was something you couldn't teach, and you practiced constantly to be ready for the moment when instinct was all you had to rely on. Kelly had heard too many stories of cops emptying entire magazines without ever striking a suspect. If that happened to someone like Brixton, he would be dead. Plain and simple.

Kelly felt herself firing, her vision having adjusted enough to the darkness of the woods to spot motion flashing amid the trees to the left. Brixton was pouring out more bullets to the right as enemy fire coughed flecks of mud, gravel, and stones into their faces, stinging both of them. On Brixton's side, she heard a few gasps, then the telltale crackling *clump* of a body pitching down into the brush.

The bark on a thin, knobby tree just to her left exploded under a barrage of fire trained on her. Kelly remembered her training enough to aim her return fire straight into its point of origin. She was firing blind, though, with no bullets to waste. And yet she had no choice but to shoot back.

Brixton pulled her down with him under the ledge, the two of them sinking into the mud, muck, and standing water.

"On your stomach! Crawl! Crawl that way!" Brixton was whispering, but his words banged about her like he was shouting them. "Stay between the trees! I'll be right behind you. Stay low, you hear me! Crawl! Keep yourself small as possible. Go!"

His final words reached Kelly as a single, unbroken thought.

CrawlKeepyourselfsmallaspossibleGo!

Kelly crawled, pushed forward on her elbows through the muck, across the leaf-riddled ground. The noise she was making as she rustled through the leaves seemed louder than the sound of the gunshots that had started up behind her. Whether it was the enemy's or Brixton's, she couldn't tell for sure.

Who were they? How had they found them?

Clawing forward on her stomach made Kelly think she had dragged herself into a world in which she had no business, a world full of men who lived their lives in secret, hiding from what they'd done, but always ready to do more.

Like the professor.

Brixton was different. He was straddling those two worlds until the one he'd known with SITQUAL came calling again, pulling him back full bore. He was the gunfighter who tried to hang up his guns but couldn't because his old life kept reaching for him.

The gunfire behind her echoed through the thinning trees and brush, making it seem like it was coming in a constant stream. Kelly kept at it, crawling on, following Brixton's instructions and trying not to think much beyond the next foot, until rustling nearby told her she wasn't alone.

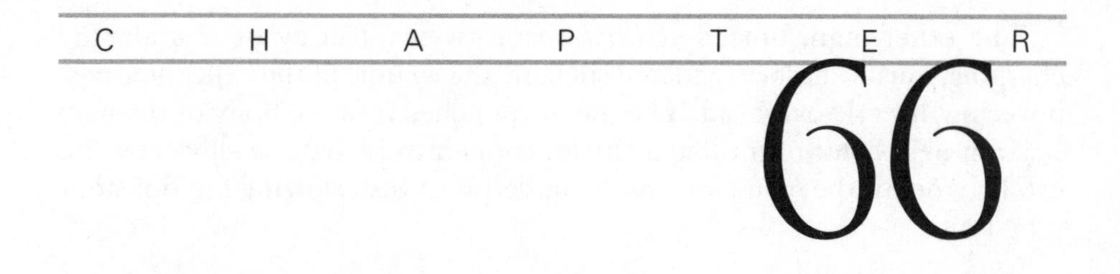

CHAPTER 66

CARNEYS POINT TOWNSHIP, NEW JERSEY

Brixton didn't feel like he was there, didn't feel like he was anywhere. It was like the kind of out-of-body experience he had heard of but never experienced. The gunfight had an odd, dreamlike quality to it, one waking moment folding into the next in splotchy fashion, skipping time.

He'd been through it before; it was always the same and always different. The pistol kicking in his hand, his mental clock keeping time with bullets. He left himself with six, knowing he'd need at least that many to save Loftus, and pushed backward. The ground seemed to move with him, shielding him from sight, darkness making for the best possible camouflage.

He felt the enemy surge past him in a clump of steps that crackled atop the ground cover, not close but not far away either. Brixton was able to spot two stragglers backing up in the general path taken by the others, just in case this was all a ruse set to allow him to make his way back up the embankment to the road, where an ambush would be waiting.

They should have spaced themselves tighter. That alone was enough to tell Brixton these men might have been good at what they did but were hardly on the level of the kind of special operators he'd worked with in SITQUAL, ex-Special Forces types who knew combat better than the back of their hands and wore their experience in eyes that never changed.

Brixton pushed himself on, angling to the side, testing the limits of these two men's peripheral vision. Gunfights tended to narrow that vision, along with just about everything else, the mind drawing the body back to the bare necessities required to function. He thought he caught the distant flutter of a helicopter overhead, welcomed it for concealing the sound of his approach even more.

He came in from the side on the first man, the ground immediately behind him strewn with stray rocks. Clambering over them would have given him away, had it not been for the growing *wop-wop-wop* of the helicopter. Brixton's hand closed on a rock when he was ten feet away; he started to climb to his feet when he was five. The man had no concept of his presence before Brixton brought the rock down and shattered his skull.

He didn't bother trying to strip the pistol from the man's grasp. Instead, he jerked his entire arm upward, controlling the pistol and at the same time holding the man's limp frame before him for cover.

The other man, braced against a tree twenty feet away, was already charging, muzzle flashes rendered silent by the volume of the helicopter now hovering directly overhead. The bullets punched into the body of the man Brixton held before him like a shield, enough to throw the shooter's aim off. Brixton hit the man twice in the bulletproof vest, slowing but not stopping him.

Click.

The attacker's gun.

Click.

The gun attached to the arm Brixton was holding up.

The attacker uttered deep wheezes of breath as he lunged, evidence of the damage done to his ribs beneath the Kevlar that had saved him.

Brixton pushed the body of the man he was holding out forward, the move little more than a distraction meant to slow his attacker. But it also disguised Brixton tearing the twelve-inch KA-BAR knife from the sheath clipped to the dead man's belt. The shiny-hued blade struggled to gleam in the darkness as Brixton brought it forward in an upper thrust that sliced deep and took root beneath the attacker's flak jacket. The man froze, stiffened, and crumpled to the ground.

Then Brixton turned and ran away from the now descending chopper, a spotlight circling from it that looked like the beam was shining down from heaven itself.

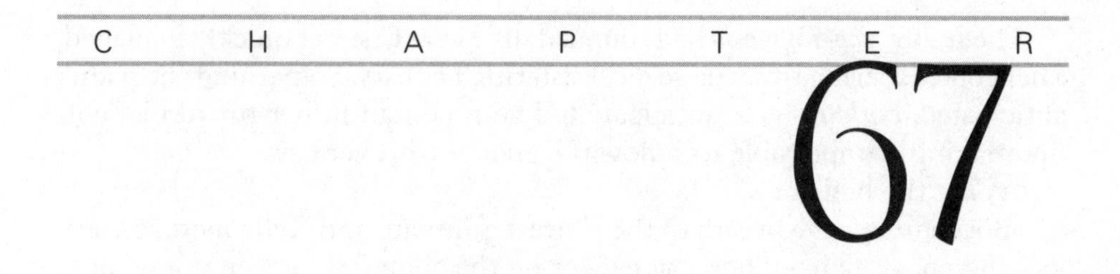

CHAPTER 67

CARNEYS POINT TOWNSHIP, NEW JERSEY

Kelly found herself in a blighted area of the woods, a gaping clearing populated by skeletal trees and dead brush that held the distant scent of char from either a forest fire or a controlled burn. The symmetry of the blighted area made her think the latter, even as she realized concealment was no longer an option.

She could see mist before the faces of the gunmen with each breath they took. It looked to be coming in shallow, rapid heaves, which indicated they had beaten her to this char-scented clearing, believing they were on her trail. She had no bullets left, and the silencing of the gunfire from back where she had left Brixton filled Kelly with dread that he had already been felled.

Clearly, their work had drawn attention from the wrong quarters, the forces behind whatever they were in the process of uncovering determined to stop them in their tracks. Ever practical in her thinking, Kelly had never believed in such conspiracies, and she even counted herself among the few who believed Lee Harvey Oswald had been acting alone in Dallas.

She heard the rustling of shoes or boots draw closer. There was nothing she could do besides press herself into the ground cover as deeply as she could manage. Hiding in plain sight, in her dark clothing under a moonless sky represented her greatest hope.

Kelly kept her face pressed down against the burned-out, parched, and stale ground. She was not about to move, even in the slightest, for fear of alerting the enemy to her presence. She had only her ears to rely on, and they told her there were four men searching for her in this blighted section of the woods.

Kelly felt the spray of dried flecks of brush against her back, evidence that the nearest of the men was just a few feet away. If she could sweep his legs out and take him down to the ground, maybe she could disable him and take hold of his weapon to use against the other three.

Maybe.

The rustling stopped, Kelly's heart hammering against her chest in the certainty he had spotted her. She wondered if he was raising his pistol, aiming it down to end things here and now, wondered if she would hear or feel anything. But then the rustling started anew. Kelly gauged his position and prepared to pounce and bring him down to the ground.

The heavy *wop-wop-wop* had sounded distant at first but quickly loudened, a helicopter soaring over the scene, blistering her ears. Something she hadn't anticipated, *couldn't* have anticipated. The final nail in her proverbial coffin, making it impossible to follow the enemy with her ears.

"What the hell . . ."

Spoken under the breath of the nearest gunman, and Kelly pictured him looking up, away from her, not expecting the chopper's presence any more than she had been. A bright spotlight began cutting swaths through the darkness, vaguely visible even with her face pressed into the ground.

She heard more mutters, then the louder voices of men trying to make sense of what was happening. Kelly felt the spotlight pass over her, holding briefly to reveal her supine frame, which otherwise had been cloaked in the darkness.

With no choice now, she jerked upward. Against an agonizing cramp in her calf, she lurched forward and tackled that nearest gunman at the knees, taking him from behind and pitching him face-first into the hard ground riddled with thin fissures. He landed facedown with a thud and Kelly pounced atop him.

She caught the glow of his pistol when the spotlight skirted its steel, lying just out of reach, to her right. Kelly rolled off the man just as a fresh spray of bullets kicked up chunks of the ground, the other gunmen firing indiscriminately, as if they didn't care which of the churning frames they hit.

The gunfire stopped when the man she'd toppled let out a cry and a gasp, giving her enough time to get a firm hold on the pistol, even as she rolled and kept rolling. She came to a halt on her stomach, firing in the next moment at the shadows revealed at the outskirts of the spotlight's spill.

Kelly kept firing until a second man was down, leaving two more. But then one dropped, as if the ground had been yanked out from under him, and another keeled over like a felled tree. Only then did she realize the slide on her pistol had locked open. The deafening sounds of the helicopter had drowned out her own shots—and those of someone else, who had taken out the remaining two gunmen.

Then she felt a hand grasp her by the collar and hoist her to her feet.

"Come on!" said Brixton.

Brixton shoved Loftus behind him, having managed to save those six bullets before making his desperate dash in her wake. Emerging into the skeletal clearing, dead itself, he felt as if he'd rewound the clock a decade and was back in this hot spot or that, shooting it out with one bad guy or another. The locations blurred, the enemies too, tonight just more of the same.

The rest of the gunmen he'd fled from, back near the start of the woods, came in a series of dizzying dark blurs, their shadows elongated in shape by the spotlight of the chopper now hovering directly overhead. Brixton fired, his aim confused by those shadows and blurry shapes in motion. Two men down, but only two bullets left for the remaining stream of them. Loftus was still braced behind him as he measured off his next shots, taking on one challenge before facing the next. A third man was downed, with at least four still to go, and no bullets left for them. Those four gunmen were pouring into the clearing with the realization that the advantage belonged to them. No reason to space or conceal themselves.

Brixton backed up against Loftus to shield her with his frame, searching for a counter where none existed.

Pfffttt . . . Pffffttt . . . Pfffttt.

The gunshots echoed from above, the sound virtually lost to the chopper's rotor wash, which was kicking ground debris into a blinding swirl through the air.

Pfffttt . . . Pffffttt . . . Pfffttt.

More shots as the debris cloud cleared enough for Brixton to spot four downed bodies where four gunmen had just been standing. He turned his gaze up to the chopper, saw a rope ladder being lowered through the open hold door. A gunman with a scoped rifle was peering downward and sweeping it about in search of any stray targets.

Brixton pushed Loftus onto the ladder first and held it steady as she climbed awkwardly against its listing sway. He held his breath until a disembodied pair of hands jerked her inside the rear hold of what he now recognized as a military-style Black Hawk.

Brixton grabbed the topmost rung of the ladder he could reach and climbed without pause, partially blinded by the swirl of debris and deafened by the roar of the chopper. He finally reached the top and felt the same pair of disembodied hands yank him up the rest of the way into the rear hold.

He tumbled to the floor and found himself looking up at the familiar sight of a man with a light complexion, a khaki suit, and a hat that he remembered all too well.

"Nice to see you again, Brixton," said Panama.

C H A P T E R

68

CARNEYS POINT TOWNSHIP, NEW JERSEY

Why am I not surprised you're involved in this?" Panama continued.

Brixton took his eyes off him long enough to embrace Loftus. Her hair smelled of char, just like the desolate, dying woods from which they'd just been lifted.

"You just happen to be in the area, Panama?"

"Sure, Brixton. Out for a leisurely ride in my Black Hawk when I spotted a couple heroes in need." His steely eyes fixed on Loftus. "Should I call you 'Detective' or 'Officer'?"

"Neither. I seemed to have burned a lot of bridges lately."

"Something you have in common with Mr. Brixton here." Then, to Brixton, he said, "I assume you have questions."

"A whole bunch."

"So do I."

Brixton had made more than his share of trips in such craft, normally in numbers below the eleven-troop capacity, which could be stretched to as high as fourteen, depending on how much gear they were toting. He noticed a man—in a wheelchair, of all things—in the back of the Black Hawk's cargo compartment.

He looked back at Panama. "Let's start with what I'm guessing we have in common: the White Death."

"You never cease to amaze me, Brixton."

"This coming from the man who hung me out to dry the last time we worked together."

"I had no choice. Somebody broke security and with it our communications chain."

"Excuses, excuses," Brixton said.

"Hey, we won, didn't we?"

"The country did."

"As it must again, Brixton. As we must ensure that it does."

With that, Panama turned to the man in the wheelchair.

"Dr. Lutayne, meet Robert Brixton, who seems to revel in playing hero."

"The world could certainly use one," the man in the wheelchair said from the back of the cargo hold, as the Black Hawk soared on.

Brixton made sure the restraints holding him in his jump seat were properly fastened, then moved his eyes to the four men in black tactical gear, who had seemed to melt into the scenery. They were typical of the kind of top special operators he'd worked with as part of SITQUAL. Loftus sat belted in next to him, not sure of her place here or comfortable enough to add her thoughts yet.

"When did you get your own chopper and security team, Panama?" Brixton asked. "I thought you preferred working alone."

"I prefer whatever the circumstances call for. We're all hands on deck on this one, for obvious reasons."

"How'd you find me, by the way?"

"Same way the team our enemy assembled did, I imagine: by tracking either your cell phone or your now abandoned BMW."

"You can track a car?" Loftus asked him.

"Only if it has a navigation system installed, which is pretty much all of them these days. I also had a contrite conversation with the professor."

"I should have figured the two of you would have swapped phone numbers at some point."

"I've got his. Mine changes too often to bother giving it out. Keeping the same phone number is like standing in the same place for too long; it makes you vulnerable."

"Never mind that," Brixton told him. "Who is this enemy you mentioned? Who tried to kill us back there?"

The word *us* drew Panama's attention back to Loftus. "I don't know a lot about you, Detective, but what I've learned, I liked. And I'm going to assume, since you're working with Brixton here, that you don't mind getting your hands dirty."

"Which keeps getting me in trouble," Kelly said, breaking her silence.

"Another admirable feature. When you tire of Mr. Brixton here trying to get you killed, let me know and I'll see if I can find a place for you." Panama flashed the slightest of smiles. "As for the notion of this enemy, let's start with Senator Byron Fitch, who pretends to be an independent when he's actually a dyed-in-the-wool reactionary. A man who'd like to take a blowtorch to the country and widen the divisions that already exist. That's putting it mildly. A more accurate way to put it is that he's actively fomenting a second civil war. All that's stopping him is the fact that it's a sixty-forty, even a seventy-thirty, country, and not in his favor."

Brixton finally grasped where all this was leading. "And don't tell me, that's where the White Death comes in. That's the game changer to flip the ratio."

"And then some. Dr. Lutayne and I just returned from Utah, where somebody sucked ten thousand gallons of the White Death from what should have been its final resting place. A microscopic portion of that, as you've already figured out, was used to kill those seven high school students."

Brixton nodded, feeling the Black Hawk shaking in a patch of unsettled air. "The victims turned a boy named Daniel Wilhyte into a human piñata. We have proof that he poisoned them with—"

"Fake coupons to a local coffee shop," Panama completed for him. "Or so I was informed by the high school principal, Mr. Cleese. As soon as he told me he'd been visited by investigators from the EPA, I had a feeling it was you, even before he confirmed that from a photo I showed him. By the way, he'd like his school reopened."

"So he told us," said Brixton. "And what exactly brought you to Cleese? And to me?"

"The same thing that brought me to Dr. Lutayne," Panama said, gesturing toward the man in the wheelchair. "You recall how I described my job, the first time we met?"

Brixton remembered the professor mentioning the work of a botanist having been behind the development of the so-called White Death, and his mind settled on this man being him. "Something about plugging holes in the figurative walls that surround the country," he said, holding his gaze on Lutayne.

"Close enough. And one of those holes, a gaping one, was the death of those seven high school students."

Brixton nodded again. "Within twenty-four hours, by a poison no one could identify."

"It was identified, Brixton, just not made public. As was the poison that put your friend's daughter in a coma and killed her supervisor at the Washington offices of the Centers for Disease Control. One and the same, I might add."

"Information that was also held back."

"Need-to-know basis only," Panama confirmed. "But the poisoning of the high school students had dug a big enough hole on its own. You mentioned the boy they bullied, Daniel Wilhyte. What do you know about his father, Deacon Frank?"

Brixton gazed toward Kelly Loftus, who was starting to look airsick. Maybe her first time in a chopper like this one. "Only what Loftus told me. He owns a big dairy farm in rural Maryland, son of one of the original televangelists, who opted not to follow in his father's footsteps."

"In one important way he did, though. That being building an army in the form of the faithful. A loyal base who will hang on his every word and support his every action."

"You're talking about the crazies out there, militias that are growing everywhere."

"Haters, Brixton. Believers in nothing besides the concoctions of their own twisted minds. The only thing they'd rather do than see the country burn is to be the ones holding the match. I've taken on terrorists who've slipped through the same cracks, and this lot concerns me plenty more than those, especially in the long term, given that there are so goddamn many of them, from so many disparate groups, which Deacon Frank has made it his life mission to bring together. And the White Death has provided the glue to make them all stick."

Brixton nodded, fitting the pieces together for himself. "Okay, so Fitch and this Frank Wilhyte have an army at their disposal—I get that. What I don't get is how they learned about the White Death vanishing off the face of the earth five years ago."

Panama hesitated, as if figuring out the best way to answer Brixton's question. "Go back to that shooting on the Capitol steps."

Brixton didn't nod this time. "Committed by a mentally disturbed man named Philip Rappaport. But the eighteen he killed didn't include the man he was gunning for," he said, recalling the video assemblage Jesus Arriaga had managed to put together. "Because he'd come there to kill Senator Byron Fitch."

Panama looked impressed. "You're truly good at this, Brixton. You should consider joining Ms. Loftus in my employ."

"I haven't made my decision yet," Loftus interjected defensively.

"You don't have a lot of other options available right now, do you?" Then he turned back to Brixton. "You were asking me how Fitch and Wilhyte learned of the White Death's existence and subsequent vanishing in transit. A soldier who was part of the security team for Dr. Lutayne's operation in Utah came to his home state's senator Byron Fitch out of guilt, no longer able to keep the secret about the White Death's disappearance. He'd already developed severe anxiety and symptoms of post-traumatic stress disorder over what he'd been party to, even before the deaths of those high school students alerted him to the fact that the White Death was back."

"Oh, man," Brixton managed, fitting the final piece into place.

"Indeed. The former soldier who effectively served up the White Death on a silver platter for Fitch and Wilhyte was Philip Rappaport."

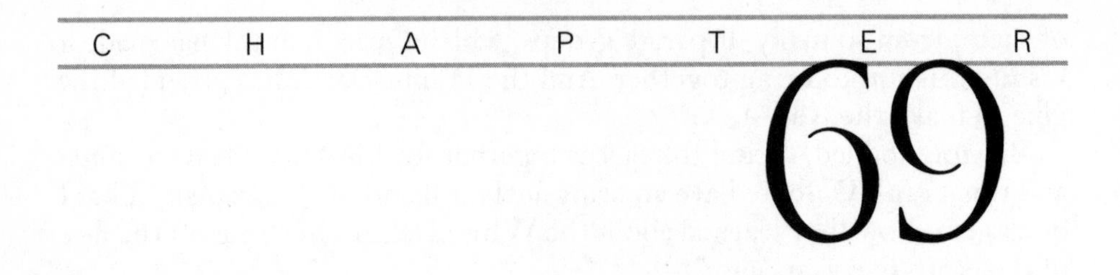

CHAPTER 69

OVER NEW JERSEY

Brixton viewed the final picture he'd assembled in his mind. Rappaport had likely approached Fitch some months back, a year or more maybe, and shared with him the secret he could no longer keep, fully expecting the senator to use his resources to move mountains—literally, if that's what it took—to find and dispose of the White Death once and for all.

Well, the senator had found it, all right, likely in tandem with Frank Wilhyte, but disposal had never entered into the equation. The two men were united in their mission to use the nation's divided nature for their own purposes, and now they had the means to leave a trail of death, chaos, and anarchy from coast to coast. A wet dream for the radical right fringe of the nation, the prospects of which drew an actual shiver from Brixton.

"They're going to use the White Death to ignite their civil war, aren't they?" he asked Panama.

"Not so much ignite as to win before it even gets started. Win by default, because the primary population centers of their perceived enemy—cities—will be decimated by the White Death, the whole country rendered virtually unrecognizable, overnight in some cases. And who do you suppose will ride in on their not-so-white horses to save the day?"

"The militias controlled by Deacon Frank Wilhyte," Loftus responded.

"Enough said," Brixton told Panama. "So why haven't you moved? Why are Fitch and Wilhyte still out there instead of sitting in Guantanamo or someplace comparable?"

"I'd like to say it's because we have no definitive proof and that's not the way we do business."

"But that would be a lie."

"So I won't bother saying it, Brixton. Instead, I'll say we can't do anything, or move on anyone, until the White Death is secure."

"Something I'm confused about," Loftus interjected. "It took somewhere around twenty-four hours for those high school kids to die, but the effects on the daughter of Brixton's friend and her supervisor were immediate. Why the difference?"

"That's a question better directed at Dr. Lutayne," Panama prompted.

Lutayne wheeled himself a bit more forward, unsteady in his chair as the Black Hawk tilted from side to side. "How much can I say?" he asked Panama.

"We're among friends here, Doctor."

"In that case, I can tell you that it's been determined that the victims from the CDC's office in Washington were poisoned via inhalation. From the analysis I've seen, it appears that just enough of the White Death was added to a pair of coffees they'd ordered with their lunch. They never drank a sip; the steam rising out of the cardboard cups would have delivered the poison."

"Except one died and one didn't," Brixton noted.

"Any number of factors could explain that. Most likely the woman was farther away from her cup than the man was from his," Lutayne elaborated. "There's no way to be absolutely sure, although that's what scrutiny of the crime scene itself suggests. The more overriding point is that with that kind of airborne delivery mechanism, the randomness of proximity and potential dissipation become huge factors. But those who are exposed in that manner suffer immediate and catastrophic effects."

"As opposed to people dying over a more gradual progression of time," Loftus picked up. "In which case it would be damn near impossible to ascertain when, where, and how they'd been poisoned."

"Not 'damn near,'" Lutayne corrected. "Impossible, period. Investigators would have nothing to go on, and by the time they got even an inkling of what they were facing, it would be too late. The whole country would be exposed, at least the primary targeted areas."

Brixton could see Loftus's eyes flashing at that, making sense of what Lutayne was saying. "You're suggesting that Wilhyte's kid, Daniel, came up with a superior delivery mechanism with those laminated coupons."

Lutayne nodded. "Infinitely superior, in fact, since the White Death delivered transdermally by touch instead of inhalation offers the perfect mechanism for any bio attack. Imagine contaminating mail that way, or newspapers, or money, or a million—maybe ten million—coupons like the one this kid came up with. A single touch would be all it would take."

"Fitch and Wilhyte get their second civil war," Panama picked up from there, his words aimed at Brixton. "And there's only one thing scarier than those prospects."

"What's that?"

"They might win." Panama stopped, then started again. "We have no idea where the White Death is being stored or the location of the lab where it's being made operational. Other than what Dr. Lutayne and I have just explained, we know nothing at all."

Brixton felt his stomach quaking up a storm, nothing to do with the turbulence the Black Hawk had encountered. "So how do we stop them?" he asked, hearing his own words as if someone else had spoken them.

"Glad you asked, Brixton. Glad you asked."

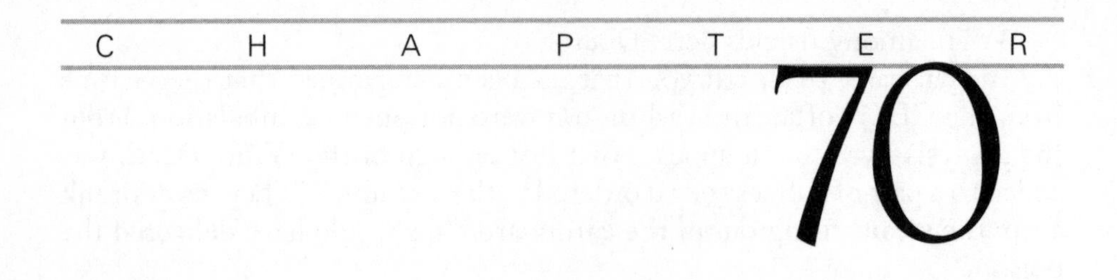

CHAPTER 70

OLDTOWN, MARYLAND

"What a clusterfuck," was the first thing Senator Byron Fitch said after he was escorted by one of Deacon Frank's security guards into the farm's processing plant, where the freshly pumped milk was flash pasteurized.

"It gets a little noisy in here," Deacon Frank said over the tinny roar of the machines along the line, handing Fitch a pair of earplugs. "You might want to pop those in so you don't do any damage."

Fitch took the earplugs but kept them in his hand instead of inserting them into his ear canals. "Where are the bottles?"

"Getting filled at another station along the line. What you're looking at here is bulk production. My milk gets trucked to the cooperative, where it's mixed with the milk of maybe a dozen or more other dairy farmers."

"So you can't buy strictly Wilhyte milk?"

"Not unless you frequent a store we supply our own bottles to, or sign up for daily delivery to your home."

"That doesn't seem fair," Fitch told him.

"Plenty about life isn't fair, like my daddy getting gunned down. Dying on the ground after one of his own services."

"Never mind that. You want to explain to me instead how things went so wrong last night in New Jersey and what we're going to do about it?"

Deacon Frank moved along the production line, following the tubes pumping vast amounts of milk from one station to the next before ultimately dispensing it into fifty-gallon jugs at this part of the line. The jugs were then transported in a constant stream into the freight depot, where they were summarily loaded into the backs of his refrigerated trucks.

With just over a thousand cows, his dairy farm was considered relatively small in comparison to the giants that boasted upward of fifteen thousand. The milk jugs were destined for smaller accounts that serviced mom-and-pop outlets under a variety of generic brand names. Deacon Frank also maintained a fleet of milk tanker trucks that were filled via hoses along an outdoor loading dock. Those hoses ran from the pasteurizing and finishing machines through an underground warren into a garage at the far end of his processing plant. Trucks backed up in the proper slots to be either manually or robotically filled. The milk tanks would then transport the vast bulk of his product to packagers supplying the larger dairy companies. It frustrated Deacon Frank no end that somebody could be drinking a big brand name in Chicago without any clue it was milk from his cows right here in Maryland.

"I let my cows graze," he said, instead of answering the senator's question directly, "even though stall feeding makes a lot more sense these days for a variety of reasons I won't bore you with. I just don't think cows can be at their best, produce their best milk, all cooped up like that with no room to roam. I got just a few local commercial accounts where you can buy my milk fresh, in addition to my fleet of trucks that make daily home deliveries. People who try it tell me they can taste a difference."

"A happy cow is a productive cow," Fitch intoned. "Is that what you're saying?"

"Look, I got a robotic system that can milk a hundred udders at once, so I'm not against the modern ways. But animals have a right to their lives, to not be confined to a tiny corral, because it's better for the consumer. You see where I'm going with this?"

"No."

"Here's the rub, Senator. The people left standing when all this goes down are like cows kept in those corrals. They deserve their freedom, too. They deserve to live without feeling they've been stuffed into a corral that's getting smaller and smaller. That's who we're doing this for. That's why it matters."

"I'm thinking we need to reconsider things," Fitch said, his voice tightening and eyes narrowing.

"You mean the timetable?"

"I mean the whole plan. After last night—a clusterfuck, like I said."

"My people are still sorting things out, Senator."

"What's to sort out? You set up an ambush and lost every single one of your men in the process. What happened to strength in numbers? I knew you should have let me handle it."

"Maybe you were right. Maybe these pain-in-the-asses were just flat-out better than we had reason to believe."

"Because you underestimated them," Fitch said, in the alternative. "Because maybe you picked the wrong men for the job, all those toy soldiers you've got used to shooting at cardboard cutouts instead of flesh and blood."

"That doesn't mean we need to scrap the whole plan, Senator. Quite the opposite, in fact."

"How you figure?"

"You were concerned these genuine pain-in-the-asses were on our trail and coming fast. Assuming that's true, we better move quick so it won't matter."

What Deacon Frank failed to elaborate on the series of setbacks, one after another, suffered by his experts in the lab. Daniel was there now, demonstrating how he'd turned coupons for some coffee place into weapons that killed on contact. They needed to replicate what the boy had done, on a massive scale, everything planned so that people started dying in waves at the same general time from coast to coast. Deacon Frank knew politicians were of a mind to run for the hills when times got tough, which certainly filled the bill here.

"I don't think you're getting my point, Deacon Frank."

"Maybe because you haven't made one."

"Then let me reiterate: this doesn't go off without my say-so."

"Is that a fact?"

Fitch nodded. "You need what I bring to the table and you know it. I'm the one running political interference for you, remember? I'm the one who's going to champion the cause of those militia men who are going to flood the target zones with guns, ready to restore and keep order. We're talking about a societal decimation on the scale of the asteroid that wiped out the dinosaurs. Do I need to remind you of that?"

"You need to stop using terms like 'societal decimation,'" Deacon Frank told him. "Try a whole lot of people, in the millions and millions, dropping dead. Give this country the fresh start we're both after."

They'd reached the part of the sprawling production line where three separate spinning devices wheeled old-fashioned glass milk bottles in front of a spigot that dispensed the freshly pasteurized milk. These bottles were sent down another section of the line, where they were capped and boxed and loaded onto similarly old-fashioned milk trucks that would deliver them to Deacon Frank's commercial accounts and to the families on his regular delivery schedule. That part of his business was a money loser for sure, but it reminded him of his own childhood, bringing in the icy milk bottles from the milk box on the porch every morning. Nothing had ever tasted better. He figured that was a tradition worth continuing, even if did hurt his bottom line.

Pretty soon, such things wouldn't matter anyway.

"We'll fix this," Deacon Frank assured the senator. "I should have given the job to better men, professionals at this sort of thing. I should have gone outside the family. But everything's twenty-twenty in hindsight and all we can do now is set things right. And we have no idea what this Robert Brixton and Kelly Loftus know, what they've managed to put together."

"But we do know they've got law enforcement backgrounds, considerable ones even, especially Brixton. This isn't their first rodeo, in other words."

"They're on their own, Senator."

"Which didn't stop them from managing just fine last night. How many they take out? Eight? Ten maybe?"

A dozen, Deacon Frank thought, not bothering to correct Fitch. "Done and gone. I'll make some calls. Get this done by men who make their living doing it."

Deacon Frank's phone buzzed with the call signal for the front gate.

"Deacon Frank here," he said.

"You got a visitor, sir," a guard's voice came back. "He says he's a detective. Man by the name of Robert Brixton."

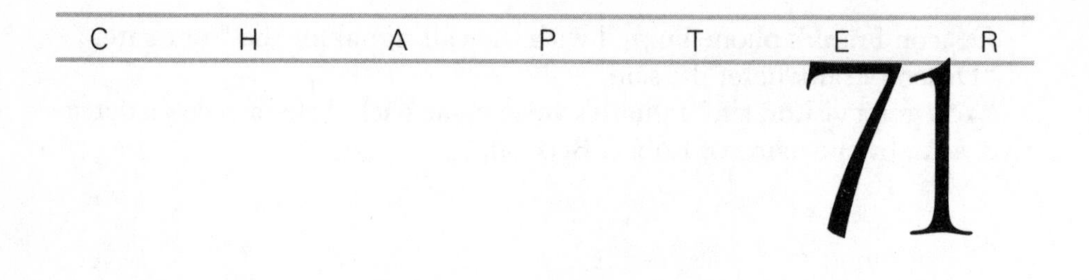

CHAPTER 71

OLDTOWN, MARYLAND

Brixton spotted Deacon Frank Wilhyte zooming toward the front gate in a golf cart, looking more like he was heading out for a round than running a dairy farm. He cut an impressive figure even from a distance. Full head of black hair, with a shadow of beard stubble growing evident, the closer he drew. Tall, with natural bulk, but carrying little fat. Having now studied pictures of his more famous father, the Reverend Dean Atlas Wilhyte, Brixton found himself amazed by the resemblance. More like twins than father and son. Add his father's thick mustache to the mix and they would be spitting images of each other.

Brixton got his first look at the man's eyes and expression when he slid the cart to a stop and shifted his long legs out. Those eyes looked as black as his hair. The pupils seemed overly large, on the verge of swallowing the whites, which were made even more pronounced by being set deep in his head, the sockets looking almost recessed. Deacon Frank carried a smirk as his default expression, a slight narrowing of his eyes, as if he was perpetually squinting—or maybe just seeing the world in a different way.

"You say you're a detective?" Deacon Frank greeted him.

THE NIGHT BEFORE

Deacon's not a name; it's a title of sorts," Panama had explained to Brixton and Loftus, after the chopper had set down at Andrews Air Force Base.

They had landed off in an area dedicated to government air traffic, both private jet and helicopter. A pair of SUVs was waiting on the tarmac for them, lights off to avoid drawing any attention. Panama had led Brixton and Loftus into one, taking the front passenger seat and leaving the middle row to them.

"You need to smoke him out," Panama told Brixton. "Rattle his cage and force him to show his hand."

Brixton almost laughed. "Anything else while I'm at it?"

"I've seen you work, Brixton. Maybe I've got more faith in you than you deserve, but that's on me. You've eaten people for lunch who were a whole lot tougher than Deacon Frank Wilhyte."

"None of them had a weapon that could kill tens of millions of people at the drop of a hat."

Panama smiled tightly, nodding as if Brixton had made his point for him. "Precisely why we've got to get him to move the White Death out from wherever it's hidden. He thinks we're onto him and his plan, he'll figure he has no choice."

"Even though we're not onto the specifics of his plan at all."

"He's planning to kill an awful lot of people, Brixton. How much more specific do you need it than that? You smoke him out and I'll work the fire extinguisher. How's that sound? Oh, and by the way, we moved your fiancée to a hotel."

"You *what*?"

"I got her a suite. You can thank me later."

Deacon Frank had about four inches on Brixton. He wore boots under his khaki pants, which were frayed along the cuffs. They practically hung off his waist, leaving Brixton to wonder if he'd donned a belt this morning.

The guards had told Brixton to park his car off to the side, in clear view of a sign hanging over the gate that read "Atlas Dairy Farm." He watched Deacon Frank walk through the open gate, passing beneath the sign that honored his father, and join Brixton out of earshot of the guards.

"You didn't answer my question, Mr. Brixton," Wilhyte was saying now. "You a detective or not?"

"Private detective, actually," he told Deacon Frank, flashing his actual ID for a change. "I've been retained by the parents of the seven boys from the Baltimore Mulighet High School who died tragically last month. I believe your son attends that school, Mr. Wilhyte."

The tall, lithe man before him smirked. "You wouldn't be here if you didn't already know the answer to that. And call me Deacon Frank. Everybody does. And what have those unfortunate folks retained you to do?"

"Look into the deaths of their sons to determine potential culpability."

"You think somebody killed them?"

"The parents didn't hire me for what I think; they hired me for what *they* think. And they aren't satisfied with the results of the investigation."

"I heard those boys were poisoned," Deacon Frank said. "Contamination of some sort at that school. That's why it got shut down."

"The investigation has produced no evidence whatsoever of that. And the parents want to make sure all possibilities are considered, given that fact."

"Okay, so what does my son have to do with this? From where I'm standing, he was lucky not to have ended up as a victim himself."

"Were you aware that the victims were bullying your son?"

"It happens with kids this age. So what?"

"Your son never told you?"

"What's to tell? It was his problem, and I didn't teach him to run to daddy every time he has a problem."

"So you had an idea about the abuse?"

Deacon Frank backed up a step, eyes narrowing even further. "I don't consider it abuse. I consider it part of growing up. Rules of the road."

"All seven of those boys are dead now. Do you have any rules that account for that?"

Deacon Frank managed a smirk. "They got a higher power to answer to for their behavior now."

"It doesn't sound like their deaths bother you much," Brixton noted flatly.

"Why should they? I never even met any of them."

Brixton hardened his tone. "Because of what you just said, how it could have been your son."

"But it wasn't, was it? Maybe there's a message in that. Maybe their deaths weren't tragic accidents at all but punishment dispensed from on high. That's what my daddy would have said."

"Your father died tragically too, didn't he?"

Deacon Frank nodded, the motion not disturbing a single hair. "Shot in the midst of a robbery. Looked like he tried to fight back instead of hand the money over willingly, Dick."

"The name's Robert."

"The term *dick* for a detective dates back to before *Dick Tracy*, to 1908 or so. I used to read the comics when I was kid. You should take the comparison as a compliment, maybe thank me for it."

"I'd like to speak to your son," Brixton told him instead.

"What for?"

"I'm interviewing a number of students associated with the victims."

"Associated in what way?"

"They'd been victims of bullying at the hands of the same kids."

That seemed to make Deacon Frank relax a bit, playing his role just as Brixton was playing his. Cat and mouse, the roles rotating, each needing to say just enough.

"How 'bout we take a ride up to my production plant? I've got something I'd like to show you, Dick."

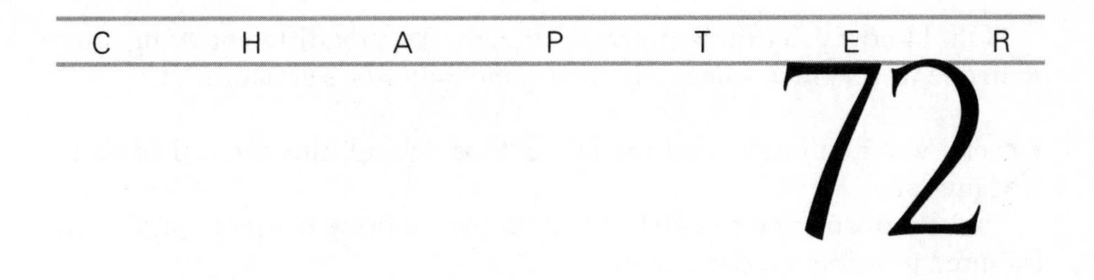

CHAPTER 72

WASHINGTON, DC

Byron Fitch was sweating up a storm by the time he reached his office. Might as well have been August instead of November, and he'd just come in from a walk in the Washington humidity, highest of any he'd ever felt anywhere in his life.

He'd driven off Deacon Frank's property through the service gate used by the milk trucks coming and going. Perspired the whole way to the Capitol, where he left the Lexus SUV in a No Parking zone on a street adjoining the Russell Senate Office Building, not caring if it got towed. He had bigger things on his mind, like how to extricate himself from this mess with Deacon Frank Wilhyte, cursing the day he'd listened to the crazy story told to him by Sergeant Philip Rappaport. He should have known where something like this was going to end up, but he couldn't help himself. The potential had just been too great.

Upon entering his suite of offices, he stormed past his assistants, ignoring whatever they were trying to tell him, which must have included the fact that somebody was waiting outside his office for him. A woman flashing an ID wallet with badge attached.

"Detective Kelly Loftus of the Capitol Police, Senator. I was wondering if I could have a few minutes of your time."

THE NIGHT BEFORE

What about me?" Kelly had asked the man Brixton called Panama, from the backseat of the SUV.

"How'd you like to take a run at the other man who almost got you killed tonight?"

"Sign me up."

Panama nodded, clearly impressed. "Don't forget about my offer to add you to my team."

"I thought you didn't have a team, Panama," Brixton interjected.

"That's why I need to add to it." He rotated his gaze back to Kelly. "Divide and conquer, Detective. We peel Senator Byron Fitch off from his buddy Deacon Frank and see where that goes."

"I think I can handle that."

"Oh, I know you can. Be warned, though. It's a lot different going after someone who's killed somebody than somebody who's about to."

Kelly watched Fitch close the office door behind him and didn't waste any time.

"Some information has surfaced about the shooting on the Capitol steps I wanted to bring to your attention."

Fitch looked confused. "I thought the FBI was running lead on that."

"This came up rather suddenly and their manpower is stretched to the limit. They asked me to follow it up, and since you narrowly escaped with your life, I figured this was something you needed to hear."

They remained standing, Fitch moving closer to a vent for the air-conditioning. His hair was mussed and his face was shiny. He was wearing a charcoal-colored suit that was darker in places where the perspiration had soaked through.

"I'm listening."

"I know you're a busy man, Senator, so I'll get right to the point. Indications have surfaced that you were the intended target of the shooting."

Kelly could tell from his reaction that the revelation threw Fitch a bit, producing exactly the effect she'd hoped for. He backed up and plopped down in a chair, alongside another, matching one. He didn't offer it to her and Kelly didn't take it.

"Were you acquainted with the shooter, Philip Rappaport, Senator?"

"Not that I recall. But he was from Maryland, which makes him a constituent."

"And you don't recall having any contact with him?"

"I just told you I didn't."

Kelly flipped open a memo pad Fitch hadn't noticed she was holding. "That's strange, Senator, because Rappaport placed several calls to your office."

"Well, like I said, he was a constituent."

Kelly moved a bit to the side so the sun shining in through an adjacent window would strike him in the eyes. "Can you think of any reason why Rappaport would want you dead, Senator?"

"I told you, I don't even know the man."

"Actually, you said you don't recall meeting him."

Fitch squinted at her through the sun in his eyes. "You're not recording this, or taking any notes."

"I have a very good memory. And like I said, we're just having a conversation here."

"Then keep talking."

"Do you know a man named Frank Wilhyte?"

"I've heard of him. He goes by Deacon Frank. I believe our paths have crossed a few times. He's another of my constituents," Fitch added, as an afterthought.

"Are you aware of any connection between Deacon Frank Wilhyte and Philip Rappaport?"

"Where are you going with this?"

"Are you aware that Philip Rappaport served in the army?"

"How could I be?"

"He was assigned to a base in Utah between 2007 and 2017. Does that ring any bells?"

"Should it?"

"I thought it might, since you've served for more than a decade on both the Appropriations and Defense committees."

"We fund a lot of military bases, Detective."

"Tooele Army Depot was different, dedicated to the storage of bio and chemical weapons. You may recall a mad scramble there in late 2016 and early 2017 to dispose of their entire stockpile before the incoming administration could get their hands on it."

"I recall no such thing."

Kelly took a slight step closer to him. "What about the fact that part of that stockpile went missing?"

Fitch squirmed in his chair. "First I've heard of it."

"You can probably see why I'm asking you all this."

"No, I can't."

"Sergeant Philip Rappaport was assigned to that base in Utah. I just figured your connection with him might have something to do with that, and maybe with that stockpile that went missing."

Fitch angled his frame toward the door, a clear signal for Kelly to head through it. "I have a packed schedule the rest of the day, Detective. Why don't we pick this up tomorrow?"

"I only have a few more questions."

He rose and tried to lead her to the door, but Kelly didn't budge.

"You see, Senator, we believe Rappaport may have been involved somehow with the disappearance of the shipment that went missing from Utah. We thought his connection to you may have involved that somehow."

"How many times do I have to tell you—"

"I'm just trying to get some clarity here. Given that it's a matter of national security, I'm sure you understand."

Senator Fitch's face had grown so red it looked sunburned. "No, I'm afraid I don't understand. What I want you to understand is that I'm calling your chief the moment you leave this office to see if the Capitol Police would like to see a cut in its funding. How's that sit with you?"

"Senator, eighteen people died on the Capitol steps Monday afternoon, killed by a shooter we believe was gunning for you. I'm just doing my job."

Fitch's eyes were like lasers. "I'm sure you are." He jerked open the door. "Now, if you don't mind . . ."

She started through it. "Me walking out of here won't end things, sir."

"Really, *Detective*."

In that moment, Kelly knew he'd been playing her. No choice now but to let him continue.

"You think I don't know who you are, Ms. Loftus? You got drummed out of the Baltimore Police Department and the same is about to happen with the Capitol Police. I'd look for a career outside of law enforcement, if I were you."

And he slammed the door behind her.

Kelly could hardly wait to place the call to Panama, stopping just outside the Russell Senate Office Building, out of earshot of all.

"Was he sufficiently spooked, Detective?"

"And then some. If Washington had hills, Senator Fitch would be running for them."

"Then the trap is baited. The only question is whether he'll take it."

"Oh, he will," Kelly assured him.

"You know Fitch?"

"I know suspects."

"I'll inform our mutual friend Brixton."

"Is he still with Wilhyte?"

"By all accounts. And, Detective? That job offer's still open, once all this is over."

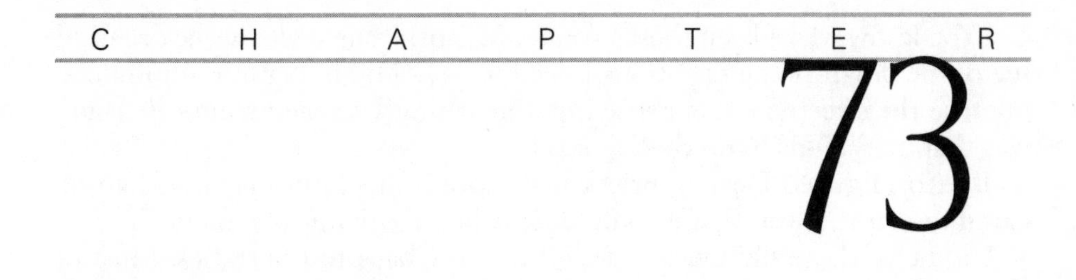

CHAPTER 73

OLDTOWN, MARYLAND

Brixton rode alongside Deacon Frank in his golf cart, holding on to whatever he could grasp throughout the rolling, rocking ride with the man who seemed determined to throw him. Perhaps appropriate, since that's exactly what Brixton had come here this morning to do to him.

The ride took them around the back of Deacon Frank's manufacturing plant to a fenced-in area, beyond which rested a sprawling, windowless building with big bay doors that told Brixton it was some kind of garage. Deacon Frank leaned over and entered a passcode on the keypad. The chain-link gate, topped by barbed wire, slid open.

Brixton spotted a fleet of home delivery milk trucks bearing the Atlas Dairy name. The rest of the fleet apparently was still in the field, dropping off a supply of milk in old-fashioned bottles of the type that adorned the trucks' sides as part of the logo.

Wilhyte turned the golf cart around and churned it to a halt.

"Let's take a walk, Mr. Brixton."

Deacon Frank led Brixton through one of the open bays, into a sprawling space that smelled of tire rubber and gasoline vapors. The bright ceiling-mounted lights were reflected by a concrete floor topped with a shiny polyurethane finish that looked clean enough to eat off. In addition to automated forklifts loading trucks with dull gray milk canisters was a fleet of tank trucks designed to carry milk in bulk. Most of them were made of gleaming stainless steel that shone beneath those bright lights, looking like slightly smaller versions of oil tankers. A ladder strung down the side of each truck joined up with what Brixton figured must be a catwalk that ran along each milk carrier's top, where hoses were rigged to spigots to fill or drain the tanks.

Another section of the garage held the remnants of an older fleet of milk tankers, which were maybe two-thirds the size of the more modern ones. At first glance, Brixton figured each of the older tanks contained two chambers, one for each hatch built into the top, looking from floor level like something out of an old submarine movie. The old trucks were parked by themselves toward the back of the garage, in an area the bright lighting barely reached. They looked more like museum pieces than functional vehicles.

"You know why I keep these around, Mr. Brixton? Because they remind me of the down-home traditions I need to uphold. I'm big into reminders, because they keep me from straying. One thing I learned from my daddy was that man tends to do that, to stray."

Brixton figured Deacon Frank had more of his father in him than he cared to admit, given that it sounded like he was giving a sermon.

"Some of those old trucks date all the way back to the sixties. Most of them aren't roadworthy anymore, but I keep them around because people were different back then. Sure, we had our problems, but folks could tell down from up, left from right, right from wrong. Color televisions were just making their mark at that time, but you know something, Mr. Brixton? The world was better in black-and-white, where you didn't need a program to tell the players, when people didn't sign their names with *He/His* or *She/Her* after them. What does that shit even mean? If anybody who worked for me asked me to do it, I'd fire them on the spot. There was a time we could tell a man or woman just by looking at them. Now I guess it's open to interpretation."

Brixton remained silent, letting Deacon Frank expound on the thing that had brought him to this point. Then he said, "I'm here on behalf of the parents of those murdered kids. That's not open to interpretation at all."

"And you know the worst thing? All this *He/Him*, *She/Her* stuff is typical of the whole damn country, which has lost its identity, too. My daddy was a bastard. My daddy never met a man he didn't try to twist to his own ends. But you know what? He was somebody who genuinely believed he was holding the last of this country together as it was falling apart around him." Deacon Frank retreated a few steps, eyeing Brixton in the spotlight spill of one of the ceiling-mounted fixtures. "You look like you got some grit, sir; like a man who's been in more than his share of scrapes. Have I got that right?"

"A few scrapes, anyway."

Deacon Frank looked at him knowingly. "I'd say plenty more than a few, and I'm betting you got into those scrapes because you believed in something. But I'm also going to venture that you believed in it less as time went on, since nothing was black-and-white anymore. The world, and the country, became a shitty place to live in once the word *relative* started getting thrown around like a football. When I was growing up, twenty million more families got their milk set in a box on their porch every day before dawn. The more those milk boxes disappeared, the more this country did, too."

"We were talking about those kids, Mr. Wilhyte, the ones who got poisoned to death," Brixton interjected, feeling it was time.

"And we still are. And if those parents you're working for still had milk boxes on their front porches, maybe their kids would still be alive today, Mr. Brixton. That's a fact."

"Those parents believe their boys were murdered. They want to know if one of their schoolmates was responsible."

Deacon Frank stiffened, his eyes widening. "You talking about my son?"

Brixton stopped himself from nodding. "Not necessarily. Not at all really. But maybe he knows something that can help me. Maybe he heard something, saw something."

"He hated those boys. They made his life miserable."

"You're giving him a motive."

"And what's wrong with that?" Deacon Frank had raised his voice enough to echo through the tinny, cavernous confines of the garage that had been built up against the dairy's processing plant for easy loading. "Used to be a good fight could solve everything. Now, nothing solves anything. The shit just keeps coming at you. My daddy saw that, you know. He built his mansion over a basement reinforced with steel, lead, and rebar, where ten people could live for a hundred years, once the world finally went dark. He never said *if*; it was always *when*. Maybe he was lucky to die before that happened."

"The light's still burning, Mr. Wilhyte."

Deacon Frank almost looked like he wanted to laugh. "Is it? Is it really? Sure, we don't need to hide out in a bomb shelter for the next hundred years, because it's a different kind of bomb that went off, one that caught us before we even knew it had exploded. Hell, an asteroid wiping out all life on earth for the second time would be regarded as a mercy killing at this point."

Brixton watched him waver slightly at that, as if he'd realized he'd said too much, given too much away.

"You tell those parents there's nothing I or my son can do to help them. And you can also tell them that Deacon Frank Wilhyte is sorry for their loss and that better days are ahead."

"You sure about that, Mr. Wilhyte?"

Deacon Frank nodded. "Yes, Mr. Brixton, I am."

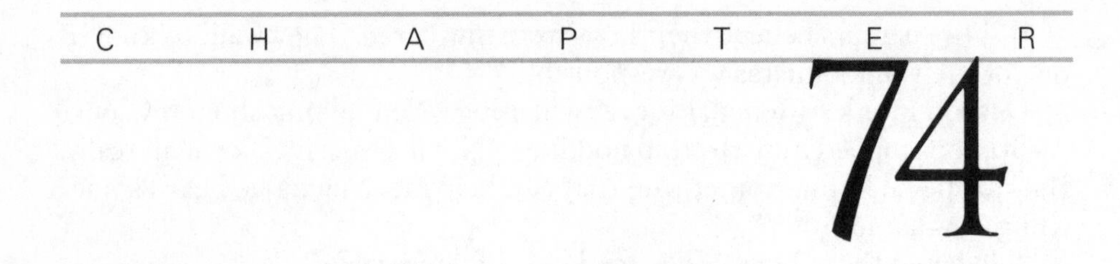

CHAPTER 74

OLDTOWN, MARYLAND

Deacon Frank drove Brixton back to the front gate and watched him drive off. His phone had been buzzing in his pocket constantly for some time and he finally yanked it out to find a dozen missed calls from Senator Bryon Fitch.

He answered the thirteenth.

"That Capitol Police bitch was just in my office."

"Hello again to you too, Senator."

"Are you listening to me? She pays me a visit at the same time this Brixton shows up to see you? What the hell you call that?"

"They're baiting us, you dumb son of a bitch."

"Because you let Brixton slip away last night, insisted you'd handle it yourself, when I could have sent the Navy SEALs in."

"This isn't just Brixton, Senator. Someone's pulling his strings."

"Yeah? Who? I'd know about an operation like that coming through traditional channels."

"Somebody outside traditional channels, then."

"All the more reason we need to take precautions, Deacon Frank."

"I agree with you there. Be back to you with a plan later."

"What's wrong with now?"

"I need to weigh the options, not do something rash that plays right into their hands. Be like a magician and misdirect them."

"Do you ever stop and listen to yourself? I mean, Jesus Christ, you complain about your father and you ramble on as much as he did."

"Leave my father out of this, Senator."

"How about your lame-ass son? Your father fucked you all up, and you fucked your son all up, and look where that got us. I believe I made a serious mistake making you my first call after Rappaport spilled his guts to me. I thought he was crazy as it gets, a total loon."

"Then it's a good thing I didn't feel the same way, isn't it?"

"Like I said, I'm not too sure about that, Deacon Frank. We need to take a mulligan on this. Reboot our thinking and make our move."

"On that much, we agree," Deacon Frank lied.

It came easy to him because he knew Fitch was lying to him, too. Planning his own self-preservation, thinking of himself first, foremost, and only.

Just like Reverend Rand Atlas Wilhyte seeing him as nothing more than a figure standing by the exit holding a collection basket. Twenty-two years old, still doing the same thing he'd done as a little boy. Reverend Rand torturing him the same way those bullies had tortured Daniel. Sticking his very soul in that same scalding water that had left his hand a blistered and puckered mess.

But Daniel had become his savior. Taking his revenge on those boys had opened a door through which tens of millions more could now follow. Talk about cosmic intervention being visited upon him as it had never been visited upon his pious father. He had never needed Senator Byron Fitch, as president or anything else. It was Fitch who needed him. Things get a little hot and the man runs for the hills. He was as replaceable as a pair of underwear. Deacon Frank probably had a thousand politicians on his contacts list, any of whom he could enlist in Fitch's place.

Daniel was showing his experts how he'd used a few drops of the White Death to kill those bullies so the same means could be used to set this country right, once and for all. Get it done and get it right. And without Fitch as an anchor holding him back, he could get it done fast.

"Tell you what," he said to Senator Byron Fitch. "Let me figure out how best to dial this back and reset things. Let's meet up tonight. Your place okay? Say, around midnight?"

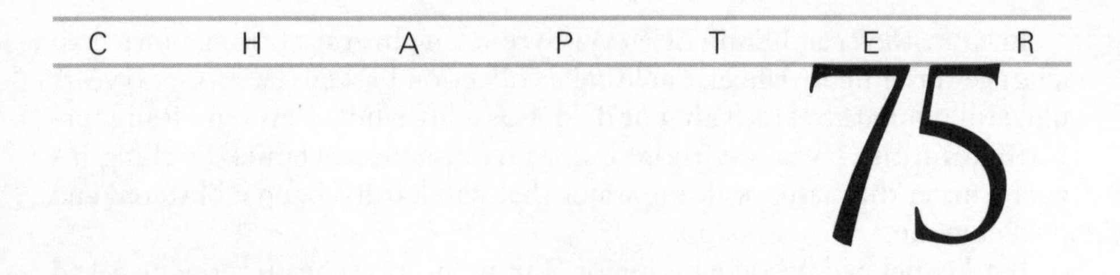

CHAPTER 75

WASHINGTON, DC

"You can't do this to me, Robert!" Flo practically screamed at him, as soon as he was through the door to the suite at the Mayflower Hotel. "You promised! I was worried out of my mind!"

Brixton didn't remember promising anything in particular in that respect, but he still apologized to her. Profusely.

"Men showed up at my door," she moaned, after practically falling into his grasp. "They wouldn't even let me pack a bag."

He stroked her hair. "I'm sorry."

She eased herself away from him, Brixton still holding her by the shoulders. "Can you at least tell me what this is about?"

"No."

"You promised not to do that again, either."

"Would it help if I told you I'm after the people who tried to kill Mac's daughter, who are responsible for my grandson almost getting killed?"

Flo seemed to back off. "So long as it's true."

"It is."

"Okay, can you tell me how serious this is?"

"Very," was all Brixton could say.

Flo shook her head, more exasperated than disgusted. "How do you keep finding these things, Robert?"

"They seem to keep finding me."

She sucked in some breath and let it out slightly. "Is that your way of saying you can't promise this won't happen again?"

"Right now, I'm focused on what's happening today."

"I thought we were past that."

"Past what, Flo?"

"Not thinking about tomorrow until we get there. It's your default mode, Robert, hyperfocusing on the present so you don't have to think about the future."

"It got me home from a lot of missions," Brixton reminded her, remaining calm.

"And now you're on another. And after this one, there'll be another, and another after that, and another, and another, and another. . . . Why don't you tell me to stop, that I'm wrong?"

Brixton took her gently by the shoulders. "Because you're not. You just described the man you fell in love with. When I let myself become someone else, you moved to New York."

He could see Flo wavering, watched her lips quivering as she formed her next words. "So what am I supposed to say to that?"

"Nothing," Brixton said, and kissed her.

He felt her arms closing around him. He was lost in Flo's embrace and never wanted her to let go.

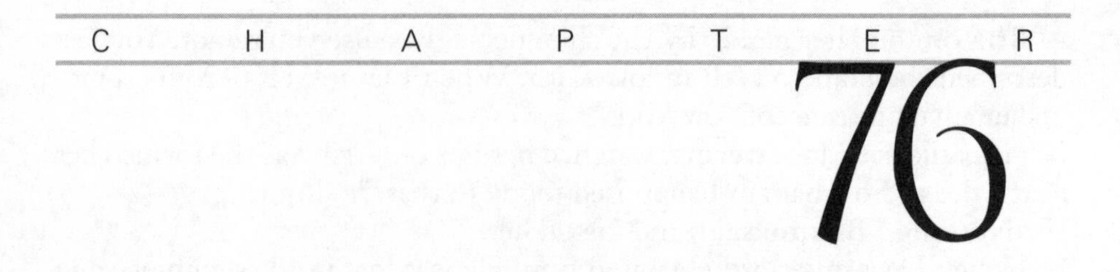

CHAPTER 76

WASHINGTON, DC

Both of you should give serious thought to joining my team," Panama said, later that Saturday. They were meeting on the top floor of an office building that had remained all but empty of tenants after COVID.

"Decent salary and benefits?" Brixton asked him, stopping just short of a wink.

"We kind of make things up as we go along. You know, like fill in the blanks."

"Makes up for the fact that we probably won't live long enough to take advantage of the retirement plan."

"There is that," Panama said, coming as close to a grin as he could. "Yes."

When Panama called this meeting, Brixton had expected more people to be in attendance, had expected a full briefing on what was coming next, with all the bells and whistles. What he got instead was an office that took minimalism to a whole new level. It had not a single piece of furniture, except for a folding table and four matching folding chairs, all colored a basic green. They hadn't bothered to take them, chose to remain standing instead. And no one else had joined them to review the particulars of the plan to put Deacon Frank Wilhyte out of business for good.

"What happens now?" Loftus wondered.

"Tomorrow we take both Wilhyte and Fitch into custody, after we've secured the White Death."

Loftus weighed his wording. "I notice you didn't say 'We're going to arrest.'"

"We like to keep our options open, Detective," Panama said, leaving it there, as his eyes moved to Brixton. "I don't like that look."

"I'm worried."

"We all should be, Brixton."

"I'm talking about the plan. Everything depends on the White Death being stored in those old milk trucks I spotted in Wilhyte's garage."

"Maybe I'm psychic."

"Or maybe there's something you're not telling us."

"Like what?"

"Like maybe you've got somebody inside Deacon Frank's operation.

Maybe you found that particular crack in the wall a while back, and recent events helped you fill in the blanks."

Panama didn't meet his gaze right away. "Glad to hear you think so highly of me, Brixton. Make believe I'm guessing. Make believe I'm just figuring that's the most likely scenario, plain and simple. And until the shooting six days ago, Wilhyte had no reason to believe there was any chance of his plans being compromised. He never knew he'd be facing this moment. We should consider ourselves fortunate."

"Eight kids were killed on the Capitol steps, Panama, and my grandson was almost number nine. Excuse me if I don't consider myself fortunate."

Panama didn't argue the point. "Then it's a good thing Wilhyte doesn't know about my involvement, isn't it? That makes me the wild card here. Deacon Frank knows he's got problems, he just doesn't know how big they are. If I were a drinking or smoking man, I'd be lighting up and pouring." He looked from Brixton to Loftus, then back again. "You can either join me or walk away. And since neither of you is the walking away type, let's talk about what happens from here."

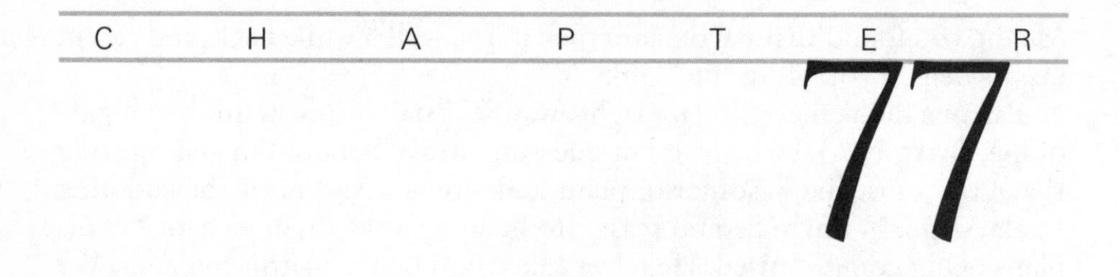

CHAPTER 77

OLDTOWN, MARYLAND

Deacon Frank's morning ritual never varied. He was up with the dawn to shepherd his fleet of refrigerated trucks out on their daily delivery rounds, to leave fresh milk inside the milk boxes on customers' porches. There also were the tank trucks, which would take yesterday's supply to the consolidators, who sold milk in bulk to packagers that didn't own their own dairies and did no more than slap their labels on the fruit of other people's labor. Finally, there were the smaller vans packed with the future contents of select stores' commercial refrigerators, sold at a premium, since bottles labeled "Atlas Dairy" could not be found in any of the big chain stores, at least not under that name. People buying another, generic brand at maybe a third of the price could be drinking the same milk and never know it.

Every day was the same, the routine forming the epicenter of his life, but Sundays were his favorite. Sundays made him feel like a young boy again, still enamored by his father's charm and charisma. He always wore a dress shirt and tie on Sundays—though the tie was a clip-on until he was around sixteen, which was the source of considerable embarrassment. He had fond memories of the services they held throughout the South and the Midwest, barnstorming those parts of the country that were friendlier to old-fashioned revival meetings.

And on this particular Sunday, Daniel would be by his side, his own son accompanying Deacon Frank throughout this historic day. Robert Brixton and whoever was behind him had played their cards. Now it was time for Deacon Frank to play his.

"Da-a-ad," Daniel uttered behind a yawn, as the line of gleaming milk tanks rolled through the gates in military-like formation.

"Stop your whining, son, and enjoy the sights."

Getting the boy out of bed had been a big enough chore to make Deacon Frank regret deciding to take Daniel along with him, literally, for the ride. They stood side by side in this crisp morning air that smelled like fall, watching the line of old-fashioned milk trucks follow the tankers from the garage, en route to serving five thousand homes in a fifty-mile radius. The milk trucks were trailed by transit vans that would take the milk bottled right here on the premises to select commercial accounts, many of which promoted, on all their social media and beyond, the fact that they sold Atlas Dairy milk.

"That's a lot of trucks," Daniel said, whistling. "I never realized you had this many."

"Well, I surely do, son."

"Wow."

Was the boy actually impressed? Amazing how their relationship had changed these past few days, all because of what Daniel had done to those boys who bullied him. It was hard to look at his thin frame, sagging hips, and sleepy eyes that were more comfortable in front of a video game and picture a killer. But a man's character, Reverend Rand always said, is the sum of his deeds, so clearly Deacon Frank had done more than his share of misjudging here. The ease with which the boy had killed would allow his father to do the same, though on a much grander scale. Robert Brixton had said just enough yesterday to assure Deacon Frank that whoever Brixton was fronting for didn't have shit on him. Nothing they could have proven, or the whole 82nd Airborne would have descended on the farm, instead of a single man.

"What happens now?" Daniel asked him, his doe eyes wide.

Deacon Frank's gaze wandered to the line of ancient milk trucks over in the corner of the garage. "We take a drive, son."

Brixton had started his morning in the predawn hours, with Panama, in the same office space as the day before. It had been devoid of any furnishings; now it was crammed with video screens, modems and routers galore, along with personnel working behind laptops. Panama's world was about doing things on the fly, popping in and out of places like he was never there at all, in stark contrast to the way his officially designated counterparts at the CIA, NSA, DIA, FBI, and other agencies had to deal with budgets and the thorny issue of accountability. It wasn't thorny for Panama, of course, because he didn't seem accountable to anyone.

"Thanks for keeping me in the loop," Brixton said to him.

"I owed you that much. Once we get rolling, though . . ."

"I'll be in the wind, gone well before that."

"I like the fact that you're driven, aren't in the habit of taking no for an answer."

"Thank you."

"I wasn't finished," Panama told him. "I also hate the fact that you're driven, aren't in the habit of taking no for an answer. That causes trouble, problems."

"I'm out of this, Panama."

"You're never out of anything, but yes, you're out of this. When it's done, we can have a long discussion about your future. For now, it's still the present."

The door to the office opened and one of Panama's security men in black tactical gear entered, escorting Kelly Loftus.

"I hope you don't mind me inviting Detective Loftus to join the festivities," Panama said to Brixton.

"Still the present for her, too, I imagine."

"Indeed. But I've got a special assignment for her, one better handled from the inside than the out."

"What's that?"

"Arresting Senator Byron Fitch."

"Something she'll definitely enjoy."

Panama gave Brixton a longer look, something that passed for respect crossing his expression. "Are you going to be able to sit back and watch the aftermath of this all unfold on television?"

"I don't have a choice, do I? In fact, I was just leaving."

Panama didn't look like he was buying that. "You've done your part, Brixton. Let it go."

"You didn't meet Deacon Frank Wilhyte up close and personal, Panama. You didn't get a feeling for the man like I did."

"What's that mean, exactly?"

"I'll let you know later."

The interior of the old milk truck smelled its age—a mixture of rust, stale vinyl, and dust. The dashboard didn't contain much more than a speedometer and a few gauges forever locked in place. The steering wheel was thin and knobby, and the inside of the windshield was caked with a layer of grime so old and worn into the glass that no amount of solvent could remove the stain.

When it came to this and the two matching relics on either side, no expense had gone into upkeep, much less restoration. No upgrades for what the eye could see, that is. What couldn't be seen was something else again.

The entire engine compartment had been replaced, and so had the transmission. The tanks, with their dull gray finishes marred by the dents and dings from decades spent on the road, had all been retrofitted with an interior skin. The trio of trucks were now armored and reinforced with a Kevlar-like compound that made military vehicles impervious to rocket or mortar attacks. Pretty close to impregnable. Deacon Frank had transferred the White Death into them as soon as the pair of sleek, shiny, retrofitted tanker trucks had made the trip here safely from Utah. To make everyone on the road keep their distance and avoid approaching those tankers at all costs, he'd had radioactive warning signs placed all over each of them. No cop in his right mind would pull over a tanker truck hauling radioactive waste—or something even worse.

Deacon Frank fired up the engine. Daniel did a double take at the rumbling growl from the six hundred–horsepower under the hood.

"Wow," the boy uttered.

"Today's going to be the day for that, son," his father told him. "Buckle up."

Daniel did as he was told, though it was just a lap belt on this ancient-issue vehicle.

"Your turn," he said to his father.

Deacon Frank shook his head. "Uh-uh. Not for me. The one lesson I got left from my daddy is 'Trust in the Lord's protection.' He never wore a seat belt in his life, even on airplanes. Believed such things were affronts to God, tempting the fate already chosen."

"Maybe that's why he got mugged."

"He claimed he trusted in God so much that he didn't believe in caution. He made me walk across the street with him a bunch of times against a green light. Pissed off some drivers mightily."

Deacon Frank and Daniel would be riding the lead former milk tanker, followed by two others with a pair of his most trusted men in each. The men were among the first he had met in his travels. It wasn't rare to find former soldiers among the ranks of the militias and movements in which he moved, just rare to find good ones, no matter how well intentioned. A pair of big black SUVs, with ample armed backup inside, would take lead and follow positions.

To avoid attracting attention, Deacon Frank had mapped out a route that would take them through the foothills and into the lower stretch of the mountains, climbing routes that spiraled up from the Cumberland Narrows pass into the flatter lands of the Monongahela River valley, which originally had been traversed by fur traders and trappers. That rarely traveled pass would take up the bulk of their journey, leading to a brief stretch spent on the precarious mountain roads that would have been washed out with winter runoff had this been spring. It had been a dry fall, though, greatly reducing the precariousness of the drive.

"Where we going, exactly?" Daniel asked.

"You're going to love it," he told his son, instead of answering his question. "It'll be even better than a video game."

Kelly watched the makeshift command post spring to life in the last of the predawn darkness. A drone Panama had hovering over Deacon Frank Wilhyte's Atlas Dairy Farm was broadcasting a seemingly endless line of milk trucks, milk tankers, and transit vans with the Atlas Dairy logo painted on their sides as they emerged from the garage, all heading for Maryland Route 51, after which they would roll out to both the east and the west before taking the most convenient spur to begin their delivery routes. Route 51 was like a tree sprouting dozens of branches that connected with remote rural towns as well as with the main arteries that accessed the greater part of the dairy's customer base.

"All right, let's get this show on the road," Panama said to his team, as the convoy of milk tanks poured out of the garage. Though the group had been hastily assembled, it seemed nothing less than professional and expert.

Panama was an enigma in her mind, to say the least. Then again, Kelly thought, so was everything about this part of the government—the clandestine part, the part everybody knew was there but allowed themselves to ignore. Panama was classic Washington, almost the stuff of cliché, a man with no name, no portfolio, and no defined job other than as some kind of sentinel manning a metaphorical wall that made no sense to her, either.

That said, it wasn't hard for Kelly to figure out the purpose of all these men and machines. Get in, get it done, get out—that was the mantra that Panama lived by.

"All right," he said again, "let's keep our focus on the milk tanks and ping each and every one. Light 'em up so we can track them, three to each screen."

Either the same or a different drone was matching the convoy's general pace down Route 51. Its view was narrowed to a close-up on the convoy, including the whole of one milk tank truck and part of another. Panama was obviously proceeding on the assumption that the White Death was contained in one or more of the trucks, believing that a combination of Brixton's and Kelly's efforts to spook Wilhyte and Fitch had forced this move.

As she watched, the drone shot invisible lasers downward. This tagged each of the milk tankers, assigning them to computer screens and enabling the team to track their every move.

"I've got more drones in the air, Detective," Panama explained, suddenly by her side. "A fleet of them. I also have teams ready to move separately on each and every one of those trucks. According to the count, thirty-one tankers left that garage, none of them destined to reach their destinations. Deacon Frank Wilhyte is going to have a lot of spoiled milk on his hands."

Kelly didn't bother asking Panama where such manpower had come from, because she knew he wouldn't tell her the truth. Instead, she followed more of the monitors, which were filling with shots of the trucks after they'd been tagged. Obviously, his considerable fleet of drones was already on station. The darkness was an untold blessing, since it made detection all but impossible.

"So, Detective," Panama said to her, "have you given my offer any thought?"

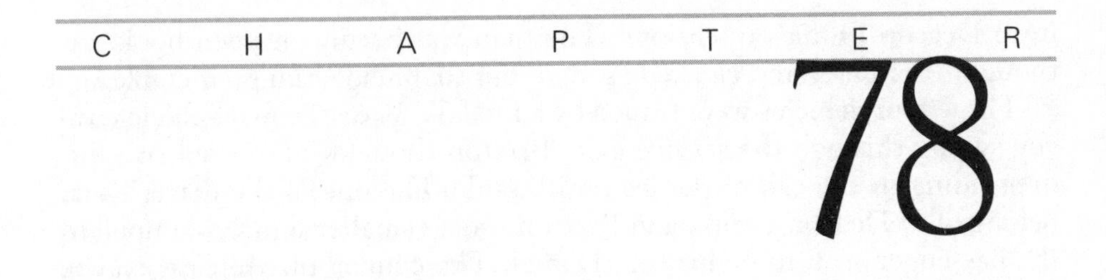

CHAPTER 78

OLDTOWN, MARYLAND

Brixton parked within easy view of the Atlas Dairy Farm, the massive black truck he'd rented straddling the shoulder and the soft grassy surface that bordered the wooded grounds on the other side of the road. After abandoning his shot-up BMW two nights before, he had planned to rent a vehicle that didn't stand out nearly as much. He had hoped an SUV would be available but had opted for this roaring monster because it was the only one that came in black. Just in case.

And now "just in case" was happening.

The BMW had been recovered, but Panama had arranged for its repair and temporary storage. Brixton was grateful for that much, not being of a mind to explain to any inquiring law enforcement authorities the shattered windshield and bullet-pocked steel.

He had pulled off the road just as a seemingly endless convoy of Atlas Dairy vehicles poured onto Route 51, most going east, though a smattering headed west. The line was so long that it reminded Brixton of watching freight trains pass as a boy; they had sometimes stretched for miles. The Atlas Dairy trucks didn't stretch that far, but it seemed like it, from his vantage point.

His plan was to stay here until no other vehicles emerged, possible stragglers trying to slip away without Panama's drones being any the wiser. Brixton couldn't accurately articulate the notions he had formed about Deacon Frank from their terse conversation yesterday. It wasn't what he said so much as *how* he said it. He was a man always a step ahead of the game, anticipating his enemy's moves instead of being spooked into action by them. Panama didn't need to know Brixton was here. If Brixton was wrong, he was wasting his time. If it turned out his suspicions were correct, well, that was what plan B was for.

Just under a half hour had passed since the last gleaming new milk tanker had rolled into the dawn, when one of the garage bay doors rose open mechanically. Brixton imagined he could hear the whir. The exterior lights had been turned off, but he didn't need them to see a big black SUV emerge first, followed by three of the relic milk tank trucks Deacon Frank had boastfully pointed out to him yesterday. That's what had keyed Brixton in to Deacon Frank's intentions. The man was hardly an open book, his thoughts as murky and cloaked as mud, but that made him predictable.

These four vehicles were trailed by a final SUV. As the five-vehicle convoy swung through the service gate, Brixton thought he spotted two figures riding in the cab of the lead milk tank. The one in the driver's seat belonged to Deacon Frank, and Brixton took a smaller figure, slumped in the passenger seat, to be his son, Daniel. The convoy turned east, maybe five hundred yards ahead of him, avoiding the main roads that the newer milk tank trucks were headed for. Two nights ago, Panama had mentioned how Deacon Frank Wilhyte had spent the past several years ingratiating himself with a big portion of the nearly two hundred militia movements operating across the country, no doubt addressing their ranks while saving his best for the men who commanded the throngs of gun nuts that needed only the slightest of rationales to start shooting. By all accounts, that meant he'd been preparing for whatever was coming well before he'd known the White Death even existed.

Philip Rappaport, a soldier assigned to Tooele Army Depot in Utah, must have told his story about the White Death, which had long haunted him, to his home state senator, expecting Byron Fitch to do the right thing by locating it and making sure it never fell into the wrong hands. Fitch clearly had found it, but then he had proceeded to place it in the worst hands imaginable. The poisonings at Baltimore Mulighet High School must have alerted Rappaport to the truth of Fitch's betrayal, and when Fitch ignored him, Rappaport had called the Washington offices of the Centers for Disease Control to report his suspicions. Brixton pictured Alexandra taking the call, listening to Rappaport's bizarre claims instead of rejecting them out of hand. Maybe following up on them enough to confirm at least a bit of his story, before reaching out to Fitch for his side of it.

Brixton squeezed the wheel tighter, thinking about the man responsible for the deaths of seven high school kids, for the murder of Alexandra's supervisor, and for putting Mac's daughter into a coma.

That was all the motivation he needed to pull out a safe distance behind the convoy, leaving the big truck's lights off.

OLDTOWN, MARYLAND

You know what separates success from failure, son? Always have a backup plan, and a backup to that backup plan. You never know when things are gonna go south, so always figure on them doing just that.

That was another piece of advice the Reverend Rand Atlas Wilhyte had given Deacon Frank, one of the few he'd taken to heart and kept close to him all these years. This time of year, the Cumberland Narrows pass offered a clear route up into the northernmost spur of the Blue Ridge Mountains, which hung over the Monongahela valley. Maryland in general, and Allegany County in particular, boasted its share of large and well-known caves, which made for great tourist attractions and popular spelunking sites. The lower reaches of the Blue Ridge range, meanwhile, featured a smattering of caves too small and undistinguished to be included on any maps or known to any tourists. In fact, the mouths of these could easily be covered and camouflaged to appear as if they'd never existed at all. The caves stayed cool enough in summer but never got too cold in the winter, though the latter quality was not relevant to Deacon Frank, since the old milk tanks and the White Death they contained wouldn't be here through the winter months.

Hell, they might not be here even through Thanksgiving.

He knew time was a factor, now that he'd reached the wrong people's radar. Deacon Frank had already sent a coded message to the groups that his funding had taken to the next level in terms of training, recruitment, and weapons. More than enough men to secure the cities after order broke down and chaos reigned. Those cities were a blight on America's soul, and the way Deacon Frank figured it, he didn't need to go after the suburbs, since so many who called the suburbs home also called themselves commuters. And guess where they commuted to?

"You say something, Dad?" he heard Daniel asking him.

He cleared his throat, tightening his grasp on the wheel to fully lift himself from the trance he'd slipped into.

"I was asking you about history."

Daniel wrinkled his nose. "I don't like history."

"You're talking about studying it, son. I'm talking about *making* it."

The boy nodded, getting the idea.

"Remember that gun I showed you the other day?"

"You said you killed a man with it."

"I did indeed, and I never once regretted it, not even for a minute. It's something you and I got in common, something we've both experienced. Tell me something, son, and be honest: Do you regret what you did to those boys?"

Daniel swallowed hard and shook his head.

"Like I said, two peas in a pod in that respect. I never took you to a ball game, we never even played catch, just like it was for my father and me. The difference being your grandpa and I had nothing in common, while you and I got a whole lot, except for the fact that I only took one life, while you took seven. Thing I want you to take from that is that one life's the same as ten, a hundred, a thousand, even a million, so long as you feel what you're doing is right and just, as both of us did when we popped our cherries."

"I showed your lab guys how to do it," Daniel said, triumph ringing in his voice. "We did some tests, and the stuff worked on everything we treated it with."

Deacon Frank smiled, letting his pride in his son's achievement shine through. "So I heard. You got any thoughts on what we should contaminate with your miracle juice when the time comes?"

"Cash is the first thing that comes to mind. Pretty much everybody touches cash. But it's not like we can walk into the Federal Reserve and start spraying."

"You leave that to me, son."

"I had another thought."

"What?"

"Toys. Well, not the toys themselves but the packages they come in. All parents buy toys for their kids, right?"

The Reverend Rand had never bought Deacon Frank a single one, even at Christmas.

"Right, Dad?" Daniel repeated.

"Something else to run up the flagpole."

"It's probably not going to be one thing, but a whole bunch of them," the boy explained.

"They told me that, too, son. And however the shit hits the fan, I want you to think about those boys who made your life a living hell. Because all those other lives we're taking are no different from theirs or the one I took. You hear me?"

The boy nodded.

"And one more thing, son."

Daniel looked at Deacon Frank expectantly.

"Don't tell your mother."

They both smiled. Together.

WASHINGTON, DC

Panama was checking his watch and, Kelly figured, comparing it with the time on his iPhone, which was contained in a case that looked like it could stop a bullet.

On the screens set atop tables that formed a U in the loftlike office space, the gleaming milk trucks rode into the first of the light, the world coming to life around them. Half of them had already peeled off, and she watched the rest of them follow suit, heading along their preplanned delivery routes, along which Panama had set up the roadblocks and strike teams that would end today's delivery runs prematurely, leaving a lot of disappointed customers.

Then Kelly spotted something change in Panama's expression—the first time she'd noticed this since they met.

"They're off course," he said, maybe to her. "None proceeding as planned."

She watched him touch some kind of communications unit coiled behind his ear.

"All strike teams, targets are rerouting. Prepare for new instructions and stand by." Then Panama looked toward Kelly. "And I've a job for you, too, Detective."

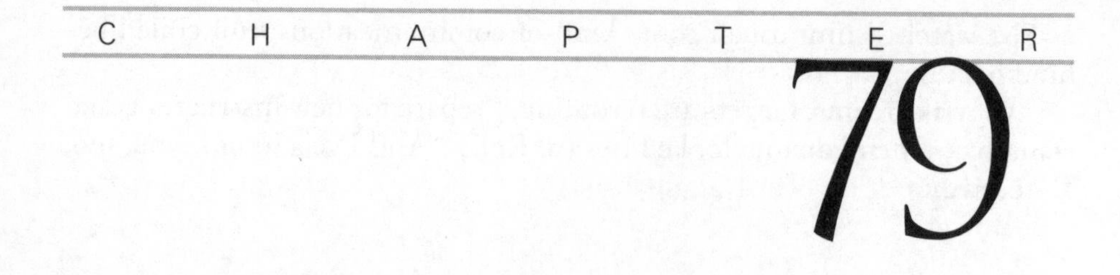

CHAPTER 79

CUMBERLAND NARROWS PASS

Brixton gave the big truck gas, feeling more like he was driving a jet. Seven miles per gallon had never felt so good. With the first of the light brightening the sky, he had fallen too far behind the convoy. He felt the grasp of dread that the vehicles had already turned off onto a side road or broken off altogether.

He breathed easier when he spotted the SUV bringing up the rear turn-off onto the Cumberland Narrows pass. This would take the convoy up a narrow mountain road with a precarious, unsecured edge, beyond which was nothing but a steep drop into the North Branch of the Potomac River. It made no sense to him that Deacon Frank Wilhyte would choose such a precarious route, even if he wanted to bypass the main roads. He felt dread clutch him again, fearing that maybe the trucks had spotted him and were changing plans on the fly.

Unless this route actually held a destination, some place to hide the milk tanks in which the White Death was now stored.

He resisted the temptation to give the big truck more gas, willed himself to keep his distance from the convoy so as not to be visible from any point of the twisting mountain road, which followed the contours of a lower spur of the Blue Ridge range. Brixton kept his distance, wondering where the convoy might emerge on the other side. The volume of the big truck's engine rose as the steep grade demanded more power around a bend that briefly revealed the Potomac River below.

And that's when he saw the trailing SUV. A pair of gunmen was hanging out the windows, one on each side, holding M4 assault rifles.

We have engaged the target!" Deacon Frank heard through the static on the old-fashioned dash-mounted radio. "Repeat, target engaged!"

It took a few moments for him to realize it wasn't static intermixed with the words, but gunfire. Deacon Frank pictured all those 5.56-millimeter shells tearing the pain-in-the-ass Brixton apart, shredding him into pieces.

He'd deal with the ramifications later. For now, the only priority was to ditch the ancient, retrofitted milk tanks in the caves he'd already selected for them along the lower reaches of the Blue Ridge Mountains. Layers of camouflage were already in place to cover the mouths of each cave and make them indistinguishable from the surrounding landscape. But first he'd ordered his trailing security team to hold its ground and set an ambush, on the chance—more of an expectation—that Brixton was following.

And now he had come.

"Gunshots," he heard Daniel say from the passenger seat. "Who they shooting at?"

"Somebody bad, son. Somebody bad."

Brixton screeched to a halt and ducked under the dash just in time, managing to free his nine-millimeter pistol, which under these circumstances was the equivalent of taking on a tank with a flyswatter. He felt shattered windshield glass raining down upon him, heard the hollow, metallic clang of bullets hitting the truck's heavy steel frame, the thwack of one side mirror being blown off, and then the other.

He could have risen enough to return fire, but another plan was forming in his mind, born of his experience escorting protectees through hostile territory for SITQUAL. This wasn't his first ambush, only the first that had found him alone, without a trailing vehicle or a chopper keeping pace overhead.

Use what you got.

It was a well-honed lesson in the world of special ops, and right now he had a weapon far more imposing and deadly than the sixteen bullets in his SIG Sauer.

The truck itself.

Brixton again willed himself to be patient. The gunfire had stopped. He heard the grind of the SUV's doors opening, then the patter of heavy steps heading his way. The gunmen were coming to check their handiwork, all but certain he was dead.

The big truck's engine was still humming, not even a sputter. It felt level, and he hadn't heard or felt the telltale pop of any tire being shot out from under him. Still, he had to do this blind; there was no way to chance a glance over the dashboard until the very last moment.

He positioned himself low in the driver's seat, his frame twisted at an odd angle. Hands on the steering wheel, foot on the accelerator. Nothing else really mattered, besides the contours of the road, for which he had to trust his memory. Brixton counted out the seconds, waited for the thud of those heavy footsteps to find his ears again, then floored the pedal.

It felt like somebody was pushing hard against his chest, gravity shoving him backward as the big truck shot forward. He pulled his gaze over the dashboard and saw both gunmen lurching to the side, an instant too late. He clipped the one on the right hard enough to send him flying off the side of the mountain and struck the one on the left flush, hurling him up and over the big truck. The crunching sound that followed was likely from the man's broken body landing on the pavement behind him.

Brixton had no further time for thinking, just steadied the truck, gave it more gas, and shot forward in the wake of the rest of the convoy.

The command center had taken on a frantic, almost desperate tone. The activity on all the screens was exceeded only by instructions being shouted into unseen microphones. Drones captured images of strike teams racing into new positions to intercept the milk tankers, which now were gleaming under the strengthening morning sunlight. Each screen became the focal point of a controlled form of chaos, complete with distance grids that the strike team coordinators used to advise their men of precisely how far they were from their intended targets.

Kelly watched Panama hold his footing, his eyes constantly moving from one screen to another, confident enough in his team to not be hovering over them. The first assaults went off without a hitch, the tankers on their dedicated screens twisting to a stop, their drivers being summarily jerked out from the cabs and face-planted into the roadbed. Meanwhile, more masked, black-clad commandos rushed up to secure the tanks. In each case, one leaped up behind the wheel while a near twin joined him in the cab to ride shotgun.

The milk tanker was driven off.

The driver hauled away.

The scene repeated again and again.

"Time to go to work, Detective," Panama said to her.

"Do I need a warrant?"

He smiled.

Deacon Frank felt the way his father must have felt when an entire congregation packed into a ripe-smelling tent leaped to its feet in response to something that had flowed from his mouth with the ease of water. He continued pushing the tank truck on, careful to avoid riding too close to the SUV at the head of the convoy, waiting for a voice to garble out news of Brixton's demise.

He waited. And waited some more.

Something clawed at his insides, a feeling like the world was out of joint.

"Dad," Daniel said from next to him.

He had forgotten the boy was even there, was starting to regret even bringing him along, when he heard something—more like *felt* something. The world, which already seemed out joint, froze up for a moment before a blistering screech burned his ears and a blur of motion flashed in his grime-riddled side-view mirrors, which revealed an impossible sight: the rearmost tank truck swerving off the side of the road and plunging downward.

The trailing SUV was stopped in the middle of the road, and Brixton glimpsed another pair of men scrambling into the front seat. More bullets poured his way, leaving him no choice but to barrel straight on, crashing into the stopped vehicle, which felt weightless before the massive scale of the big truck. It featured an extended bumper that absorbed some of the shock, but the impact nonetheless crinkled the forward portion of the hood.

He shoved the SUV on, twisting the steering wheel sharply to the right to send the other truck into a whirling pirouette that spun it straight off the road. He knew in that moment what he had to do, as words from the professor echoed in his mind.

The White Death's only weakness, if you want to call it that, is the fact that its potency dilutes in water.

Like the Potomac River.

One of the gunmen inside the SUV scrambled to get behind the wheel, but it was too late to regain control or pull away, as the two vehicles, riding in tandem, gained rapidly on the milk tank truck at the rear of the convoy.

The driver's panic sent the SUV into a spin that left it sideways across the road, still being shoved on by Brixton's pickup. More gunfire peppered the windshield. Brixton again ducked low in the driver's seat, while keeping his eyes over the dash, utilizing the driving acumen he'd learned for SITQUAL to force the SUV to the right and then angle his own wheels to push it over the edge.

He kept working the wheel and the pedal in tandem, righting his angle and slamming into the trailing tank truck on an angle that tipped its nose toward the road's edge. Brixton felt his truck's massive tires struggling for purchase as he plowed it forward, until the old tank truck with unintelligible letters stretched across its side disappeared over the edge. There in one breath, and gone the next.

Wasting no time, Brixton gave the big truck more gas, the next tank truck in line growing in his sights.

Fall back! We need to fall back!" the driver of the lead SUV screeched at Deacon Frank, after the rearmost milk tanker and the trailing SUV plunged from view one after the other.

But the road was too narrow to do anything but barrel on. No way his truck and the SUV could switch places to allow him to pull away. In his side-view mirror, he was able to grab glimpses of a big black truck with a busted-up grille and shattered windshield being driven by a crazy man.

Brixton.

He wondered if this was what the Reverend Rand Atlas Wilhyte had been thinking when he spotted the gun that would kill him. The hopelessness, the utter sense of failure and weakness, the feeling that all you have done has not been enough. A third of the White Death was gone, but he still had two more tanks, more than enough to get the job done.

Until he didn't. The second relic milk tanker was there and then it was gone, a blur seeming to take flight and then disappear through the trees, taking a blanket of their shedding leaves with it over the edge and following the first truck into the Potomac River below. The crazy man Brixton was coming up fast now, nothing left between him and Deacon Frank.

"Reach under the seat," he told his son, "and grab me my shotgun."

The big truck was listing to the right now, a tie rod or something snapped on that side. Brixton compensated with the steering wheel and the gas, the big truck fighting him, shaking up a storm he could feel in his core.

He had to remind himself to breathe, as he slowly closed on the final milk truck, driven by Deacon Frank, whose son was in the passenger seat. Brixton couldn't let the boy's presence deter him; there was too much at stake to let conscience intervene. Maybe that was why Deacon Frank had brought the boy along for the ride, kind of like insurance.

Beyond the final milk truck, the lead SUV fought the road in search of a clear line of fire. Brixton spotted gunmen in black tactical gear hanging out the windows, trying to find a clear line of sight past Wilhyte's tanker, but the contours of the road defied them as they rode the curves farther up the mountain. The driver seemed to lose control for a split second, overcorrecting to the left, which flattened the man hanging out that window against the rock face.

Brixton grimaced at the sight. The man's remains were left dangling out the window, his hands scraping at the roadbed. Stunned, the driver overcorrected again, to the right this time, and lost control, sending the SUV straight into Deacon Frank's path.

The final milk tanker T-boned the SUV and sent it whirling across the road. The SUV picked up speed as it churned toward the edge and then dropped out of sight. The impact sent the milk tanker twirling into a squealing spin that left it canted sideways across the road. Brixton glimpsed Deacon Frank poking a sawed-off shotgun out his window and fire four rounds in rapid succession, one of which blew out Brixton's left front tire in a hissing blast.

The big truck heaved right, then left, then right again, Brixton fighting for control. He tried to work his brakes, the antilock system engaging too late to stop it from angling for the edge. He felt the right front wheel teeter, then the left, only air beneath one and then the other, until he worked the wheel and accelerator in tandem to regain the road.

He realized Deacon Frank had opened fire again with his sawed-off, but this time Brixton didn't duck beneath the dashboard for cover. Instead, he gave the big truck all the gas it would take, screeching forward straight into the line of fire and slamming into Deacon Frank's milk tanker on an angle that forced it into a violent, 360 degree spin across the mountain road.

Before him, the milk tanker thudded to a halt, back end higher than the hood because its front tires had been left hanging over the edge. Yet there was Deacon Frank, hanging out his window and steadying the sawed-off again.

This time, Brixton dropped below the dashboard just before the next shot turned the headrest he'd just been propped against into a pincushion, stuffing showering the interior like snow. He thought he might have screamed. His foot stamped down reflexively, pressing the accelerator pedal all the way to the floor. He felt the big truck lurch ahead, bucking as it barreled straight for Deacon Frank's milk tanker.

Deacon Frank felt the jolting crash separate him from his twelve-gauge, realized the front of his tanker was dipping farther downward, though it was frozen for the moment, as its rear tires locked on a rocky extension of the ridge. He gave the truck gas to try to coax it into reverse, but that resulted in the tires starting to slip again.

"Dad!"

"We're getting out of here, son. Just hold still!"

Deacon Frank threw open his door, twisted toward his son, and reached over to pull the boy out with him, but Daniel wouldn't budge from the passenger seat.

"Dad!"

The boy had been snared by the damn seat belt! Deacon Frank kept pressing the release button but the old latch refused to give. It was seized up solid.

"Please, Dad! Please!"

The boy was pleading, wailing, sobbing, as the truck lurched farther downward, the precarious grip of its rear tires starting to slip. Deacon Frank looked at Daniel.

Daniel looked back.

"I'm sorry, son. I'm so goddamned sorry."

The boy reached out to him as Deacon Frank threw himself out the driver's door in the last moment before the rear tires gave up the last of their hold. He hit the roadbed hard just as the milk tanker, and the last of the White Death, pitched over the edge, its nose angled in line with the river below.

Deacon Frank rolled once, then again, and a third time on impact with the asphalt. He grabbed a glance at the big black truck, which looked like some kind of iron dinosaur, and saw a bloodied Robert Brixton looking dead behind the wheel, as Deacon Frank thought he heard the last of his son's screams.

Brixton didn't know if he had lost consciousness or had merely been lost in a daze. He remembered finding his driver's door jammed, remembered tumbling through the window and hitting the pavement hard. His battered truck was the only vehicle on the road; the others, including Deacon

Frank's milk tank truck, had been lost over the side to the watery graves promised by the Potomac River.

He knew Wilhyte had survived. Couldn't say how he knew, he just did. Brixton was suddenly aware of bird sounds and the river running below, before he finally gave up his hold on the light and let the darkness take him.

By all accounts, Senator Byron Fitch must have been home. The aides at his office insisted they'd been unable to reach him all morning. So Kelly drove out to his home in the Bradley Manor–Longwood neighborhood of Bethesda, just inside the Beltway, where Bradley Boulevard crosses over.

When knocking and ringing the bell produced no result, she circled around the house and found a set of French doors that opened into what looked like the senator's home office. The doors were locked, so she found a rock to break the glass closest to the latch, reached in cautiously, and unlocked it.

Entering the house, she found herself in the largest home library she'd ever seen, her eyes gaping at the magnificent collection of books that covered the entirety of three of the room's walls. Fitch's desk was centered against the fourth wall, which was dominated by photographs and other memorabilia.

Kelly approached, noting the blood and brain splatter that coated a good portion of the side wall, where the bookshelves ended at a big bay window. The glass was a gory mess. She found the senator lying on the floor, the top of his head mostly blown off by the .45 that lay on the other side of the chair, where it had slipped from his hand before the chair tipped over.

She realized her phone was ringing and she drew it to her ear with a trembling hand.

"You arrest Fitch?" Panama asked her, before she'd even had a chance to say hello.

"Not exactly," Kelly told him.

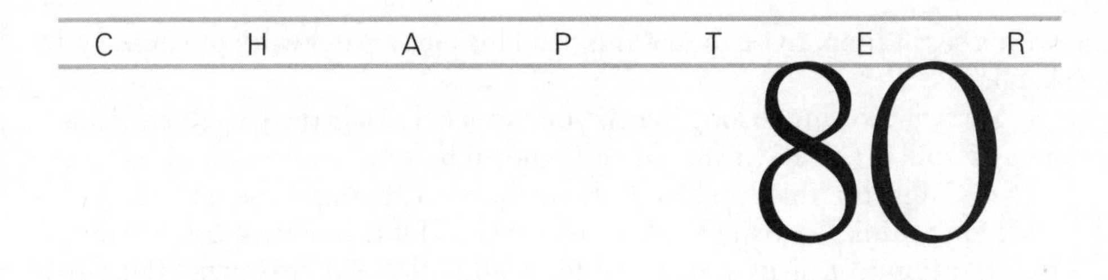

CHAPTER 80

OLDTOWN, MARYLAND

Deacon Frank had made it home on foot, covering fifteen miles. He was beaten, dejected, and mourning the loss of a son he'd pretty much ignored until a few days ago. Three more days had passed with him in full cleanup mode to deal with all the chaos. He hadn't told his ex-wife about Daniel yet, waiting to concoct a proper story with the help of the army of lawyers that had replaced his army of gunmen. Maybe he'd tell her the boy ran away and take things from there. It wasn't much of a story, but it beat planning his son's funeral. Better the world think Daniel was still alive.

Subordinates took care of shutting down the lab and sending his scientists on their way. None of them was about to talk; they were fully aware of their own complicity in what had nearly come to pass. The last remaining samples of the White Death they'd been working on were destroyed in an explosion that blew the building to smithereens, leaving absolutely nothing behind.

For the whole of those three days, Deacon Frank waited for a visit from the authorities—the FBI, most likely. But that never came. His lawyers insisted they had nothing on him anyway, just a lot of pieces they wouldn't be able to fit together. And with any luck at all, Daniel's body would never be found and the story of the kid running away would stick.

In fact, he was more worried about Brixton than about anyone or anything else, except that Brixton hadn't shown up yet, either, and Deacon Frank started to wonder if he had died behind the wheel of his smashed-up truck along the Cumberland Narrows pass. That just might end things here and leave Deacon Frank and his minions to fight another day, as the saying went.

And then he got a call from the front gate that Robert Brixton had just arrived.

Brixton felt Kelly Loftus hovering near him as he emerged from her car and tucked the single crutch under his arm on the side where he'd been grazed twice by bullets he hadn't even felt. Everything ached, whenever and however he moved, leaving a perpetual grimace stretched over his face.

He spotted Deacon Frank ride up in his golf cart, felt Loftus tense at the sight of him. Deacon Frank stepped out of the cart and walked toward them with a slight limp, his arm in a sling and his face a patchwork of gauze and bandages.

"Sorry it took me so long, but as you can see, I'm a little banged up. Took a nasty spill off an RV. I should have known better."

"Yes," Brixton told him, "you should have." Leaving it there.

"Don't think I've had the pleasure, ma'am," Deacon Frank said, turning his attention to Loftus and trying for a smile that didn't come. "The two of you together or something?"

Brixton held his gaze. "We're here to take you into custody, Mr. Wilhyte."

"I told you, Brixton, that everybody calls me Deacon Frank."

"We're taking him into custody, too."

Brixton couldn't believe the man's calm, knowing he'd taken every step to cover his tracks and erase the events of three days ago.

"You're responsible for the death of your own son, Deacon Frank," Brixton accused him.

"Come again? Do you know something about my son? Because he up and ran away a couple days back. I've got people tracking him right now. Hey, you're a private investigator, right? Maybe I should have called you."

Brixton hobbled closer to him. "Stow the bullshit. We're not here about what happened on the Cumberland Narrows pass."

Deacon Frank pretended not to hear him. "Come again?" he said, hooking a hand behind his ear. "My eardrums got damaged in the fall off that RV. Hey, it looks like you got yourself banged up too, friend. What happened?"

"We're here to arrest you for the murder of Senator Byron Fitch, Mr. Wilhyte," Loftus jumped in, freeing the handcuffs from her belt, same pair she'd carried as a homicide cop in Baltimore.

This time, Deacon Frank didn't bother to pretend he couldn't hear. "That's about the dumbest thing I ever heard. It was all over the news. Man committed suicide; blew his own brains out."

Loftus approached him, ignoring the guards, whose hands had slipped a little closer to their pistols. "Here's the thing, Mr. Wilhyte. We managed to recover the bullet from the forty-five Senator Fitch supposedly used to do the deed. That bullet turned out to be a perfect match for one that killed another man, twenty years ago, a man by the name of Reverend Rand Atlas Wilhyte. Maybe you've heard of him."

E P I L O G U E

It was the best Thanksgiving Brixton could ever remember, a packed house at Mac and Annabel's apartment that included his entire family. And there was plenty to give thanks for, what with Alexandra Parks having been released from the hospital two days before, though with a long recovery ahead of her. She claimed to have no appetite and then proceeded to fill her plate three times at the buffet.

Mac had insisted that Brixton invite Kelly Loftus, too, who was glad not to be spending the holiday alone. She sat directly across from Brixton and Flo Combes, with Brixton's grandson, Max, seated on the other side of him. He had no idea what had happened to Deacon Frank Wilhyte in the weeks since he and Loftus had facilitated his arrest. They both found it interesting, even instructive, that from the time they handed him over to Panama there had been no publicity, court appearance, perp walk, or anything whatsoever involving the justice system. Deacon Frank, it seemed, had fallen off the face of the earth.

Not that they were surprised.

Before they sat down, Alexandra had eased Brixton aside. She was moving a bit gingerly and struggling for energy and endurance as she continued her recovery from being exposed to the White Death, but her smile could still dominate a room.

She hugged him, out of nowhere. "Thanks, Uncle Robert."

"For what, Alex?" he asked, after they'd separated.

"You caught the men behind this, and I'm not just talking about what happened to me. You stopped something terrible from happening. You saved . . . well, I can't even begin to think about how many lives. Guess I should have told you the whole truth when we met for lunch."

"You did tell me the truth. You just didn't tell me everything."

Alexandra looked at him with the same narrowed gaze she'd flashed repeatedly when they'd first met. "And what if I had?"

He shrugged. "One thing I've learned in this world is never to ask that kind of question, or to try to answer it."

"And what world is that?" she asked him, picking up on his use of the term.

"The one you got a glimpse into when you took that call from Philip Rappaport."

She sighed, holding on to a chair to keep her balance. "That glimpse was enough to tell me I don't want to see any more."

"It's not for everybody," Brixton told her.

Alexandra looked down, then up again. "Can you tell me what you did, how it ended?"

Brixton nodded. "Whenever you're ready. You deserve that much."

"These things don't always finish happily, do they?"

Brixton thought about the death of Daniel Wilhyte and the lives of the seven classmates who'd bullied him, which the boy had taken. He thought about the men who'd died in the New Jersey woods and Deacon Frank's guards in those two SUVs. He thought about Max saving a classmate's life, and the other classmates who'd perished on the steps of the Capitol. He could qualify nothing related to that as even remotely happy.

"No, they don't," he told Alexandra. "But everything's relative."

Back at the table, Mac tapped a spoon against his water glass to get everyone's attention.

"Normally," he started, when everyone else's conversations slipped into silence, "we go around the table and ask everyone to say what they're thankful for. We've all been through a tough stretch, so this year let me speak for everyone. It's been a strange year for sure, but here we are, all together." Mac reached over and took Alexandra's hand. "I'm thankful for my new daughter, who I get to enjoy minus the diaper changing and chauffeuring around. And I'm thankful for everyone at this table, just because you're here."

The clapping continued until the doorbell rang and Mac rose to answer it.

"It's for you, Robert," he said, reappearing moments later. "You and Kelly."

Feeling a twinge of foreboding, the two of them moved to the front foyer, where Panama was standing, hat in hand, revealing white hair flecked with strands of gray, still holding the hat's contours.

"Thought I'd stop by, see how the two of you were doing."

Neither Brixton nor Loftus asked him how he knew where they were.

"Usually the doorman calls on the intercom to tell Mac he's got a visitor," Brixton noted.

"Usually," Panama said, leaving it there. "You know the most precious resource there is, Brixton? It's time, because time is finite, the hardest to secure and easiest to disrupt or destroy. That's what Deacon Frank Wilhyte would have done if he hadn't been stopped—so much time stripped from so many."

"Should we ask what became of him, exactly?" Loftus asked him.

"A murder trial isn't good enough for some men," Panama told her, again leaving it there, and both of them knew better than to press the issue further.

But there was one thing Brixton *did* want to press with Panama.

"You knew all along how this would turn out, didn't you? You knew Wilhyte would try to decoy you and you knew I'd be there to pick up the slack."

"In my experience, Brixton, assessing a person is no different than hitting the bull's-eye on a shooting range, and it can save a hell of a lot more lives, to boot."

"What if you were wrong?"

"About you?" Panama shook his head. "Nah. You're an idealist, the most predictable type of all. The kind of guy who runs into the water when someone yells 'Shark!' to make sure everyone else gets out safely. So call it a chance I was willing to take. But that's in the past. It's the future I'm here about—yours, both of you. You've seen how I work and how important that work is. There's no shortage of Deacon Frank Wilhytes in the world, but there is a shortage of those capable of dealing with them. It's not just about knowing where the bodies are buried, Brixton; it's about the willingness to plant some more in the ground with them."

"Interesting way to put it," Brixton noted.

Panama looked toward Loftus. "You can have your job back with the Capitol Police or go back to work homicide in Baltimore, if you want. Just say the word. But I'm offering you a third alternative."

"Can I think about it?" she asked him.

"Of course," he said, after pausing briefly.

"Care to join us?" Brixton asked him. "There's plenty of food, if you're hungry. For the men you left downstairs, too."

Panama smiled. "They've already eaten."

"What about you?"

"Would you believe I'm needed elsewhere?"

"On Thanksgiving?"

"Fresh cracks in the wall wait for no man. Different day, same story."

"Hope it has a happy ending."

Panama fitted his hat back into place. It was riding the top of his brow in a way that framed his entire face in shadows as his lips flirted with the semblance of a smile.

"Everything's relative, Brixton," he said. "Everything's relative."

ACKNOWLEDGMENTS

Longtime fans of the Capital Crimes books, as well as readers familiar with my work, will note that this is only my second effort in Margaret Truman's fabulous series, and I find myself extremely fortunate to have inherited that mantle from the great Don Bain.

Many thanks to our mutual agent, Bob Diforio, for giving me the opportunity, and to TDA founder and chairman, Tom Doherty, for trusting me with one of mystery-thriller fiction's most iconic brands. Both Tom and Forge's publisher, Linda Quinton, are dear friends who still publish books "the way they should be published," to quote my late agent, the legendary Toni Mendez. The great Bob Gleason is there for me at every turn. Editing may be a lost art, but not here thanks to him, and I think you'll enjoy all of my books, including this one, much more as a result.

Thanks also to Robert Davis, Anna Merz, and my great copyeditor, Todd Manza. I'm also eternally in debt to Russell Trakhtenberg, who designed a cover that perfectly complements the story I told the best way I know how.

No one is more important to assuring that than Jeff Ayers—there is indeed a reason why I call him "the Wizard," and his sage advice on this book was more vital than ever. Thanks, again, to Jeff's wife, Terry Ayers, for making my scientific jargon sound much better than it did originally. And a special thanks to Carolyn O'Keefe for help with the Baltimore locales and culture.

Check back at www.jonlandbooks.com for updates or to drop me a line, and please follow me on Twitter @JonDLand. And if we haven't met in such pages before, I hope we will again soon, perhaps in my Texas Ranger Caitlin Strong thrillers I hope you'll check out online or at your favorite bookstore.